MURDER TAKES A CRUISE

ROBERT W. GREGG

INFINITY
PUBLISHING

ISBN 978-1-4958-1038-1
Library of Congress Control Number: 2016907294

Published April 2016

INFINITY PUBLISHING
1094 New DeHaven Street, Suite 100
West Conshohocken, PA 19428-2713
Toll-free (877) BUY BOOK
Local Phone (610) 941-9999
Fax (610) 941-9959
Info@buybooksontheweb.com
www.buybooksontheweb.com

DEDICATION OF 'MURDER TAKES A CRUISE'

It is with great personal pleasure that I dedicate this book to my four wonderful grandchildren - Kevin, Amy, Brian, and McKinley - and wish them happiness and success in the years that lie ahead.

PROLOGUE

Carol and Kevin, along with many of their fellow passengers, stood at the rail of the cruise ship, looking down at the quay where a dozen or so people, most of them members of the crew, were tending to assorted tasks or simply idling, waiting for instructions. Kevin checked his watch for the third time since they had left their cabin. It was now 5:23, nearly an hour after the ship's bulletin had said they would lift anchor and head for Martinique.

A short man whose uniform identified him as a member of the ship's crew walked past. Kevin turned away from the rail and caught up with him.

"Say," he said, "what seems to be holding us up?"

The man hesitated, then shrugged his shoulders.

"Don't know." He obviously didn't want to engage this passenger in a discussion of whatever problem had caused their departure to be delayed. He managed a slight smile and kept on walking toward the stern of the ship.

Kevin pursued him.

"When do they expect us to be under way?" He addressed the question to the crew member's back.

"I'm sure there will be an announcement," was the answer. The man disappeared through a door that said Crew Members Only.

"We could still be sightseeing," Kevin said as he rejoined Carol. "If we'd known we'd still be in port, we might have been able to get over to the windward side of the island to take a look at the rough surf."

"Stop worrying," Carol said. "It probably won't be more than a few more minutes, and they wouldn't have wanted to round us all up again."

Kevin thought about it. He had recently read a number of stories about 'trouble at sea,' problems that had plagued cruise liners in the Caribbean. The ship on which they were now standing had an excellent reputation, and he doubted that it was about to be the topic of a disaster story in the *New York Times*. A virus of some kind or other could, of course, strike the passengers and crew, but if that were the problem they would already have been aware of it. The dining room would have had more vacant tables, servers would have been wearing gloves, the public address system would have warned afflicted people to remain in their cabins.

Then another thought occurred to him. What if passengers who had taken a shore excursion had not yet returned to the ship? Local transportation on some of the Caribbean islands was reputed to leave something to be desired. Barbados should be better than most of its neighbors, but there are always exceptions. On the other hand, he remembered reading somewhere that cruise ships were not in the habit of waiting around for delinquent passengers. In his imagination he saw people running frantically down the pier only to see the stern of their ship slowly disappearing into the sunset.

These thoughts were interrupted by the voice of the ship's captain. There was barely a hint of an accent, and his words struck Kevin as both avuncular and stern.

'This is your captain speaking. I am sure you have been wondering why we are still docked in Bridgetown. The answer is that one of your fellow passengers has not followed our departure instructions. Those instructions made it clear that the *Azure Sea* would sail at 4:30 local time and that all passengers should return to it no later than 3:45. Normally, we would have sailed for Martinique at the announced departure time. In this case, however, we have made valiant efforts to locate the missing passenger. Unfortunately, we have been unsuccessful and we cannot delay our departure further. I must inform you that it is rarely possible for the ship to delay its departure, as we have done today. Therefore, I strongly urge each and every passenger to pay extra close attention to instructions telling you when you *must* be back on the ship."

The captain fell silent for what seemed like a minute. When he spoke again, his words were clipped and succinct.

"The *Azure Sea* shall be underway in five minutes."

"So that's it," Kevin said. "We've been going nowhere because someone was having so much fun he forgot that we were sailing this afternoon. They should sock him with a surcharge for his carelessness."

Carol turned toward Kevin, looking pensive.

"What if it wasn't his fault? Or hers. Maybe he or she had an accident and wasn't able to let the captain know. Five minutes late, that I could understand. But an hour? Doesn't that make you suspicious?"

"Well, one thing's for certain. It's going to cause our delinquent passenger a pretty penny to get some local pilot to fly him to Martinique to meet the ship. I'm glad it's not you or me."

"Me, too. What do you say we head for the Horizon Bar and see if we can find out who it is who went missing. Somebody's bound to know."

"As for who, you're probably right. I've got a hunch, though, that why won't be so easy."

CHAPTER 1

Carol put her book down and went to the window. She didn't have to go out onto the deck to know that it was cold outside. The first month of winter was nearly over, but Carol saw little evidence that the days were getting longer. The sky was grey and a light snow had started to fall. At least the lake wasn't entirely frozen over.

She hadn't seen Kevin since they had gone their separate ways after the cruise. She would like to call him now, but unfortunately he would be teaching his seminar. For the first time in a long time, Carol was feeling sorry for herself and regretting it. They had made peace with their situation several years earlier, and all things considered they were enjoying a good life in spite of the months of separation dictated by their jobs, several hundred miles apart. What is more, they had only recently returned from the Caribbean which had been satisfying in every sense of the word.

Why not leaf through the pictures they had taken on the cruise? It was more likely to lift her spirits than returning to the book she had been reading. It had had good reviews, but like so many of today's best sellers it was a downer, a lengthy recital of the woes of a dysfunctional family. The pictures they had taken in Martinique, St. Lucia, Antigua - they would remind her of blue skies, soft sands, charming people. And of the mystery of the passenger who had missed their ship's departure from Barbados.

Carol went into the study, collected the photo scrapbook she had been putting together, and resumed her seat on the couch. Her purpose had been nothing more than stimulating pleasant thoughts about a cruise they had finally taken after several years of threatening to do so. The scrapbook fell open to a page which she had labeled Barbados. Of course. Although they had enjoyed all of the islands they had visited, Barbados seemed to have assumed pride of place because of their delayed departure.

Carol flipped through the pictures of Barbados' delightful sights until she got to the one that was most intriguing. Actually, the picture had not been taken anywhere on the island itself, but on board the *Azure Sea*. She didn't even know exactly when or where in the course of the cruise the picture had been taken. Some passenger had volunteered to snap Kevin and her standing in front of an attractive bar. There were two other people in the picture, the bartender, wearing a colorful shirt and busily engaged in shaking what was presumably a rum drink, and a less conspicuous man in the background.

Had the ship not been delayed because of the missing passenger, it is doubtful that this particular picture would have earned a place in the scrapbook. But the man in the background turned out to be the passenger who had missed the ship's departure. They hadn't known that when the picture was taken, but after they had left Bridgetown he was inevitably the principal subject of conversation. Photos began to circulate, and eventually - actually while they were docked in Martinique - they discovered that the man in the background of the bar shot was the one who had missed the *Azure Sea* in Barbados. Not only had he not made the trip from Bridgetown to Martinique on board the ship. He had not made the trip by air. In fact, he never caught up with his fellow passengers. What they knew about him was that his name was Franklin Pierce and that he had been traveling with a small group of people who had apparently been friends in college. None of them seemed to have any idea what had happened to him. Mr. Pierce had simply disappeared.

It was 9:11 and Carol was getting ready for bed when the phone rang.

"Hi, it's me." It was Kevin. He sounded excited.

"Hi yourself. I was going to call and then remembered it was Thursday and you had a seminar."

"I'm not calling to tell you how brilliant I was. I have news. News about Barbados. They found Pierce. I read it in one of those little stories in the back of the *Times* - you know, just a couple of inches, a space filler."

"I was thinking about Pierce myself. Figured he'd turn up eventually. What was he doing?"

"Nothing. He was dead."

Carol was now wide awake.

"Dead?" She didn't sound as if she quite believed what she was hearing.

"That's right. No details, just that the Barbadian authorities had found his body. At least we now know why he didn't make it back to the ship."

"No word about natural causes versus foul play?"

"None. The whole story couldn't have been more than than 75 words long. Why am I not surprised that my sheriff is already speculating about foul play?"

"My interest is not professional, Kevin. I'm just curious."

"That's good, because I'm sure your jurisdiction doesn't extend to the windward islands. Anyway, I doubt that it strikes the *Times* as a big story. Maybe there'll be a follow up in a day or two, but I wouldn't bet on it. I promise to keep my eyes open."

"Thanks."

They exchanged a few more words, then called it a night. But Carol couldn't get Kevin's news off her mind. Instead of falling asleep at a good hour, she found herself weighing the odds that a man she'd never met, one Franklin Pierce, had been murdered in far off Barbados.

CHAPTER 2

The alarm clock told her it was time to get up and face the day. Unfortunately, it had been a bad night and Carol wanted only to bury her head in her pillow and go back to sleep. Still groggy, she had trouble remembering why sleep had been so elusive. And then it came to her. It had everything to do with Kevin's call and his news that the man who had missed their ship's departure from Bridgetown was dead.

She forced herself to get up, and to swear that she was going to stop losing sleep speculating about a case that was not on her agenda and never would be. She looked at her face in the bathroom mirror. Who was this woman who was staring back at her? Certainly not the rational person who was always urging her colleagues not to let themselves get side-tracked. She splashed cold water on her face and set off for the kitchen and coffee.

When Carol reached the office, she was still tired, but her mind was now clear and ready to deal with whatever local problems she was likely to find in her in-basket. Ms. Franks had already arrived and the coffee pot was already steaming. Carol poured herself another cup and began making notes for the squad meeting.

Less than an hour later her officers had scattered on their appointed rounds and she was reading a report her deputy, Sam Bridges, had prepared for her on a decidedly unneighborly conflict between two neighbors on Berringer Point.

The phone rang and, as usual, she ignored it. If it was for her, JoAnne would find out who was calling and give her a heads up. It was nearly two minutes later that JoAnne buzzed her.

"It's for you, a woman who says she's Abbey Lipscomb."

"It took her quite awhile to let you know who she is," Carol observed. "What does she want?"

"That's what took her so long to tell me. Actually, she didn't really tell me what she wants. She seems to think that she shouldn't be bothering you, but she hopes you can tell her what she should do."

"Do about what?" This was the kind of call Carol didn't like.

"About somebody named Pierce. She says he's dead."

Pierce. The man who had deprived her of a good night's sleep? The man who had disappeared in Barbados and, according to Kevin and the *New York Times,* had subsequently been found dead?

"Go ahead and put her through to me," Carol said, now curious to find out whether Pierce was who she thought he might be, and if so why Lipscomb was calling the sheriff for advice.

"You are Sheriff Kelleher?" she asked before introducing herself. She sounded as if she wouldn't be surprised by a denial.

"Yes, this is Sheriff Kelleher. How is it that I can help you?"

"I don't know. It's about -" Carol heard a noise, something falling. This was followed by some words she couldn't understand, and more noise. The woman was apparently trying to pick up whatever had fallen, probably the phone, and was having difficulty doing so.

"Sorry about that. I'm having a bad time, aren't I? I was just trying to put the phone to my other ear and I lost it. I probably should be talking to you face to face, but you know how it is - you're busy, and, well, I'm just confused. The news about Mr. Pierce came as such a shock. I can't imagine that you can help me, but maybe being a sheriff you'd know something about how things like this are handled."

This conversation was going nowhere.

"My assistant says your name is Abbey Lipscomb. Is that right?"

"Yes, Lipscomb. And you're probably wondering who this Mr. Pierce is. We're old friends, which is why, I suppose, this is such shocking news."

"Mrs. Lipscomb," Carol interrupted. She had no idea whether the caller was a Mrs. or a Ms., but she needed to get to the point. "Where are you calling from?"

"Just over the hill. Do you know where Blalock Point is?"

Of course she knew where Blalock Point was. It was on Crooked Lake and not much more than a 35 minute drive from where she was sitting.

"Yes, I do. But I didn't know that you lived here on the lake. Perhaps we should get together."

"You'd be willing to take the time to see me?"

"You suggested that a face to face conversation would be better than the telephone, and I agree with you."

"Well, if you're sure it's all right. Where is your office?"

"If you don't mind, I'd prefer to come over to your place. Just tell me the number and when would be convenient."

It took another apology or two before they agreed that the sheriff would be there at 10:30.

Carol made the trip in exactly 27 minutes.

Chapter 3

The woman who came to the door looked considerably younger than Carol had expected. Certainly no older than 50, probably closer to 40. Unprepossessing, her only distinguishing feature was a pronounced limp. She wore no ring, which didn't guarantee that she wasn't married but persuaded Carol to refer to her as Ms. rather than Mrs.

"Delighted to meet you, Ms. Lipscomb," she said as they shook hands.

"You're very kind to help me, sheriff. I'm really not sure that you can, but I couldn't think of anyone else to ask. Won't you come in?"

It didn't take but a minute or two for Carol to decide, rightly or wrongly, that Ms. Lipscomb was indeed single. She saw nothing in the living room that suggested a man had ever shared the small rambler. The profusion of plants, quilts and throws, small porcelain dolls and dogs, and numerous copies of the *Readers Digest* made the room one of the busiest Carol could remember seeing.

Ms. Lipscomb made a production out of serving coffee and chocolate biscotti. Carol had been in the busy Lipscomb living room for nearly a quarter of an hour before her hostess finally got around to the reason for their meeting.

"Perhaps I should explain myself," she said, to which Carol nodded in assent. "Franklin Pierce and I were friends for many years, going back to our undergraduate years at Syracuse. People used to kid him. About his name, I mean. His parents probably thought it was a compliment to name him after an American president, but unfortunately Franklin Pierce was one of our worst presidents, even worse than those other nonentities before the Civil War. No matter, Franklin took all the kidding in stride, even to the point of telling stories about his namesake. But that's not what I want to talk about."

Carol found Ms. Lipscomb's comments about Pierce's name interesting, but welcomed her admission that it wasn't the reason for this little get together on Blalock Point.

"You see, Franklin was one of a group of Syracuse graduates who get together every so often. Those get togethers aren't really exactly reunions. They just involve people all of whom knew each other in college and still live in upstate New York. I used to be part of the group, but I don't get around very well since the accident. Anyway, the group decided to take a cruise this winter. They kept me posted about their plans, even if everyone knew I couldn't go along."

Although Carol still had plenty of coffee in her cup, Abbey Lipscomb suddenly decided she should put her hostess's cap on again.

"Would you like a refill? I would."

"If it's no trouble, I'd be delighted." Abbey retreated to the kitchen while Carol marveled at the fact that she was about to learn something about the man who had caused the *Azure Sea* to leave Barbados for Martinique an hour behind schedule.

"Now let's see, where was I? Oh, yes, the Caribbean cruise. The *Azure Sea*. I'm not a hundred percent sure who all was going. Stevens, Westerman, Pringle I think. The Craigs, I'm pretty sure they were along, too. It doesn't really matter, does it? There were probably eight. All of them had stayed or settled in the upstate area after college. Franklin lived in Newark. That's Newark, New York, not New Jersey. It's up near Rochester. Jim Westerman, he's further east, not far from Cooperstown, if I remember correctly. They're from all over the area, Binghamton, Elmira - you know, the southern tier. Like I said, what started this group thing is that we're all upstaters with a Syracuse University background.

"Anyway, if I can make a long story short, they were sailing from Fort Lauderdale. I don't know much of anything about most of their travel plans. But Franklin, he thought it'd be nice to stop by and say hello to an old friend who wouldn't be on the ship. That's me. He drove to the city for his flight by way of Crooked Lake, and we had a pleasant little reunion of our own right here. The last time I saw him we were sitting just about where you and I are right now."

For the first time since Carol had arrived at the Lipscomb house, Abbey started to tear up. There had been no hint as to the nature of her relationship with Franklin Pierce. Carol half expected that Abbey was about to enlighten her, but the moment passed without further comment.

"Which brings me to why I called you, sheriff. Franklin told me he'd send me cards from their ports of call, but none ever arrived. At first I thought it was just a matter of mail service on those little islands being slow. But when nearly a week after the cruise was over and I still hadn't heard from Franklin, I really began to worry. It turns out that I had good reason to. It was three days ago that I got a phone call. It was from Barbados, and the man identified himself as Inspector Williams. It seemed strange, a name like Williams and no Hispanic accent."

Carol wasn't about to remind Ms. Lipscomb that the inspector had an English name because Barbados had been a British colony. Better to let her get on with the business of explaining what the inspector's call had been about.

"And what was it that Inspector Williams wanted to tell you?" she asked, anxious for the woman to get to the point.

"That Franklin was dead."

"How did it happen that he called you?"

"When they found his body, there was a post card he'd written to me in his pocket. The inspector said that his wallet was missing and that the cruise line had no record of next of kin, just the Newark address. They'd have had no way of knowing that Franklin had no next of kin. He'd never married, and he had no siblings. So their best lead was that post card he never mailed to me."

"It must have been a painful conversation, you learning that Mr. Pierce was dead."

Mrs. Lipscomb shook her head.

"Oh, yes, it was painful, very painful. For me, of course, although the inspector sounded - what's the word, beleaguered?That's really why I wanted to talk to you."

"Why don't you tell me about your conversation with the inspector."

"Like I said, he wanted me to know that Franklin was dead. What's really important, though, is that he said he had been killed."

Ms. Lipscomb voice left no doubt about how shocking this information had been.

"That's terrible," Carol said, not choosing to divulge the fact that she was already aware that Pierce was dead. That he had been killed, however, was big news. "But what is it that you think I can do?"

"I'm not really sure, but like that inspector, you're in the law enforcement business. We haven't met - before today that is - but I know something about what you've done in apprehending our criminal element. So I thought maybe you could help people in Barbados catch Franklin's killer. They're just a little island, after all. They won't have the kind of experience you've had. Besides, the people Franklin was traveling with are all from around here where you could question them or whatever it takes to identify who killed him."

Oh, no, Carol thought. The nemesis of Crooked Lake's killers to the rescue. How little Abbey Lipscomb knows.

"I'm not sure I understand. Did this inspector who called tell you that whoever killed Franklin was one of his fellow Syracuse alumni group?"

"No, he didn't really talk about it. I think it was just a courtesy call because of the post card. But he did sound beleaguered, as if he was having a hard time. And I can understand that, what with Franklin's killer now all the way up here in western New York."

"How do you know that one of your old group killed him?" She had just said that the inspector hadn't elaborated about Pierce's death, which meant that Abbey either has a vivid imagination or she thinks she may know something important about Franklin's relationships with the other tour group members.

"Well I suppose I don't *know* that one of them killed Franklin. But isn't it logical? I wouldn't think that the natives in places like that go around killing tourists off a cruise boat."

It was rapidly becoming clear that Abbey Lipscomb had formed some opinions about her friend's death and had decided that Cumberland County's sheriff was the person to right this egregious wrong.

"I see," Carol said, now certain that what she said next would be a great disappointment to Abbey Lipscomb. "I'm afraid that what I think you're suggesting is impossible. Barbados is a sovereign country. If there's a problem, they'll be in touch with our State Department. Cumberland County has no diplomatic relations with Barbados. The fact that I was a fellow passenger of Mr. Pierce on the *Azure Sea* gives me no authority to intervene in Inspector Williams' investigation. If I knew something about what Mr. Pierce did when he went ashore on our last day in Bridgetown, I would feel a responsibility to share that information with the inspector. But I'd never met Mr. Pierce, never even heard of him in fact, not until after he missed the ship when it sailed from Barbados. Do you understand?"

Ms. Lipscomb was staring at the sheriff as if she were looking at an animal from some medieval bestiary.

"Are you telling me that you were on Franklin's cruise ship?" she asked, obviously non-plussed.

"Yes, I was. I assumed that's why you thought I might be able to help the inspector."

"This is unbelievable, sheriff," she said, her voice betraying considerable excitement. "I had no idea you were on the same cruise as Franklin. So you must have known all about his disappearance."

"The *Azure Sea's* departure was delayed for an hour because a passenger hadn't returned to the ship. It wasn't until later, when everyone began talking about the so-called missing man, that I learned his name was Pierce."

It was obvious that Lipscomb was still trying to make sense of this new and surprising information.

"But if you were right there, it makes even more sense that you could help Inspector Williams," she said.

"Why would that be? All I know about Mr. Pierce I learned without ever meeting him. Most of it I've learned today from you. The police on Barbados surely know far more than I do about what happened to him."

Suddenly Abbey Lipscomb's eyes lit up.

"That may be so, but they don't know anything about Franklin's group. The cruise was over and they had gone home before Franklin's body was found. So there's no way Inspector Williams or his people would have questioned them."

Carol was reasonably certain that Franklin's friends had been questioned by officials on the cruise ship and whatever they had learned about his whereabouts had been shared with the Barbados authorities. But in a sense Abbey was right. The other members of the tour group would have been questioned before his body had been discovered, and the purpose of those questions would have been solely to ascertain whether any of them knew what his plans for the day might have been.

"Don't you see," Ms. Lipscomb continued. "Barbados isn't going to send their police all the way up here to quiz the other members of the group about what happened. You can do it!"

Carol decided it was time to be a bit more direct.

"As I have said, Ms. Lipscomb, it would be irresponsible of me to assume that investigating Mr. Pierce's death is my responsibility. I have important duties right here that the county government and our citizens expect me to concentrate on. I am sorry about your friend, but you really must let the Barbados police handle the case."

"I suppose I should apologize," the sad faced woman finally said. "I thought I was doing the right thing."

"There is no reason to apologize," Carol said. "I'm the one who should apologize for not being able to do what you ask. We live in a complicated world. Working with the police of a nearby county can sometimes be a challenge; working with a foreign country is unfortunately another story altogether."

As she drove back to her office, Carol found herself hoping that the Barbadian police would indeed be able to solve the mystery of Franklin Pierce's death. But she was also congratulating herself that it was their task, not hers. The very thought of interrogating a flock of strangers, none of them Crooked Lake residents, about something that had happened in the distant Caribbean had briefly given her heartburn.

CHAPTER 4

"It was just bad luck," Inspector Brathwaite said for perhaps the third time.

"I'll never buy the 'bad luck' argument." Inspector Williams was stirring his coffee vigorously. "We could have spotted him more than once. Now it looks like we may have to deal with some small town American sheriff, just in case the man's killer was one of his shipboard partners. Which you and I know he wasn't."

"I don't know why you're so sure it was some drunken bajan who did it."

"Because tourists don't come here to kill each other. When has that ever happened? Some dumb local thought he had an easy mark and things went wrong. At least we won't have to embarrass ourselves by getting the State Department involved."

"Just who is this sheriff?"

"Good question. Washington says she seems to have had some experience with capital crime, but I didn't want it to look like we needed help, so it was mostly just a quick bio check. I hope I'm not going to regret sending that post card to the Lipscomb woman. If it weren't for her, I'd never have heard of this sheriff."

"You don't mean that, Cyril. It was the decent thing to do, and you always do the decent thing."

Williams knew that his colleague was right. But he wasn't enthusiastic about involving an American sheriff in his investigation. He would have politely dismissed Ms. Lipscomb's adamant insistence that he had to talk with the woman if it hadn't been for the fact that she had been on the *Azure Sea* with Mr. Pierce. A mere coincidence, apparently, but conceivably a fortuitous one. He very much doubted that the sheriff would have anything to contribute, having convinced himself that the killer would turn out to be a local. But he knew that unless they made an arrest fairly soon, he would have to reconsider the possibility that one of Pierce's tour mates might be guilty.

"I suppose I'd better call her," he said. He stared at the Royal Barbados Police Force plaque on the wall. "What have I gotten myself into?"

Inspector Williams said a grumpy 'good-bye' to Brathwaite and shuffled down the hall to his own office. He'd held the rank of inspector for over four years, and at no time in those four years had he ever embarrassed the RBPF or incurred the displeasure of any of the cruise lines whose ships regularly docked in Bridgetown. Pierce was surely not the first passenger to miss a scheduled departure time. But he was unfortunately the first whose failure to board his ship was because he had been killed while on shore, presumably by one of the inspector's countrymen. It was already becoming a black eye for the force. And for Barbados.

It was now more than 89 hours since Franklin Pierce's body had been discovered on the steps from the old ruined Harrysmith House down to the water. It wasn't in one of the country's more travelled areas. If the killer had done his work on the windward side of the island, why hadn't he left the body on the beach at Bathsheba? Or on a trail in Joe's River Forest? It would have been discovered much sooner. On the other hand, he knew that he himself was partially at fault. As the officer in charge, he had first concentrated the search for Pierce in and around Bridgetown. Given the shops and restaurants and its proximity to the dock, it had seemed like the most logical place to begin.

He consulted his notes, which now included the phone number of the sheriff of Cumberland County, and then made the call. While the phone in this unfamiliar rural area in upstate New York rang, the inspector forced himself to sit up straight in his chair and put a smile on his face. He was determined to be pleasant, to give the sheriff no reason to know how unenthusiastic he was to be asking for her help.

"This the Sheriff's office. What may I do for you?" Jo Anne, of course, had no idea that the this was a call that would have a dramatic impact on her boss's schedule for weeks to come.

"This is Inspector Cyril Williams of the Royal Barbados Police Force." The voice had an almost lyrical lilt to it. "I need to talk with the sheriff. I understand that her name is Kelleher."

JoAnne knew that the sheriff had recently been on a cruise in the Caribbean. She had even had a brief conversation with her about the disappearance of one of her shipmates in Barbados. But Carol had not shared with her what she had learned from Abbey Lipscomb. Why would someone in authority in that far away Caribbean island be calling Carol? Perhaps they had found something she had left behind when she was in Barbados. Perhaps. But it seemed unlikely that such a discovery would be reported by a long distance phone call from someone who called himself an inspector.

When JoAnne told the sheriff who was on the line, Carol was not surprised. She had half expected the Lipscomb woman to get back in touch with Inspector Williams. What was worse, she had very probably told him that the sheriff was in a position to help him identify Franklin Pierce's killer. Otherwise, it was unlikely that the inspector would be on the phone to the sheriff's office in Cumberland County.

"Hello, this is Sheriff Kelleher. How may I help you?"

"I'm sure you weren't expecting a call from a member of the Barbados police, sheriff. Let me explain." Carol found the voice fascinating. Soft, honey toned. If pressed, she would have called it mesmerizing.

"I am investigating a murder, a murder of someone you know. He was a passenger on the cruise ship *Azure Sea* which docked here in Barbados several weeks ago. It is my understanding that you were on that same cruise."

"Excuse me, inspector," Carol interrupted. "I did take a cruise recently on the *Azure Sea*, and I spent a lovely day in your country. I have since learned that one of the other passengers on that cruise never made it back to the ship on the day of its departure because he had been killed while on shore. But I did not know this man. We had never met. Most of what little I know about him is the result of a conversation with a friend of his. Her name is Abbey Lipscomb. I am assuming that Ms. Lipscomb is the person who gave you my name."

"Perhaps I misunderstood Ms. Lipscomb. About you knowing this man, I mean. His name, by the way, is Franklin Pierce."

Carol had decided to act innocent, to let the inspector explain his reason for calling.

"So I understand. But why are you calling me?"

"Perhaps we should begin by my asking a few questions. I know you must be very busy, but may I take a few minutes of your time?"

"I suppose that would depend on the nature of your questions, but why don't you try me."

"Thank you, sheriff. This is very kind of you." Carol could hear what sounded like papers being shuffled. Inspector Williams was trying to conjure up a picture of the person he was speaking to.

"Let me begin by asking you about Ms. Lipscomb. She claims to be a resident of a place called Crooked Lake in New York State, and she says that you are the person responsible for maintaining law and order there, which means that you and I are in the same profession. She also speaks very highly of your reputation. It may seem like a strange question, but if I may, how would you describe your relationship with Ms. Lipscomb?"

"Until a couple of days ago I did not know Ms. Lipscomb at all. I had never heard of her, much less met her. But what you want to know, I assume, is why she called you and why she brought my name up in her conversation with you. I have been sheriff in this jurisdiction for just over a decade. This is basically a rural area, with a relatively small population, so it is not surprising that Ms. Lipscomb, like most people who live here, knows who I am. When she learned that Mr. Pierce, an old friend of hers, had been killed - she said that you were the one who gave her the news - she had the idea that I might be able to help you discover who killed him."

"Yes, that's what she told me," the inspector said. Carol thought his voice sounded doubtful.

"I explained to her that a crime in Barbados was well outside my jurisdiction. But Ms. Lipscomb is, shall we say, tenacious. She had formerly been a member of the tour group that Mr. Pierce was traveling with. In fact, she would have been with them but for a physical problem. For some reason, she seems to have decided that he might have been killed by one of his friends."

Carol realized that 'killed by one of his friends' was perhaps not the best way to put what Ms. Lipscomb had said.

"You should know that not only do I know nothing about Mr. Pierce, I know nothing about the people in his small tour group. I have no idea why Ms. Lipscomb got the idea that one of those people might have been responsible for Pierce's death. She didn't tell me anything about the members of the group who were on the cruise, other than that they had all attended Syracuse University and occasionally took trips together. Inasmuch as I had no intention of becoming involved in the matter, I didn't ask her about them."

A question occurred to Carol.

"Ms. Lipscomb must have called you and spoken with you a second time, after her meeting with me. Did she mention the name of a specific member of the tour group that she suspects of killing Pierce?"

"No. Quite the contrary, my impression is that she has simply decided that she may not know this group of friends as well as she thought she did, and that there might have been bad blood between one of them and Mr. Pierce. In any event, she is now obsessed with the idea that you are the one to find out who that someone is. She went on at great length, explaining that members of the group live close to where you also live and work, so that it would be easy for you to interrogate all of them and use your considerable skills to identify the killer."

My considerable skills. Carol realized that she was very annoyed with Abbey Lipscomb. The woman must have given the inspector a glowing and almost certainly inflated account of her handling of Crooked Lake's recent murders. But she was also, and to her surprise, annoyed with Inspector Williams as well. He hadn't said it, but she thought that his use of the 'considerable skills' phrase had a sardonic ring to it.

"I think we may be back to my earlier question, inspector. Why are you calling me?"

"May I be perfectly frank, sheriff?" Williams sounded uncomfortable, which in fact he was. He didn't wait for Carol to tell him that she would be grateful if he were frank. "As you know, this is indeed a matter for the Royal Barbados Police Force. I believe that Mr. Pierce's death was caused, not by one of his traveling companions, but by a Barbadian. I don't have to tell you that there are bad people who take advantage of others everywhere. We like to think that such people are few and far between here in Barbados, but there is the occasional mugging, a tourist is robbed, things like that. Do you understand?"

The inspector wanted the sheriff to know that Barbados was a safe place, but that once in a blue moon there was an exception.

"Unfortunately, we haven't found the culprit yet. So I do not have the luxury of dismissing out of hand Ms. Lipscomb's theory. I am sure she is wrong, but I have decided that it might be useful to talk with Mr. Pierce's companions. I am hoping that you may be willing to help me do that."

Inspector Williams paused. Carol waited. Helping him would be much more complicated than simply volunteering to make the acquaintance of a number of Syracuse alums who had recently taken a Caribbean cruise.

"I am in no position to travel to where these people live," he said. He was simply stating a fact, not apologizing for what he was obviously about to ask the sheriff to do. "But it is my understanding that the people Mr. Pierce was traveling with all live in the same area that you do. I know that it would be an imposition, but I would be most grateful if you would consent to talk with each of these people, learn what you can about their relationship with Mr. Pierce, and find out what they were doing on their last day in Barbados. I suppose you could say that you would be serving as my eyes and ears."

Ears, yes, Carol thought. She was doubtful when it came to eyes.

Inspector Williams hastened to elaborate on his request.

"We here in Bridgetown cannot, of course, compensate you adequately for your assistance, but I can assure you that there would be a modest remuneration. I know that you were in my country only a matter of weeks ago, but I believe that it's desirable for you to come back so that we could meet and so that I could show you where we found Mr. Pierce's body and how one would presumably have gotten there from Bridgetown."

He paused, as if to let the magnitude of the task sink in.

"It is quite possible, Sheriff Kelleher, that none of this will be necessary. As I have said, I am still optimistic that we shall have arrested a bajan - sorry, a local Barbadian - shortly. But I am hoping that you will be willing to do what I have suggested. I am sure that your friend Ms. Lipscomb would also be greatly pleased."

Carol wanted to repeat that Abbey Lipscomb was not her friend, but didn't wish to sound cranky. She had decided about six minutes ago that she was going to agree to help Inspector Williams. Whether doing so would be a courtesy to a friendly neighboring country or simply an unanticipated adventure she wasn't sure.

"When would you like me to come to Bridgetown?" she asked.

"I'm sure you understand how urgent things are for us," Williams said. "I have made a tentative reservation for you to fly down from New York the day after tomorrow."

How thoughtful, Carol thought. He's giving me time to pack my bag. This time it was the sheriff who was asking what she had gotten herself into.

CHAPTER 5

Carol sat at her desk, trying to organize her thoughts. She had told Abbey Lipscomb that becoming part of the investigation of Franklin Pierce's death was none of her business. She had enough on her plate right here on Crooked Lake without taking on the work of the Royal Barbados Police Force. And she had meant every word of it. But she had just told Inspector Williams that she would do what she had told Abbey she would not do. Moreover, she had told him that she would start doing it right away. There was no getting around it, she had been talked into a task that was in no way a part of her responsibility, a task that could well prove to be a major thief of her time.

It was, of course, one thing to say no to a citizen of Cumberland County whom she didn't even know and quite another to say no to a Barbadian official who was asking for her help in his official capacity. What was bothering her at the moment was that she had agreed to do as he asked without consulting her superiors in the county government. Not to mention failing to discuss it with her own husband, who was dutifully teaching his classes down in the city. What would he think? And then there was Deputy Sheriff Bridges, just down the hall. What would he think when she told him that he might well be acting sheriff for who knows how long. And unofficially at that.

She was about to get up and go tell Sam what was going on, but she sat back down and wiped what appeared to be sweat from her brow. For the first time that she could remember, Carol felt the beginning of a panic attack. She took a few deep breaths and tried to console herself with the thought that the inspector believed Franklin Pierce's killer was a local Barbadian. The need for her services would vanish in a day or two with word that an arrest had been made, that the case was well on its way to a solution back in Barbados. Thanks for being willing to help out, but we don't need you. Unfortunately, that thought did not have the calming effect she had hoped for. She had already agreed to fly to Barbados the day after tomorrow, and the odds that her trip would be aborted within the next 24 hours by news that the killer was in jail in Bridgetown seemed remote. More importantly, what if the inspector's belief that the crime had been committed by what he called a bajan was nothing but a ploy to convince her that it was unlikely she would actually be needed?

After a few more deep breaths, Carol got up once again and went to Sam's office. They talked for the better part of 45 minutes, during which time she did her best neither to overstate the situation nor dismiss it as but a minor challenge to their routines. Sam took the news, as he did most things, in a relatively matter of fact manner. It was only the occasional wry smile that made it clear that he knew that Carol was just being Carol.

That having been taken care of, she apprised JoAnne of the situation and had her check on flights that would put her in the city in time for a flight to Bridgetown.The rest of the afternoon she devoted to worrying about what she was doing and, necessarily, about what she would not be doing.

"Hi, Kevin. How are things down there?"

Carol knew that her husband didn't have an evening seminar, and he didn't usually take in a concert or an opera on a week night. As she had expected, he was at home, presumably grading papers.

"To what do I owe the pleasure?" he said, his voice suddenly more upbeat than when he'd answered the phone.

"How would you like to meet me at JFK for a drink between flights on Monday?"

"Between flights? I don't know what you're talking about."

"I know. That's why I called. I'm taking a short trip and it will take me through the city, so I thought we could share a glass of wine and a kiss before I headed back upstate."

"Well, this is news. Where are you going? I don't recall any travel plans on either of our schedules."

"Where I'm going is Barbados. How's that for a surprise? Two visits to that enchanted island in one winter. Not bad, huh?"

"If I didn't know better, I'd tell you to put the cork back in the bottle. What's this about Barbados? I thought we'd already done that."

"We did, and I loved it. But I'm sure you remember the man who didn't make it back to the cruise ship. You're the one who told me he didn't make it because he was dead. It turns out he was dead because somebody had killed him, and the Royal Barbados Police Force wants me to help discover his killer."

Carol let that sink in.

"I can't believe this. You've been invited to be an honorary member of the Barbados police? I'm sure it's a compliment, but for God's sake why?"

"If you're standing up, sit down and I'll tell you the whole story, or at least what I know of it at the moment."

Their conversation lasted for nearly an hour, at which point she reiterated her suggestion that they get together at the airport while she waited for her connecting flight to the Corning/Elmira airport.

"How about postponing that last leg of your trip and spending a day or two in my apartment. We could turn your newly minted international notoriety into something special."

"I was sure you'd ask, but the answer has to be no. I'd love to, but I'll have been doing pro bono work at the expense of my job, and if I want to keep the job I'd better be putting my sheriff's hat back on."

"Don't say I didn't try," Kevin said. "Oh well, we've still got a long weekend during my spring break, right?"

"We do, but last time I checked my calendar you were planning to come to the lake then."

"I know. But do me a favor, wrap up this Barbados caper in a hurry so you don't have to be running off to Bridgeport again while I'm at the cottage."

"That's my plan. Right now I have to pack my bag and get some sleep. Love you - good night."

Getting some sleep proved to be the more difficult of the two tasks. There was too much else occupying her mind, such as composing a carefully worded letter to the county authorities, a letter in which she emphasized that she would be accepting no money from the RBPF, only the round trip air fare, and that she would discharge her commitment quickly. By the time she had fallen asleep she still hadn't figured out how to make 'quickly' more specific.

CHAPTER 6

There were only a handful of people waiting for the passengers to disembark from the plane, so it was not difficult for Carol to spot Inspector Williams, the man with whom she would be working to solve the killing of Franklin Pierce. His uniform gave him away. But even had he been wearing mufti, she would have recognized Williams, even if she had formed no idea from their telephone conversation what he would look like. He towered over the rest of those greeting the plane, several inches above six feet tall, every bit the authority figure. He was totally bald, and his beautiful mahogany skin glistened in the mid-afternoon sun.

His face broke into a smile as he spotted Carol. He had no better idea of what she would look like than she did of him, and the fact that she was wearing a beige pant suit, not a policeman's uniform, didn't help. But years spent cultivating the art of sizing up strangers made the call an easy one.

"Officer Kelleher," he said as he stepped through the small crowd and extended his hand. "Welcome to Barbados. Rumor has it that this is your second visit this winter."

Carol returned the inspector's smile.

"I must confess to some ambivalence about this second visit, but how could I not say yes to your appeal for help in the Pierce case."

"Yes, I know." The smile faded temporarily. "What we are doing is somewhat unusual. Here, let me take your bag."

Carol was quite able to manage the small suitcase, thanks to the fact that it had wheels and was lightly packed. But she sensed that in this case protocol called for her to turn it over to the inspector.

"My car is just around the corner over there," he said. "I'll take you to your motel, but perhaps we can first make a brief stop at my office. It's only a few blocks away."

A quarter of an hour later the right hand drive vehicle had pulled into the parking lot of a pink stucco building which bore the RBPF shield above its entrance. In just over another three minutes they were seated in Inspector Williams' office and tea had been ordered.

"The best way to bring you up to date on the Pierce case is to drive to where we found his body and to other places where we think he or his friends may have spent time the day when he didn't make it back to the ship. Given the hour, I think it would be best if we did that tomorrow."

The inspector reached into his desk drawer and pulled out a detailed map of Barbados.

"How well would you say you know our island, sheriff?"

"Not well, I'm afraid. We only had the one day here, and other than Bridgetown, the Gun Hill Signal Station, and a plantation or two we didn't wander far afield. My husband had wanted us to spend part of the day on the windward side, but frankly we didn't budget our time very well and we never made it."

"That's a shame. You would have enjoyed Bathsheba. But that's beside the point. What matters is that you will need a reasonably good mental picture of the island if you are to question all of those people who were in Mr. Piece's tour group."

He looked at Carol as if to gauge whether she understood his point.

"Of course. It's been my understanding that that's why I'm back in Barbados."

"Good. We aren't all that big a place, and I think we can skip the northern parishes."

"Where, may I ask," Carol asked, "was it that you found Mr. Pierce?"

"To our surprise it was in St. Philip parish, which is at the southeastern end of the island."

He spread the map out on the desk and pointed to a place where the island country bulged out into the Atlantic.

"Do you know how he got there?" Carol asked. "Car rental, taxi? I assume it's beyond walking distance."

What Carol was beginning to think of as a perpetual smile vanished from Inspector Williams' face. She regretted asking what was really an obvious question.

"Unfortunately, we aren't sure." He didn't choose to elaborate. "Chances are somebody passed him on the road and offered him a ride."

Carol was processing what the inspector had said and hadn't said. It was likely that he had already talked to all of the rental companies and checked the records of whoever operated the island's fleet of cabs. Now he was unhappy to have to report that he still didn't know how Pierce had ended up where he did. For the first time Carol had a feeling that the inspector was embarrassed for the RBPF, worried that this sheriff from a small town in the United States would be forming a negative opinion of him and his ability to police this small Caribbean country.

She decided it was time to call it a day.

"Inasmuch as I'm going to be taking most of your time tomorrow, why don't I check in at the motel and let you get back to your own agenda. Is that okay with you?"

"Certainly. I only brought you here so you could have a look at my office. It's not luxurious, as you can see. In any event, you'll be needing some down time after your flight, so let's head for the motel."

Once again Carol let the inspector take her bag, and they set off for what would be her home away from home for the next couple of nights. Bridgetown is not a large place, but they had only been on its streets for a couple of minutes before she had lost her bearings. It turned out that the motel was in a less crowded and less noisy neighborhood than she remembered from the cruise. She had no idea whether it had been selected because the RBPF was being solicitous of a fellow policeman from the United States. Perhaps rooms were simply scarce at this time of year, and she had been assigned a room in what was available.

The desk clerk was obviously impressed when the tall figure of a police inspector deposited Carol's bag and issued a stern warning to take good care of her. Williams did not, however, linger or show any interest in escorting the sheriff to her room.

"Have a good evening," he said, raising his right hand to his forehead in a mock salute. "I shall be here at 9 o'clock. In the morning, that is. We have quite a bit of ground to cover."

It was clear to Carol that the desk clerk had been studying her carefully. She wondered what he would make of the brief scene he had just witnessed in the lobby.

———

If this was what she had to do, she wanted to brush aside her reservations, still strong, and get started. She had set the alarm for 7, but she was awake far before that and ready for whatever the day would bring well before 8. Inspector Williams entered the motel lobby promptly at 9, just as he had said he would. The smile was back, but somehow it didn't look as if he meant it..

"I've brought along a driver," he said. "He's green, but he knows the roads as well as I do, and we'll cover more ground if I can concentrate on your Mr. Pierce rather than the roads and Barbados traffic."

Barbados traffic was already heavy, the streets full of vehicles large and small, many of them painted with bright colors. The inspector, after a few 'how did you sleep,' 'did you have a good breakfast' questions, put on his tour guide hat to explain the difference between the many yellow and blue vans and those that were white with a maroon stripe. Carol didn't say so, but she was privately pleased that she and Kevin had not chosen to ride in one of the multi-colored open-sided buses that periodically blocked their path as they headed east across the island.

Once out of Bridgetown, they gathered speed as they headed for the place where Franklin Pierce's body had been found. Carol had the map of Barbados spread across her lap, trying to match names on it with places on the roadside. Williams said little other than occasionally giving her a progress report on the number of miles left before they reached Harrysmith.

He had explained that their first destination carried that name at both a old ruined 'great house' and the beach below it. Carol did not want to revisit the question she had raised the day before, the question of how Pierce had probably traveled from Bridgetown to the place where he had been found and presumably met his death. But as the miles slipped by, the more certain she was that he had not walked there. He might have rented a bicycle, but even that began to look unlikely. Barbados was not a large island - the map gave its dimensions as roughly 14 by 21 miles. But it was large enough to discourage cruise ship passengers from setting off to see the sights on foot. By the time they reached the Harrysmith house, Carol was virtually certain that Pierce had driven or been driven to it. Williams had presumably reached the same conclusion.

There was no other vehicle in sight when they parked near what was left of the old house. Undoubtedly they would have company later in the day, but Carol was ready to believe that this was not high on the list of destinations for most tourists. She had no idea how popular it was with the locals.

"Let's walk around to the ocean side," the inspector said. "The view is quite spectacular, and there's a stone step path down to the beach. It was on that path that we found the body."

Although the inspector didn't seem interested in taking her through the house, she peeked into what was left of it in several places, enough to provide ample evidence that it was now virtually roofless and otherwise a victim of decades of wind and weather. And total neglect. The path to the beach was not marked, and was in fact partly overgrown, but the inspector knew exactly where he was going and they were soon at the cliff edge.

"There are several beaches down there," he said. "That's Harrysmith at our feet, Bottom Beach next to it. From here on north to Bathsheba and beyond are the true windward beaches, rough surf, great rock formations. This one is one of the smallest."

Williams was obviously pleased to take a minute to rhapsodize about the country's beautiful east coast. But almost as quickly as he had begun to wax ecstatic about the beaches, he turned sober and, urging the sheriff to watch her footing, started down the stone path. It was hemmed in by dense foliage on both sides, much of it in the form of a large rubbery leafed plant Carol didn't recognize.

A third of the way to the beach, the inspector stopped and waited for her to catch up.

"Right there," he said, pointing to the side of path. "That's where we found him. These sea grape plants make a great hiding place. Those leaves are the damnedest things, practically a green blanket. They're tough, too. Whoever did it managed to stuff him under the sea grapes so you'd never know he was there unless you took a machete to them. Of course they'e all over our shores, and we didn't figure he'd be over here. This isn't one of Barbados' top ten attractions. I'd have bet on Bathsheba, but I'd have been wrong."

Carol was interested that the inspector had in effect admitted that he'd lost what might have been several valuable days before he turned his attention to Harrysmith House and beach.

"I realize I've never asked how Mr. Pierce met his death. How was he killed?"

"It was a pretty primitive killing. No gun, no knife. The killer did a neck snap on him." The inspector looked at Carol to see if she understood what he was talking about. "You know, a guy grabs the victim's head, gives it a sharp twist, breaks his neck."

"I thought that only happens in the movies. It would take an awfully strong man, and even then death would be problematic."

"I know," the inspector said, aware that the sheriff knew what she was talking about. "The killer wasn't taking any chances. He made sure Pierce was dead. Smashed in his head. Not sure what the guy who did it used, but it was heavy enough to do the job."

"Where did it happen? I mean, do you think he was killed right about here, on the path, or was there anything to suggest he might have been lugged down from the old house or up from the beach?"

Williams looked down at where Carol was prodding under the sea grape leaves. He had been concerned that she would ask a lot of questions, and she seemed to be ready to do just that. Of course to do the job he had asked her to do, she would need to know everything he had learned in his frustrating investigation. Nonetheless, he sounded as if he was irritated.

"It's most likely the killing took place right where we're standing. I have trouble picturing the killer moving the body up from the beach. Or down from up there, for that matter," he added, jerking his head toward the Harrysmith House. "Of course Pierce could have been moved some distance if the killer was a big, strong man. In any event, this is where he was eventually found - it was the odor that did it."

"About how big would you say Pierce was?"

Williams was surprised by the question.

"I thought you knew him," he said, but immediately remembered that she had denied any knowledge of Pierce and his traveling partners. "Oh, sorry, you didn't know any of them, did you?"

"No, I'm afraid not."

"Well, then, about Pierce, he was about 5 foot eight or nine, and probably hit the scales at 165 or thereabouts."

"So it would have been *possible* to move him - what would it be, 100 yards?"

"It would depend on the killer, and I don't know any more about him than you do."

Carol wanted to ask if there had been any sign that the body had been moved, such as blood on the stones, but she didn't put that question to the inspector. It would only create the impression that she might have doubts about his ability to conduct an investigation.

"One thing that seems clear to me," she did say, "is that the killer was lucky that there was no one else around to watch him beat Mr. Pierce to death. And that suggests that it may not have been a pre-meditated killing, but rather a spur of the moment act made possible by the fact that there were no other tourists or locals in the vicinity. That would be consistent with your argument that the Harrysmith area isn't a top ten attraction here in Barbados."

Once again, Carol was conscious of the way the inspector was looking at her. Maybe he isn't resentful of what I have to say, she thought. Hopefully he's discovering that, to his surprise, I may make a good partner.

"Okay, this is where it happened," Williams said. "Let's get back to the car and head up the coast. I want to show you a few places where some of Mr. Pierce's group may have gone that day. It could help you decide whether they're telling the truth or making it up."

They were soon on the way to Bathsheba.

CHAPTER 7

Once again Williams' green driver, now identified as Clarence, took them over roads that Carol had trouble following on the map. The inspector spoke up whenever he thought a particular road or roadside landmark would be useful for the sheriff to keep in mind, but for the most part he remained silent until they approached Bathsheba.

"You understand," the inspector said, "that the places I'll be showing you won't begin to cover all the attractions that Mr. Pierce's friends might have visited when their ship docked here. There's necessarily quite a bit of guess work involved in where we're going today. You'd have to be here at least a week to see most of the top tourists attractions, and there's no guarantee that even then you wouldn't miss a place where one or more of that group spent the day."

Carol had given enough thought to the problem to realize that the inspector wasn't simply engaged in promoting Barbados.

"Why don't you let me in on what decided you on the places we will be visiting?" she asked.

"Some of it is geography, the rest hunches based on government records and local wisdom. For example, I mentioned that we wouldn't be going up to the north end of the island. It's not that I'm indifferent to St. Lucy parish, but I have trouble imaging that someone would spend his day up there *and* also go to St. Philip to kill Pierce. They're at opposite ends of the country. That's the geography angle. My hunches are just that, but I like to think they're based on common sense. Unless these people you're going to be talking to have been to Barbados before, the odds are they'd hit the spots that command the most attention on the internet. Which is one of the reasons we're going to Bathsheba next. We'll stop there and then check out Hunte's Gardens and a couple of my other hunches while we're in the area."

"You realize, I assume, that you're in the process of talking me into a longer visit than I had planned."

Inspector Williams looked momentarily ill at ease.

"Don't worry, inspector," Carol said, "I'm not going to be a further charge on your budget. Just the flight. And frankly, my responsibilities to my own government won't let me stay beyond tomorrow. I'd love to, but it's simply impossible."

"It's a difficult mission you've undertaken, isn't it?"

"How so?" Carol asked, surprised by the inspector's remark.

"You say you don't know any of these people, including Pierce. And you don't know where any of them spent their day on Barbados. Yet you have agreed to take time from your usual schedule to try to figure out whether one of them killed Mr. Pierce. It sounds like a daunting assignment to me."

"But it was you who persuaded me to do it," she said defensively.

"I know. Perhaps I was wrong."

The conversation was taking an interesting turn, but it was interrupted by Clarence.

"We're here, sir. Where would you like me to go?"

Williams turned around in his seat.

"Let's do the *Palm Cove*," he said. "Just head for the beach and turn left at the roundabout. "

He turned back toward Carol.

"Why don't we stop and have an early lunch. You'll have a good view of the beach and our famous rocks. Okay?"

"Sure. Whatever you say."

They had good seats and a good view, and the lunch proved to be as good as the inspector had advertised. A few words were exchanged, but it was obvious that Williams was giving the sheriff an opportunity to soak up the atmosphere of one of Barbados' best locations. But Carol was interested in his 'perhaps I was wrong' comment which he had never explained.

"If you don't mind, inspector," she said, "I'd like to go back to what we were talking about before we decided to have lunch. You had suggested that you thought my assignment in the Pierce case was a daunting one. But when I reminded you that you had asked me to do it, you said you might have been wrong. Why is that?"

"Let me be frank, sheriff. I have been quite confident from the beginning that Mr. Pierce had been killed by one of my fellow bajans. But the Lipscomb woman kept insisting that the killer could be one of his colleagues. Inasmuch as I still wasn't able to confirm my suspicion, I guess I took the path of least resistance and told Ms. Lipscomb that I'd ask you to work with me. It was an easy thing for me to say, wasn't it? All it would cost my department was one round trip air fare. I wouldn't have to go anywhere. You'd be the one whose routine would be put on hold. It was when we were over at Harrysmith this morning that I think I first saw this from your point of view."

It sounded like an apology. Carol thought it best to assure him that no apology was necessary.

"That's kind of you to say, inspector, but you needn't worry. I could have declined your invitation." She thought that 'invitation' was the right way to put it. After all, he could not have ordered her to join his investigation. "In any event, I can agree with you that Ms. Lipscomb is tenacious. When I get back, I intend to spend more time with her. She may know more than she thinks she does about the fellow members of Mr. Pierce's tour group."

Williams found his smile again.

"I wish you luck," he said, sounding somewhat relieved.

———

When they resumed their partial tour of the island, Clarence took them to a number of places which the inspector insisted were the most likely spots for tourists to visit.

"Like I said, we can't cover everything. I'm skipping the popular party-boat tours and the snorkeling and diving. That may be a mistake, but those things tend to attract the younger set, people in their late 20s and 30s. Otherwise, it's pretty much guess work. Some tourists spend their time with the plants and the animals - always hoping to see our monkeys. We won't stop at Gun Hill - you said you were there. I think we can forget the rum visitors' centers, too. So while we're near Bathsheba, we'll take a quick look at Hunte's and the botanic garden and then head back toward Bridgetown via the Flower Forest."

"That sounds like a full afternoon," Carol said.

"It is. I've included one more top ten tourist stop. That's Harrison's Cave. My suggestion is that when you get back home you rustle up Barbados on your computer and spend some time reading websites with pictures. There'll be a ton of them."

Carol shook her head.

"I never believed I'd learn a lot by taking another trip to your country. Other than meeting you, of course. It has been a pleasure. You've talked about your hunches. Mine is that I'll learn more about Pierce's tour group from their personalities than from what they saw or didn't see while they were here. You know, it's how comfortably they respond to questions, those little vibes people give off when they're in a room with a police officer."

"Makes sense," Williams said. "Anyhow, it won't hurt to see at least some of the places these people will have seen. Who knows, somebody may inadvertently give the lie to the claim he was at Harrison's Cave by placing it near the airport."

The afternoon went by quickly, and every place they visited or drove through reminded her of how many things she and Kevin had missed on their cruise. She made a few notes, but mostly tried to keep track of relationships by consulting her map as they drove from one spot to another.

When they got back to her motel, Carol had to acknowledge to herself that she was tired. The inspector offered to take her to dinner, but she demurred.

"I think I need to kick my shoes off for an hour and then limit myself to a quick snack. A few hours of sleep and I'll head for the airport."

"No taxi, please, sheriff. I'll pick you up. But I don't seem to have your departure time in my memory bank. When must you be at the airport?"

"Sorry, but I'll be calling a taxi. My flight leaves at four something in the a.m., and I have no intention of prevailing on your good will at such an ungodly hour. It's also the departure hour that persuaded me to say no to your kind offer of dinner."

Inspector Williams looked shocked, as well he might have. Obviously a secretary had booked the flight, but the inspector thoughtfully declined to blame her for the result. Perhaps Barbados and the airlines had collaborated to dissuade tourists from leaving.

"I had no idea," he said. "Which means that this is good-bye and good luck."

He stepped closer for a quick *faire la bise*. Carol was surprised at the cheek to cheek kiss, but so was Williams. The sheriff knew of the custom, but it wasn't the American way. It was common in the islands, but the inspector knew instantly that his intentions might be misunderstood.

They pulled apart and within seconds both were laughing.

"Do you know the movie *Casablanca*?" Carol asked.

"Of course. Who doesn't?"

"Well, if I may quote Bogart, I think this is the beginning of a beautiful friendship."

"Thank you, sheriff. I know we shall be staying in touch. Say hello to Ms. Lipscomb and have a safe flight."

Carol watched him as he returned to his car. The desk clerk watched Carol watching the inspector. What he thought of what he was seeing he didn't say.

Chapter 8

Carol spent most of the flight back to JFK catching up on her sleep. When she came to somewhere not far north of Washington, her thoughts turned inevitably to what she had learned from her trip to Barbados. Her conclusion: not much.

But no, that wasn't correct. Nor fair. Her initial impression of Inspector Williams had been neutral, perhaps slightly unpleasant. He had been superficially friendly, but she hadn't been able to dismiss the feeling that he didn't like to have to deal with the presence in his work life of another law enforcement officer. She ran the possible reasons for this impression through her mind. He was used to working alone? He resented the fact that he had to share his investigation of the Pierce case with an American official? He was so sure that the killer was a Barbadian that he felt he was wasting his time? Even that he had an aversion to working with a woman?

The last of these explanations she tended to dismiss as unimportant. She had had enough experience with gender bias in her career as a lawyer and a law enforcement official to take it in stride. Besides, the inspector had never said anything which would give credence to the view that he was opposed to women in his field of work. Moreover, he had been considerably more pleasant, or at least more forthcoming, as the day wore on, which had softened her impression of him. When they had parted the previous evening he had seemed weary, but she thought it was because the Pierce case was proving frustrating rather than that she was somehow a cross he had to bear.

No matter, she was now on her way back to Crooked Lake and a much colder winter. And there was the prospect of spending an hour with Kevin while she waited for her connecting flight. She peered out the window, only to find that she could see nothing. The cloud cover had not dissipated in several hours, and probably would not lift before landing. For some reason she had not checked on the weather forecast for upstate New York; she hoped that there would be no problem in completing her trip home from Barbados.

It proved to be a business-as-usual landing, and in due course she found herself in a lounge with Kevin. He spotted her before she saw him, and came quickly across the room to embrace her in a big and welcome hug.

"Couldn't get enough of Barbados, could you?" he said as he released her from the hug.

"I like it, but you look much better," Carol said as she caught her breath.

"Come on. I'll walk you down to the bar. How much time do you have?"

"More than an hour. Enough to give you the highlights."

Most of the conversation over their Chardonnays focussed on the inspector, with the occasional side excursion into Carol's comments on what they had to see if and when they took another trip to the Caribbean.

"What next?" Kevin finally asked.

"To be perfectly honest, I haven't given it as much thought as I should - as I'm going to have to. But it's pretty clear that I'm going to need more time with Abbey Lipscomb. She's the one that made this trip necessary. There's no question about it, if it hadn't been for her I'd never have been back to Barbados. The inspector said as much. So I'll be spending more time with her than with all the rest of this mysterious tour group. There has to be more to her conviction that one of Pierce's cruise mates killed him than she's let on. I'm not even sure she know's why. I'll have to dig it out of her."

"You are going to have those fellow upstate passengers of ours on the carpet, though, aren't you?"

"Oh, yes, but not until Lipscomb tells me everything she can about each of them. By the way, any advice about how you'd do it? I mean, do I meet them all as a group first, or do I question them one by one?"

"Thanks for the opportunity to provide some input," Kevin said, chuckling as he said it. "Unfortunately, my answer is I don't know. You like the one at a time approach. That I know from experience. But I guess I'd wait until you've quizzed the Lipscomb woman first. Not that it's her call, but I'd bet you'll have a better sense of how to proceed after you've quizzed her."

"Glad we agree on that. My current plan, very much subject to revision of course, is to see if Lipscomb will arrange to have them all meet at her house. Let's call it a memorial get-together for Franklin Pierce. Needless to say, I'll be there. My reason can't be because I'm after Pierce's killer. Too soon. Better to explain it by saying I was on the cruise, too, and like everyone else was interested in what happened. If you were at the lake, you could sit in with me, but I guess I'll have to fly solo."

"Maybe not. What if I could wangle a couple of days leave? I'm sure I've got some unused sick days. Besides, my assistant is quite able to take my classes for a day or two."

Carol rolled her eyes good naturedly.

"I have a long memory, Kevin. Need I remind you of that assistant who almost nipped our romance in the bud?"

"Ancient history, Carol. Anyway, this one is a guy. Jeremy Hurley. But seriously, I could be there with enough notice."

"Let's take it one step at a time. I haven't even had my debriefing with Lipscomb."

The familiar banter continued until Carol had to head for her flight to the Corning/Elmira airport. Kevin walked her to the departure area, kissed her good-bye, and demanded regular updates on his wife's first international case.

"I'll call, just like I always do. But remember, this isn't my case. My job is to stay out of Inspector Williams' way."

"Good luck with that," he called after her as she went through the gate.

CHAPTER 9

When Carol's plane set down at the small airport some 40 miles from Southport, she welcomed the landing with a huge sigh of relief. It had been an unusually bumpy ride, with strong turbulence keeping her on edge for much of the last two hundred miles. She had never been afraid of flying, but this last leg of her return trip from Barbados had been a strong test of that attitude.

Her welcome home became even more unpleasant when she stepped off the plane, only to be buffeted by winds which she felt certain were somewhere in the 40 to 50 mph range. Not much snow was falling, but what lay on the ground had been whipped into a near blinding blizzard. By the time she reached her car, she was regretting that she had not worn something warmer or thought to pack gloves. The contrast to Barbados was dramatic.

Never one to exceed the speed limit unless involved in an emergency, Carol was even more cautious than usual all the way back to the cottage. At times the snow was blinding, and by the time she had parked the car and unlocked the back door she thought she knew what people meant when they said they felt like a nervous wreck. Having turned up the thermostat, she headed for the kitchen to start a pot of coffee. It wasn't until she had taken off her coat that she remembered that she hadn't picked up the mail from its box behind the cottage. Not to worry, she said to herself. Coffee first.

The overcast and the windblown snow made it deceptively dark outside, but in fact it was only mid-afternoon, thanks to the pre-dawn departure from Bridgetown. When the coffee was ready, Carol took her cup to Kevin's study and turned on the radio for a weather forecast. She found it interesting that she hadn't given a thought to the weather since leaving for Barbados, whereas now it was very much on her mind. There was a five minute wait for the Rochester weatherman, but when he gave his report it was obvious that the region was about to be hit with a major storm. The weatherman sounded as if he were delighted to be the harbinger of good news. The next day's TV shows would carry endless shots of newscasters standing in snowbanks as the occasional brave driver crept by. Carol was not so happy. She was used to the snow and the cold of upstate New York. It came with the territory. But she was anxious to put her post-Barbados plans into action, beginning with a serious conversation with Abbey Lipscomb. It could still be possible, but she knew that these winter storms had a way of disrupting the best laid plans of mice and men.

Carol called the office and was assured by JoAnne that everything was under control, but that the predictable road accidents were starting to occur and that Sam had added an officer to the duty crew. That done, she turned her attention to Ms. Lipscomb. The tour group member who had stayed home answered the phone, as Carol had expected she would.

"Ms. Lipscomb, or should I say Abbey, this is Sheriff Kelleher."

"Oh, how wonderful!" was the reply. "I knew you must have gone to Barbados, but I had no idea when you'd be back."

"I arrived not much more than an hour ago, and I wanted to let you know that I have met your friend, the inspector, and am anxious to begin the task that you and he have planned for me."

She knew that she had just stretched the truth in several directions. Inspector Williams was not Abbey's friend, and to say that they had decided what she would be doing in the investigation of Franklin Pierce's death was not entirely accurate. Now that she was back on her home turf, she would be doing things the way she thought best. In fact, that was the reason for her call. Nonetheless, she wanted to cultivate a good relationship with Ms. Lipscomb, inasmuch as she had plans of her own for the woman on Blalock Point.

"I'm so eager to hear what you learned, sheriff. I'm sure you have lots of things to tend to. Your department must be all backed up. But we shall have to get together just as soon as you have a minute. I'd urge tomorrow for tea if I didn't know that you'd be terribly busy."

Carol had no intention of telling her that, while she was indeed busy, her very reliable deputy sheriff would not have allowed things to become 'all backed up.' Instead she used the weather situation to give herself some leeway.

"I, too, am eager to bring you up to date. Normally I'd be delighted to come over for tea tomorrow, but the weather forecast isn't a good one, so I think it's best to wait and see how bad this storm will be. I do, however, have a question for you. You don't have to answer it right now, but I'd appreciate it if you'd do something for me."

"Of course. Anything you need, sheriff."

Carol had decided to bring the Syracuse alumni group to the Lipscomb cottage. She was quite sure that Abbey would fall in with her plan to host a memorial get together that would give her - and Kevin, if he was determined to come to the lake for a day or two - a chance to meet their fellow passengers on the *Azure Sea*. She had no illusions about how easy such a gathering would be to arrange, much less whether all of the group would be able to attend. But she intended to do all she could to make it happen. What she did not intend to do was broach the subject over the phone. Better to do that over tea.

"What I'd like you to do, Ms. Lipscomb, is make a list for me of the names of all the members of your alumni group. I mean everyone who usually participates in these periodic trips. While you're at it, their addresses will be helpful. As you know, I would like to speak with each of them. But please, don't tell them I'll be in touch. There's no reason at this point for them to know anything about me. As far as they are concerned, the only people investigating Mr. Pierce's death are members of the Royal Barbados Police Force, and as we know, Inspector Williams and his colleagues are a long way away and very unlikely to pay us a visit in upstate New York."

"I rather thought that you'd want to know who was on the cruise. I've already called them all to report that the inspector had called and told me what had happened. That was all right, wasn't it?"

"Of course. You were reporting as a friend. I hope, though, that you didn't tell anyone that the Cumberland County sheriff was to be involved in the investigation."

Ms. Lipscomb hesitated.

"I don't think so. I may have, but I'm pretty sure your name never came up."

"If it did, there's nothing we can do about it now. Other than not mentioning it again. Do you understand?"

"Oh, yes. But I will have that list for you right away. Shall I put in the mail?"

"Please, no. This is between us, just you and me, face to face, over tea if possible. And soon. Okay?"

"Yes, sheriff. And thank you."

Carol gave Kevin a quick call that evening to assure him that she was home safely. Not long later she called it a day and climbed into the sack, her mind full of conflicting thoughts about the Pierce case. She would not only be working with Inspector Williams of the RBPF. She would have yet another partner, the much less reliable Abbey Lipscomb.

Chapter 10

It was Carol's habit to move quickly in the morning. She liked to be among the first to arrive at the office, although JoAnne typically made it impossible for her to be the very first. This morning, for some reason, she felt no such compulsion to hurry. It was nearly 48 hours since she had slipped into light, colorful summer clothes and met the inspector for their trip to Harrysmith and several of Barbados' more attractive features. Today was another story.

A hot cup of coffee in hand, she stood at the living room window, looking out at the lake. The storm had come and gone, taking the strong wind with it. Snowfall had been less than predicted, and the skies were mostly clear. But Crooked Lake was still enduring a cold snap. The outside thermometer registered 17 above. It wasn't necessary to go out onto the beach or even the deck to see that the lake was largely frozen over, at least in the immediate area of Blue Water Point. There was no blue water to be seen, and someone was camped in a chair ice fishing some distance out from their shore line.

The cottage was warm and a rare breakfast omelet was nearly ready, yet Carol had already decided that, no matter how cold it was, she was going to take a brisk walk down the point before heading for the office. Sam, JoAnne, and the others would understand. By the time she had dressed and bundled up in her warmest winter togs, the sun was beginning to appear over the bluff. When first she stepped out onto the deck, the cold air took her breath away but didn't change her plans.

She had set no limits on how far she would walk, but by the time she was back at the cottage she had covered nearly a mile and enjoyed every minute of it. Barbados had been pleasant, actually delightful. And wonderfully warm, of course. But Carol realized that she loved the change of seasons, something the Caribbean islands knew nothing of. She had expected to miss Barbados. But as had been the case when they got back from the cruise, she was glad to be home.

The snow plows had done their work and she was sure that visiting Abbey Lipscomb would not be a problem. But she was in no hurry to set that part of her day in motion. First things first, and first things meant giving Sam a report on her trip. Not that there was much to tell, but he'd be curious and was entitled to know what his boss had been up to now that her portfolio included international law and order.

Carol's drive to Cumberland was a welcome home treat. The snow was still a glistening white and traffic was light. She almost experienced a let down when she pulled into the parking lot. It was nearly empty. Sam's last squad meeting had ended and the officers had scattered on their assignments around the county, leaving only JoAnne, Sam, and Tommy Byrnes to greet her.

"Welcome home," JoAnne said in her familiar cheerful voice. "Have a good time?"

"You should know," Carol said, "that this wasn't a vacation. It just happens that this time our case de jour had its origins in the sunny Caribbean. There was no time for swimming in the ocean."

"I'm so sorry." JoAnne produced what she hoped was an appropriately downcast face.

"Everything okay here?"

"Absolutely. We never missed a beat."

Sam heard this exchange and joined them.

"Glad to have you back, but it would have been nice if you'd brought along some warmer weather."

"It's against the law down there to take it with you," Carol joked. "But what's new here?"

"Nothing but a few cars getting run off the road by the weather. Business as usual, I'd say. Oh, and Officer Dockery arrested Judge Hempel for speeding. She hadn't heard that we're not supposed to do that."

"I trust she's not upset with herself," Carol said.

"Not Dockery. She's staking out a claim as a real 'by the book' officer. I think she'd pull you over if given half a chance."

"Give me a minute and then come down to the office. I'll give you a quick report on what I did over the last couple of days. Nothing that qualifies as significant, but you should hear it anyway."

As she stopped for a cup of coffee en route to her office, Byrnes stuck his head out of his door to add his welcome back to Sam's and JoAnne's. Okay, Carol thought, now let's get to work.

As promised, the sheriff's briefing of Bridges took little time and supplied him with little information of great importance.

"The work begins back here, not down in Barbados. I hope to do what I can as quickly as I can and then close the book on this one. The RBPF inspector could make my day by calling to say he'd caught the killer. One of what he calls his bajans - that's local lingo for Barbadians."

"By the way, too bad you had to come home to a snow storm."

"I loved it, Sam. Splendid antidote to murder under the sea grapes."

"Sea grapes? What are you talking about?"

"It's not important. Just that the victim was found under a local plant called a sea grape."

"Oh." Sam could think of nothing else to say to that. "Well, good luck. I'm here if you need me."

"I know. Thanks."

Carol closed her office door and contemplated the conversation she would have with Abbey Lipscomb. She didn't know what hours she kept, but decided to wait until 11 o'clock, by which time the woman was almost certain to be up and about. To her surprise, she found it difficult to concentrate on anything else and ended up making the call at 10:45.

Ms. Lipscomb answered the phone so quickly that Carol assumed that she had been hovering over it, awaiting the call.

"It's so wonderful to hear from you, sheriff. I was hoping it would be you."

"Tell me, did the snowplows clear Blalock Point? Is the road passable over there?"

"Oh, goodness yes. The storm was pretty much a false alarm. May I count on you for tea today?"

"I'd love that. Please don't go to any trouble. Just tell me when would be convenient."

"Anytime it fits your schedule, sheriff. Anytime."

Carol wanted to say she'd come over right now, but thought it wise to create the illusion that she had a tight schedule. Moreover, late morning wasn't exactly tea time.

"Can we make it 3:30?" she asked.

"3:30 it shall be."

And so it was, giving the sheriff several hours in which to make notes which she doubted she'd need and to nibble on her finger nails.

CHAPTER 11

"I'm so glad you're going to be the one to track down Franklin's killer," Abbey said when they had settled down in the crowded living room with their tea and scones.

"Please, Ms. Lipscomb, we have no evidence that one of your group of alums was responsible for his death. The inspector down in Barbados is fairly confident that one of his countrymen is the killer. All I'll be doing is learning what I can about Mr. Pierce's companions on the cruise. Which is why I have asked you to get me started by giving me their names and addresses. After all, they are all strangers to me."

"I know. The inspector sees this differently than I do, and I know he could be right. But I have an uncomfortable feeling that it will be one of Franklin's so-called friends."

"You have never told me why you feel that way," Carol said, determined to get right to the point. "I'm here to collect the list you prepared for me and to enjoy your tea and scones, which, by the way, are excellent. But you won't be surprised that I'm also anxious to hear you explain your hunch about Pierce's killer. You have told me that this small alumni group consisted of friends - not just those who went on the cruise, but you, too. Am I not right that you would have been on the cruise if it hadn't been that walking is a challenge for you?"

"That's true. I haven't been quite right since I fell and broke my hip last fall. They say that cruising is the easiest way to travel, but it's no fun to stay on the ship in every port. You want to get off and walk around, and I'm in no position to do that."

"I understand. So these people are your friends as well as Mr. Pierce's. Why would you assume that one of them would want to kill him? Or perhaps I should ask why you'd have been perfectly happy to travel with someone whom you suspected of harboring that much hatred for a member of your group?"

"I suppose it sounds strange. But haven't you ever had a feeling that you couldn't quite explain? A feeling that something is wrong."

"Of course. It's a common problem. But you've had a number of days to examine this feeling. I have trouble believing that it isn't related to something you've experienced with the group, or something you've heard about one or more of its members. Friends don't suddenly morph into killers. Why don't you dig into your memory and see if you can't help me understand why you think Mr. Pierce's killer could be one of his traveling companions."

"But I have given it thought. Actually, a lot of thought. And I can't think of anything that explains what I'm sure is the case."

Carol had always been of the view that people know more than they think they know. But there was something about Abbey's demeanor that suggested that that might not be the case this time. On the other hand it was possible that she was deliberately refusing to be candid. That she knew of whom she was suspicious but for reasons of her own was not prepared to name him. Was it even possible that she was reluctant to point a figure at a long time friend but hoped that the sheriff would do it for her, thereby saving her from an act of betrayal?

"Okay, let's set that aside for now. I need to know who were the members of the alumni group who were traveling with Mr. Pierce. Could I see your list?"

"I put it together last night. At first I thought Nancy Brubaker was on the cruise, but it turns out I was wrong. Otherwise, I'm sure it's accurate. Here."

Abbey handed a neatly type written list of eight names to Carol.

None of the names meant anything to the sheriff, although their addresses confirmed Abbey's claim that they all lived in upstate New York.

"Let's call this the reunion group," Carol said. "Is everyone here?"

"Everyone except Nancy and me. There were a couple more of us a few years ago, but one of them moved to Texas and the other just dropped out."

"They're all Syracuse alums, right?"

"Not Mrs. Bickle. Her husband is, of course, but he wanted her to be included and there didn't seem to be a good reason to tell her she couldn't join us."

"When did the rest of you all graduate from Syracuse?"

"We were class of 1985," Abbey said. "But no, that's not entirely true. Harry Pringle was a year ahead of the rest of us."

"How was it that the reunion group got started? Class reunions I can understand, but this was obviously different. Do you remember whose idea it was for you upstaters to start these annual get togethers?"

"Well, they haven't been exactly annual affairs," Abbey corrected the sheriff. "Every two or three years would be closer. But Franklin and I, you might say we were the founding fathers."

"It was a nice idea, Ms. Lipscomb. But what prompted you and Mr. Pierce to do it? I presume that you were all close in college."

"That's true in a way, although we had different majors and went on to different careers. The way I remember it, it probably started with Christmas cards. Not that everyone sent cards to the others every year, but, well, one thing led to another and we just began to find ourselves communicating. Somehow the fact that we'd never left our upstate roots made a difference."

"Would you say that all of you had similar interests? I mean outside of your professions. Or maybe I should say similar personalities - say similar backgrounds, a good sense of humor. How about political views?"

Abbey thought about this for a moment.

"There's probably some truth in what you say. I mean most of us were good Republicans, although Harry was a liberal through and through. We all had a thing for SU basketball, although that could hardly count for all the reunions, could it?"

Carol studied the list as they talked, and soon found herself remembering the names and beginning to link each of them to their addresses.

There were eight names on the list. Two couples, John and Ann Bickle of Skaneateles and Stuart and Betty Craig of Cortland, plus Jim Westerman of Cooperstown, Harry Pringle of Syracuse, Roger Edgar of Elmira, and Bess Stevens of Binghamton.

"Would you say that you are still fairly close to all of these people?" Carol asked.

"Of course I don't see any of them regularly, but I guess I'd say we're close, or as close as one can be when we live in different places and have our own jobs to take care of."

"By the way, what is your job?"

Abbey smiled.

"Don't laugh. You might say I'm a geek. I may not look like one, but I help people set up websites and trouble shoot their computer problems. Who'd have thought it? I majored in European history."

This information surprised Carol. Before she was through with the Pierce case, she'd know what all of the people on the list did for a living. Unless Inspector Williams preempted her participation in the case by arresting a bajan. It was time to raise the subject of a memorial service for Franklin Pierce.

"If I'm to be a useful partner of Inspector Williams, Abbey, I'm going to have to meet all the people on your list. I could do it one at a time by traveling to where they live. And I may still need to do that. But it wouldn't be an efficient use of my time. I have a plan, and it depends on your cooperation."

Ms. Lipscomb's face lit up. It was obvious that she was anxious to cooperate. Carol wasn't sure she'd be as anxious to do so once the plan had been presented.

"You've spoken to these people and let them know that Mr. Pierce was killed during the cruise ship's stop on Barbados. I think that a memorial service for him would now be appropriate. Informal, nothing more. Not in a church, but right here in your home. A weekend makes sense, inasmuch as your friends have jobs to attend to. The way I read your list, everyone with the possible exception of Mr. Westerman over in Coopertown is close enough to make the trip in just a couple of hours. I would very much like to be present. It would give me a chance to meet them, watch them interact, listen to them talk about Mr. Pierce and events on Barbados."

"I couldn't promise that they'd all be here, but it sounds like a great idea, sheriff. I'm not sure I'd know how to do a memorial service, but with your help we could probably make it seem appropriately proper."

"It wouldn't have to be proper. I'm not thinking of anything religious, just an opportunity for Mr. Pierce's friends to gather and talk about him."

"Sort of what they call the celebration of a life, is that what you mean?"

"Precisely. I'd be the fly on the wall, forming opinions of these people I've never met."

"But they're smart. At least everybody but Bess Stevens is. They'd be suspicious of you."

"If they knew I was a sheriff, perhaps one or more of them might be. But I'd be there only because I'm your friend and neighbor, and I just happened to have been on the same cruise. I know you aren't sure whether you mentioned to any of them that I might be joining the investigation of Mr. Pierce's death. But even if you did, none of them knows me or even knows what I look like. I think we could do it. And I believe we *must* do it."

"Oh dear, this is exciting, isn't it," Ms. Lipscomb said. And she did indeed sound excited.

"I'd prefer not to think of it as exciting, but rather as a thoughtful gesture on behalf of an old friend. One where we should be casual, not acting as if we were waiting to pounce on a killer. Do you think you could do it?"

"What would you like me to do?"

"The most important thing is to find a weekend, reasonably close if possible, when all of them, or at least most of them, would be be able and willing to come to Crooked Lake. What's your sense of it? Do you think they would be willing to come over for a memorial to Mr. Pierce?"

"Oh, yes, in principle. Of course the weather could be a problem, or some of them could have obligations that would get in the way. But I'm optimistic I could get at least five or six to come - providing the weather cooperates. If you like, I'll get on the phone right away, starting tonight. There's no point in my setting a date until I've sounded them out."

"That sounds good, Ms. Lipscomb. Just do your best to make it feel like you'd appreciate it if everyone came. And like I said, no mention of me. Okay? This has been a very useful meeting and I want to thank you, but I really have to get going. Please let me know how the memorial is shaping up. I'll be available any time."

"You can count on me. I'm very grateful you agreed to help that inspector, sheriff. I'm sure he's grateful, too."

Carol left gripping Abbey's list in her hand. As soon as she got back to the office, she'd have Officer Byrnes see if he couldn't track down more information about each of the members of what she was coming to think of as the Barbados Eight.

CHAPTER 12

The sheriff had been gone for four days, but Inspector Williams was having trouble putting her out of his mind. He was still convinced that her involvement in the Pierce case was unnecessary, that the man who had done away with the passenger on the *Azure Sea* was one of his own benighted countrymen. He had not looked forward to her visit, even if he himself had been the one to invite her. He had been proper and had even tried to be courteous, but he realized that he must have given her the impression that he was less than pleased with the task of showing her around the island.

He was conscious of making an effort late in her brief visit to act friendlier, but he feared that she would have seen that effort as transparently false.

"You're looking a bit grim today," Inspector Brathwaite said. "Coming down with something?"

"Of course not. When have you ever known me to be sick?"

"Maybe it's my imagination, Cyril, but we go back quite a few years and let me tell you, you're not yourself. Want to talk about it?"

"Not really, but it's the sheriff from New York who was here the other day."

"I thought you said she seemed to know what she was doing."

"That's the problem. It's not her, but what she's doing. And what she's doing is wasting her time. That's my fault. What kind of a fool am I to let somebody I've never met talk me into involving the sheriff in our investigation of this damned Pierce affair. Ever had a guilty conscience? Well, I've got one right now."

"I haven't noticed that you're ready to put a bunch of no good bajans in a line up, Cyril. Your sheriff could yet do you some good."

"Could be," he admitted, "but I'm still feeling guilty."

This inconclusive conversation came to an abrupt end with a sharp rap on the door.

"Come in," Brathwaite hollered, and Constable Alleyne entered, looking excited.

"What can we do for you, constable?" The two inspectors asked, almost in unison.

"I think you should come with me, sir," he said, directing his remark to Inspector Williams.

"Where would we be going?"

"Just over to the bus terminal. There's someone you ought to see."

"About what?" The inspector sounded as if he'd rather continue sharing his feelings about the sheriff with Inspector Brathwaite.

"It's about that man who missed his cruise ship and got himself killed."

Williams was instantly interested and on his feet.

"Who is it that wants to see me?"

"He's a bus driver."

"Okay, let's go"

As his colleague was leaving the office, Inspector Brathwaite couldn't resist a parting shot.

"I thought you'd covered all the bus driver leads, Cyril."

"I have. This will be a wild goose chase."

He slammed the door.

Ten minutes later they were at the Fairchild Street bus terminal. It was a busy corner of Bridgetown, and its proximity to the Parliament guaranteed that there would be a lot of tourists in the area. The constable pulled into a place which said, quite clearly, that parking was limited to emergency vehicles. Both he and the inspector took it for granted that they had an emergency to cope with.

"He said he would be inside," Constable Alleyne said.

But he wasn't. He was sitting on a outside bench, and when he saw the constable and his companion he got up and walked over to the police car.

"You must be the inspector," he said to the inspector.

"I am. And you are -?"

"I'm Andy, Andy Baptiste."

"Good. Now why don't we go back to the bench and you can tell me what you wanted to talk with me about."

But the bench had filled up, so the inspector suggested they use the car.

"Now," the inspector began, "I take it you're a bus driver and you have something to tell me that pertains to the cruise passenger who was killed a couple of weeks ago. Was he on your bus?"

"I don't know, sir. There's lots of people on the bus, all the time, and I wouldn't know what he looked like."

"I thought you were going to tell me something about the man who was killed."

"I don't think I can do that. Sorry, sir. But word's out that he was found out by Harrysmith Beach, and I may know something about that."

"Well, come on lad, let's hear it."

"The day the man missed his ship and got killed, another man tried to get on my bus and said he wanted to go to Harrysmith. But that's not my route and I told him to find some other way to get there. He wasn't nice about it, so I pulled some bajan on him."

Baptiste laughed and repeated his admonition to the man who wanted to go to Harrysmith not to let himself get ripped off.

"Dun let nobody jook you in the eye." I said. "The bus people thought it was funny. The white man, he didn't."

"The man who wanted to go to Harrysmith was white?"

"Yeah, and all red from the sun."

For the first time since he'd been put on the case, Inspector Williams experienced a strange feeling: a woman named Abbey Lipscomb might possibly be right.

But no, hundreds of people could be looking for a ride to Harrysmith, some of them black, some of them white. He remembered, however, his own words. It would have taken a large, strong man to have killed Franklin Pierce.

"Tell me about this man who wanted a ride to Harrysmith." he said.

"Like I said, he was white and had been out in the sun too long."

"Yes, yes, but what else can you tell me? Tall? Short? Young? Closer to my age? You know, what did he look like other than sunburned?"

Baptiste looked puzzled.

"Hard to say. There were a lot of people in the way. He was outside, shouting at me. It was the white skin, the red face that stood out."

"Surely you can remember if he was a big man."

"I think so," came the answer, now less certain. "But I'm not sure. The man ahead of him in the queue was big, I know that, much bigger than me. In fact he was really in the way, made it hard to see the white man."

Williams, so recently thinking he might have some critical information, had trouble containing his frustration.

"Did he say why he wanted to get to Harrysmith? Was he meeting someone?"

"He didn't say anything about it to me." An idea occurred to him. "Maybe he said something to other people in the queue. You'd have to ask."

The inspector closed his eyes and sighed. Asking unknown 'other people' who had been in a queue somewhere in Bridgetown nearly two weeks earlier would be impossible.

"By the way," he asked, more out of a reluctance to admit defeat than anything else, "how is it that you wanted to tell me this?"

"Everybody's saying that the dead man was found at Harrysmith, so I thought you'd want to know about people going to Harrysmith."

Yes, the inspector said to himself, but you don't seem to have anything to tell me except that a man wanted to go there. A man you can't even describe.

"I appreciate your willingness to help, Mr. Baptiste. If you remember anything else about this man, please get in touch with me. Right away."

It was all the inspector could do to keep his temper under control on the drive back to RBPF headquarters. It wasn't the constable's fault, and there was no reason to take his frustration out on him.

Inspector Brathwaite had known his colleague long enough to know when things weren't going well.

"Just a wild goose chase, eh?" he said. "Well, I've got another lead for you. Call came in just after you left for the bus station. It was the manager over at *Chesney's*. There's a guy that hangs out over there a lot, never buys anything. A real pauper, dirt poor. Anyway, this time he drops nearly three hundred US dollars. The manager thought it was strange, worth giving us a heads up."

Williams knew exactly what Brathwaite and the manager of *Chesney's* were thinking: those dollars had been stolen, and just possibly they came from Pierce's wallet, which conveniently had not been left on his body.

"Interesting. Why didn't the store tell us about this sooner?"

"Actually, they moved pretty fast. It didn't happen until this morning."

What might have passed for a look of excitement on Inspector Williams' face vanished.

"Shit! This has nothing to do with the Pierce case. Can you imagine this poor bajan killing him, lifting his wallet, and then waiting weeks before spending the money? He'd have been so eager to spend all that cash he'd have been at *Chesney's* or someplace else in an hour."

"You can't be sure of that," Brathwaite said. "Maybe he's a smart bajan, figures it's better to let things cool down before he starts spending his ill-gotten bills."

"Don't worry, I'll check into it. But I'm getting tired of leads that turn out to be dead ends."

The inspector had good reason to be skeptical. So far nothing remotely significant had resulted from all the time he had spent with taxi companies, tour guides, and various people known to be keen observers of the local scene. He'd dutifully add *Chesney's* to his list, but he wouldn't hold his breath.

CHAPTER 13

For several years, Officer Tommy Byrnes had proved his value to the Cumberland County Sheriff's Department less by arresting speeders and scofflaws than by ferreting out information on his computer about persons of interest to his boss. His latest assignment, thanks to the fact that Carol was now interested in a crime committed in Barbados, was to learn as much as he could about eight upstate New Yorkers who had recently visited that Caribbean island country.

Inasmuch as none of these eight people were celebrities or otherwise notorious, it was not an easy assignment. In fact, for one of the eight people it was to prove particularly frustrating. But perseverance, supplemented by some luck, led to the acquisition of new information about the other seven, although neither Tommy nor Carol had any idea whether any of that information was important.

Tommy had said he would keep working on Jim Westerman, the member of the group who seemed to be most elusive. Apparently he had majored in Lit and had had a brief success as an author. Otherwise his life was largely a blank. But Carol was anxious to look at what he had discovered about the others, and it was late in the afternoon of February 9th that she closed her office door and opened the 'Pierce File.'

Roger Edgar was both first on Tommy's list and the member of the group who lived closest to Crooked Lake. Elmira. It had been only a short time ago that she had used the small airport which it shared with Corning for her trip to and from Barbados. She wished she had thought to ask Abbey Lipscomb if she had pictures of these people. None of their names gave her the slightest sense of what they would look like. But Tommy's notes did tell her that Edgar was a dermatologist and that he had stayed in Syracuse for his MD. In addition to his private practice, he apparently enjoyed privileges at Elmira's principal hospital and medical center. There was a paragraph identifying a few elements of his background, including an award he had earned a few years earlier as one of the top dermatologists in the state's southern tier. To her surprise, Tommy had been unable to find any reference to a spouse or to children. She realized as she set the 'Edgar page' aside that she would have to see and hear him before she could presume to know him at all. In fact, that would almost certainly be the case with every member of the Barbados Eight.

The second page of Tommy's file was devoted to Harry Pringle, who alone of those in the file had settled in the city where he had gone to college. As she started to read on, however, it became obvious that that wasn't quite accurate. Pringle had started his post-college life in Toledo, Ohio, only to move to Syracuse some two years later. The apparent reason for this 'return to roots' had something to do with a woman, although Tommy's notes did not elaborate. His marriage to Dorothy Furman had produced two children, one boy and one girl. The file said that Harry was a mechanical engineer who worked for one of Syracuse's larger firms, but there was nothing which explained just what he did there.

Two down, five to go, including two married couples. Unlike Dorothy Pringle, the other wives were members of the reunion group and had been on the fatal cruise. Carol recalled that Mrs. Bickle was the one member of the group who was not an SU alum. For no reason she could justify to herself, she set the Bickles aside for the moment and turned to the Craigs, both members of Syracuse's class of 1985.

Their file was considerably longer than the others and, although Tommy had made no comments to that effect, it seemed to suggest that the Craigs might have had a more interesting life. Carol immediately corrected herself. Maybe it was just because they had traveled further, done more things which sounded interesting to her, than Edgar or Pringle. They had both grown up in Cortland, New York, a small town farther east beyond the Finger Lakes, and had gone back to Cortland after graduation. They had both become school teachers, Stuart of math and Betty of English. Stuart had even added to his classroom duties the responsibility of coaching the school's soccer team. Both of them had earned the praise of their students and the community in which they lived, as evidenced by a couple of awards they had won (and in one case shared). But unlike the other files, their's spoke to a life of travel and their love of the great outdoors. Carol read a long list of places where they had camped, climbed mountains, and skied, both together and later with their two kids. It was obvious that they had put all of this together for their website; they had wanted to share a happy life with others. Or at least that is what it looked like. Carol remembered why she was doing this, and reminded herself that it was too soon to form impressions of people she had never seen.

Which brought her to John and Ann Bickle. It covered the important things, but was much briefer than the report on the Craigs. Ann, according to Abbey the only member of the reunion group who hadn't matriculated at Syracuse, had completed a bachelor's at Skidmore three years after John's graduation. They had married seven years after he received his BS, by which time he had settled in Skaneateles, Ann's home town. So, like the others, he had chosen to stay near his university. But unlike them, he seemed not to have had a clear sense of what he wanted to do; not surprisingly, he subsequently changed careers a number of times. Tommy's report didn't dwell on this except to say that he was currently a carpenter who crafted elegant tables and chairs. Ann was listed as a homemaker.

Finally, Carol picked up Tommy's comments on Bess Stevens, the only single female in the reunion group. She had saved her for last, she realized, because she regarded Stevens as among the people least likely to have been the killer. The way the inspector had described things, it would have taken someone with considerable strength to dispatch Pierce, which Carol had reflexively thought of as a man. Betty Craig and Ann Bickle were also women, of course, but she was interested primarily in their husbands. But she soon found herself rethinking her assumption that the killer had to be a man. Not only was it possible that a woman had put a man up to using a neck snap on Pierce at Harrysmith. A woman might have had the strength and knowledge to do it herself. What brought her to that view was the fact that Ms. Stevens - there was no mention of a marriage in Tommy's notes - was a physical therapist who also had acquired something of a reputation as a boxer and was even teaching a few women the finer points of that sport. Carol remembered her reaction to Clint Eastwood's *Million*

Dollar Baby. Hillary Swank had been good in the title role, but she had found herself totally disinterested in a film about women boxing. Indeed, she and Kevin had discussed it and had both admitted that boxing by either sex turned them off. However, Bess Stevens' reputation as an amateur boxer was the only thing in her file that had received much attention.

Carol detected no pattern in these files. But why should she? If and when Tommy was able to produce a longer report on Jim Westerman, it was very likely that a pattern would still be undiscernible. For the moment at least, these people were still only members of a group of college graduates who took trips together now and then.

Once again she found herself wishing she had pictures of these people. She picked up the phone and dialed the now familiar number on Blalock Point.

"Hello, Ms. Lipscomb. This is the sheriff."

"Two minds in the same channel. I was going to call you."

"With news about a date for the memorial, I hope. Let me ask my question before I forget why I was calling. Would you happen to have photographs of the members of your reunion group?"

"Oh, dear. I'm not sure that I do. I have our yearbook, but of course that shows you what we all looked like 30 years ago. I think I may have saved a few Christmas cards. Not sure where they'd be. As you may have noticed, I'm not the best organized person on Crooked Lake. But I'll take a look and let you know what I can find."

"I'd appreciate that. You were going to call. Was it about Mr. Pierce's memorial?"

"Nothing final, but I thought you'd like to know how it's going. I've talked to everyone except Jim Westerman. I can't seem to reach him. The others think it's a nice idea, but it may be difficult to find a date. The Craigs have a pretty full calendar, and Roger has a medical convention we'll·have to work around. But I'm optimistic. Like I said, everyone agrees it's the right thing to do and they all seem to appreciate my willingness to be the hostess."

"Thanks for the update, Abbey. And let me know if you have any photos of your friends."

Carol was of the opinion that she was unlikely to learn more from photos than she was from Officer Byrnes' reports. She hoped that Inspector Williams would be calling soon to tell her that one of his bajans did it.

Chapter 14

Jim Westerman's phone rang for the third time that afternoon. He started to reach for it, but caught himself before he picked the phone up. Caller ID told him that Abbey Lipscomb was trying to reach him.

"Damn! She's certainly persistent," he said out loud as he read Abbey Lipscomb's name. He had no interest in talking with her, not today, not any day. This time the phone rang ten times. The last time it had been fifteen. Why won't she accept the fact that I'm not home, that I'm in France or who knows where?

He had been doing his best to burn bridges to people he was tired of hearing from, and it hadn't been easy. Once you've established contacts they not only never leave you alone, they tend to multiply. It wasn't that Abbey was a bad person. She was simply a sometime friend who called or e-mailed him too often, usually for what he considered no good reason. He didn't mind the occasional trip with old college acquaintances, such as the recent Caribbean cruise, provided he never had to share a room or a cabin and could always be alone when he wanted to be. But Abbey, who hadn't been on the cruise, had tried to reach him at least five times in the weeks since he had gotten back to Cooperstown. Five times!

Her calls were one of the reasons he was trying to distance himself from people. He knew, however, that there was a much more important reason for what he had been doing. It went back further than the creation of the alumni reunion group, and it had come dangerously close to ruining his life.

He had always wanted to be an author. He was the rare male member of several writing classes at Syracuse. His professors had encouraged him and, while never telling him he was a natural, a gifted writer, they had typically graded his efforts with an A or at least a B+. His financial circumstances, thanks to his father, permitted him the luxury of devoting his early post-college years to working on a novel. He had not been in a hurry to send the book off to an agent or a publisher, preferring to polish several drafts until he thought he had it right. He had been warned that he might face a number of rejections before someone accepted it, but to his surprise the third house to receive it had agreed to publish. Such a relatively rapid acceptance from an unpublished author buoyed his confidence.

The novel, which bore the title *The Mohican Boy,* was admittedly a tribute to James Fenimore Cooper, the famous American author who had lived only a few miles from Westerman's home on Otsego Lake near Cooperstown. *The Mohican Boy* proved to be a winner, earning a number of good reviews and launching him on what looked as if it would be a fine career. Unfortunately, one successful book does not guarantee long term success either in sales or critical reviews. Two years later he published a second book, also an historical novel and also set in the Cooperstown area. Unlike *The Mohican Boy*, it was drubbed by the critics, who found the plot dull and turgid, the characters mere cardboard figures, and the writing style both pretentious and sloppy. Bad reviews do not always lead to weak sales, and may not have been responsible in this case, but Westerman's royalties also took a precipitous nose dive with the publication of *The Loyalists and the Iroquois.*

Undaunted, Jim went right to work on a third novel, believing that he had not been sufficiently diligent with editing in book two. This time, *The Frigate Compass* took three years to finish and allowed him to set the story several decades later than its predecessors. But if he expected it to recapture the success of *The Mohican Boy,* he was grievously disappointed. He might have settled for a further decline in sales if the book had enjoyed a *succes d'estime.* But that was not to be. The reviews not only repeated the attack on *The Loyalists and the Iroquois.* They went so far as to use the occasion to re-review *The Mohican Boy*, saying that it had been seriously overrated and that Westerman was nothing more than a hack (one well known critic actually called him that).

The result was that the fledgling author crept into his shell, never to write another book. He worked intermittently on other subjects, but his efforts always came to naught and he came to hate the fact that he had ever written anything but *The Mohican Boy.* After all, the so-called authorities on the literary canon remained in awe of *To Kill a Mockingbird*, and it was his understanding that the author, Harper Lee, had never published another book. If he had stopped after *The Mohican Boy*, he might now be spoken of in the same breath as Lee. But it was too late. His other books had given the critics the opportunity to disparage *The Mohican Boy* as a much overrated fluke.

He managed to switch his mind from his failed career as a writer back to the omnipresent Abbey Lipscomb. She hadn't been the one to inform him that Franklin Pierce was officially dead. Caller ID had seen to that. It was Stuart Craig. He should never have answered Stuart's call, but he had, and needless to say Stuart's source had been Abbey, who was obviously enjoying her role as the bearer of bad news. So Jim knew what she was now up to. She was going to hold a memorial service for Franklin Pierce. She was going to be mourner-in-chief.

Which left Jim very much on the spot. He couldn't pretend that he knew nothing about the memorial service. But the last place he wanted to be when the service took place was in Abbey's parlor, looking somber, fighting back tears as members of the reunion group remembered Franklin and his endearing ways. He could, he suppose, plead a need to be out of town, even out of the country, although Abbey and others might well be suspicious of such an excuse. On the other hand, if he missed the memorial service he would miss the inevitable conversation about what had happened to Pierce, about who his killer might be. And that was a conversation he wanted very much to hear. The very improbability of Franklin's murder would almost certainly lead to speculation, and once his fellow passengers on the fatal cruise started to speculate, wasn't it possible that his absence would prompt someone in the room to say something like 'how about Jim Westerman?'

He got up from the desk and walked angrily to the kitchen to collect another beer. It wasn't that he particularly wanted another beer. What he wanted was some help in solving the problem of what to do about the memorial service. He hated the idea of attending, but he also could not afford to miss what might be said there about Franklin

Pierce and his violent death in far off Barbados. Unfortunately, he could think of no way in which such help would be forthcoming. It was more likely that he'd be starting his fourth novel. Again. And he knew that that wasn't about to happen. Jim Westerman slammed the refrigerator door.

CHAPTER 15

It was after Carol had read Officer Byrnes' notes on the reunion group for the third time that she realized that there was something she had overlooked. It was so obvious that she couldn't believe she had missed it. The file pages in Tommy's report included information on everyone who had accompanied Franklin Pierce except for Jim Westerman. But the file Tommy had prepared did not cover Pierce himself. Carol had been so focussed on the reunion members who theoretically might have killed Pierce that she had failed to seek data on the victim. Yet she knew that she had to know more about Pierce if she were to understand his death, unless, that is, he had in fact been killed by a drunken bajan.

She sought out Tommy the next morning.

"Your sketches on my Barbados Eight are going to be very helpful. At least that's what I think this morning. Time will tell. But I haven't given you enough to do. We're going to need information on one more person. You think you're up to this?"

"Why wouldn't I be? Unless he turns out to be a phantom like Westerman. Who do you have in mind?"

Carol gave him Pierce's name and explained why anything he dug up might be useful.

"By itself, more information about him probably won't mean much. But when we look at it along side what we know about the others, it may suggest a connection. If one of the group on the cruise killed him, it's more likely that there'd already been some bad blood between them than that one was a Yankee fan and the other hated the Bronx Bombers."

The quest for more information about Pierce might also lead to Lipscomb, and that was something that Carol could take care of herself. She called Abbey as soon as she'd given Tommy his marching orders.

"I hope I'm not calling too early," she said, although she wasn't really concerned about catching Abbey in her pajamas and housecoat.

"No, no. I'm an early bird. At least most of the time." She didn't say whether today qualified as the norm or the exception.

"Good, because I need to ask a few more questions about your friend Franklin Pierce. I've been more interested in the other members of your group, the ones who theoretically could have had something to do with his death. As a result, I haven't really thought much about the victim himself. Perhaps he had done something that alienated one of the others."

"I can't imagine him doing something like that," Abbey said.

"Anyway, let me ask those questions. In the first place, I'm afraid I don't even know what he did for a living."

"I'm sure it has nothing to do with his death, but he ran a place up in Newark. It's called *Upstate Consignments.* I'm sure you know all about consignment shops, but about a year ago Franklin got the idea that he'd also like to use his shop as a kind of showcase for his SU alumni friends. I know it sounds a bit weird, but it tells you how much he liked our little group. What he's been doing is creating a display that tells his customers about each of us. He's been hounding us to scour our attics and come up with things that we'd be willing to part with. I know that he got John Bickle to donate one of those little cabinets he's crafted."

Carol didn't know a lot about consignment stores, but she knew enough to realize that Pierce's plan to showcase his friends might pose a few problems. One of those friends might create furniture in his spare time, but others might have little to show for their extracurricular activities other than letters to the editor of a local paper.

"How about you?" she asked Abbey. "What did you donate?"

Abbey laughed.

"Nothing. Well, nothing much. He took a drawing I did back when I was trying my hand at being an artist. Needless to say, I never became an artist. Otherwise, all he has were photos going back to my childhood, a couple of favorite books my mother read to me when I was little, a Broadway playbill autographed by Angela Lansbury, and a pair of baby shoes."

"No offense, Abbey, but I can't imagine that he'd get much for any of those things."

"I don't think he wants to sell them. They're just part of what he calls his 'Alumni Corner.' It's more like a gimmick than anything else."

"Have you seen this 'Alumni Corner?'"

"No, and frankly I haven't been in any hurry to see it. Anyway, he hadn't finished it before he died, and now it will never be finished."

"How do you think Mr. Pierce did with his consignment store? I've always figured places like that didn't bring in much money, unless you acted as a middle man for wealthy people."

"You'd be right about that. Franklin worked about as hard as anybody I know, but financially he was on the margin. Never complained about it, though. He liked to tinker, as he did with the 'Alumni Corner.' But I don't think he ever earned big money. His life was sort of like mine. A good week every now and then that lets you breathe easier, followed by a month when you thought the income would never start flowing again."

"That sounds frustrating."

"It is for me. But like I said, Franklin never complained." Carol thought she heard Abbey snuffling. "I'm missing him, sheriff. Already. We never got together more than two or three times a year, but it's going to be a lot harder with Franklin gone than with people I see every week."

"Any progress on a date for the memorial?" At least this was something within Abbey's control.

"Not quite, but I think it'll be March 15. That's a Sunday, and it will do for everyone but Roger and Jim. Don't know why I never get a call back from him."

Carol assumed that 'him' in this case meant Westerman.

"Do you suppose that Mr. Westerman dreads something like this so much that he finds it easier not to know what's on your mind?"

"But he doesn't know that I'm calling him about a memorial service."

"Perhaps. But what if the idea has occurred to him and he's decided that it's simply better not to know?"

"I don't know. If he lived as close as Elmira, I'd drive down there and go to his house. It'd be like serving a summons."

Abbey smiled at the comparison.

"Look, I have to go. Thanks for the head's up on Franklin's business. I think I'll take a drive up to Newark one of these days. Assuming the consignment shop is open. Have you heard anything about it?"

"I have no idea what's going to happen to it, but when I called the young man Franklin pays to keep an eye on it, he said he'd hold onto the keys until the owner of the building decides what he wants to do. Name's Grimley, he'll let you in. Let me give you a number."

Carol copied the phone number. She was curious about the strange decision to have the consignment shop become a tribute of sorts to the reunion group, but she could think of no reason why it would have any bearing on Franklin Pierce's case. She might take a look at it some day when she had to be in Rochester and had time on her hands, but not now. Considering the many things she had to attend to in Cumberland County, Carol's decision not to pay a visit to *Upstate Consignments* was, of course, a logical one. It was also to have important consequences, consequences she could not have imagined as she turned her attention to her crowded in-basket.

Chapter 16

Carol was beginning to feel like Abbey Lipscomb's siamese twin. It was early afternoon, and they had already spoken on the phone twice. If one were to add the number of conversations since her return from Barbados, the number would be closer to -

She didn't finish the thought, thanks to the telephone.

"Sheriff, it's Abbey again."

"Hello, Abbey." She knew she must sound tired.

"I wanted to clear it with you before I sent out the invitation, but March 15th looks good. I told you this morning that everyone but Jim Westerman and Rodger Edgar was on board for that date. Roger called me just an hour ago and says he's juggled his schedule and can now join us. That's everyone but Jim, and I can't make him answer his phone. What I'll do is mail him, telling him what we're doing and when and tossing in a heartfelt plea that he join us. At the very least I want him to know that he'll be missed. Do you think we can go ahead without him?"

"We've been over this before, and I don't think it makes sense to let him stand in the way of holding a memorial service. My guess is that by this time he knows, or at least suspects, what you're doing. So by all means go ahead with the March 15 date; otherwise he wins this stand-off. And remember, I'll be seeing him, talking to him, even if I have to spend time in Cooperstown."

"Glad you feel this way, sheriff. So we're on for the 15th?"

"We are. And I'll be there. It's possible that somebody will recognize me. After all, we were all together for ten days, on deck, in the dining room, even the spa. It's a risk we have to run. But we don't panic if it happens. I'm still a lake friend, and I'm there because I, too, was on the cruise. We aren't hiding anything. Yes, I'm a sheriff, but what I do up here has nothing to do with what's going on in Barbados. And there's no reason why any of your friends should think otherwise. Just remember, be natural. As for me, I don't expect to say much of anything. That would be intruding on their grief. I'll be taking mental notes, but they won't know that."

Abbey sounded nervous.

"I've never been in one of these undercover affairs," she said. "I just don't want to give us away."

"Try not to think of it that way, Abbey. Honoring Mr. Pierce is a natural thing to be doing. So is inviting me. The only person who might think we've set a trap would be the killer, and I'm still pretty sure that the one who did it is a going to be a Barbadian. But let's just say, for the purposes of argument, that one of your friends *is* the killer. If that's the case, we want him to give himself away. So we'd want him to act suspicious, wouldn't we?"

Abbey understood the sheriff's logic, but she still didn't sound comfortable.

Carol decided to change the subject.

"You were going to do what you could to find pictures of the reunion group. Any luck?"

"Some. Not as much as you'd want, of course."

"How would it be if I drove by your cottage and picked up what you have."

"Of course, I'll be here all day tomorrow."

"I was thinking about today. Would it be okay if I stopped by in half an hour? I won't stay."

"Of course. I'll just be watching TV."

"I promise not to interrupt."

It was barely half an hour later that the sheriff collected the Syracuse yearbook and a manila folder which contained several newspaper clippings and a few photos of the kind that people send at the Christmas season.

"Not much here, I'm afraid," Abbey said. "The yearbook's not much help. We've all aged. Anyway, I've put a big X next to the pictures of our members. Everyone's here, somewhere or other, even Ann Bickle. She's the one who didn't attend Syracuse, but she's in a group photo her husband took several years ago at Cape May."

True to her word, Carol didn't linger, letting Abbey get back to her TV show.

Once back at the office, the sheriff set about the task of putting names and faces together. As was her habit, Carol pulled a yellow pad out of the desk drawer in the study and made notes that captured the most recognizable features of the group that had accompanied Pierce on the Caribbean cruise.

'John Bickle: hard to tell about his height, but he looks to be in good shape and he still has a full head of dark hair - glasses, even back in college days - smile in yearbook looks forced

'Ann Bickle: no yearbook photo, but other pics suggest she's her husband's height, maybe slightly taller - face and hair-do unremarkable - she wouldn't stand out in a crowd

'Stuart Craig: class photo makes him look like a young Robert DeNiro - should see a dentist for his bite - said to be an outdoorsman, but pics offer no clue - looks like he'll be bald before he retires

'Betty Craig: no clothes horse this one - best smile of the lot, makes ordinary face come alive - informal pics suggest she has a sense of humor

'Roger Edgar: yearbook photo makes him look older than the others - and more serious - does that and horned rimmed glasses foreshadow his medical career? - otherwise, bland features

'Harry Pringle: based on photos, he's the best-looking guy in the group, although it looks like he can't decide how much facial hair he wants - one informal pic says he may also be the tallest

'Bess Stevens: someone who looks for all the world like the boxer she claims to be - a blank face, but self aware'

After reading her own notes a second time, Carol was ready to toss them into the wastebasket. What had she learned? Virtually nothing. The class photos were only head shots, and they were all somewhere around thirty years old. The Christmas pictures, when available, were uniformly 'happy family' shots that, on reflection, provided surprisingly little insight into the people Carol was supposed to be interested in. The informal shots hinted at personality, but not everyone among the Barbados Eight was represented, and informal didn't mean that they hadn't been posed. Even such basic matters as height were hard to pin down.

Carol was annoyed with her own efforts to read something important into the pictures. That Bess Stevens was self-aware. That John Bickle's smile in his yearbook photo was forced. That Betty Craig had a sense of humor. The more she thought about it, the more she was convinced that she was taking her role in the case too seriously. Why not simply meet them all on March 15th and let what they have to say about Pierce and their day in Barbados shape her opinion of each of them?

She decided not to put her notes in the circular file, opting instead for the small but growing folder labeled the Pierce case. Having done that, she silently apologized to Robert DeNiro for comparing him to Stuart Craig. Or was it the other way around? Carol made a deliberate decision to forget about Barbados and spend what was left of the day on Crooked Lake issues.

CHAPTER 17

Inspector Williams was normally a happy man, and a major reason was that he had a happy marriage. One of the principal reasons that he and Marva got along so well was that the inspector made it a practice not to bring his job home with him at night. His wife was proud of what he did, but he had long ago sensed that she preferred not to be burdened with detailed accounts of the problems that inevitably cropped up in his line of work. For that matter, he also welcomed the opportunity to set aside the day's vicissitudes when he closed his office door and headed home each evening.

But the murder of Franklin Pierce - or rather the inability of the RBPF to solve it - had begun to take a toll on life in the Williams household. It wasn't only Marva who was having trouble adjusting to the change in the inspector's mood. Their daughters, accustomed to cheerful dinner hours, were clearly puzzled when he frequently seemed withdrawn, unwilling or unable to join in the conviviality they knew and loved. It wasn't that the inspector was unaware of what was going on. But he found it increasingly difficult to shrug off the lack of progress in tracking down Pierce's killer.

"Hi," he said as he wrapped his arms around his wife that evening. "Hope you had a better one than I did."

"Still no progress?" she asked, but she had known the answer the minute Cyril walked through the door.

"I'm afraid not. But I promise to talk about something else." He tried to put on a smile; the result didn't qualify as a success.

"I hate to be the bearer of more bad news," Marva announced, "but you had a call today. I thought he should have rung you up at the office, but he said it was urgent. I have the impression he thinks you'd take it more seriously if he called you at home, although why that should be I have no idea."

"It's bad enough that I'm overwhelmed by this case. I sure don't need people to be bothering you at home. What's this man's name?"

"He didn't say, just wanted you to get back to him as soon as you can."

"No clue what he was calling about?"

"Not a one. I'm no judge of such things, but I'd swear that he wanted to sound mysterious."

"I'm so sorry, honey. Why don't you pour me something while I change. I'll see what I can do to make the call a quick one."

The inspector didn't look optimistic that he'd succeed.

Dressed in shorts, polo shirt and sandals, Scotch in hand, he sat down at his desk and dialed the number his wife had handed him.

The voice that answered him was a deep bass, one of the lowest he could ever recall hearing.

"Inspector Williams, how kind of you to get back to me." Kind? His caller had virtually commanded that he call as soon as he got home.

"Yes, this is Inspector Williams. And whom am I speaking to?"

"Peter Harper. We've never met, but that doesn't matter. What does matter is that you have been searching for the man who killed that tourist last month, the one whose body you found on the Harrysmith beach. I'm calling because I know who did it, and I know you'd want to know."

This man with the deep bass voice wasn't the first person to tell RBPF that he knew the identity of Pierce's killer. Williams hadn't been keeping count, but he was sure that the caller was at least the ninth. It was apparently common in such cases for several members of the citizenry to come forward with names. Some were patently seekers after notoriety. Others thought they had seen or heard something that pointed to the guilty party. There had even been a case or two where the person claiming to know something really might know what he was talking about.

The inspector had had too many false alarms in this case to experience any quickening of his heart beat.

"We always welcome such information," he said, trying to sound grateful for the call without leaving the impression that he was excited. "Whom do you believe is the killer in this case?"

"I'd much prefer not to name names over the phone. I'm sure you can appreciate why I'm a bit reticent."

"Yes, of course," the inspector replied, although he didn't know why Mr. Harper was so reticent. "But I would like to meet with you as soon as possible. You presumably know where the RBPF building is. Why don't we set a time for us to meet there, preferably tomorrow."

"If you don't mind, I would rather meet you somewhere else, not in police headquarters. Perhaps we could get out of Bridgetown entirely. Why not make it some place that's not crowded, you know, away from the tourist crowd."

This interest in privacy puzzled the inspector. What was Harper's problem with a crowd? With the RBPF? For that matter, what was his problem with the telephone? Surely he didn't believe that the inspector's phone was being tapped by the killer. No point in sounding annoyed, however. He did some quick thinking and came up with what should be an acceptable place.

"Okay. Let's meet at the Holetown Monument. We can find a quiet place near there, I'm sure."

Harper was obviously considering this suggestion. But he decided that it would do, and they began to discuss the matter of when. The inspector was anxious to bring what he thought of as an unnecessarily complicated conversation to an end.

"I must get off the phone, Mr. Harper, and unfortunately tomorrow is going to be a busy day. So let's make it 9:30 at the Monument. I'm looking forward to meeting you. We're in agreement, right?"

Once again, Harper hesitated. But his interest in sharing his knowledge of the killer was obviously more important than further haggling.

"That should be fine. I'll be there at 9:30. How will I recognize you?"

"I imagine I'll be the only person hanging around the Monument at that hour. It shouldn't be difficult."

Whether because of the pending meeting with Mr. Harper, even if it turned out to be another false alarm, Cyril felt temporarily in better spirits. For a change, he and Marva actually enjoyed their happy hour.

———

Peter Harper and Inspector Williams found each other in Holetown without any difficulty, and shortly thereafter were sitting at a sidewalk cafe, drinking coffee. The deep voice had led the inspector to expect that Harper would be a big man. He turned out to be a head shorter than Williams, an unprepossessing but obviously nervous figure.

"Well, here we are," the inspector said. "Nobody close enough to overhear us. As you can imagine, I'm very anxious to learn whom you believe is responsible for the death of the cruise ship passenger."

Harper leaned forward, as if to make sure that no eavesdropper overheard him.

"It's Ralph Blackman. Do you know him?"

"I don't think so, but I'm not absolutely sure. I know a couple of Blackman families. You'll have to tell me more. How is it that you know he's the one who killed Mr. Pierce?"

"It's an unusual story, inspector. I overheard him at a bar."

That didn't strike Inspector Williams as a promising explanation, and he said so.

"Are you familiar with *The Rockaway* in Hastings?" Harper asked.

"I know it. Not well."

"I often stop off there after work, and that's what I did last night. It was early, crowd still thin. I took a seat at the end of the bar, ordered a scotch, and settled down to read the paper. There were two men down the bar a few chairs, probably doing what I was doing. We weren't paying any attention to each other, but I got the impression that they were excited. At least one of them was. I didn't hear everything they said, but the one who seemed excited said something about a cruise ship. You know, the *Azure Sea*. That got my attention because of the story about the passenger who got himself killed. I didn't want to look too curious, but I listened more carefully. He took out a wallet - I mean the man who was doing most of the talking. But it wasn't his. He said he'd found it on Harrysmith Beach."

Harper took a sip of his coffee, watching the inspector to see how he was reacting to his story. The inspector nodded, waiting for his companion to continue.

"Now this isn't word for word what was said, but I know I've got the important things right. It seems the wallet had been tossed into a trash basket. Or rather he thought that's what had happened. Only it missed and must have landed on the ground. It was pretty much buried in the sand under those sea grapes that grow along the beach.

"That's when it got interesting. This man, he's Blackman, opened the wallet and they agreed there was no cash in it. But it seems it did have other stuff - driver's license, credit cards, the things you put in a wallet. And it was Pierce's."

"Blackman said so? He specifically said the wallet had cards that told him it belonged to Pierce?"

"Right. And you could tell he was excited. It was like he'd found something really important. The other man said he should give the wallet to the police."

If what Harper was saying was true, if he had really heard all of this, it was possible that the Pierce case had just taken a big step forward.

"But Blackman said he couldn't do that. They'd - I mean you people in the RBPF - would immediately assume he was the killer. They sort of argued about that, but the man with the wallet made it clear he was keeping the wallet. After awhile they quieted down and in another ten minutes or so they left the bar."

"How do you know the man with the wallet was Ralph Blackman?"

"I asked the bar tender. He said the two men were Blackman and Andy Browne."

"And you're sure the one with the story about finding the wallet was Blackman?"

"I am. He's the one who was drinking whiskey."

Harper's story might fall apart with one or two pointed questions, but Inspector Williams knew what he was going to be doing as soon as he left Holetown for the return trip to Bridgetown. But one more thing was on his mind.

"Where do you work, Mr. Harper?"

"Scotiabank on Broad Street. I'm the branch manager. Why? Is there a problem?"

"No, no. Just curious. How would you describe Mr. Blackman and his friend?"

"What do you mean?"

"What kind of jobs would you guess they have?"

"Oh, I see. Like me, I guess. Professionals. They seemed to be friends, but they never used bajan, at least not that I remember. Maybe they weren't all that close."

"It's probably not important. At least Blackman didn't strike you as someone who might be a common pickpocket."

"Definitely not. I don't think he was making any of it up."

"Is there anything else I should know?" Williams asked.

Harper suddenly looked uncomfortable.

"I'm not sure how to say this, inspector. But I've been wondering if there might be any reward money. I was thinking that you might not know anything about Blackman if we hadn't had this meeting."

The inspector was surprised, but realized that he probably shouldn't have been.

"I haven't had time to think about that, Mr. Harper. In fact, I don't even know what official policy is. But I do appreciate it that you've shared this information with me. It's potentially very important. By the way, I'm going to ask you to come by RBPF and make a formal statement. No problem, I hope?"

Harper didn't like the idea, but he knew that if he didn't do what the inspector asked there would be no chance of a reward. He nodded yes, and the two men returned to their cars and headed back to Bridgetown.

———

By 4:30 that afternoon, Inspector Williams had located Ralph Blackman's address, made the necessary inquiries, and secured the necessary papers. He took two constables with him and set of for the Blackman residence.

The man who claimed to have found Franklin Pierce's wallet had not yet come home, and his wife was visibly torn by fear and indignation when the inspector announced that he had a warrant to search the house. It took less than ten minutes for Constable Ayres to find the wallet.

"I'm sorry, Mrs. Blackman, to be an inconvenience. But we shall have to make ourselves comfortable until your husband gets home. Please do not call him. I would rather be the one to explain why we are here."

Just a few minutes less than an hour later, Ralph Blackman walked through the front door and called out a cheerful 'hi, honey.'

Inspector Williams rose from the chair nearest the door to meet the man of the house, whose smile had already disappeared.

"Mr. Blackman," he said, "I'm going to ask you to accompany me down to headquarters. We need to talk about Franklin Pierce. I think you know who he is. Or perhaps I should say who he was."

Chapter 18

"If you were in my shoes, what would you do?"

The inspector had been worrying about it since the previous evening and his lengthy and inconclusive interrogation of Ralph Blackman.

"I assume you're talking about your American sheriff," Inspector Brathwaite said.

"I am. I shouldn't have involved her in this business in the first place. Now that Blackman's in our cross-hairs, maybe it's time to tell the sheriff to go back to policing her own jurisdiction."

"I don't have the impression that Blackman is guilty of anything except poor judgment. No question, he'd have been wiser to have told you he'd found Pierce's wallet. But he hasn't confessed to killing him, and from what you tell me he's not going to."

"Oh, come on. We've just had one night. He'll come around."

Inspector Brathwaite laughed.

"And how do you expect to get a confession out of him, Cyril? Thumbscrews? You couldn't operate like that it you had to. Good God, man, if you weren't a cop you'd be a priest! Besides, you don't have any evidence that Blackman killed Pierce for his wallet. He could have come by it like he says he did."

"I don't buy it. Somebody throws a wallet at a beach trash container and misses, what would he do? What would *you* do? You'd pick it up and make sure it went in the trash. The story makes no sense at all."

"But if Blackman really is the killer, why wouldn't he have deep-sixed the wallet? He had the whole Atlantic Ocean right there in front of him. What's the point in keeping the wallet? I know you've been assuming the killer is some dumb bajan, but Blackman's a responsible mid-level official in the Finance Ministry. Why would he be coshing a tourist for a few Yankee dollars?"

"We'll be looking into his finances, Adam. Look, you know I can't swear that Blackman murdered Pierce. I think he did and I'm going to make him sweat. But the way the wind's blowing, I don't see how I can keep that sheriff tied up in this damn case."

"Well, you asked what I'd do, and I told you. I'm sure she'd be grateful if you told her she's no longer needed, but it's your call."

"Thanks for the advice." Inspector Williams didn't look as if the advice had made him happy.

He thought about it for the next several hours, but he knew he was postponing the inevitable. He knew it was his responsibility to let the sheriff know that he was now more than ever confident that the culprit in the *Azure Sea* disaster was a fellow Barbadian. He wouldn't go so far as to 'take her off the case.' He'd leave it to her as to what she would do. But he was sure that his report would have the effect of bringing to an end the strange international arrangement which someone named Abbey Lipscomb had recently set in motion.

Carol was not in her office when the inspector made an effort to contact her. But he made certain that he would be in his office when she returned his call.

"Hello, sheriff," he said, doing what he could to make his tone of voice sound positive. "I thought it was time I reported to you on how things stand in the Pierce case. How have you been?"

"Busy," she replied, "but people in our line of work are always busy, aren't they?"

It was his call, his report, so Carol chose not to ask questions. Williams did the talking. He gave her a detailed account of the Blackman development, being careful to avoid making claims he couldn't substantiate while making it clear that he believed he had the investigation into Pierce's murder well under control.

"So you see," he said by way of summing up, "it seems only fair to let you know that your friend Ms. Lipscomb's fears now seem unwarranted. I have always felt guilty about talking you into joining this investigation. Apprehending the killer was always my responsibility, but I would have been happy to have you on my team had it been necessary."

"Thank you, inspector. I have always assumed that it was your investigation, not mine. But ironically it appears that I shall continue to be interested in the matter, and the reason is Ms. Lipscomb, if not in quite the way I originally thought."

"I'm afraid I don't understand," the inspector said.

"I have had several conversations with Ms. Lipscomb, and it was obvious from the beginning that she wanted me to be involved because of the possibility that Mr. Pierce might have been killed by one of his traveling companions, all of whom are now back in the United States. She and I have discussed this a number of times, and she has never been able to explain why she thinks any one of them might be guilty. You and I have talked about this before. But I have come to the conclusion that this concern of hers is not just a matter of guesswork. I am now convinced that there was a relationship between Mr. Pierce and another member of his tour group which might have led to his death. The problem is that Ms. Lipscomb literally can't put her finger on that relationship. It's an elusive something, something her mind tells her wasn't particularly important but something that keeps bothering her. This is a common problem, as I'm sure you know, inspector. We all know things we don't know we know. In any event, I doubt that I'll be able to forget about the Pierce case until I've figured out what that something is."

"I see." Carol had no idea what the inspector thought he saw.

"My point is that I appreciate your willingness for me to forget all about Pierce and his traveling companions and concentrate on law and order up here on a small lake you've never seen. Or even heard of until a few weeks ago. But I can't do that. In fact, I shall be meeting the members of this tour group very soon. If I learn anything which you might be interested in, I'll let you know. So don't worry that I'm wasting my time. You may well be right. You probably are. But I discovered long ago that when I'm confronted with a puzzle which keeps me awake at night, I just can't seem to let it go."

"You are actually experiencing sleepless nights?"

"It's not quite that bad, but yes, some nights are worse than others."

"I didn't know, sheriff. I'm sorry."

"Don't worry about me. It's probably you who'll be needing a good night's sleep before this is over."

When Carol hung up the phone, she was more certain than she had been following the inspector's first phone call from Barbados that she had committed herself for the duration of the Pierce case. The first time she had been worried that she had made a mistake to please both Abbey Lipscomb and Inspector Williams. This time she was sure that she had made the right decision, and she had made it for herself.

CHAPTER 19

Madison College had entered the period of the academic year that was widely thought of, by students and faculty alike, as the doldrums. Both calendar and weather said it was still winter, and spring break was still weeks away. The zest with which Kevin had approached his classes following the cruise had vanished, to be replaced by lectures which he regarded as uninspired and a general lassitude which even his best students found it hard to conceal. He tried to pep up his opera course by substituting Alben Berg's 20th century shocker, *Lulu*, for a Rossini pot-boiler. He had hoped that this story of sex-obsessed decadence, ending with the eponymous Lulu dead at the hands of Jack the Ripper, would stir the class to vigorous debate. It did no such thing, leading instead to two students dropping the course.

Fortunately, he thought, there would be a phone call from Crooked Lake any day now letting him know when the memorial service for Franklin Pierce would be held. He had already alerted his teaching assistant to his forthcoming absence. It wouldn't be for more than a four day weekend and would probably involve no more than two classes at most, but the prospect that he would soon be meeting and watching Pierce's fellow reunioners kept him going through the doldrums.

As was their habit, he and Carol talked on the phone at least once a week, and it was on a particularly gloomy late February day that she interrupted one of TV's innumerable cop shows with a call from the cottage.

"Let me guess. You're grading papers? No, it's too early in the semester for that. You're trying to get another research paper of your own off the ground? Sorry. I should know better, shouldn't I? Why don't you tell me?"

"I'm warding off mind-numbing boredom by trying to figure out which of several losers killed a guy who was going to testify against the mob. You do it so much better than they do it on TV."

"The difference between what I do and what my fictional counterparts do is that they get it done in 60 minutes. When did I ever close a case in less than four or five months, and then only if I'm lucky?"

"Which means that you aren't calling to tell me that you've wrapped up the Pierce case."

"No way. Actually, Inspector Williams down in Barbados has tried to persuade me to forget all about Pierce. He's feeling guilty that he dragged me into it. He still thinks the guilty party is going to be one of his fellow Barbadians. He may well be right, but I've signed on to this one for the duration. Not quite sure why, but something's bothering my friend Abbey, and because it's bothering her it's bothering me."

"I'm glad to hear it. And you won't be surprised to hear that I hope your inspector is wrong. If he's right, we'll be sidelined, with all the action down in the Caribbean."

"*We'll* be sidelined? Let me remind you, Kevin, that you aren't anywhere near the half way mark in your spring semester. I'd like to think that when the inspector finds out who killed Mr. Pierce - or when I do, for that matter, you'll still be down in the city reading term papers or grading finals."

"I hope you haven't forgotten that there's a memorial service coming up and that I'll be back at the lake to give you a hand in analyzing Pierce's traveling companions."

"I was going to talk with you about that," Carol said.

"A date's been set?" Kevin sounded excited.

"It has, but that's not my point."

"When's it going to be? My arrangements are tentative, and I'll need to firm them up."

"I'm sorry, Kevin, but I'll be handling this myself. I've given it a lot of thought, and I think your presence isn't a good idea."

"What are you talking about? I thought we'd agreed that I'd come up to the lake so the two of us could take stock of these SU alums."

"We talked about it, and I know you'd like to be here. But, please, hear me out."

"I don't want to hear you out, Carol. I want to hear Pierce's friends, enemies, whatever they are, myself."

"Hey, we're a team, remember? That means we listen to each other. I'm the one who was asked by Inspector Williams to handle the US end of this investigation. Believe me, if I thought I could help him catch Pierce's killer by having you at my side in Abbey Lipscomb's parlor, I'd send you an engraved invitation. But I'm going to be there as a friend of Abbey's, not as one half of a couple who traveled on the *Azure Sea* with the SU reunion group. Somebody in the group may recognize me and start asking questions. That's the risk I run. But if they see both of us, the odds that someone will remember the lovey-dovey couple who were always smooching on the deck or in the pool will go up exponentially. In due course the truth will out, but right now my objective is to form some opinions of these people when they don't yet know I was on the cruise or that I'm a police officer. Don't you see?"

"No, I don't. We weren't the only smoochers on the ship. You know that. Remember that mousy blond whose D-cup landed right in the middle of her mashed potatoes when she leaned across the table to kiss her spouse?"

"Yes, but I'm sure we were the most obvious ones. Two people actually asked me if we were honeymooning."

"If we were, the honeymoon is over if I'm excluded from the memorial service."

"Nice try, Kevin. Look, I've already reserved a place for you in our investigation."

"It had better be good," he said, not quite sure whether to sound upset or interested.

"One of the group seems to be determined not to respond to Abbey's e-mails or phone calls. So it's a safe bet he will not be attending the memorial. If he won't come to Crooked Lake, somebody's got to go over to Cooperstown. That's where he lives. I've already missed too many days at the office, so I'm deputizing you."

Kevin let that sink in.

"I'm not sure why it's okay for me to see Mr. X but not the rest of the Syracuse gang. And what if he bars the door, won't let me in?"

"I thought I'd answered your first question. Anyway, by the time you see Westerman - that's his name, Jim Westerman -chances are that our identities will no longer be a secret. As for his barring the door, I'll think of something. Or you will. Why don't you put your thinking cap on, like tonight. Maybe he's got a thing about the Baseball Hall of Fame. Or the Glimmerglass Opera Festival. Bet you didn't know I knew they were in Cooperstown, did you?"

"You always amaze me, Carol. For what it's worth, though, Glimmerglass doesn't start until July and baseball's Hall of Fame ceremony is also in late July. I figured you'd need my help sooner than that. Otherwise your inspector friend will already have made an arrest."

"Oh, come on, Kevin, I'm not that dumb. You won't be seeing Westerman in July. You'll be seeing him in just a week or two. If you want to use your meeting to get the low down on Glimmerglass or Hall of Fame tickets, be my guest. You might even claim to be writing a travel feature for the *Times* on two of our great lakes, Crooked and Otsego."

"So you want me to visit Cooperstown soon?"

"I do. The memorial service is to be on March 15th - invitations only, mind you. If Westerman doesn't surprise us by showing up unannounced, I'd suggest you make the trip the following weekend. And I expect you to put together an itinerary that includes the cottage on Blue Water Point. How about making me your first stop. That way I can give you the low down on what I learned as the fly on the wall at Abbey's."

"You've made my day. Sorry to be so stubborn about the memorial service."

"No problem," Carol said. "I knew I was playing the better hand."

CHAPTER 20

Once Kevin had been disabused of the idea that he'd be present at Franklin Pierce's memorial service, Carol turned her attention to Abbey Lipscomb. The woman wasn't exactly a control freak, but she was accustomed to being in charge of things she was interested in, and she was very much interested in saying good-bye to Franklin Pierce. The upstate alums would be gathering at Abbey's house because Abbey was a long time friend and had invited them. She would have decided on an appropriate farewell ceremony, prepared whatever they ate and drank, and otherwise orchestrated the whole affair.

The problem was that it was Carol who needed to be in charge. She would have to use the memorial service to acquire as much knowledge as she could of each of the 'guests,' none of whom she knew, all of whom she would be observing and, if possible, questioning for the first time. It would in all probability be the only opportunity she would have to form impressions of the group as they interacted with one another. If she was to be of any help to Inspector Williams, she would have to set the rules and insist upon Abbey's compliance with them. It would not be an easy task.

"Abbey, it's Carol," she said when Ms. Lipscomb answered the phone. "We need to talk, and I was wondering if I could come over to your cottage. Today is preferable."

"Of course, sheriff. I have to see my doctor at 10:30, but after that I'm free."

"When do you expect to be back from the doctor's?"

"No later than 11:30. It's just a routine check-up on how my hip is doing."

"Good. I'll be there at 11:30. If you're not back just yet, I'll wait in the car. We have to discuss how we're going to handle things this Saturday."

"I'm sure there won't be any problem. These are old friends."

Yes, Carol thought, old friends. Except for the fact that one of these old friends may have killed another of your old friends.

Abbey's confidence that her appointment with the doctor would be brief turned out to be overly optimistic. It wasn't until ten of twelve that she pulled up next to Carol's car.

"So sorry," she said. "He had a little emergency. You must be cold, sitting out here all this time. I'll get us some hot chocolate."

"That's quite all right. My heater was working fine."

It wasn't long before Abbey had delivered on her promise of hot chocolate. Carol had spent the time trying to imagine how all the SU alums would be able to find seats in the crowded parlor. She considered offering her assistance in rearranging the furniture, but decided that such an offer could easily be misconstrued as criticism.

"Now, about the memorial service," Abbey said, "I think everything is under control. Everyone should be here by noon, and we should have it all wrapped up by three at the latest so that everybody can get home at a reasonable hour. Only the Craigs are staying over. In a B & B down in Southport, I believe. I'll have various things ready for an informal lunch, so that's all taken care of. It's better for it not to go on too long. Otherwise, these things tend to get maudlin."

Carol wondered how many of 'these things' Abbey had attended. It hadn't occurred to her that the gathering on Saturday might be maudlin.

"As we both know," she said, "I'm here because the Barbados police want me here, in case Mr. Pierce's killer happens to be one of his colleagues from the tour group. So I must be in a position to learn as much as I can about all of them. That will be possible only if you help me. You know I do not know any of these people. So our first order of business Saturday is for you to make sure I quickly figure out who's who. You're going to have to introduce all of them to me. Don't overdo it, just explain that I'm a friend from the Crooked Lake area, and that I'm here to help you take care of the food and drink. And I mean it. I'm the good neighbor who's here to bring things in from the kitchen, take drink orders, give a friend a helping hand during a trying afternoon. Got it?"

Abbey nodded her head tentatively.

"But what's critical is that I learn who everybody is. I'll be responsible for associating a name with things like height, weight, complexion, voice level, and so on. For the most part I'll stay out of the conversation. After all, they're your friends, not mine. The tragedy of Mr. Pierce's death is why *they're* here, not me. If I do say anything, it will be because I'm trying to clarify something that seems important to me as Inspector Williams's investigative partner."

"And you don't want them to know you were on the cruise?"

"I'm hoping that none of them recognizes me. But if somebody does, don't act surprised. Be natural, say yes, I was on the ship - you invited me to help you because you knew I'd be interested. And just in case somebody remembers that I had a husband on that cruise, that's okay. I'll volunteer that he's interested, just like I am. Obviously I hope that nobody remembers us from the cruise, but if they do it's not a big deal."

"What if someone asks if you're a sheriff?"

"I can't imagine why anyone would think that. Kevin and I never talked about it while we were on the trip. But if someone happens to ask that question, let me handle it."

"It sounds like we're doing two things for Franklin - saying good-bye and catching his killer."

"I'm not sure about catching a killer, but looking for one, yes. What I'm saying is that this is about much more than saying good-bye to your friend. We both know that; we've known it since you urged the inspector to let me help him. I just wanted to make sure we have our signals straight, especially in view of the fact that I won't be talking much during - what shall we call it, the ceremony?"

"That's too fancy, don't you think? All I planned on doing was asking each of them to offer a few words in appreciation of Franklin. Give them a chance to say something about their memories of him. I may have my suspicions, but I'd rather not get into the issue of how he died or who might have killed him. It's better, don't you think, to treat it like he just had a heart attack or something like that?"

"Probably so, although I wouldn't be surprised if some of the group raised the subject. It will have been on all their minds. and of course I'd be glad to hear them speculate. But you're right. It might be better if you let it come up naturally, rather than asking them to share their thoughts about it. In fact, I'll be interested in who's anxious to talk about what happened in Barbados. Or for that matter, who doesn't seem interested in talking about it."

"Do you expect to learn anything?" Abbey asked.

"I have no expectations. What happens will happen." Carol chuckled. "Now there's a cliche for you. But there's a good chance that I'll have learned something, even if I don't know it at the time. We have to remember that this is just the beginning of what could be a long process."

What happens will happen. But Carol's greatest concern was that Abbey would get in the way, that she would over-manage the memorial when she should stay out of the way. It was, of course, impossible, but she had to acknowledge that she would prefer that Abbey not be there.

Chapter 21

Carol and Abbey were enjoying a late morning cup of coffee in the Lipscomb kitchen, waiting for the first of the alumni group to arrive. Abbey seemed completely relaxed. If she was wondering who of the seven 'mourners' might be Franklin Pierce's murderer, she neither said so nor acted as if it mattered. The sheriff marveled at the hostess's calm. Had their roles been reversed, she knew she would have been engaged in some frantic last minute guessing as to the identity of the guilty party. Unless, of course, Abbey had never seriously entertained the idea that Franklin's killer had been on the cruise, and if that were the case she would have to go back to the beginning and rethink everything that had happened since the discovery of Franklin's body.

Without prompting, Abbey had cleared surfaces in the parlor and made sure that there was a place for everyone to sit. Carol would have sworn that there would be no place for it, but room had been found for a card table and it now contained several platters with finger food, crudites, and cookies, as well as glasses which would presumably be filled from bottles of this and that which were still in the fridge. With so little room for the guests to walk about, it was clear to Carol that she would be the server de jour. She was studying the layout, deciding how best to navigate through the cramped parlor, when the first of the visitors' cars drove up.

Abbey was on her feet more quickly than Carol thought possible in view of her bad hip.

"It's the Craigs," she said. "They're the couple from Cortland, both high school teachers."

Carol watched as they climbed out of their car and walked across the lawn toward the porch. She recalled the few available pictures of them and Tommy's thumb-nail sketches, and was surprised at how well they matched her expectations. Her one disappointment was that Stuart looked nothing like a young Robert DeNiro.

"Welcome, welcome," Abbey announced. "Somebody has to be first, and you're it. Let me introduce my lakeside friend, Carol Kelleher. Carol, this is Betty and Stuart Craig."

The Craigs' smiled, reminding her that Mr. Craig had a bad bite. The photos had also suggested that Mrs. Craig had a warm smile that hinted at a sense of humor, and the woman at the door seemed to confirm that impression.

Coats were shed, and Carol, Abbey's 'maid for the day,' deposited them in a nearby first floor bedroom. Cups of hot coffee followed, and it was but a few minutes before Carol found herself on the sideline while friends from undergraduate days resumed an acquaintanceship that went back many years. It was a pattern that would repeat itself each time another member of the reunion group drove up. It gave Carol an opportunity to compare these people with their photos and Officer Byrnes' sketches. To her surprise, it wasn't hard to guess the identities of each of the newcomers. By the time everyone had arrived, the sheriff was confident that she knew exactly who was who. None of them looked like a murderer.

Carol tried to follow the conversation, which inevitably became more difficult as it became two and then three conversations and Abbey needed her help in the kitchen. Everyone was polite to her, but they paid her little attention. Until Roger Edgar, apparently aware that he and his colleagues were for the most part ignoring her, made an effort to include her in the conversation.

"I'm sorry, Miss Kelleher, we don't mean to be thoughtless. Why don't you join our little circle. What is it you do around Crooked Lake except help Abbey take care of her guests?"

It was a perfectly polite and understandable question. For obvious reasons, Carol didn't wish to answer it.

She smiled and shook her head.

"Nothing very interesting, Dr. Edgar. Abbey thought she'd need some help today, and here I am."

"Oh, for goodness sake," Abbey erupted. "No need to be shy. Carol is our Olivia Benson. She happens to be -"

The hostess caught herself in mid-sentence. For the briefest of seconds it looked as if she might spill her coffee. She broke into a cough. Bess Stevens was out of her seat and at Abbey's side, anxious to help. But Carol knew that Abbey needed no help. Her coughing jag was her way of covering the fact that she had made a mistake. In her eagerness to speak up for the sheriff she had momentarily forgotten that the 'clever' reference to the police detective on *Law and Order: SVU* would give away her friend's profession. She had been about to be even more specific when she realized what she was doing.

Carol had never been that confident of Abbey's ability to satisfactorily explain her new found lake friend. Now the truth was out, unless nobody else in the room had even heard of Olivia Benson, and that was extremely unlikely. She made a quick decision to tell the truth. At least some of it.

"Are you all right, Abbey?" she asked. "Don't scare us like that. What she was telling you, I think, is that she gets a kick out of having the local sheriff as a friend and is afraid that I'm too modest to admit it. It's really no big deal. My Dad was sheriff here in this county, and when he passed away I was asked if I would be willing to take his place. I'd grown up here, loved the place, and just couldn't bring myself to say no. So I guess you could say I've been Ms. Law and Order around here for the last ten years. It's not that exciting a profession, ticketing speeders, making sure that fishermen have their licenses. In any event, I really am here today to help Abbey say good-bye to someone I understand is an old friend of all of you."

Carol was mentally crossing her fingers. She considered telling the assembled SU alums that she had been on the *Azure Sea* with them, but chose not to. She did not consider saying anything about her role as a partner of the Royal Barbados Police Force in its investigation of Franklin Pierce's murder. She hoped that the conversation would quickly turn to other things and eventually to remembrances of the man who had sailed to Barbados, never to come back.

She fended off several questions about what it was like to be a sheriff, but Abbey, hoping to undo any damage she might have done, shifted the subject of conversation back to Franklin by persuading each of her colleagues to say a few words in appreciation of him.

Ann Bickle, the only non-SU alum among them, chose not to speak, as did Bess Stevens. The others, for the most part, confined themselves to predictable comments - his death a terrible tragedy, a beautiful life cut short, a decent man who had never had a bad word for anyone, a loyal alum whose support for his alma mater put the others to shame, the man who more than anyone else was responsible for their reunions. Carol found the remarks depressing. In almost every case they failed to rise above boiler plate, and in only one instance did a speech contain words which seemed to reflect personal knowledge of the deceased. The speaker whose remarks came closest to hinting at a personal relationship was Harry Pringle, and it was doubtful that those remarks would have suggested such a relationship had not all of the others been so bland and uninspiring.

Pringle, who struck Carol as the best looking person in the room, otherwise stood out for the reason that he had, at some time in his life, disfigured his left hand. One of the fingers was missing, a fact which he seemed self-conscious about. At least he had a tendency reflexively to tuck his left hand under his right arm from time to time as he spoke. He was also the only member of the group who expressed regret that the consignment business had been such a let down for Pierce, a man he claimed deserved much better.

By the time the crudities and finger food were gone and the fridge had given up almost all of its wine and soft drinks, the assembled mourners were beginning to get restless. They had done what they had come to do: pay their respects to Franklin Pierce, the man who had been largely responsible for creating the group's occasional reunions and who had attended what would be his final reunion just two months earlier. Carol had attended enough such events to be sure that it was time to bring the afternoon to an end. Abbey also realized that, having said good-bye to Pierce, it was probably time for people to say good-bye to their hostess and each other and head for home. But she didn't want the day to end, which resulted in producing another pot of coffee and attempting to jump start more conversations. The effort to keep the memorial service going came to an end when the Bickles asked for their coats and said they had to be on their way. Their initiative led quickly to a round of goodbyes (everyone had the presence of mind to include Carol, and most of them even referred to her as the sheriff). By 3:20 Abbey and Carol had the cottage to themselves.

"I'll help you clean up," Carol said, "if you don't mind."

"Thanks, but I'm going to need to lie down." Abbey used the excuse of her hip, but Carol was sure that she needed to be alone. It had not been the kind of affair that Abbey had hoped for. What is more, she realized that she had committed a serious faux pas, giving away the fact that Carol was a sheriff. She started to apologize, but Carol cut her off, insisting that it really didn't matter, that it would have become common knowledge soon enough anyway.

For the first time since she had met her, Carol felt sorry for Ms. Lipscomb. The woman had been responsible for getting her involved in the investigation of Franklin Pierce's death, and the eagerness of her guests to cut short the memorial service made it clear that many, perhaps most of them, were as tired of Abbey as she was. Yet it was impossible not to commiserate with her. She had had a bad winter. And Carol was in a good position to know that whatever the calendar said, this winter was a long way from over.

Chapter 22

John Bickle had been ready to leave the Lipscomb cottage at least an hour before he and Ann made the move which started the exodus from Abbey Lipscomb's Crooked Lake residence. Once on the road, however, he was in no hurry to get back to their own cottage at the northern end of Skaneateles Lake. Instead of heading directly for Geneva and route 20, he selected one tertiary road after another, a course which took them on a tour of the eastern Finger Lakes. The skies were clear and the roads were dry, although there were still large patches of snow on the ground. Neither Ann nor John had much to say, Ann because she was not in a mood to annoy her husband by criticizing this latest 'episode' in the saga of the SU alumni group. John's problem was that something about the afternoon at Abbey's was bothering him.

It was John who finally broke a long silence as they neared Auburn.

"It's about that sheriff," he said. "Did she look familiar to you?"

Ann Bickle had almost fallen asleep.

"I'm sorry. What did you say?"

"I was asking about Abbey's friend, the one she says is a sheriff. I have a feeling that I know her, or at least that I have seen her somewhere. How about you?"

"I'm only half awake, but I don't think I've ever met her. Try me again after I've had a wake-up coffee."

"Isn't it annoying when you swear you know someone but can't figure out why?"

"I guess so, but it doesn't happen to me very often. There was, of course, that girl in the *Safeway* check out line I was sure was Katniss, you know, *The Hunger Games* star, but no one else looked excited so I knew I was wrong."

"You're terrible at names, Ann. That was Jennifer Lawrence, or rather it wasn't Jennifer Lawrence. I'm not talking about celebrities. I'm taking about everyday people we've seen but can't remember. I know I've seen Abbey's friend the sheriff before."

"Well, it'll probably come to you one of these days."

"I hope so. It's driving me crazy."

Ann was now wide awake, and regretting all over again that she had agreed to accompany her husband to the memorial service. Only it hadn't been a memorial service, only a boring several hours with people most of whom she didn't much care for. She should never have let John talk her into joining his group of SU alums. She wasn't a Syracuse graduate, so she hadn't known any of these people in college. With the possible exception of Betty Craig, she didn't think of the members of the group as friends, only as acquaintances who went on trips together every year or two. She had shared her feelings about it with John on a number of occasions, and doing so had invariably upset him. She had decided not to bring the subject up again, but now that she was alert she knew she could no longer pretend that she had enjoyed the day.

"What did you think of our little ceremony at Abbey's?" she asked, trying to make sure her voice didn't sound sarcastic.

"About what I expected," John answered. "She probably thought it would be some sort of catharsis, but you don't get that just by having people tell you what a great guy Franklin was. It had to be done, and I'm not surprised that Abbey's the one who did it. Or tried to. But we still have no idea who killed Franklin, and considering that it's now in the hands of the Barbados police we may never know. Funny thing, isn't it? It was too late. If we'd gotten together back when we heard about the murder, there wouldn't have been a dry eye in the cottage. As it is, we'd all gone back to business as usual, and the drive over to Crooked Lake was an inconvenience we had to fit into our schedules. But it was also too soon. If we'd just heard that Franklin's killer had been caught, it would have been a big event, almost a joyful one, not the flat, dutiful one we just left."

Ann was surprised. She didn't think she'd ever heard her husband speak in paragraphs instead of terse sentences before. What is more, he had expressed a view very similar to her own.

"Would you rather we had stayed home?" she asked.

"No. We had to be there. You saw how they reacted to Jim Westerman's absence. Maybe he had his reasons, but not showing up, not even letting Abbey know why he couldn't be there, it left a bad taste in everyone's mouth. I mean, what kind of friend does that?"

"That's the trouble, John. We aren't friends. Why are we kidding ourselves? College was years ago, we were kids, we weren't married, had none of our own - what brought us together was frat parties, campus pranks, keeping our GPAs more or less respectable. Now what? Adults, yanked out of our routines every couple of years because Franklin or Abbey or somebody thinks we should remember the good old days. And here we are, pretending to mourn someone I barely know and someone you thought you knew half a lifetime ago. Good grief, for all you know Pierce was a phony, someone who cheated on his exams and raped a coed or two along the way."

"Ann, if you can't say something pleasant, then please shut up." John was suddenly angry. "We're talking about a friend, and you're accusing him of rape."

"I'm doing nothing of the kind. He's not a friend and I'm not accusing him of rape. I'm just tired of this pretense that we're all buddy-buddy, this ritual pretense that we can recreate the good old days. Forget that I wasn't part of the Syracuse wonder years. Sorry that fate sent me to Skidmore. Other than the fact that you call SU alma mater, what is it that keeps this charade alive? If you haven't noticed, nobody's in a funk because Pierce didn't make the ship when it sailed from Bridgetown. Predictably sad, of course, but that's just because they knew him when."

John's hands gripped the steering wheel tightly.

"Let's cut this out, right now, before we lose our tempers."

"Of course," Ann said. "The Group must come first."

Both of them lapsed, once more, into silence. But John spent most of the remaining miles to Skaneateles thinking about what his wife had said about the handful of college friends of whom he was a part. And more particularly about Franklin Pierce. Who was Pierce, or rather who had Pierce been?

Their recently deceased colleague - not a friend, for John was trying to picture him from Ann's point of view - had never been close during their college days. They had known each other, but he had known many other Syracusans who had not become members of the group. They had taken one - no, on reflection it had been two - classes together, but the classes had been large and Franklin was a relatively non-descript unattractive guy who would have remained anonymous had it not been for his penchant for quirky behavior. John recalled a time when Franklin, bored like everyone else by a pedantic lecturer, had donned a Halloween mask and taken to nodding his head vigorously from his seat in the back row. A common bond could have been their fraternity, but they had not belonged to the same fraternity. In fact, John couldn't remember what fraternity Franklin had belonged to.

The small alumni group had, nonetheless, been Franklin's idea. He might have had the same idea had they all attended Yale and hailed from cities and towns across Connecticut. But the idea had taken root in Syracuse, and they had done any number of things together, some successful, some a near disaster, ever since. Through it all, he and Franklin had never become close. Their differing personalities tended to preclude a personal friendship, and it had not been until fairly recently that they had done more than smiled, shaken hands, and spent a few minutes talking about the glory days of SU football. That had changed when Franklin had surprised him by sending him an e-mail which addressed his well known hobby, wood crafting.

John's career had been in accounting, but he had never particularly liked his job as a CPA and his income from it had never come close to the figure he had imagined in college. Sometime along the way he had taken up furniture making in his garage as an escape from his real job, and it had gradually become virtually an alternate career. He discovered that he had a skill he didn't know he had, invested in some state of the art equipment, and converted the garage into a full-time workshop. They had not parked either of the family cars in the garage for at least seven years, causing an occasional family row when their neighborhood experienced a heavy snow.

Franklin had learned of his hobby through a casual conversation on the last group jaunt before what would prove to be the fatal one. In any event, a subsequent e-mail had made an unusual suggestion to which he had given some thought, leading to an eventual meeting at the consignment shop in Newark. It seems that Franklin had decided to dedicate a corner of the shop to the group, presenting materials pertinent to their lives and work, and would like to have a small John Bickle built table or chair for the exhibit. Would I be willing to donate one?

It seemed like a no-brainer, provided that they could agree on how to split the money from a sale. He did do a bit of wondering as to what the equivalent money-making item could be for the other group members, and based on what he knew about them decided that he alone stood to profit from Franklin's idea. But the fact that he might make some money and get some free advertising for his 'hobby' carried the day, and he had put what he considered an attractive small corner cupboard in his car and driven to Newark the previous October. The project to which he was contributing hadn't yet gotten off the ground, although Franklin had showed him where it would be and spoke glowingly of how it would look when it was finished.

He had given the consignment project and his cupboard little thought in the intervening months. The sole exception was a brief conversation on board the *Azure Sea,* at which time Franklin sounded upbeat and expressed his opinion that he expected it to open by June. Now, as he drove the final miles to their Skaneateles home, he actually found himself thinking about the cupboard. And about the consignment shop where he had left it back in the fall. He knew nothing about Franklin's family situation. As far as he knew, he had never married, and if he were married his wife had never been a member of the group. Was the consignment shop still in business, and if so who was running it? He realized that he had Franklin's phone number somewhere; he'd look for it when they got home. If necessary, he'd take a drive over to Newark and see what was going on at *Upstate Consignments.*

Chapter 23

Had the memorial service been a fiasco? Carol's initial reaction was that it had been. It had certainly not given her any significant insights into the local dramatis personae of the Pierce case. She now had a much better sense of what they all looked like, not that that was much help. At least it gave her a better mental picture of each of them, which could help when it came to storing additional information as it became available. But she had no illusions as to how easy it would be to acquire additional information. She had hoped that somebody - hopefully several somebodies - in the group would have said something that provided a clue as to just who they really were. It hadn't happened, however.

She had at first been upset that Abbey had given away her police connection. But there had been no point in criticizing her for it in front of the group, and on reflection she had decided that it didn't really matter. She had always assumed that it would become general knowledge before long. Nobody had said that she looked familiar, which might have led to a discussion of the passenger list on the *Azure Sea*, but even that didn't bother her very much. And unless Abbey really forgot herself, none of them would know anything about her role as Inspector Williams' partner.

Nonetheless, Carol had trouble putting the memorial service out of her mind. Nothing that had been said had prompted Abbey to remember what it was that made her think that someone in the group might have borne Franklin ill will. And nothing she had heard made her suspicious of any of them, unless it was the general lack of enthusiasm in what they had to say about their recently deceased colleague. Pringle had been something of an exception, but that was only because he had spoken of

Pierce as Frankie and mentioned Christmas cards. There had not been a single word about the nature of any personal or professional relationship. It was as if the only thing they had in common was that they traveled together occasionally. Nothing was said about what was supposedly the origin of those travels, a common Syracuse University background. Had they been close friends back then? Carol was inclined to doubt it. Otherwise, somebody would have been likely to bring up a memorable event, a professor they had hated or loved, a campus crisis, a game that nobody could forget. Of course Westerman was not there, whether as a result of a conflict or indifference, she didn't know. Maybe she should make an effort to find out. No, that was going to be Kevin's responsibility. In fact, it was time to give him a call and discuss the matter.

Carol had written his schedule down, but had not memorized it. When she got home she went to the desk and, after a few moments of unsuccessful rummaging, found a small notebook labeled 'Kevin.' It turned out to be what she wanted, but it occurred to her that her husband deserved a better repository of data pertinent to his other life. The small notebook made it clear that he didn't teach on weekends, but she already knew that. There was also no reference to any meetings or 'an evening at the opera.' In any event, it wasn't yet quite evening. She'd call now.

"Hi, it's me," she said when he picked up. "Thought I'd touch a base."

"Love you! Let me cut to the chase and tell you I'll be arriving on Thursday. Does that work for you?"

"It works for me. I'm not sure how well it will work for you. As we expected, Westerman didn't make it to the memorial service today. We can try to reach him by phone (no cell info available), but considering how hard he has been for Abbey Lipscomb to reach, I wouldn't bet on making a connection. So our problem - your problem, I should say - is that you may drive over to Cooperstown and find that he's nowhere around. Which means a long trip for nothing."

"Hey, I'll be seeing you. I'd hardly call cozying up with my wife for a couple of days a long trip for nothing."

"I'm looking forward to that part of it, too, but we're both hoping that we discover whether Westerman's the one who did it to Franklin Pierce."

"I have a hunch that he's been playing possum and that I'll catch him when he's not expecting company."

"I sure hope so, because you'll be putting a whale of a lot of miles on the Camry."

"No point speculating about it today. Why don't you tell me about the farewell to Pierce."

"I wish there were more to tell. As a memorial, it was a bust. Moreover, the people were uniformly dull. I'm in no position to say whether they're just naturally that way or chose to be opaque. If the latter, Abbey may be onto something. But the bottom line is that no one said anything which gave me a clue as to their relationship with Pierce. It was almost like a conspiracy of silence."

"Now there's an idea. What if they conspired to do away with Pierce and drew straws to determine who'd do the deed?"

"Kevin, I hope you aren't heading off to Cooperstown with any such nonsense in your head. It's still my opinion, just as it is the inspector's, that the killer is a Barbadian. He even thinks he has a lead."

"Well, we'll be able to hash things out Thursday night. I'm sure you know something about Westerman, or if not maybe Officer Byrnes can help you. All I'll need is a few facts that will let me get a conversation started. Remember, I can play the Hall of Fame and Glimmerglass cards."

"You'd make a good detective but for one thing. You think it's too easy. Believe me, and I've been there for nearly twelve years now, it's never easy."

"I'm only trying to accentuate the positive."

"Good. Oh, by the way, Abbey let the cat out of the bag. She as much as told the group that I'm a sheriff. Fortunately, no one said anything to suggest he or she remembers me from the cruise. I have the feeling, though, that my cover will be blown before long."

"I assume that I'm not to tell Westerman that I was on the ship or that I'm married to a sheriff, right?"

"It may not matter, but, yes, you're in Cooperstown to learn what you can about him, not to feed him information about me. If I can change the subject for a minute, how's everything down there?"

"Same old, same old. But that's not really fair. My Beethoven to Mahler course is humming along pretty well, better than usual. And I saw a smashing production of an early Rossini opera at the Met the other night. It's a lonely life, but there are occasional compensations."

The conversation bounced around from opera to weather to the problems of bachelor housekeeping until Carol eventually called it a day.

"It's only four more days, and I promise to have a fire on the grate and steaks in the fridge. Let's hope that snow doesn't interrupt your plans."

"It better not. So you can count on me by four."

"I love you, and I can't wait."

"Me either."

CHAPTER 24

Inspector Williams had left the door to his office ajar, and the man in the corridor cautiously pushed it open a few inches and peered into the inspector's inner sanctum.

"Do come in, Mr. Blackman. Right on time."

"I hope you are keeping notes on just how cooperative I am being with your investigation," the man said. "Needless to say, I am very anxious to help you find the man who killed the tourist, but this will be the third time I have been summoned to your office."

"Yes, and it's quite likely that there will be a fourth. Please come on in and have a seat. Would you like some coffee?"

"Thank you, but no thanks."

Ralph Blackman took a seat. He looked as if he were making a conscious effort to be stoical.

"And how have you been sleeping, if I may be so bold as to ask?"

"I assume you are asking because you think I have a guilty conscience. As I have said repeatedly, my conscience is clear. Getting a good night's sleep is another story, and it has everything to do with the fact that you believe I am the person who killed Mr. Pierce. I will sleep better when you realize that I know nothing about his death and am telling you the truth."

The inspector smiled and shrugged.

"As I have told you, this is what we do. Learning the truth requires that I ask lots of questions."

"That I can understand, inspector, but you keep asking the same questions."

"I suppose I do. It's a bad habit. But let's get started. Why don't you tell me when it was that you visited Harrysmith beach and discovered Mr. Pierce's wallet?"

"I'm sure you have it on that pad in front of you, but I'll be glad to repeat myself. I was there last Sunday. In fact, I go there often on Sunday morning. It's very restful."

"Were you alone?"

"I was. And my wife knew where I was. I told her when I left the house. Have you asked her?"

"Of course, and she confirms your story. Unfortunately, she confirms your story that you were there last Sunday, whereas I'm interested in another, much earlier date. The date when the *Azure Sea* was docked here, the day when Mr. Pierce lost his life."

"But it was last Sunday when I found the wallet. We've been over this several times."

"Yes, I think we have. But as you yourself have said, you like Harrysmith. Restful, I think that's what you call it. You've been there often. How about the day the *Azure Sea* was in dock?"

"As I've told you, I go to Harrysmith on Sundays. I don't even remember what day of the week it was when the ship was in port. But it was a weekday, and I was at work."

"Of course, it was a workday. You'll forgive me, but I took the liberty of consulting your boss. He agrees you were at work that day; at least he has no record of you taking leave or a sick day. But there doesn't seem to be any way of accounting for very hour of that day. We can't pinpoint the exact time of Mr. Pierce's death, so we have to consider the possibility that he was killed at almost anytime between mid-morning and fairly late in the day. Did you take a long lunch? Go for a walk? Do anything unusual that day?"

"How do you expect me to remember something like that? It was weeks go. It's also beside the point. As I've said over and over again, I found the wallet last Sunday."

The inspector shifted the focus of his questions.

"Where exactly did you say you found the wallet?"

Blackman sighed a sigh of exasperation.

"On the beach, near the trash can they use to collect the unsightly junk people throw away. It was pretty much buried in the sand. When I first saw it, it didn't even look like a wallet. More like a dead sea grape leaf."

"Yes, I think that's what you told me when first we met. How do you explain it being there? You must have asked yourself why a wallet, especially a wallet with no money in it, was underfoot on Harrysmith beach."

"If it had had any money, I suppose I'd have assumed somebody dropped it. But because it didn't, I guessed - and I mean I *guessed* - that it might have been taken by a pickpocket, somebody who'd lifted it, taken the money, then tossed it away."

"Sounds like a reasonable guess. But why couldn't you be that pickpocket?"

"I'm not trying to be smart, but let me count the ways. In the first place, like just about everyone else in Barbados, I knew that this tourist passenger had been killed back in January. But now it's March. How could I have picked his pocket two months ago - sorry, killed him for his money two months ago - and then found the wallet that I had presumably gotten rid of way back then? More importantly, I am not a pickpocket. I'm a respected government employee with a good salary. If you check my bank, you'll find that I am doing quite well and have no need to rob anybody, fellow citizens or tourists."

"Pardon the interruption, but isn't it possible that you kept the wallet for all that time and then decided to pretend you'd found it last weekend? And as for your good bank account, not all robbers are dirt poor. Some have money problems because they have to feed their addiction. Others are simply kleptomaniacs."

Blackman's temper was about to explode.

"You will probably keep on making inquiries about my private life, but I can assure you that you will find nothing to suggest that I am a drug addict or a kleptomaniac."

"That's good to hear. Do you have any other ideas as to how that wallet came to be on the Harrysmith beach last weeked?"

"Yes, I do, because I've thought about almost nothing else since I first met you. I know nothing about such things, but when you're trying to find ways to prove your innocence brainstorming can be helpful. So how about this? Pierce was killed by one of his fellow passengers. Don't ask me why, I'm just brainstorming. The tourist who killed him wanted the RBPF to suspect a poor bajan who was low on cash. So the tourist throws the wallet, now without money, on the beach, hoping you will find it and conclude that the killer was this poor bajan. The tourist sails away, home free. How's that for a crazy idea?"

Inspector Williams had actually given some thought to that very same crazy idea and dismissed it. Now here was a local suspect, the most likely candidate for Pierce's murderer to date, offering it as a possible alternative explanation of what had happened.

"Very interesting. Unfortunately, RBPF didn't find the wallet, you did. And instead of turning it over to us, you decided to keep it. In light of the good it might have done you to bring to me, why did you hang on to the wallet?"

"In retrospect it wasn't a good idea. But my crazy idea, which is still crazy by the way, didn't come to me until you began to interrogate me almost on a daily basis. I figured you'd suspect me of Pierce's killing, so I kept the wallet. Maybe you'd catch the killer and the lost wallet would no longer be relevant. In any event, I never gave it much thought. I just kept it."

"Bad decision, Mr. Blackman."

"You learned I had the wallet because someone heard me talking about it to a friend. Do you honestly think I would have told people I had the wallet if in fact I'd killed Pierce? I like to think I'm smarter than that."

"You might be surprised how many people think they're smarter than they are. Even the best and the brightest make unforced errors from time to time."

The interrogation came to an end shortly thereafter, and Inspector Williams tried to act the friendly cop as he smiled, shook hands, and ushered Blackman out of the office. For the better part of the next half hour, however, he sat quietly at his desk and thought about the state of the inquiry into Franklin Pierce's death. His colleague, Inspector Brathwaite, had kidded him about his interrogation technique, low keyed, unthreatening. He'd even said that if Cyril hadn't been a policeman, he'd have been a priest. It was a joke they shared. Brathwaite knew that Cyril had a brother who was a priest; Williams knew that one priest per family was enough.

The trouble with Ralph Blackman as a suspect in the murder of Franklin Pierce was not only that so far there was nothing in the evidence that provided grounds for charging him. More than that, the inspector had a growing feeling that Blackman, in spite of the 'fortuitous' discovery of the wallet, would turn out to be innocent. Yes, his judgment about what to do with the wallet left much to be desired. But instead of making the inspector more convinced that he was on the right track, three meetings with him had shaken his conviction that at last the guilty party was virtually within his grasp. He was not about to tell Inspector Brathwaite of his change of heart, but he knew he was ready to set the Blackman file aside and begin again his quest for the real killer.

Chapter 25

Kevin had one final meeting with his teaching assistant, making sure he had plans for his classes and CDs and films, should they be needed in one of his courses. It wasn't until he was settled into his car and had left the city heading west that the near disaster involving a previous TA came to mind. That assistant was Jennifer Laseur, an attractive young violinist who, unfortunately had an unreciprocated crush on him. His mistake had been to carelessly refer to her as 'he' in a conversation with Carol. When his future wife found out that he was a she, and what's more, a she who had designs on him, she had very nearly put an end to their budding romance. It had been a costly lesson.

But now, a decade later, they could laugh about it. And he had been much more careful in his choice of TAs. His thoughts turned to his pending trip to Cooperstown for a meeting with someone named Jim Westerman. He had never met Westerman, knew only that he had been part of the group of Syracuse alums who had been on the *Azure Sea* with them, and needed to be tracked down in his lair on Otsego Lake because he had been impossible to reach otherwise.

His initial reaction to the information that Abbey Lipscomb had been unable to reach Mr. Westerman for several long weeks was that he was off on some kind of trip. But Abbey had convinced Carol that he was more likely simply to be ignoring her efforts to make contact. If she were wrong, the trip to Cooperstown would be a waste of time. If she were right and he had an opportunity to talk with him, the problem would be to try to get to the root of Westerman's make believe disappearing act. Either way, he would have the pleasure of a couple of days with Carol, something they had too few of during the off season when he was down in the city teaching music history at Madison College.

As was his wont, Kevin entertained himself on the long drive with CDs of his favorite operas. That and kind, lovely thoughts about Carol. It was nearly five o'clock when he pulled in behind the cottage on Blue Water Point and was delighted that she was already home. The kiss at the back door was considerably more than perfunctory. Carol eventually broke it off and suggested that they go inside where the temperature was much warmer. The steaks were excellent, and their bed, which was both larger and more comfortable that the one they had shared on the cruise, was put to the use Kevin had envisioned on the drive from the city. The conversation about Westerman didn't take long, partly because Carol knew so little about him and in no small part because they had trouble getting their minds and hands off each other.

The following morning as Kevin was finishing breakfast and getting ready to leave, he put a question to Carol.

"It seems to me that in cases like this I'm always toward the back in the queue. How come I'm the one going to visit Westerman, not Bridges or one of your other men?"

"My other officers, Kevin. Remember that Miss Dockery is now part of the roster. But it's you not Bridges for the simple reason that the Pierce case isn't really my responsibility. His death occurred way down in Barbados and none of the parties lives in Cumberland County, so I'd be cheating the government that pays me if I used my staff to conduct this investigation. I took leave for my flight down to Bridgetown, and I'm doing my best to schedule business related to what happened there on weekends. It may take a bit of sleight of hand, but I'm doing my best to play it by the book. I hope you aren't disappointed."

Kevin smiled.

"Of course not. Perhaps you should consider tackling more international or at least interstate crimes."

"Absolutely not. This is an exception, and I intend that it shall be a one of a kind exception. Don't you think you should be going?"

"What's on your docket for the day?" he asked as he transferred his dishes to the sink.

"The usual. But Saturday I'm taking an early trip up to Newark to take a peek at Pierce's consignment shop. I'm not sure why, but I have a hunch it could be important. Anyway, that's what I'm up to."

"You won't be here when I get back?"

"Oh, yes, barring a snow storm. It'll take you longer to drive back to the cottage from Cooperstown than it will for me to make it back from Newark."

"I sure hope so."

"Come on, hit the road. And drive carefully. Oh, and please do not give my regards to Jim Westerman. If you run into any problems, you know how to reach me."

A good-bye kiss and Kevin was off.

Cooperstown is not exactly in the middle of nowhere, but the corner of the state it occupies is not heavily populated, nor is it on the thruway or other major interstate highways. Kevin was enjoying the opportunity to drive relatively secondary roads and observe small town America as he wound his way eastward toward what he hoped would be an interesting meeting with the man who was apparently the most reclusive of the SU alumni group.

Once in Cooperstown, Kevin looked for what might pass for a local institution where he could ask questions about local residents without seeming to be someone with a suspect agenda. He considered a pharmacy and a fast food restaurant, but found the right place when he spotted a place with the word INFORMATION in big letters over the front door. Of course Cooperstown, in view of its distinguished attractions, would have an information center. The question was whether it would be open in the late winter. Fortunately it was.

"Good afternoon. What may I do for you?" The question was asked by an attractive woman with graying hair. She stood behind a counter on which stood a rack of pamphlets describing Cooperstown's many features.

"Hello," Kevin said. "I'm just driving through, but I happen to love both opera and baseball and thought I'd look into the possibility of coming back this summer. I'm sure it's a busy season here."

"It certainly is, especially when Glimmerglass is up and running."

"I don't really know anyone who lives here, but I know of a man named Westerman and I thought I might stop and say hello, provided he's in town. Do you know him?"

"Not personally, but he's a long time resident."

"Might it be possible for you to help me locate his home?"

"Sure. Just give me a second." She stepped away from the counter, located a small phone book, and began to leaf through it. "Here it is. Oh, I remember. It's a big old white house, set quite a good distance back from the road. No way you could miss it. It has one of those old fashioned widow's walks. Unless he's taken it down, it's got a flag on a pole in the front yard - 'Don't Tread on Me.'"

The woman smiled at the thought of the flag.

"Maybe he's a history buff."

"Does that directory mention a street number?"

"It isn't exactly a street, more like the main road up the west side of the lake. I doubt you could read the number from the road, but it can't be more than a couple of miles from where we're standing."

"I appreciate your help," Kevin said. "If I miss Mr. Westerman, it's no big deal. I expect to be back for an opera or two at Glimmerglass this summer."

He drove slowly north along Lake Otsego. There had been no major snow fall recently, but some fairly large patches of it remained along the lake in most of the yards. It had been a very cold winter, and Otsego, like Crooked Lake, was still frozen over in many places. An attractive area, Kevin thought as he looked out over the lake, although he still preferred Blue Water Point and the view of the bluff from his own deck and dock.

He stopped admiring the lake and began concentrating on the homes to the left of the road. It was as the woman at the information counter had said. The big white house with the widow's walk, set well back from the road, came into view almost exactly two miles from the heart of town. The flag pole was there, but the flag was not. Instead he spotted a car parked in a circular drive in front of the house. A man was hosing it down. Jim Westerman? In all likelihood, yes. It had not been a wasted day.

As Kevin approached the house, the man with the hose in his hands stopped what he was doing and watched the Camry approach.

"Looking for something?" he said as Kevin rolled to a stop and opened the window.

"I think I may be looking for you. Would you be Jim Westerman?"

Whereas the man had looked ready to help a driver who had lost his bearings, his demeanor changed quickly. It was clear that he wasn't interested in engaging this stranger in conversation.

Kevin was prepared for this. After all, Westerman had shown no interest in coming to Crooked Lake with the other SU alums for Franklin Pierce's memorial service.

"You are Mr. Westerman?" Kevin asked as he opened the car door and stepped out onto the drive.

"Yes, but I'm sure I don't know you."

"No reason why you should, but I'm Kevin Whitman, This is the first time I've ever been to Cooperstown, but it's supposed to be one of America's great small towns. Anyway, I've been thinking of coming back this summer and thought I'd see if there's someone around the lake who could give me some advice. Someone back in the town suggested I speak with you. I'd love to have about five minutes of your time, if you think you could help me."

"Advice? What is it you want?" Westerman's manner had shifted slightly from something close to hostility to wariness.

"It's like I said, I may be back this summer. For the Hall of Fame, of course, but mostly for opera at Glimmerglass. I figured you might know something about how things are here in high season. I mean how much in advance you should order tickets, where the good places to stay are. That kind of thing."

"You might inquire of the Chamber of Commerce."

"I guess I've learned from experience that the best advice comes from the local citizenry. And the woman spoke highly of you."

"Who was this woman?"

Kevin put on a face that said he was embarrassed not to know.

"I'm afraid I never asked." But he was sure that Westerman wouldn't be washing the winter grime off his car if he had to be elsewhere. "It's the opera I'm most interested in. Festivals like that usually sell out quickly. You like opera?"

"Depends. I've seen some good productions at Glimmerglass, some not so good. They almost always do a couple of the staples, plus something modern and a musical. Maybe a rarely performed work - usually pre-Mozart. But why am I telling you this? You probably already know what's on tap for this summer."

Kevin was euphoric. Westerman may be difficult, but wonder of wonders, he seemed to like opera.

"Actually I don't," Kevin said. "Do you?" Actually he did, but when you have an opportunity to pursue your objective by asking questions, that's what you do.

To Kevin's delight, Jim Westerman unbent enough to put down the hose and, having weighed the risks to his carefully cultivated privacy, invited him in out of the cold.

"This is very kind of you," Kevin said. He meant it.

"I don't know about kind, but there's no point being rude."

There was no offer of a cup of coffee, but they did take seats in what looked like an untidy all-purpose room.

"What's your interest in opera?" Westerman asked.

It had been obvious that he had not recognized Kevin as someone he had seen on the cruise; there seemed to be no reason not to be honest about what he did for a living.

"I teach music at Madison College down in the city. Opera is my speciality."

"I'll be damned!" The conversation quickly took a predictable turn. Westerman's tastes in opera were traditional, and he did nothing to suggest he was in any sense of the word an expert. But the ice had been broken, and the coolness of his welcome in the driveway vanished. They talked for the better part of half an hour, during which time Kevin was careful not to ask again about when to buy tickets and where to book a room during the summer season. That would only suggest that it was time for him to leave.

Instead Kevin waited for what looked like a good opportunity to change the subject. It came when a sudden gust of wind rattled a nearby window.

"It sounds like winter may not be ready to give way to spring," he said.

"It has a way of hanging around too long," Westerman agreed.

"Don't you get cabin fever up here? I mean the lake looks beautiful, but lakes are for summer."

"I usually manage to get away from time to time. Even took a Caribbean cruise this winter."

It's been too easy, Kevin thought. His quarry had been home. He loved opera. He had admitted to taking a cruise in the Caribbean that winter. He had done almost everything except acknowledge knowing Franklin Pierce and missing Abbey Lipscomb's memorial service for him.

"That sounds like a good idea. I ought to do it one of these years myself. Where'd you go?"

"The usual stops, all the way from St. Thomas down to Grenada and back."

"Good ship?"

"First rate. The *Azure Sea*. Ever hear of it?"

Kevin looked as if he were trying to remember something.

"I'm not sure. It sounds vaguely familiar." He started to change the subject, then interrupted himself. "Wait a minute. There was a ship - I think I read it in the *Times'* travel section - where some passenger got left behind on one of the islands and was found dead days later. My memory for names is lousy. Does that sound like it could have been the *Azure Sea*?"

"Not that I know of. I'm sure I'd have heard if something like that had happened."

Kevin did not know whether to be surprised or not, but he knew that what he had just heard from Jim Westerman might be important to the investigation of Franklin Pierce's death.

As suddenly as Westerman had become relatively friendly and talkative, his persona reverted to that of the frosty car washer. Or something close to it.

"I'm sorry, Mr. Whitman," he said. "This has been very pleasant, but I completely forgot that I had promised a friend that I would lend him my jigsaw for a project he's working on. I should have been over there the better part of an hour ago. I hate to cut you off, but I'd better run."

"No problem. I'm the one who's intruded on your day, and I apologize. It's always pleasant to meet another opera fan. I'll take your advice and get in touch with the Chamber of Commerce about a good B & B for when I come back for Glimmerglass."

It had been a leisurely chat, but now they both found themselves beating a hasty retreat to their cars. Kevin climbed into the Camry and set off down the drive, Westerman close behind him. If the reclusive member of the SU alumni group was really taking his jigsaw to his friend, it was obvious that it must already have been in the car.

CHAPTER 26

It was too late in the day for Kevin to set off for Crooked Lake, much as he would have liked to get back to Carol and report on his unexpectedly interesting meeting with Jim Westerman. Chances were that she would already have gone to bed had he made the return trip that evening. Instead he checked into a motel in Cooperstown and found a restaurant that served credible fish and chips.

He would have preferred to read a bit before turning off the light, but had neglected to bring a book with him and hadn't had the nerve to ask Westerman if he might borrow a book he'd seen in the big white house with a widow's walk. Actually what he had seen there were at least four copies of the same book. If it hadn't been for Westerman's sudden announcement that he had just remembered a promise to loan a friend his jigsaw, Kevin would have inquired about that book. He would have done so because the book's author was sitting right across from him.

Carol hadn't known much about Westerman, but thanks to Officer Byrnes' research she was aware that he had done some professional writing. The proof lay within arm's length of where he had been sitting, close enough that he could easily read the title and ascertain that the author was indeed Westerman. *The Mohican Boy*. He had never heard of it, but inasmuch as his task was to learn all he could about the man he made a mental note to check in out at a library and see what he thought of it. What had interested him at the time was that so many copies of the book were on display. Had he ordered multiple copies to present to friends? Or were they merely evidence that he was showing off to visitors the fact that he had actually published a book?

Lacking a book, Kevin watched an hour of uninspired TV and went to bed early. He would rise early and get a good start for the trip back to the cottage.

Carol's reason for 'early to bed' was that she, too, planned to be away at a good hour in the morning. She wanted to be home before Kevin returned, and barring a problem in gaining access to *Upstate Consignments,* that would be no problem if she hit the road by eight a.m.

She had called Mr. Grimley that afternoon and made arrangements for him to meet her and open the consignment shop. While he had initially seemed unsure of whether he should allow her access to the place, he quickly yielded to her forceful lecture on the importance of cooperating with a police investigation of Mr. Pierce's untimely death. Thus it was that she met Grimley at the Newark store at precisely 9:45. She would have been even earlier had she not taken a wrong turn on the outskirts of Newark. Grimley turned out to be a young man still in his twenties. When asked to explain what his responsibilities were with respect to the consignment shop, he admitted that he knew virtually nothing about what to expect or when. He had, of course, heard that Mr. Pierce was dead, but he seemed not to know that he had no family or close relatives.

"Oh. I see," he said when Carol explained this to him. "Nobody knows what to do with this place, is that it?"

"The owner of the property is probably giving it some thought as we speak," Carol assured him. "Let's take a look."

Upstate Consignments was located in an unprepossessing building distinguished mostly by an unattractive green paint job and, incongruously, a large blue and yellow sign which was missing two of its letters. Once inside, however, Carol was impressed by the layout and the goods which Pierce had collected and displayed. The place gave off an odor which spoke to its having been closed for many weeks, but otherwise it looked ready to open for business. That, unfortunately, would not be happening for quite some time, if at all. The area to the right of the doorway, in what was a recessed corner, was covered by what looked like a very large drop cloth that had been suspended from one of the rafters by a combination of ropes and hooks. It blocked off an area which Carol estimated to be about the size of a small bedroom. Inasmuch as nothing else in the place looked like what Abbey had described as Franklin's tribute to the Syracuse alumni group, she assumed that it was behind the drop cloth.

"Mr. Grimley, let's see what we can do about removing that tarp or whatever it is. I'm interested in the entire store, but it's what I think lies back there that's most important."

Grimley looked confused, which he was, but Carol forced the issue, insisting he try first one and then another strategy until the drop cloth collapsed onto the floor, revealing two tables and several triangular shaped scaffolds, most of them empty.

"What have we here?" she asked, not expecting an answer from the young man who had been charged with keeping strangers out of *Upstate Consignments*.

It was obvious that whatever Pierce's intentions had been, he had barely begun to act on them. Piled on one of the tables was a stack of photos, while on the other was a small collection of miscellaneous odds and ends. Carol quickly scanned some of the photos. Most were head shots of the SU alums. The others were group pictures, apparently of trips they had taken together. One was labeled Ocean City, 2004, another The Greenbrier, 1999. She would look them over more carefully later. It was the items on the other table that interested her more.

Pierce had apparently made it a practice to coax members of the group to donate personal memorabilia and evidence of their accomplishments, and at least some of the group had agreed to do so. There were a number of framed plaques attesting to degrees and memberships, plus a number of newspaper articles, some framed, others not. Like the photos, they would have to be gone through more carefully to ascertain to whom they had belonged before entering Pierce's collection. Not so with several books. Three of them carried James Westerman's name in bold letters on the cover. A fourth was by an author whose name was not familiar to Carol, but it had been signed and inscribed to Betty Craig. Standing under one of the tables was the small cabinet which John Bickle was alleged to have created in his spare time.

It was a pathetic collection, even if one discounted items like Abbey Lipscomb's baby shoes. The cabinet would have to stay where it was for the time being, but Carol knew she would have to pack up everything else and take it back to the lake with her. Without a more thorough examination she couldn't be sure, but she very much doubted that everyone in the group had contributed something. As it was, what lay in front of her wouldn't fill more than a small corner of what was already a small room.

"I need to take a look around the place," Carol said. "There must be a work room somewhere, a place where he packs and unpacks things, stores stuff that doesn't belong on the floor. Probably down there at the other end."

Grimley was by now quite willing to do whatever the sheriff had in mind. They worked their way through the merchandise until they reached a door in a long wall on which were mounted many old prints and several sets of antlers which had seen better days. Carol tried the door, and to her relief it was unlocked. What lay behind it was indeed Pierce's work room. Two things interested her. One was a business file, the other empty boxes.

"Make yourself comfortable. I'm going to be awhile."

Grimley made himself comfortable in a desk chair while she set about the task of searching the file for information regarding the alumni corner. What she found was a fairly voluminous correspondence with the other members of the Syracuse group plus a detailed list of all donations up to the time of the cruise. Carol rustled up an empty box and transferred all of the relevant papers to it. She proceeded to inspect the room, looking for anything else of possible relevance to her mission. She found nothing.

"Okay, this box is going to my car, and we're going to have to scrounge up several more boxes to pack up the stuff that was behind that drop cloth. Let's get started."

It took another half hour, by which time the patrol car contained four boxes full of things from the late Franklin Pierce's consignment shop.

"You've been very helpful, Mr. Grimley," Carol said as they left the building and he relocked the door. "There's no reason for you to discuss what we've been doing with anyone. I can assure you that it's all very proper."

It hadn't taken Officer Byrnes long to track down the owner of the building where *Upstate Consignments* was located, and Carol had already dutifully explained to him that Mr. Pierce had died (no details divulged) and that she was diligently searching for his next of kin (without divulging that it was almost certain that he had none). Pierce had been up to date with his rent payments, and the owner, a man named Singleton, had seemed temporarily willing to leave things in the sheriff's hands as long as the place remained under lock and key. Newark, of course, lies in Wayne County, and the sheriff to whom Mr. Singleton had entrusted matters had no jurisdiction there. That fact would almost certainly come to his attention sooner or later. In the meanwhile, Carol would take full advantage of the carte blanche she had been given.

If without formal authority I can help the sovereign country of Barbados to find a murderer, she thought, I can certainly do so in a neighboring county in the state of New York.

CHAPTER 27

Carol got back to the cottage much before Kevin did, much as she had said she would. Not only that, she had carried all of the boxes inside and unpacked them. The papers from Franklin Pierce's file had been placed on Kevin's desk, where she had divided them into two piles, one containing documents relating to the consignment shop's business, the other to Franklin's efforts to mount a tribute to the Syracuse alumni group. The living room, usually the neatest in the cottage, was now the repository of the three boxes of memorabilia which had been donated to Franklin for the display which was slowly taking shape on the tables behind the drop cloth.

She had chosen to leave the mess in the living room alone while she sorted the papers on Kevin's desk. She was in the process of going through Pierce's correspondence with Harry Pringle when Kevin announced himself.

"Good grief, what a mess!" he said.

"With any luck it'll all be in a good cause," she said as she rushed into his arms. "Can you believe we've been doing what we've been doing to help Barbados' finest catch a killer?"

"After my little adventure in Cooperstown, I'm ready to believe just about anything. Here, let me get out of this coat. And I don't notice that you've put a log on the fire."

"That's supposed to be a man's job. But the truth is I've been too eager to take a good look at what I found in that consignment shop."

"I take it you think you've scored."

"No idea. I've barely started my inventory. How about you?"

"I wish I knew. I don't have any stuff like you do, but I've got a number of impressions. Just give me a few minutes. I haven't had a rest room stop since Binghamton, and I want to get out of my boots. Then I'll tackle the fireplace. Why don't you see if there's some wine in the fridge?"

Carol moved things around so they could sit on the couch, and Kevin, who had not only taken off his boots but changed sweaters as well, soon had a fire going on the grate.

"Let's compare notes first, then you can help me with the files. They ought to tell us something about Pierce's big plan. Which, by the way, looks to me more like a pipe dream."

"You were going to produce some wine," Kevin said.

"I did. There just wasn't any place to set it down. Be right back."

"This looks like it's going to be show and tell," Carol said when she returned. "I'll show, you'll tell. You go first."

"As you have surely guessed, Jim Westerman was home and, after a cautious start, he turned out to be quite a talkative guy. I'm afraid I don't have anything like a bottom line opinion of who he really is or why he chose not to make the memorial service. But at least he didn't slam the door in my face. I caught him washing the grime off his car, so he didn't have a chance to pretend he wasn't home. Like we agreed, I played the 'love your beautiful town' guy, looking for information. And who'd have believed it, he loves opera."

"So, you lucked out."

"I like to think I could have lured him into conversation even if his all-time TV favorite is *Gilligan's Island.* But yes, we talked quite a bit about the Glimmerglass festival, which I assured him was a big part of my summer schedule. I was ready to talk baseball, but he showed no interest in the Hall of Fame, so we didn't go there. Anyway, it was a pleasant conversation, mostly about opera. Trouble is, that isn't a topic which is much help in figuring out where he fits in Pierce's group of alums. So I made some innocuous comment about how people up that way cope with cabin fever in the winter. And damned if he didn't say he'd beaten cabin fever, just this winter, by taking a cruise. It was like the opera business, he just came right out with it, no prompting."

"You did luck out, didn't you?"

"Yes and no. He had no trouble when I asked which ship. It was the *Azure Sea.* It was then that I guess I got greedy. I told him I'd read somewhere that that was the name of the ship one of whose passengers got left behind somewhere and was later found dead. And guess what? He said he'd never heard of anything like that happening, knew nothing about it. And that was it. Within three minutes he suddenly remembered something he had to do. We went from a reasonably animated conversation to 'times up, got to go.'"

"I wouldn't say you lost him because you got greedy," Carol said, sounding cautiously excited. "You asked the right question. What's important is that he claims to know nothing about Pierce's death in Barbados, which is simply a flat out lie. Now why would he deny knowing about it? He could deny it because he obviously didn't know you knew he was lying. But *why?* What's the point? When you think about it, almost everyone on that ship would be aware of what happened. Certainly all of the SU alums would know."

"Westerman knew we were in dangerous waters," Kevin said. "Any semblance of a pleasant conversation ended then and there. And for what I suspect was a bogus reason. He claimed he'd promised to deliver one of those jigsaws people use to shape wood to a friend of his, but he drove off without it. At least I think he did. I wish I'd had a chance to ask him how Pierce had died. Then he'd have had an opportunity to cook up another lie."

"Are you sure he didn't think you looked familiar?"

"If he did, he's a real magician. He had no problem with talking about the *Azure Sea,* just the death of a passenger. And I never mentioned Pierce by name. Except for that, I never saw or heard anything that would suggest that he's got something to hide. He seemed natural, maybe not normally friendly but not someone who's on his guard. By the way, you didn't mention that he's an author. There were several copies of a book he'd written lying around. *The Mohican Boy*. Ever hear of it?"

"Not until today. There was a copy of it in Pierce's unfinished display case, along with two other books he's written."

"That title - appropriate, don't you think? Cooperstown, home of *The Last of the Mohicans* and *The Mohican Boy.* Maybe I'll see if the library has a copy."

"I've got enough on my plate without reading Westerman. So I gather you didn't learn anything that makes him a prime suspect for Pierce's murder."

"No. The lie doesn't make sense, but I'm damned if I can see how it's relevant to our case. Sorry, to *your* case. Or is it that Inspector's case? Do you think you should call Bridgetown and tell him about it?"

"Not just yet," Carol said. "I'd rather read all of Pierce's file on the display at *Upstate Consignments* first. I was looking at his correspondence with Pringle when you arrived, and that's just the first of the group. I'm not sure there's anything helpful there, but it might be interesting to see how they all responded to Pierce's appeal for donations. For that matter, I haven't really looked carefully at what's been donated. I'll call Inspector Williams when I've gone through everything."

"Why don't we tackle those files after dinner? Sounds like good bedtime reading."

"That's what I'd planned to do. I haven't finished Pringle, but I've seen enough to know how Pierce floated his idea. At least what he put on paper. There were probably some phone calls as well. Pringle didn't sound very enthusiastic from what I've read."

Kevin refilled their glasses and asked Carol of her impression of the consignment shop.

She shrugged.

"Okay. Fair collection, other than what was to be his Syracuse alumni corner. Frankly, I doubt it would ever have come to fruition. Which raises another big question: what's going to happen to the place now? According to Abbey, Franklin had no family and no close relatives, and I suspect she knows whereof she speaks. In any event, there isn't going to be any SU display, no matter what happens to the shop itself."

"You don't suppose that's why Pierce was killed, do you? I mean to make sure his plan would never be realized?"

"I've heard of lots of reasons for murder," Carol said, making no effort to suppress her smile, "but never anything as far out as that. You can't be serious."

"Let's say semi-serious. No, I take that back. It's too crazy, especially when you factor in that it was done in Barbados. It's just that at the moment I can't think of any other reason why one of the members of the group would have done it."

"And that's one of the reasons why I'm still convinced that the killer is going to be what the Inspector calls a bajan. That's his opinion, and one of these days he'll be on the phone to let me know that they've caught him."

"But you still want to go through those files, don't you?"

"I'm afraid so, so let's have dinner and then get busy."

CHAPTER 28

It was another chilly March evening. Carol could only remember twice in the month when the daytime temperature had climbed above the freezing mark.

"It's barely above 20," she called out to Kevin when she came back in from the deck. "I grew up with days like this, but I'm really ready for spring."

"Me, too. But I assume you're still ready to tackle these files you filched from the consignment shop."

"I didn't filch them, Kevin. I borrowed them."

"What if they provide evidence that leads to Pierce's killer? I'd keep them if I were you. Who's to know?"

"Let's read them before we decide what to do with them. I'm going back to Pringle, and you can start with the cabinet maker. We'll work through the lot of them and then swap files."

"What are the rules?"

"I'd suggest we resist the temptation to comment on everything that sounds interesting. Just highlight the juicy parts and save our reactions until we've read them all. Okay?"

"It's your investigation."

"Unfortunately. So here are your files: Edgar, Stevens the therapist-boxer, the Bickles - he's the one who makes furniture, and the woman who didn't take the cruise, Brubaker. I'll take Pringle, Westerman, the Craigs, and Abbey Lipscomb."

It was just past 7:30 when they settled down with their reading assignments for the evening. Kevin finished his stack of files first, looked over his notes, and retired to the bedroom for a few minutes of TV.

"You can come out now," Carol announced a little later. "Time to switch these SU alums."

This time it was Carol who finished first. By 8:54 both of them had read all the files. It was time to compare notes.

"What do you think?" she asked.

"Pierce had a hare-brained idea, if you ask me. And he loves redundancy. Every one of the files contains a copy of the letter he wrote explaining what he was up to and why they all should want to take part. It didn't take long to cut my reading time by a third. It's my impression that he had two things in mind. He was trying to pull off a promotional stunt for his alumni group, although why he thought that was a good idea puzzles me. And he was obviously playing on the vanity of the members of the group. No point speculating on why he wanted to mount a display at the shop. He simply asserts that he wanted to do it. But he miscalculated badly on the vanity issue. Nobody sounded like he was anxious to toot his own horn."

"I'm not so sure about that," Carol said."The problem is that most of them didn't think they had things that would make it look as if they had a successful career. Just look at what they donated to Pierce's cause and you can see why they felt that way. Sure, there were exceptions, like Dr. Edgar's diplomas and rewards, but what amounts to success or even a good life is often intangible. Anyway, in the end most of them came up with something."

"I found those who didn't more interesting. Westerman in particular. Pierce has three of his books, but his note tells us that he got them himself. Westerman was adamant that he wasn't going to contribute two of those books. That curt note of his, you saw it. 'I bought up all the copies in print and made it clear they weren't to be reprinted.' It was just his bad luck that Pierce ignored his wishes and was able to get his hands on those books."

"It would probably be a waste of time to read them, especially the ones he didn't want Pierce to use. But I'd like to see if I can figure out why he had a problem with them."

"Well, they're now in my possession, right over there in that old Merlot wine box. There's no question about it, Westerman is a problem. The books, the memorial service, his lie that he didn't know anything about what happened to Pierce on Barbados. The one I'm most interested in, however, is Harry Pringle. It's the way he talks about a woman other than his wife in his initial reply to Pierce's letter that's interesting. Let me read the part that intrigues me. It's in that pile in your lap."

Kevin pulled it out of the pile and passed it to Carol.

She found it on the top of page two of a relatively short letter.

"Here it is," she said. "'Of course we wouldn't be corresponding about this if I'd stayed in Toledo. I'd never have been part of your upstate New York gang. But I didn't stay in Toledo, and you know as well as I do why I didn't because you know all about Terry Barkley. Dorothy never wanted to be part of the group, but Terry might have. Dorothy and I are doing fine, thank you, but a guy's first love is always something special, and Terry was special. So I think you can understand why I can't muster much interest in what you have in mind.'"

Kevin looked thoughtful.

"I see what you mean. I didn't pay it enough attention, especially to his comment that Pierce knew all about the Barkley woman. I wonder what that's supposed to mean? One thing we've learned from these files is that we're going to have to talk to these people."

"You're in the middle of the spring semester at Madison," Carol said. "So I'm the one who's going to have to talk to them. Of course I've always known that, but what some of them have to say for themselves in these files makes it even more obvious. And more urgent. What is it with this Terry Barkley? With Westerman's strange behavior? And how about the woman boxer, Stevens? She didn't just say no to Pierce, she was borderline unpleasant to him. Here we have a group of college friends who've been taking trips together for years, and now we're learning that trouble may have been festering under the surface."

"I'd say that Pierce's murder made that very clear," Kevin said.

"That would assume that one of these SU alums killed him, and we don't know that. The inspector doesn't think so."

"The inspector doesn't know anything about Pierce's tour group."

"But maybe Abbey Lipscomb does." Carol was looking pensive. "The reason I'm in this business up to my neck isn't because Inspector Williams wants me to be, it's because there's something about these people that's bothering her, and she doesn't know what it is. It's possible that clues to that something are here in those files we've been gong through. Let's take them, one by one, and see what we have."

Kevin looked at his watch.

"I'll give it a try, but I'm tired. I should have taken the thruway home from Cooperstown."

"Just give me fifteen minutes, okay? Start with the ones who told Pierce to count them out. That would be all of the women except Mrs. Craig - Bess Stevens, Ann Bickle, and the Brubaker woman who wasn't on the cruise. Stevens and Brubaker spoke for themselves, and John Bickle made it clear that his wife wasn't interested. I suppose you could say that the cabinet or whatever it is he's made could be a joint contribution, but I doubt it. Inasmuch as Brubaker didn't take the cruise, we can forget about her. My impression is that Ann Bickle, the only non-Syracuse grad in the group, is in the picture primarily to please her husband. Which leaves Stevens, about whom I know next to nothing. Maybe her indifference to Pierce's plan masks some deeper hostility to him, but that's pure guess-work, and I don't do guess-work. In any event, I'll have to talk with her."

"We haven't said anything about the school teachers," Kevin chimed in. "The Craigs. Their reply to Pierce's invitation was much the most enthusiastic of anyone's."

"They were also the nicest people at the memorial. Which probably proves nothing. Seemingly nice people have been known to do terrible things. I'll be interested to see what of the stuff in those boxes came from them."

It was agreed that Westerman's reply to Pierce had suggested that he was either having a bad day when he wrote it or that, without much enthusiasm, he'd see what he could do. The one thing he wouldn't do, apparently, was send copies of his second and third published novels.

Pringle's response had been straight forward, with just a hint of unpleasantness and the hard to decipher reference to his first wife. He hadn't said he would donate, nor had he said that he wouldn't. Bickle's file had been slightly thicker than the others because it reflected back and forth messages about the terms of the arrangement for the corner cupboard. His was the only case where a member of the group had some reason to believe that contributing to the display might prove to be financially beneficial.

Then there was Dr. Edgar, whose file revealed him to be serious, not very imaginative, but ready to cooperate with Franklin Pierce's plan. He promised framed copies of his degrees and expressed a willingness to give it more thought. There was nothing in the file, however, to suggest that he either welcomed the opportunity to be involved with old friends and classmates or that he had tired of the group and its trips. Carol was inclined to believe that he fell into the latter category but was, by training or temperament, too polite to say so. Kevin's observation was that he was simply opaque, which made it impossible to know the real Roger Edgar.

They both knew, or thought they knew, on the basis of what was in the files, what they would find when they examined the contents of the boxes. They decided to defer that task until morning.

"We've got a lot of work to do," Carol said. "It looks as if I can forget about relaxing weekends. Which reminds me, your spring break starts when?"

"You don't remember? You're supposed to have it circled in red on the kitchen calendar."

"Of course I remember, I was just thinking ahead to when I'd be enlisting your help again. We'll be on the road a lot."

"Let's define terms. What do you mean by a lot? Normally I'd be chomping at the bit to start interrogating your suspects, but I've been counting on something more intimate."

Carol gave him a lascivious wink.

"I think we'll find time to do some multi-tasking, don't you?"

CHAPTER 29

While Kevin was on his way back to the city and Carol was trying to decide how relevant her half of the search for Franklin Pierce's killer was, Inspector Cyril Williams down in Bridgetown was having a chat with another man named Williams. Lester Williams was no relation, but he was the owner of a small fleet of taxis and had just learned something which he thought might be of interest to the inspector.

Lester of *Lester's Taxis* had called RBPF over the weekend to inquire as to whether they were still interested in the death of the man who had missed his cruise ship. The woman who answered the phone said they were and said he should speak with Inspector Williams. The inspector, not surprisingly, was not in his office, but when he heard about the taxi company's inquiry he immediately got busy arranging for a meeting on Monday morning. It was 9:30 a.m., and that meeting was now in progress.

"You understand, inspector, that I have no idea whether what I'm going to tell you has anything to do with that missing man."

"That's all right. I want to hear what you have to tell me. By the way, the man you're referring to is not missing. He's dead."

"Well, yes, I know that. It's been in the news for weeks. But I learned something just Friday afternoon that reminded me of it. And it has occurred to me that there may be a connection. Probably not, but your men talked to me some time ago about our records for the day that ship, the *Azure Sea,* was in dock. I wasn't able to help you back then and forgot all about it. Actually, I hadn't forgotten everything, because when somebody named Quinton stopped by my garage on Friday what he had to tell me made me angry. But when I thought about it, it also made me think you ought to hear what he had told me."

The inspector was inclined to assume that this would be yet one more false alarm, but he had long since come to the conclusion that he should listen to everyone who came forward with an idea about the Pierce case.

"Please, Mr. Williams. Let's hear it. You say it has to do with a Mr. Quinton."

"Not exactly. It's Quinton who came to me, but it's Moses King that I want to talk about."

"And who is this Moses King?"

"He's one of my drivers. At least he has been. But I intend to fire him."

"I take it that he's done something that makes you think I may be interested in him."

"Yes, that's why I'm here."

"Good," the inspector said, anxious that Lester Williams get to the point. "What did he do?"

"Quinton is a friend of his. At least he knows Quinton. Apparently they got to talking recently and the way Quinton tells it, King as much as told him that a man gave him a thousand US dollars for letting him borrow his taxi."

"That's interesting," the inspector said, and meant it. "I assume that you don't allow your drivers to do something like that."

"Indeed I don't. Can you imagine - I don't need to tell you what a terrible practice that would be for a company like mine. You might never see your vehicles again, or they'd come back with damaged fenders or worse. My men know better than to let anybody else behind the wheel."

"Does Mr. King admit that he let somebody borrow his taxi and was paid handsomely for letting him take it?"

"No, he denies it, as I expected he would. But he got sort of flustered when I told him what Quinton had told me, claimed he'd been misunderstood. He insists that this man offered him money but that he refused."

"What do your records show?"

"King did turn in money that day, but that doesn't prove anything. He could have let somebody drive his car for just an hour or two, which means he could have made more than the thousand dollars. Or he could have turned in some of the thousand, just to make everything look okay. He's lying, I'm sure of it."

"How long had King been working for you?"

"About twenty months."

"Any problems over that time?" the inspector asked.

"No, he always seemed to be a responsible driver. A bit rough, if you know what I mean, and not all that smart. But he'd never done anything to make me believe he was dishonest. Not until this time. But he just couldn't resist a windfall like that."

The inspector changed the subject.

"Did King say what this man wanted to use his taxi for?"

"He says he never asked, just told the man that what he proposed wasn't allowed."

"Did he tell you what the man looked like?"

For the first time Lester Williams seemed uncomfortable.

"I probably should have insisted on more details, but I wasn't thinking about your missing man case at the time. I was just mad at King. All I remember is that he thought the guy who wanted to borrow the taxi was a tourist. But of course most of our business is tourists, so that was to be expected."

The inspector was disappointed.

"So King didn't provide any clues as to what the man looked like or sounded like? Tall? Short? Overweight? What he was wearing? Deep voice? Sound like a Yankee?."

"Not much, I'm afraid." It was obvious that the owner of *Lester's Taxis* had not thought to ask such questions.

Unfortunately, Inspector Williams thought, by now Moses King will know he's in trouble. Heaven knows how he'll respond when I question him. His namesake had said he wasn't very smart. I hope so, the inspector said to himself.

There didn't seem to be anything else to learn from Lester Williams.

"I'm going to have to talk to King. Is he still on your payroll?"

"Like I said, I'm going to have to get rid of him. But technically he's still working for me. If you want, I can send him over to RBPF as soon as I get back to the garage."

"I'd rather pick him up myself. Here, you call the garage. If he's there, tell him to wait for me; if he's not, make sure he doesn't leave again until he's seen me."

The call having been made, the two Williams's set off in tandem for *Lester's Taxis.*

Moses King didn't look happy to see his boss and a uniformed officer of RBPF waiting for him when he returned to the garage some ten minutes later. After a frosty introduction, Inspector Williams hustled him into the official car and made the return trip to headquarters

'Now, Mr. King," the inspector said when they had taken seats in his office, "I understand that you had a rather unusual day back in January. A day when you earned a thousand dollars by generously loaning your taxi to a stranger."

"No, no, I never did anything like that, your honor." King was transparently nervous upon hearing this none-too-subtle accusation so soon after he had explained to his boss that he had declined the 'car for money' deal.

"You don't need to refer to me as 'your honor.' Inspector will do just fine. But the way I hear it, a tourist wanted to borrow your taxi - wanted it enough to pay you a king's ransom in US dollars for the privilege. Oh, I'm sorry, Mr. King. I didn't mean to use your name like that."

"But it's like I told Mr. Williams, that man offered me money but I told him I couldn't take it and that I couldn't let him have the taxi. It's against policy."

The inspector smiled and shook his head.

"I know, Mr. King, but people are always doing things that are against policy. It's simply human nature. It'd be a pretty dull world if we did things by the book all the time. A thousand dollars is a lot of money. I can't imagine that you wouldn't have been tempted. By the way, I assume you're married, have a family. Is that right?"

"That's right," King said, clearly not sure why this was relevant. "We've got four kids."

"Congratulations! It's none of my business, of course, what your income is, but I've heard that, much as we love our tourists, they're a bit stingy when it comes to gratuities. In other words, a thousand dollars must have looked like a godsend."

In spite of the air conditioning, Moses King had started to sweat.

"It is a big sum, I'll admit that. But I need my job."

"So you're going to stick with your story that you never took the money and let the tourist take the car. Which reminds me, this tourist - you're certain he was a tourist?"

"Oh, yes. A white man with sun burn. The voice was American, I'm sure of that."

Describe him for me," the inspector said to King.

"Average height, average build - could have been anyone. He did have on a funny hat. I remember that. It had a big broad brim, the kind some tourists wear to keep the sun out of their face. That and the sun glasses made it hard to see his face. Anyhow, I didn't really care what he looked like, just wanted him to know I couldn't let him take my car."

"Are you aware, Mr. King, that the day we're talking about was the day that a passenger on one of the cruise ships in dock here was killed?"

"That's what Nigel Quinton told me. I'd heard people talking, but had forgotten about it until just the other day."

"Quinton, he's the man who told Mr. Williams about the thousand dollars?"

"It wasn't his fault. He misunderstood what I told him about the thousand dollars."

The inspector had already given some thought to that story. He had trouble believing that there had been a misunderstanding between King and Quinton. If they were friends, King might have shared his experience; but if they were friends, why would Quinton run to Lester Williams and tell him something that could cost King his job.

"Did the man who wanted your taxi tell you why he wanted it?"

"I don't believe so."

"You don't believe so. What does that mean? That you can't remember?"

"It was a long time ago, inspector. I was worried about the car, so I may have asked him where he was going."

"Why would you have done that? You just told me that you had no intention of loaning him the taxi or taking his thousand dollars."

Had King been a white man, his face might have turned red. As it was he stammered.

"That's not what I meant. The truth is, I can't recall what I asked him or what he said. We talked for only a minute, because I wasn't interested in his idea."

"Mr. King, I think the truth is that he did give you a thousand dollars and that you gave him the car. When did you tell him to bring the car back and where was he to bring it?"

"But -

"Don't try my patience. How long did he have the car?"

"It wasn't long at all, inspector. Less than three hours, more like two. Please, don't say anything to Mr. Williams. I paid him for a full day of passengers. The company didn't lose anything, I swear."

Moses King was by this time a very frightened man.

"Thank you, Mr. King. As you may know, I am conducting an investigation into the death of a cruise passenger. I very much hope that the man who 'borrowed' your taxi won't turn out to be the man who killed the cruise passenger. Because if he did, you will be in danger of much more than losing your job. You could help me - and yourself - by thinking very hard about the man who gave you all that money. Anything you can think of about him, let me know. Not some day, but right away. We're talking about murder. Do you understand?"

"Yes, sir."

"Good. Now we have one more bit of business to transact here. I am going to ask you to provide the RBPF with a statement of what you have finally told me this morning."

Inspector Williams called his secretary and asked her to bring in a recorder and some forms.

"This won't take long," he said. "Then you can leave. I have a very big day ahead of me, so I'll let you walk back to the garage. It isn't far, and the exercise will do you good."

CHAPTER 30

Inspector Williams had no way of knowing whether the tourist who had 'borrowed' Moses King's taxi had anything to do with the murder of Franklin Pierce. He could think of many explanations for the thousand dollar transaction. It was even possible that a rich Yankee had made a bet with a friend that he could hornswoggle some dumb bajan into giving up his cab. The inspector smiled at the thought. Hornswoggle had never been a part of his vocabulary.

But there was no use denying it: the Yankee tourist *could* have been the person who had lured Pierce to his rendezvous with death at Harrysmith. For the first time since he had agreed to let Sheriff Kelleher become involved in his investigation, the inspector was ready to take seriously Abbey Lipscomb's thesis that Pierce's killer might be a member of his alumni tour group.

For the better part of an hour he mulled over what he had learned that morning and what its possible consequences could be. When he finally decided that he should get in touch with the sheriff, he hadn't yet substituted a rich American for a poor Barbadian in his picture of the crime, but he had acknowledged that his upstate New York accomplice should be aware of this development in the Caribbean.

Initial efforts to contact the sheriff came to naught, but he persevered and eventually found himself speaking with her. The inspector was reluctant to bring up the Moses King story right away. That might give it too much credence as the key to Pierce's murder. So he asked first about how things were going with her possible suspects, now so far removed from the scene of the crime.

"I'm afraid I've learned nothing substantive, inspector," Carol admitted. "We were able to put together a memorial service for Mr. Pierce. It was the first and only time so far when all of the tour group were together. Actually not all; one man was missing. It gave me a chance to see them, get a picture of what they looked like, listen to them talk about Pierce. But frankly I saw and heard nothing which tells me that some of them bear watching. My principal impression is that the group that travelled together isn't quite as close as had been advertised. They may take trips together every so often, but if they were friends in college most of them don't act it today. Nothing unpleasant, no cutting exchanges. I don't know, maybe it was just the occasion. But then I didn't expect anyone to disparage Pierce. Incidentally, nobody recognized me from the cruise, or if they did they gave no indication that they did. They do know I'm a friend of Abbey's who also happens to be a sheriff."

"What about the one who didn't make the memorial service?" the inspector asked.

"He's apparently anti-social. Didn't respond to Abbey's outreach. I saw him a week later by driving up to his home, which is several hours away." Carol made no attempt to explain that it had actually been her husband who had made that trip. "He was pleasant enough then, but the word that comes to mind is opaque. Look, now that I've seen them all, I intend to make personal visits, ask questions I couldn't ask when they were all in the room. Questions about their relations with Pierce, questions about what they were doing and with whom in Barbados. You've been on this case for many weeks. I'm just getting started."

"Of course. I'm not trying to hurry you. I know you have your own job to do up there. In fact the real reason I called today is because I have some news. At least I think I have."

The inspector proceeded to tell the sheriff about Moses King and the deal that resulted in his making a thousand dollar windfall. Needless to say, Carol was very much interested in what she was hearing, immediately recognizing the potential importance of it to her end of the investigation of Franklin Pierce's death.

"Pardon my impatience, inspector, but do you have a description of the person who borrowed the taxi?"

"I was getting to that, and I wish I could give you a detailed picture. But I can't. Mr. King, to put it mildly, is very vague. I was suspicious at first, but the more I've thought about it the more convinced I am that he's doing the best he can to describe the man. What he says is that the man is white, sunburned, medium height, nothing distinctive about his physique - not fat, not skinny, not muscular. In other words, the epitome of average. King says he was wearing sunglasses - surprise! - and a broad brimmed hat of the kind that's designed to protect the wearer from the sun. Which made it hard to read his face. In effect he could be just about anyone, except for the fact that King insists he's an American. He's been a taxi driver long enough to have carried a lot of cruise passengers, and the majority of them come from the States, so he's probably right about that."

"Do you suppose you could get him to be a little more specific? I mean about the sunglasses and particularly the hat. I saw a lot of hats like that on the ship, and they come in different colors. You know, beige, pink, maybe a darker color. See if King can remember something like that. And sunglasses, they come in different sizes and colors. Some are so dark you can't see the eyes, some are big wrap-arounds. Inasmuch as I hope to be seeing all of Pierce's group in person, I could use detail like that."

Carol knew that none of them would be wearing hats like the one the inspector had described. Upstate New York in March and April is nothing like Barbados. But it was worth a try.

"I'll do my best. Mr. King isn't the swiftest man on the block, but with some prompting he may be able to answer your question. You understand that I have no evidence whatsoever that the man who swapped a thousand dollars for a couple hours use of King's taxi has anything to do with my case. I've argued from the day we met that our killer will turn out to be one of my people, not yours. But I haven't made much progress. So in good conscience I must acknowledge that the odds that an American did it have gone up a wee bit. Which means that you'll have to be asking questions of all the 'average' men who traveled with Mr. Pierce."

"I'm afraid I'll have to quiz the women as well, inspector. They may not have been involved with Mr. King, but it's too early to write them off as suspects."

"I thought the way Pierce was killed would pretty much eliminate the women,"he said.

"It probably does," Carol said. "But in my experience, things aren't always what they seem. Besides, one of the woman in that group is a physical therapist who has decided to become a boxer."

"A woman boxer?" The inspector sounded as if he doubted that such a thing was possible.

"That's right. I only met her the once, at the memorial service. She's quite small, but she looks as if she could handle herself in a pinch, even in a boxing ring. Who knows what things they teach physical therapists."

"I certainly hope you don't have to spend hours with all these people."

"Oh, I'm sure I'll be doing that. They live all over what we call upstate New York. And I'll be wanting to see them in their own homes, not in my office."

"You have my best wishes. I'm sorry I had to bring up the King matter, but you understand why I did."

"I do, and I thank you. Somehow I think we'll be talking many times in the weeks ahead. Unless, of course, you make an arrest first. I'm sure you can appreciate why I hope that happens."

"Damn!" Carol said to herself after saying good-bye to the inspector. Not only was she now facing a somewhat greater possibility that Pierce's killer was living within driving distance of Crooked Lake. She also had to live with the thought that Americans, so much richer than their neighbors in Barbados, were in the business of casually throwing money around. And if that weren't bad enough, they might be doing it to facilitate murder.

CHAPTER 31

The memorial service had plunged Harry Pringle into a funk. It wasn't because he was sad to be saying farewell to Franklin Pierce. It was because it had brought to the surface old memories, unhappy memories. Yes, those memories had something to do with Pierce. Quite a bit, in fact. But Pierce wasn't the central figure in those memories. That role went to a girl named Terry Barkley. He always thought of Terry as a girl, although he knew she must now be close to 50.

Try as he would to shake off the funk, he found it almost impossible. His wife had noticed. She tried to give her husband some time and space to recover, but eventually she cornered him and asked what the problem was.

"Something's bothering you. Want to talk about it?"

"Come on, Dorothy, we both know we can have moods. I seem to have one these days. I'll get over it. I always do. Maybe we should treat ourselves to a dinner out tonight. It might help."

"We ate out yesterday, and it hasn't helped."

"We did? I'd forgotten."

"You don't remember what you did less than 24 hours ago? That doesn't make sense. You're much too young to be having dementia. What's the problem?"

"There's no problem, really. Maybe it's just a hangover from that memorial service over on Crooked Lake."

"The service for Mr. Pierce? You didn't like him. I can't imagine you shutting down because you've just buried a man you've never liked."

"We didn't bury him. That happened figuratively back in January on Barbados. We just eulogized him."

"You never told me you read a eulogy."

"Well, I didn't. Not exactly. Everybody said some nice things about Pierce, then we called it a day. I probably should have stayed home."

"You didn't have to go. He meant nothing to you."

"I guess I thought it would have been rude. Abbey Lipscomb had gone to a lot of trouble to arrange it and I didn't want to let her down."

"Harry, this isn't you. You don't much care for the Lipscomb woman either. I don't think the memorial service has anything to do with how you're acting."

Pringle got up and walked about the room.

"I'm not acting, Dorothy, I'm feeling. That's a wholly different matter. Haven't you ever felt something that really upset you?"

"It's been days now. No, I take that back; it's actually been months. I thought you'd snapped out of it, but you're right back where you were last fall. You're not easy to live with, do you know that? Come out of your damned shell - tell me about it."

"It's personal. Let's just leave it alone."

It was at that moment that Dorothy Pringle uncrossed her legs and sat up in her corner of the couch.

"Don't tell me you're having a thing about that Barkley woman again." Her voice betrayed the fact that she was both sad and angry.

"I don't want to talk about it, Dorothy. It has nothing to do with you. Nothing to do with us. Like I said, I'll get over it."

"You've been getting over that woman for close to thirty years, Harry. Thirty years! We've been married for 25 of those years, and you've told me I don't know how many times that she means nothing to you. Just a college crush. We all have them. Well, I had one or two myself, but I outgrew mine, just like most people do. Why does yours have to be a middle age obsession?"

"That's not fair. And I don't want to talk about it."

Harry stopped at the foot of the stairs.

"I'm going to lie down. Maybe take a nap. Okay? Don't be judgmental, please. Like I said, I'll be all right. I love you, you know that."

Dorothy chose not to have the last word.

Harry Pringle did lie down. He did not take a nap. His mind was much too active. Not with new thoughts, but with thoughts that had kept him awake at odd hours on many days over many years, beginning in 1985.

That was his senior year at Syracuse, and his college life had been satisfying in virtually every respect. His grades, while not of Phi Beta Kappa caliber, had been very respectable. He enjoyed his fraternity, both for the friendships and the social life, including the parties that managed to leaven the academic grind. He had dated, but had no real 'girlfriend.' One fall night, after a losing football game, he had drunk a little more than he liked to think of as his quota. His date was someone whom he didn't know all that well, but she was cute and a good sport, and to his surprise they had gone to his room and had sex. There was no question but that it had been consensual. And very satisfying. But it hadn't led to a second date, much less a serious relationship. Harry had pretty much forgotten the girl's name when during a mild day in mid-March he met Terry Barkley.

This time it wasn't at a frat party. It was the library. It was fairly late, and not many students were still present. He had been assiduously studying for an exam the next day, when she got to her feet to leave. He had looked up and said something like good-night when she lost control of an armful of books, all of which landed on the floor.

Harry remembered the moment as if it had been yesterday. He had the presence of mind to jump up and help her collect her books. In the process of doing so, he really looked at her for the first time. She was a revelation. Not beautiful in a conventional sense of the word, but beautiful in ways which he had never before experienced. For the first time in his life, Harry was tongue tied.

He hadn't been sure how he'd managed it, but he rallied, introduced himself, and before the evening was over had gone with Terry to a campus coffee shop where they talked for almost an hour. He learned that she was a junior from Toledo who was majoring in biology. One thing led to another, as it often does. They had another date, as such things were called back in the day. And then another. As the spring term neared its end, he was hopelessly in love. He might have rushed things a bit had it not been for the fact that it very quickly became apparent that Terry was a very devout Christian girl. She talked freely about it, always in a way that said that she knew he would understand and respect her for her beliefs. Instead of being frustrated that she was very cautious when it came to physical intimacy, he admired her and even began to reassess what had been his own casual approach to the subject.

Whether Terry intuited what may have been on his mind or simply felt the need for a frank talk on the subject he never knew, but she surprised him one evening when they were enjoying another cup of coffee after another evening in the library.

'Harry, can I share something with you?' He could remember what she had chosen to share with him as if it had been yesterday. He had, of course, said yes, little knowing what was to follow.

'I took a vow back when I was in high school that I was going to remain a virgin until I was married. I hope this doesn't shock you, but I think I love you and - how to say this? - I just had to tell you.'

He had been shocked. But he had also been thrilled to hear her say that she loved him. Or at least that she thought she did.

'I love you, too, Terry, and that's what matters. You've made a beautiful vow. You don't know how happy I am to be with you right now.' He had started to lean across the table to kiss her, but caught himself and took her hand between his two hands instead.

'I knew you'd understand,' she said. 'Maybe you didn't make a vow like I did, but we see things the same way, don't we? I never imagined that something like this would be happening to me.'

That night Harry knew for a certainty that he was going to marry Terry, and that he would gladly defer sharing a bed with her until they were on their honeymoon. Unfortunately, that certainty collapsed only nine days later. Most people would have said a week later, but he knew it was nine days. He had counted every one of them.

It was on the ninth day, and the fraternity was having an end of semester party to make the prospect of upcoming final exams a bit less hard to deal with. It was only the second time that Terry had attended a function at the fraternity with him, and his brothers paid her the compliment of lots of attention. He knew that she was special, and he enjoyed the fact that his friends seemed to agree.

He remembered that Terry had actually had a glass of wine. She wasn't a drinker, but she had told him that she wouldn't embarrass him by sticking to coffee or a soft drink. There were, however, a fair number of others, both brothers and dates, who managed to consume quite a bit of beer, with the result that as the evening wore on the house became noisier and the conversation more uninhibited. It was almost 10:30, and he was about to take Terry back to her dorm when one of the brothers caught up with them as they edged their way toward the foyer. It was Franklin Pierce.

'Brother Pringle, don't know how I missed you this evening. If I'd known you'd have such a lovely bird of paradise in tow, I'd have come around sooner. You must be Terry,' Pierce said to her. 'I believe we met last month, back when we weren't so caffeinated from all-nighters. You're all Harry talks about.'

Pierce slapped his unamused fraternity brother on the back, almost falling down in the process of doing so. If only they had left five minutes earlier, they would have missed the obviously drunken Pierce. It was too late now, and disaster lay ahead.

'Good to see you, Franklin. We're just leaving.'

'Leaving? The night is young. Have you shown Terry your room?'

'We really have to be on our way.'

'I thought it was a house rule that you had to score before leaving a party,' Pierce said, slurring his words.

'Good night, Franklin.' He took Terry's arm and steered her toward the door.

'Hey, wait a minute. There's still time for a quick roll in the hay, Harry.' There must have been at least a dozen people within hearing range of Pierce, who was now practically shouting. 'Your little sweetheart needs to get laid, don't you, honey? Show her how it was with that cute little tart after the BC game last fall.'

For a brief moment he hadn't known whether to land a hard punch on Pierce's jaw or simply get Terry out of the frat house as fast as he could. He had chosen the latter course, but he knew that it didn't really matter. Terry walked all the way back to the dorm in silence, sobbing as if her heart would break. He had started to apologize for his boorish fraternity brother, but she had shaken her head and said something to the effect of 'not now.'

There was no good night kiss on the steps of the dormitory. There was no call the next day. He had decided to give her a day to get the terrible experience out of her system, but when she didn't make an attempt to contact him, he started trying to reach her. She answered his fifth call, claimed to be too busy with finals coming up to see him, and finally hung up when he sought to explain that his brother was nothing more than a drunken, obnoxious liar.

It was not until the day she was leaving for home after her last final exam that she saw him again. He had camped out near the dorm, hoping to see her off.

'I'm sorry Harry. It won't work. I've got to put my life back together. I hope you can do it, too. Take care.'

They were the last words he ever heard from her. And now she was dead.

CHAPTER 32

Carol had been dreading the one-on-one visits with each of the upstate New Yorkers who had taken the cruise on the *Azure Sea*. It meant time away from policing in Cumberland County and many hours on the road. It also meant that she would have to begin asking a lot of questions about what people had been doing when the ship was docked in Barbados. She was well aware that this would be a challenging task.

But her most pressing immediate problem was that she had just recently presented herself simply as a friend and neighbor of Abbey Lipscomb, and now would have to admit that she had been a fellow passenger on the *Azure Sea* and was working with the Barbadian authorities in their investigation of Franklin Pierce's death. How would the alumni group respond to this revelation? How would she explain it? There was only one way to do so, and it would necessitate some help from Inspector Williams.

Although she had no new information to pass along to the inspector, she placed a call to him the next morning.

"Inspector Williams, good to speak to you again," she said when she had been put through to him. "Any new developments down there?"

"I'm afraid not, but are you on the line because you've learned something?"

"No, and I'm doubtful that I'll learn anything unless you help me out. That's why I'm calling."

"What seems to be the trouble?"

"It's something I should have talked with you about some time ago. I'm going to need a letter from you which looks and sounds official. A letter which makes it clear that you have asked me, on behalf of the RBPF, to assist in the investigation of Mr. Pierce's death. I expect to be visiting the members of his group that were aboard the cruise ship, beginning this week, and they don't know that I'm doing this. They'll think it's strange that I'm involved in the case unless I have some document that makes it clear why. What I have in mind is something on official stationery, something that you sign, something which says that you need me to interview them because you are unable personally to come to the States to do it. No need to be too specific about what I'll be asking them, just that you need help and that the reason it's me is because I was on the cruise and come from the area where they all live. Phrase it any way you like, only make sure they won't have any reason to question what I'm doing - I'm doing it at the formal request of a friendly foreign country. Okay?"

"Of course. You shouldn't have had to ask. I'll take care of it today and use the diplomatic pouch to make sure it's in your hands right away. Is that it?"

"It is. Not quite sure when I'll have been able to see all of them, but I hope to be able to brief you soon on what they have to say about what they did and with whom while the ship was in your country. Oh, and let you know if I don't trust what any of them tell me."

"Sounds good. I don't expect miracles, sheriff, but it would be helpful if one of them comes across as suspicious, like a candidate for the guy who paid my man King a thousand dollars for the use of his taxi."

Carol didn't expect miracles either. The people she would be questioning could understandably have forgotten just what they had been doing more than two months ago in Barbados. If one of them had killed Pierce, he - or she - would have had good reason to have 'forgotten.' All she had going for her was experience dealing with people who were being less than honest. Unfortunately, detecting dishonesty was not always easy. Sometimes it was impossible.

Where to begin? She took out her ubiquitous yellow pad and started to consider whom she should visit first. Of course that could depend on who was available, but ideally she wanted to take into account how reticent or outspoken, how nervous or at ease, they were. She knew more about such things than she had before the memorial service, but she was relying on brief impressions rather than protracted observation. The truth was that she still did not know any of these people well, and some of them she hardly knew at all.

Carol was also conscious of the fact that whomever she saw first would inevitably contact some if not all of the others, meaning that the element of surprise would almost immediately become a casualty. There was nothing she could do about that. After half an hour of agonizing, she chose to start with Dr. Edgar. He had probably been the most opaque of the group at the service and hence perhaps the most formidable challenge. In some ways she would have preferred to begin with the Craigs, who were more relaxed and voluble than their colleagues. But doing so would only have postponed the more challenging task of speaking to Edgar or Westerman. It was because Kevin had already had a lengthy if largely irrelevant conversation with Westerman that she decided to lead off with Edgar.

The donations which were to have been a part of the *Upstate Consignments* display were still in their boxes at the cottage. Carol worked her way through the boxes, making an effort to keep each member's contributions together. By the time she had sorted everything out, Roger Edgar's small pile consisted of five items. In addition to a framed graduation photograph, there were two diplomas, also framed, which attested to his degrees from Syracuse University and the College of Medicine of the SUNY Upstate Medical Center, also in Syracuse. Somebody, presumably Dr. Edgar, had prepared an elaborate framed resume which detailed the highlights of his career as a dermatologist. Finally, there was a black leather bag which contained a stethoscope and several other medical items, all conspicuously old and well used.

It was obvious that Edgar wanted the world, or that part of it which would visit Franklin Pierce's consignment store, to know that he had been a successful medical doctor. There was nothing in his donations to the display to suggest a family, much less other interests or experiences. Carol wondered if Edgar was really such a one-dimensional man as these items suggested. She also found herself thinking about his connection to Pierce, and, for that matter, to the rest of the alumni group. Had he been a close friend of any of them in his undergraduate years? For that matter, was he still a friend of any of them?

These thoughts led her to a larger question to which she had been giving more and more attention as she dug deeper into the Pierce case: what was it that had held this seemingly quite disparate group together over the years? They had not struck her as close friends as she observed them at the memorial service. Why were they still taking the occasional trip together? Was it anything other than habit? That question brought her back to the issue of Abbey's feeling that something was wrong, something she couldn't put her finger on.

Carol put the yellow pad aside and returned Dr. Edgar's contributions to the consignment display to one of the boxes. She knew too little - to be honest, almost nothing - that justified further speculation. She would have to contact the doctor and arrange a meeting, hopefully at an early date. She hoped that that meeting would make such speculation more profitable. Not normally a pessimist, however, she doubted that it would.

CHAPTER 33

Dr. Edgar was still a practicing physician, so finding a time to visit him posed a problem. On the other hand, he lived closer to Crooked Lake than any of the other members of the alumni group, so Carol figured she could see him on relatively short notice. They finally arranged for her to make the trip to Elmira on Thursday afternoon, leaving the lake during rush hour and arriving at the Edgar home around six o'clock. If he was surprised by her call and a request to meet with him, he gave no evidence of it. It was almost as if she were one of his patients and he was simply finding a vacant slot in his schedule to accommodate her needs.

Either the doctor had just arrived home from his office or he was by nature formal, for he was still wearing a suit and tie.

"Good afternoon, sheriff. I'm surprised to see you again, but I must confess that I'm also intrigued. Just natural curiosity, I suppose. I can't remember a time when the person responsible for maintaining law and order came knocking at my door. And you aren't even *our* sheriff. Please come in."

"Thank you for making time for me, Dr. Edgar."

"No problem." He escorted the sheriff to a living room that didn't look as if it had been much lived in. "Have a seat. I'd offer you a drink, but I'm a teetotaler and the strongest thing in the house is non-alcoholic ginger beer. Would you care for some?"

"That would be fine, thank you."

"Well, here we are," the doctor said as he handed the sheriff her ginger beer. "Now perhaps you can enlighten me as to why I have the pleasure of your company."

"Of course. I would have tried to explain when I called, but, as you shall see, it's a bit complicated." She pulled Inspector Williams' statement from her purse and handed it to Edgar. "Better that you read this than for me to try to summarize it."

She waited while the doctor read the official looking document. His face made it clear that he was surprised by what he was reading.

"To say that I find this interesting would be an understatement," he finally said. "And to think that I probably saw you many times while we island-hopped across the Caribbean. I hope you enjoyed the cruise."

"I did. I did not, however, expect that I would be asked to play the role that the Barbadian authorities have given me. I'm still not sure I can help them. The way I understand it, the RBPF - that's what they call their law and order people - hope that by talking with Franklin Pierce's friends who were with him on the cruise I'll learn more about just what he was doing the day he was killed and hence how he met his death."

"That's what this document from an inspector in Barbados seems to be saying. I wish you luck. In my case at least, I have no idea what Franklin was doing when we were on the island."

"Which means, I gather, that you and he had different plans. Did he say anything to you about what his plans for the day were?"

Dr. Edgar produced a wan smile.

"No, he didn't. I didn't ask him; in fact, I don't believe I even saw him that morning. Wait a minute, that isn't quite right. I may have caught a glimpse of him on the deck, talking with someone. I'm not sure - it was crowded, and I was some distance away. For all I knew, he could have chosen to stay on board ship all day. Like everybody else, it wasn't until we had an explanation for our late departure that evening that I realized that he had indeed gone ashore."

"You say that for all you knew he might have decided not to go ashore. Did he frequently stay on the ship when you were in port?"

"Not that I know of. I really didn't give any thought to what he might be doing that day. Or any other day."

"It sounds as if you and Mr. Pierce weren't all that close. Is that fair?"

"We weren't, but then none of our little group are really close. Each of us goes our own way."

"If you aren't really close, how does it happen that you all travel together frequently?"

"That's a good question, one I've asked myself more than once. Force of habit? Keeping up a pretense that we're still friends? I'm really not sure."

"Had there been a time when you were close, when you actually considered yourselves good friends?"

"Another good question," he said. "I suspect that you'll get a different answer from different people. We all knew each other in college. Other than Ms. Bickle, that is. But frankly I'm not even sure any of us were all that close even in undergraduate days. As I'm sure Mrs. Lipscomb told you, the catalyst for putting together our little group was Pierce, and I always thought his rationale seemed a bit odd - you know, SU alums, upstate New Yorkers. Those aren't exactly exclusive categories. I used to think Franklin had pretty much pulled names out of a hat."

"Are there any members of the group that in your opinion might qualify as real friends?"

Once again the wan smile.

"I'd just be guessing. You should ask them yourself."

"Of course I'll be doing that. I asked what Mr. Pierce was planning that day in Barbados. How about you?"

The smile disappeared.

"Why does it matter? Your job, it says here in this document, is Pierce, not me."

Carol knew that it would come to this with every one of the SU group. But her questions could not be limited to Franklin Pierce if her purpose was to discover whether any of his colleagues could have been his killer.

"If I'm to get a good impression of things in Barbados, I'll need to know who was doing what, who might have seen something that's important. Even when it might not seem to be at first. You didn't see Pierce that day. How about the others? Did you talk with any of them about their plans? Did you spend the day, or a part of it, with any of them? I'm simply trying to recreate that day in my own mind."

Dr. Edgar knitted his brow. He was either trying to remember the day or feigning to. It was even possible that he was trying to decide whether she was seeking to trap him into saying something that would make him a suspect in Pierce's death. If he asked her whether that was the purpose of her question, she wouldn't have been surprised.

"Well, as for me, I'm afraid that I not only wasn't with Pierce, I wasn't with any of the rest of our group. You should know that we didn't spend all of our time together. In some cases, not even very much of it. Our cabins were scattered around the ship; who was where depended to a considerable extent on when we signed up and paid our deposit. Dining was an open seating affair. I only remember having dinner with Harry Pringle twice on the whole cruise; the Craigs ate with me once. I doubt I saw Bess Stevens anywhere, on the ship or off, once we left St. Maarten. The fact is, as I guess you must know by now, that I like to be alone."

"And how about shore excursions in Barbados? You were going to tell me whether you know anything about anyone else's plans."

"Pretty much what I said about Pierce. It's possible that the Bickles were going to go over to the windward side of the island. She said something like that as we were disembarking. Otherwise I'd be guessing."

"Guessing? If you didn't talk to them or overhear them, how could you guess where people might be going?"

"I didn't say they would be reliable guesses. But I'd be surprised if Westerman wasn't heading for a rum factory."

"And you? I assume that you set off by yourself, but where were you going?"

If, as seemed most unlikely, Dr. Edgar had killed Pierce, he would answer her question by naming some place far away from Harrysmith.

"I had been in Barbados twice before. There was a time when my dermatological association used to hold its biennial conferences in so-called exotic places You know, Hawaii, Costa Rica. Back in the late nineties we met once in Barbados. I'm a conscientious MD, so I didn't run around all over the island. But I did manage to see the highlights. I also took a cruise - yes, another cruise - about five years ago, and we stopped in Bridgetown. But that trip was a disaster. I got some kind of a bug and was quarantined in my cabin for almost four days. To be honest, that's a major reason why I decided to take this cruise with Franklin's alumni group. See what I missed last time."

It was an interesting and unexpected bit of history, but it didn't answer her question.

"Sorry about those days you couldn't leave your cabin, but about this winter's cruise. Where did you go in Barbados this time?"

"Nowhere in particular. Sorry to disappoint you, but that's the truth. I burn easily, and like I tell my patients, cover your head and wear lots of sunscreen. So I stayed away from the beaches, nice as they are. Mostly walked around Bridgetown. Nice town, one of the best capitals in the Caribbean."

"So you never explored any of the rest of the island?" Carol was obviously disappointed.

"Not this time."

"Any chance that one or more of your colleagues later shared with you where they had been and what they had seen?"

"I'm a medical doctor, not a policeman, but I have a sense that you're looking for evidence that one of the alumni group just might have been Pierce's killer."

It was Carol's turn to smile. And, if not to lie, to stretch the truth a bit.

"You misread me," she said. "The RBPF is of the opinion that Mr. Pierce fell victim to a local who robbed him and, when he put up a fight, killed him. They hope that one of your group may have heard or seen something that can help them track down the guilty party. I feel as if I'm playing blind man's bluff, or something very much like it. Anyway, that's why I'm here, and why I will be talking with your friends."

As this conversation went on for the better part of the next half hour, Carol had to acknowledge that Dr. Edgar was not quite as opaque as she thought he was after the memorial service. But while he was more outspoken than she had expected him to be, he had told her nothing that gave her a better picture of what went on in Barbados on that now long ago day in January. A self identified loner, the doctor had apparently spent that day (and in all likelihood many others) by himself, avoiding the other members of the group whenever possible. Or had he? Perhaps her interviews with some of the others would tell a different story. On the other hand, if he had indeed spent the day in Barbados alone, it would have been much easier for him to have met up with Pierce and been responsible for his death. If that is what happened, and she had no evidence that it had, an important question would remain unanswered. Why?

CHAPTER 34

Carol's second meeting with one of the Syracuse alums took her to Binghamton and Bess Stevens. That wasn't the way she had planned it, but messages on two other phones indicated that neither the Craigs nor Harry Pringle was available. Those messages had said nothing about being out of town, which made it likely that she could reach them later in the day. But it didn't really matter in what order she saw people, and she was anxious to establish some momentum in her investigation. So she had turned her attention to Ms. Stevens, the therapist who had taken up boxing.

Like Roger Edgar, Ms. Stevens appeared to be single.

"Hello." The woman who answered the phone said in a high voice.

"Ms. Stevens, this is Sheriff Carol Kelleher. We met just the other day at the memorial service for Franklin Pierce."

"You want to speak with Bess?"

"Oh, I'm sorry, I thought you were Bess. Yes, I need to talk with her."

"Just a sec." It took several minutes before the therapist came to the phone.

"Do I understand that this is the sheriff from over on Crooked Lake?" she asked. The question was followed by some deep breathing.

"It is. I hope I'm not interrupting, but I would like to see if there is some time when we can get together. Sometime fairly soon. I'll be glad to come to Binghamton."

"What's the problem?"

"There isn't a problem, other than Mr. Pierce's death. I'm in the process of scheduling meetings with members of the group that took the cruise on the *Azure Sea* back in January. I can explain when we meet, but the fact is that the Barbados police have asked me to talk with each of you on their behalf. Might it be possible for us to meet within the next few days if possible?"

"Has something happened regarding Franklin?"

What could she be imagining, Carol wondered.

"No, no. It's just that the inspector in charge of the investigation wants me to do what he can't do because he can't come all the way up here right now. As I said, I'll explain in more detail when I see you. How are your evenings? I'll not need more than an hour of your time."

After a long pause and more deep breathing, Ms. Stevens agreed to a meeting and the conversation turned to the practical problem of setting a date.

"Do you mind making the trip on a weekend?" she asked. "I usually play golf on weekends, but you've aroused my curiosity. I could see you either tomorrow or Sunday."

"That's great. How about tomorrow? Would late morning be okay? That would leave you time to hit the links."

"Sounds good. I'm willing to leave golf for Sunday. Do you have a pencil and paper handy? I'll give you directions."

Carol could have told her that she already had the necessary instructions for getting to everyone she needed to see, but she decided that evidence of too much advanced planning might be alarming. Better to let her believe that their meeting was simply a spur of the moment thing.

It was a longer trip than the one to Elmira to meet with Dr. Edgar, and it was also a much nastier day, with steady rain and occasional gusts of strong winds. She would have preferred to sleep in, but instead she got an early start and found the Stevens' house at 11:15, not long before the appointed hour.

Ms. Stevens had been the shortest of the group that had attended the memorial service, but when she came to the door she looked even shorter than Carol had remembered her.

"Good morning, sheriff. I see that you're without your uniform again."

"The uniform is perhaps the least favorite part of my job. It's also off-putting to a lot of people."

"Come on in. And try to ignore the chaos around you. Jerry is a great roommate, but she's no better than a C minus when it comes to neatness."

Carol was in the process of jettisoning her wet shoes when the woman who was presumably Jerry appeared from the kitchen.

"You must be the sheriff," she said. "I don't think I've ever met a sheriff. Don't worry. I won't be bothering you, but I have coffee duty today. How would you like yours?"

"This is Jerry." Ms. Stevens introduced her roommate, who Carol was guessing was more than that. "The sheriff will have it black, no sugar, if I remember what she was drinking over at the lake."

"Yes, that will be fine." Bess Stevens might well be a more formidable person than she had imagined, based on what she had observed at Abbey's.

Jerry brought the coffee and quietly disappeared, leaving the living room to Bess and the sheriff. Her hostess made no effort to comment on her roommate or to discuss further the 'chaos' she had mentioned. Carol didn't think the place looked especially chaotic.

"So, you are not only a friend of Abbey Lipscomb's. You are here on a mission for the people in Barbados. Would you care to explain?"

"I shall, but first I'd like you to read this." Carol extracted Inspector Williams' document from her purse and handed it to Ms. Stevens.

"Very interesting," was her response after reading it. "I assume that this doesn't represent a new development since the memorial service. You were there to size us up, is that the way to put it?"

Carol made no effort to choke off her laugh.

"Quite true. If I had told the whole story of my presence at Abbey's I fear I would have distracted all of you from the real purpose of the service. But as that document says, the Barbadian police would like me to learn what I can about what you remember of the day you were on the island. Who if anyone saw Mr. Pierce, talked with him, knew what he was doing that day. I talked with Dr. Edgar just the other day. Today I'm here. In the next week or two I expect to have visited with every one of you who were on that cruise. So why don't you do what you can to help me out, beginning with what you remember about the day in Barbados."

"I suppose I could tell you that it was many weeks ago, that my memory isn't all that reliable. But what's the point in doing that? I know exactly what I was doing, with whom, and, if it matters, why. I don't do much traveling, so when I do I look on it as a pretty big event. I actually keep a diary. If you like, I'll show it to you. But it isn't really necessary. I'm quite capable of telling you just what I did on every day of the cruise."

"That's remarkable. Tell me about Barbados."

"Of course. My day on Grenada was more interesting, but that's not why you're here. I tend to go to bed early, get up early, so I watched us dock that morning before breakfast. I'd arranged to go sightseeing with the Craigs. We met in the lounge where you go when you're taking a shore excursion, and those of us who had signed up for Bathsheba were among the first off the ship. We'd decided against one of the ship's tours and took a cab instead. It was a longer drive than I'd expected - I mean it's a small island, but there was a lot of traffic, most of it locals going about their daily business. Betty and I spent the day in Bathsheba, had lunch, must have taken close to a hundred pictures. The usual things tourists do. We got back around mid-afternoon."

"You said you went sight seeing with the Craigs, but that you and Betty spent the day in Bathsheba. What happened to Stuart?"

"Oh, he was feeling restless, decided to take a walk up the coast to Cattlewash. I think the name fascinated him. We met up again that afternoon and cabbed back to Bridgetown."

"Did you see any of your fellow alums?"

"Not until we got back to the ship."

"Do you know anything about what any of the rest of your group did that day?"

Bess started to respond to Carol's question when Jerry stuck her head around the corner.

"I'm on my way to the supermarket. Anything you want?"

"Not that I can think of," was the answer, but the interruption had apparently caused her to lose her train of thought.

"Damn!" she said. "But wait. I think that Westerman, he - I hate it when this happens, don't you?"

"It'll come to you," Carol said. "Sometimes it helps to switch to another subject. Why don't you tell me how it happens you became part of this Syracuse tour group?"

Bess laughed.

"That's easy, and much harder to forget. I used to be sensitive about it, but what's the point. What's past is past. It was because of Franklin, and not just because he invited me. Are you really interested?"

"I guess I am, mostly because what I observed at Ms. Lipscomb's didn't suggest that you all are that close. I don't mean you; I'm talking about the group as a whole."

"You're probably right about that. But me and Franklin, that's something else. Oh, oh - it's Franklin and me. I'll be tucked away in some retirement home before I get that right."

"Now that you're opened the door to your past, I'd like to hear about it."

"Franklin and *I*, we're a couple of odd ones. He had a reputation at SU as something of a cut-up. I think he actually enjoyed being thought of as the campus clown. As for me, I was that kid who was pretending to be a college student. I was real short, looked like I was maybe thirteen or fourteen. Anyway, we were in a freshman class together, intro to anthro or something like that, and he must have thought I was some kind of a kindred spirit. One day, out of the blue, he asked me out. Believe it or not, I'd only had one date that I can remember before that. But it sounded like fun, so I said yes."

"So you and Mr. Pierce dated in college?"

"That's not really the right word for it. We went out, but nothing happened. No, that's not true. In the process of having fun and playing touchy-feely, we both discovered ourselves. Let me cut a long story short. Franklin and I are gay, or he's gay and I'm a lesbian. Neither of us knew it, or at least admitted it to ourselves, until that night. The odd thing is that we weren't embarrassed. We found it funny. It was the beginning of a good friendship."

"Yet I believe that you have chosen not to donate any mementos to Mr. Pierce's display at his consignment shop." Carol chose not to comment; Bess would get the point.

"How would you know that?"

"It was part of my responsibility to check out the shop."

Ms. Stevens nodded, acknowledging that she understood.

"I guess there are two explanations for my failure to make a contribution," she said. "The idea just doesn't appeal to me. Even if it did, I don't really have anything that I'd want to put on display. But to be honest with you, Franklin and I aren't close any more. In fact, we haven't been for many years. Our 'relationship' was good for a laugh at first, but how much mileage is there in a college date between two homosexuals, one a guy and the other a girl?"

For some reason, Carol didn't find this surprising.

"Let me try your memory again - about what the rest of the group was doing that day in Barbados."

"Oh, yes. I can't recall what everyone was up to, but I do know that Jim said he planned to make the rounds of the rum plants and John and Ann were having a disagreement about what to do."

"That would be Jim Westerman and the Bickles, right?'

"That's right."

"Once the ship sailed, did any of them say anything else about what they'd done?"

"Not that I remember. The conversation, such as it was, was mostly about what could have happened to Franklin."

As had been the case with Dr. Edgar, Carol went back over the same ground, phrasing her questions a bit differently. Bess Stevens proved to be consistent, and what she had to say had the ring of truth. When Carol changed the subject, it was more out of curiosity than a search for information that might help solve the Pierce murder.

"You haven't said anything about your interest in boxing. How come?"

"Very simple. When you're as small as I am and need to fend off overly aggressive guys, it's a good strategy. Some people use the treadmill, others bench press. I take out my frustrations on a punching bag. Besides, my reputation as a boxer is much inflated. I've only been in the ring with another boxer twice in my life."

When she left Binghamton for the drive back to Crooked Lake, Carol had made up her mind, however tentatively, that Ms. Stevens could not have been Franklin Pierce's killer. Boxer or no boxer, she was simply too small - and too willing to be surprisingly frank.

CHAPTER 35

Lester Williams had finally fired Moses King. He had agonized over it for a few days, conscious of the fact that King's sizable family would be without a bread winner if he let him go. But in the end he had decided that forgiving a violation of one of the company's most basic rules would set a dangerous precedent, Moreover, Lester had rationalized, the nature of the islands's tourist economy made it likely that King would be able to find another job soon.

That would have been the end of the matter if the aging taxi that had earned King a thousand dollars and cost him his job hadn't 'broken down' not long after it had acquired a new driver. It hadn't literally broken down, but that's the way that Lucas George had described it.

"Mr. Williams," George said one day, "this car needs some work. Awfully sluggish, and it needs a tail light. A passenger got after me because a spring in the back seat is poking up through the seat cover. It's really broken down."

Lester knew that some of his taxis had seen better days, but he also knew that the taxi George was driving was no worse than several others in his fleet. He also knew that he hadn't given it a test drive since Moses King had loaned it out. Perhaps he should take a look at it; maybe the unauthorized driver had done something to it that accounted for its sluggishness.

And so it was that the taxi was in the shop, where one of the mechanics was working on it. He knew that he was expected to be thorough, which accounted for that fact that he didn't stop after replacing the tail light and otherwise addressing George's complaints. He fished odds and ends out of the side pockets, then turned his attention to what was on the floor, reaching back to corral whatever had gotten stuck under the driver's and passenger's seats. There was something under the driver's seat, but it seemed to have gotten caught where the seat was bolted to the floor.

"Damn it," the mechanic muttered under his breath. "Why do they do this?"

He didn't expect an answer, and he heard none. Perseverance got results, however, and when he straightened up he held a rock in his hand. It was just short of a foot in length, between two and three inches thick, and of comparably uneven dimensions in width. Andy Browne, the mechanic, was more interested in the fact that he had suffered a gash on the back of his hand while extricating the oddly shaped rock. He gave voice to another expletive and tossed it into an old oil drum that served the garage as a waste can.

"Inspector Williams, I'm sure you remember me," the man on the phone said. "*Lester's Taxis*. I'm Lester Williams."

"Oh, yes. Your man loaned his taxi to somebody for a thousand dollars."

"Do you mind if I ask you a question about that Yankee tourist who was killed back in January?"

The inspector did not like to discuss the case, but the question made him curious.

"That depends. What is your question?"

"How was he killed?"

The question surprised him, and the inspector found himself repeating it and feeling foolish that he had done so.

"Yes, I recall hearing that that man was killed somewhere over near Harrysmith. But whoever told me about it didn't know what killed him. Not who - if you'd found the killer, the whole country would have heard by this time. But how. How was he killed? You know, was he knifed? Or maybe hit over the head? What's the word? Bludgeoned?"

"I see." The inspector thought about it. The cause of death wasn't exactly a secret, but he was not in the habit of talking about it outside of the office.

"Why don't you tell me why you're asking?"

"My men have been working on that particular car, the one Mr. King used to drive. It needed some work. Anyway, my mechanic found a big odd-shaped rock stuck under the driver's seat. At first I didn't think much about it, but then it struck me as strange. Why would King need to keep a rock like that? And that started me thinking that maybe the guy he loaned it to could have been the killer and used that rock to do it. It's just a wild guess, but I had to call you and tell you about the rock."

Inspector Williams was now very interested in his namesake's question. Franklin Pierce had been the victim of a hard blow to the head. What had been used to deliver that blow they didn't know. If the man who had borrowed King's taxi had been one of Pierce's traveling companions, the rock Luther Williams had discovered in the taxi could be the murder weapon.

"First, let me thank you for calling. You've got a good head on your shoulders, Mr. Williams. Of course the rock you found in the taxi may have had nothing whatsoever to do with the killing at Harrysmith. We have no evidence that the man who borrowed the taxi was involved in any way in the murder of the tourist. But what you've suggested could be very important. You used the word bludgeoned, and that happens to be how he was killed. I hope you still have the rock you found in King's taxi."

"Yes, I do. My mechanic was going to throw it away, but I rescued it, thinking you might be interested."

He'll probably be another one who wants a reward, the inspector thought. Maybe I should see what we can do for him.

"I'll want to see this rock. But why don't you tell me about it. You say it's big?"

"Fairly big. It's close to a foot long, thick enough to make it pretty heavy. It's because it looks as if you could grab it at one end and use it to hit something that it came to me that it could be a weapon."

"Mr. Williams, I'd be very grateful if you or someone at your place of business could bring that rock over to RBPF today. I suppose that it's been handled in your garage, but I'd appreciate it if you could wrap it in a newspaper."

"You think it might have fingerprints on it?"

"I won't know about that until we have a look at it, but just in case I'd rather we avoid touching it with our own fingers. I mean yours and mine."

"This is exciting, isn't it?" Luther Williams sounded as if he were smack dab in the middle of a murder investigation. And delighted to be there. Cyril Williams was considerably more cautious. But for the first time since he'd heard the strange story about the 'thousand dollar taxi rental' he felt a surge of optimism about the Pierce case. First, he'd have a look at the rock. Second, he'd place a call to Sheriff Kelleher on Crooked Lake.

CHAPTER 36

Dinner over and the kitchen in good order, Carol collected the consignment shop files and spread them out on the kitchen table. She had decided to spend the evening hours rereading the correspondence between Pierce and members of the SU alumni group, with special attention to the Craigs.

She began by setting aside papers that pertained to Roger Edgar and Bess Stevens. She had already talked with them, and for no reason other than that she had found the Craigs the most pleasant of the people she had met at the memorial service, she had chosen to visit them next.

The Craig file was somewhat longer than the others, apparently because they had been the most responsive to Pierce's plan to create a display featuring the alums. Like the others, it opened with Franklin's letter announcing his plan and soliciting contributions. Carol set this letter aside, much as she had several others when it became clear that they were all identical. She had begun to leaf through the subsequent correspondence when she realized that something wasn't quite right. She reached across the table and picked up the letter from Franklin which she had just set aside. It was obviously a copy of the letter he had sent to everyone - yet it wasn't. It was slightly longer than the others. But no, that might not be true. She had never read all of Franklin's initial letters, just the first two she had come across. Because those two were exact replicas of each other, she had assumed that all of the others would be the same.

Why had he had more to say to the Craigs than to the others? Or to some of the others? She read the extra sentence in the letter to Betty and Stuart Craig, the public school teachers from Cortland.

'I know that you will want to support my plan. Of course I hope everyone will. But you know, better than most, that not everyone will be enthusiastic, so I am counting on you to pitch in and help me rally the laggards. After all, it's in your interest as well as mine.'

Carol tried to remember which of the initial letters she had read and taken as reason not to bother with the others. It probably didn't matter. But why was it more in the Craigs' interest to support Pierce's plan than, let's say, the Bickles'? What if anything had Franklin meant by that additional sentence?

It was curiosity as much as a conviction that it could matter that prompted her to abandon the Craigs for the moment and take a look at the letter that Franklin Pierce had first sent to all of the group members. She went through every file and extracted that letter from each one, even Abbey Lipscomb's and Nancy Brubaker's, the two members who had not taken the cruise.

As she expected, most of the letters lacked what she had begun to think of as a 'personalized sentence.' These standard letters had been sent to Lipscomb, Brubaker, Westerman, Edgar, and the Bickles. But the other three, to Harry Pringle, Bess Stevens, and the Craigs, each contained an additional sentence. Even more interesting, those paragraphs were identical: it was in their interest to support Franklin's plan.

The 'additional sentence' might turn out to mean nothing, but she wasn't about to dismiss it as irrelevant. Suddenly it was important that she read more carefully every exchange in each file. Had any of the group who had received a letter with a personalized sentence commented on it in their reply or in any other piece of correspondence? Bess Stevens had gotten a personalized sentence, but Carol had not read it. Nor could she remember Bess saying anything that could be construed as a comment on it. But she'd take another look.

Had Kevin been there, he would have headed for the fridge and the Chardonnay. Carol rarely had a drink after dinner, but tonight there would be an exception. It looked as if her evening would be a longer one that usual.

It was close to 10:30 when she finished the last of the files, and to her considerable surprise none of the three recipients of a personalized paragraph had made any reference to Pierce's strange suggestion that it was in their interest to support him. Not only had Stevens, Pringle, and the Craigs not commented on it; they had said absolutely nothing that indicated that they might know what Franklin was talking about. She thought about it for a few minutes, after which she was about ready to assume that Franklin had been doing nothing more than urging his alums to help him sell the consignment shop plan to their colleagues. Unfortunately, a small but insistent voice kept telling her that accepting that line of reasoning would be a serious mistake.

Where are you Kevin? In spite of the fact that he tended to be impulsive, she had learned to trust his ideas on matters such as this. She could, of course, call him, but it would be more satisfying if the two of them were discussing the issue face to face, with the files in front of them. Unfortunately, that would be impossible for at least another six weeks, by which time she hoped that the Pierce case would have become history, with one of Inspector Williams' bajans arrested for the murder at Harrysmith.

In the meanwhile, Carol would continue to interview - or as Sam Bridges would say, interrogate - the members of the SU alumni group who had taken the fatal cruise. At least she now had an additional line of questioning for her meeting with Stuart and Betty Craig. What did they think Franklin was talking about when he solicited their help in launching the *Upstate Consignments* display? Why was the success of the display project in their interest as well as his? She hoped that they would be forthcoming, or if not that their efforts to dissemble would be transparently unpersuasive.

CHAPTER 37

Upstate Consignments had now been closed for more than two months. Franklin Pierce's man Grimley had maintained a conscientious vigil there for much of that time, but he had never had to do more than explain to the occasional patron that the manager was out of town and the shop was temporarily closed. That was of course true, but a far cry from the whole story. But after many boring days, Grimley had taken it upon himself to take liberties with Pierce's instructions. The 'Closed for the Week' sign on the door should be sufficient to relieve him of the obligation to maintain a personal watch on the building. His conscience dictated that he should drop by from time to time to make sure that everything was in order, and he rationalized that Sheriff Kelleher's visit to the shop gave him license to cut back on his hours on duty. Surely responsibility for the place was now hers, not his.

Carol, in turn, had pretty much put *Upstate Consignments* out of her mind. She had removed everything that was of interest to the assignment Inspector Williams had given her. She had notified Cy Singleton of her visit and had explained that she had left the shop under lock and key and under the watchful eyes of Mr. Grimley. That done, she had made no further contact with the owner of the building which still bore the sign *Upstate Consignments.*

Thus it was not surprising that she was confused the next morning when JoAnne told her that a Mr. Singleton was on the phone. The name came to her just as he announced himself.

"Sheriff Kelleher? This is Cy Singleton. We spoke weeks ago, back when you called to let me know you needed access to Franklin Pierce's consignment shop on Walnut Street."

"Yes, I remember," she said.

"Don't you think it's time for you to bring me up to date?' The voice wasn't unpleasant, but the message said that he was impatient.

When Carol had called to tell him she would be visiting the consignment shop he already knew that its proprietor had died. Abbey Lipscomb had thought he should know, and had told him. But neither she nor Abbey had mentioned that he had been murdered. In fact, Abbey had told him very little, including the important fact that Franklin Pierce had no relatives and that therefore it was very likely that no one would be coming forward to take over *Upstate Consignments.* Carol had fudged the issue, telling the owner that she was in the process of tracking down Pierce's next of kin.

Now Singleton was on the line, and it was doubtful that he could be put off with more talk about a search for next of kin.

"You are quite right. I should have been in touch before this."

"I must say, I am puzzled. It never occurred to me when we spoke that you weren't sheriff of Wayne County. I should have asked more questions when we talked. I never even asked for your phone number - too busy, I suppose. Anyway, when I realized that the status of Pierce's business was still in limbo, I called our sheriff's office, and they had no idea who you were. I'm sure you can understand why I'm puzzled. Fortunately, somebody called me back subsequently to report that you're actually the sheriff of Cumberland County, which explains how I got your phone number."

"I must apologize, Mr. Singleton. It was never my purpose to mislead you. As I told you at the time, I was looking for papers which might help me get a handle on Mr. Pierce's business. Now that you are on the line, perhaps I can atone for my carelessness and bring you up to date on the matter."

"I certainly hope so."

"In the first place - and you may know this already - Mr. Pierce was on a cruise to the Caribbean when he died. He died on Barbados, one of the places the cruise ship stopped. And not only did he die; he was murdered."

Mr. Singleton interrupted.

"I assume you knew this when you asked permission to look for records in the consignment shop. That would explain why it was you, a sheriff, not an attorney, who contacted me."

"That's not quite true, Mr. Singleton. You see, the police on Barbados have asked me to help them solve this particular crime. Why me is a rather long story, and the fact that I was on the same cruise seems to have made it natural for the local police down there to seek my support. But what is important is that the people in Barbados need information that will only be available up here, where Mr. Pierce lived, not down in Barbados where he was killed."

Carol realized that her attempt to explain things to Mr. Singleton without divulging more than she wanted, or needed, to could only complicate her relationship with him. She'd have to cross her fingers and hope for the best.

"You didn't leave the consignment shop empty handed, did you?"

"No I didn't. But what I took has nothing to do with any contractual obligations Mr. Pierce had with you. I was interested in files that Mr. Pierce kept regarding a plan he had for a new display he was preparing and for items which were to be a part of that display."

"Was he planning on importing things from Barbados?"

Carol momentarily considered answering that question in the affirmative. It wasn't true, but it would help her avoid further questions that would lead to the real reason she was involved in the Pierce case, and she didn't wish to go there. At least not now. But she was also not anxious to tell such a lie.

"I'm pretty sure that he wasn't, but I must confess that there's still a great deal that I don't know."

"It has been quite a long time since Mr. Pierce's death. I laid back at first. Didn't want to rush a family coping with its grief. But nobody has come forward to tell me what they intend to do. That building is still full of the stuff that people in the consignment business collect, and I am at a point when I have to look out for my bottom line. I have to know whether the Pierce family plans to take it over and start paying the bills or what. So where do I stand?"

The moment of truth had arrived. Singleton had a right to know that there was no Pierce family. She herself had been so tied up in the search for a murderer that she had done nothing whatsoever to ascertain whether Pierce had a will, much less to find out what it might say about the disposition of the consignment shop. For the first time in a long time Carol was feeling guilty - not about what she was doing, but what she had not been doing.

And then a second thought came to mind. What if Pierce, without a family of his own, had decided to leave something to one or more of his 'friends' in the SU alumni group and the members of the group were aware of his attentions? Was it conceivable that his will had something to do with his murder in Barbados?

Chapter 38

Carol's plan to make an appointment with the Craigs in Cortland was derailed by the call from Mr. Singleton. More accurately, it was derailed by the fact that Singleton had reminded her that he still had no idea what Franklin Pierce's heirs planned to do with the consignment shop. Franklin had no heirs, and until she took steps to locate his will, assuming that he had left one, the future of the shop was likely to remain a mystery for some time to come. Of course the situation would not have been much different had she never met Abbey Lipscombe or Inspector Williams. As it was, however, the owner of the building which housed *Upstate Consignments* would hold her responsible for his problem, and she could hardly blame him.

The first thing Carol did after her conversation with Singleton was to get in touch with Abbey.

"Hi, Abbey, it's me, Sheriff Kelleher. I have a problem and wonder if you can give me a few moments of your time."

"Do you want to come over?"

"No, no, that won't be necessary. I think a few minutes on the phone should suffice."

"Well, I'm not doing anything important, so fire away."

"It's about Franklin, of course. We know he had no family - no wife, no children, no siblings, his parents deceased. Do you happen to know if beyond that there are any other living relatives with whom he had any kind of a relationship? What I'm getting at is whether there's anybody who might be a candidate to inherit the consignment store?"

"Oh, goodness, I'm afraid I wouldn't know. Franklin always made it clear to me that he didn't have any family, but I suppose everyone has a family if you look beyond the obvious candidates. He never talked about cousins several times removed or things like that. I somehow got the feeling that his situation was something of a rarity. Not only was he alone, but so were his father and his mother. I've no idea how far back you'd have to go before you'd find someone."

"I think you can see the problem. The man who owns the place which Franklin rented is getting anxious to do something about his store. Which means that we need to know if he ever made a will, and if he did to whom he willed the store. To the best of your knowledge, did Franklin have a will? I sure hope he didn't die intestate."

"Oh, dear." Carol wished Abbey wouldn't talk like that. She wasn't surprised when Abbey told her that she had never discussed a will with Franklin.

"Okay, you knew him, I didn't. In fact you probably knew him better than any of the other members of the group. If you had to hazard a guess, would you say it's likely that he made a will or that he hadn't gotten around to it?"

"I'm not a good guesser when it comes to things like that. I suppose I should have brought it up, considering that he didn't have a family. But I didn't. This really is an important matter, isn't it?"

"I suspect so. And not just for Mr. Singleton." Carol tried another tact. "Did you ever visit Mr. Pierce at his home?"

"Probably twice, but that's over a period of more than two decades. Why?"

"What's your opinion of his house? Was it orderly? Did it appear that he kept things neat, knew where things were? I'm assuming that an orderly person would be more likely to have a will than one whose house was sloppy, cluttered. That may not be true, but I'm just trying to form an opinion of him."

"I don't think I ever thought much about it. I was visiting him, not his house."

"Of course." Carol was disappointed.

"Did Franklin have a lawyer?"

Abbey sounded as if she had just failed a critical test.

"He never spoke of one. I never knew of a time when his circumstances seemed to warrant legal counsel."

"Chances are, however, that if he was thinking about a will he'd have sought out an attorney. He must have known that the absence of a family would have made legal counsel even more important."

"That could be, but Franklin wasn't a worrier. If he was concerned about such things, he never sounded it to me. I may be wrong, but there were times when I thought the absence of a family gave him more freedom, if you know what I mean. No one to second guess him, no one to challenge his ideas, his decisions."

"Okay." No point pursuing the matter further with Abbey. Carol would have to go back to Newark and work with the police there to gain access to the Pierce house. Hopefully there would be something there that would help: a will, an address or phone book with a lawyer's name, a key to a safe deposit box.

Carol soon found that Newark had a number of estate attorneys, and that the greater Rochester area had a great many more. Finding out if any of them had Franklin Pierce as a client was going to be a sizable task, entailing a great many phone calls. It didn't take her long to make the decision to drive to Newark, which she knew from her visit to the consignment store was not that far north of nearby Seneca Lake. She'd enlist the help of the local police to gain access to Franklin Pierce's home where, with any luck, she would find something that would tell her whether he had an attorney and, if so, who he was.

Unfortunately, the Newark police needed some persuasion to accede to her request for assistance in her mission.The person who took her call had heard about her; he had been the one who had told Cy Singleton that she was the sheriff of Cumberland, not Wayne, County. She recited the now old story of what had happened on Barbados and promised to present the RBPF document when she got to Newark. That seemed to convince a skeptical duty officer in the local PD to cooperate with her, as long as he or a colleague accompanied her. That might turn out to be a nuisance. On the other hand, there could be advantages in having an officer familiar with the town and its people as she went about her search for a will and an attorney.

The local policeman assigned to her turned out to be Leonard (Len) Carpenter, a genial young man who seemed to be both honored and intrigued to be riding shotgun next to a sheriff from another upstate jurisdiction. A woman sheriff at that.

Although Len got them into the Pierce's house, which Carol would have described as relatively neat, their search there came up empty. They gave it a thorough going over, but unless Franklin had chosen to create a secret hideaway under the floor somewhere (Len suggested that possibility), there was no will to be found. A desk, which appeared to be where Franklin spent many hours when he wasn't at the consignment shop, did contain an address book. But none of the entries said anything to indicate that the person named was an attorney. Carol took the address book with her, intending to check the names she found there against the roster of attorneys in the yellow pages.

The desk also contained a key to Franklin's safety deposit box, a discovery which Carol found encouraging. As a consequence they set off for the R & T Bank as soon as they had wrapped up their unsuccessful search of the house. It was much more likely that a will, if indeed there was one, was in the safety deposit box than in a secret hideaway under the floorboards. Inasmuch as neither the sheriff nor the policeman accompanying her had an account or a deposit box at the bank, it took conversations with a teller, an assistant manager, and ultimately the manager herself before Inspector Williams's artfully worded document allowed them into the inner sanctum where the deposit boxes were located. It turned out that its contents were surprisingly thin, and that once more a will was among the missing documents.

It had been a long and unproductive day. Carol thanked Officer Carpenter for his kind assistance, and headed back for Crooked Lake. If Franklin had an attorney and she could locate him, it was still possible that she would discover his will. From her own days practicing law she knew that lawyers typically retained wills they had prepared for their clients. But she was no longer optimistic that Franklin had ever written a will. Or, for that matter, that he had ever used the services of a lawyer. It probably didn't matter; the future of *Upstate Consignments* was really none of her business. She consoled herself for the wasted day by downgrading the possibility that Pierce's hypothetical will benefitted one or more of his SU alumni group. That had never been probable in any event. By the time she reached home, Carol had almost written it off as even a possibility. Almost but not quite.

CHAPTER 39

Carol's principal task, both in Inspector Williams' mind and her own, was to learn as much as she could about the surviving members of the SU tourist group who had been aboard the *Azure Sea*, including what they had done and what they had observed during their day in Barbados. Unfortunately, her pursuit of that information had been temporarily sidetracked by secondary matters, particularly the search for a will which Franklin Pierce may or may not ever have written.

Thus far she had spent time with and asked questions of Roger Edgar and Bess Stevens, neither of whom had been very enlightening. But at the time she had seen them, she hadn't realized that Stevens had been asked to contribute to Pierce's special exhibit at *Upstate Consignments* with a suggestion that it would be in her interest as well as his to do so. It would now be necessary to find an opportunity to talk to Stevens again. In the meanwhile, there was no reason why she shouldn't approach the issue more directly with the Craigs, who had also been among the recipients of this more specific letter about the new exhibit at the consignment shop. Hopefully, they would have some idea what Pierce had had in mind.

Cortland, where they lived, lay somewhere east of Binghamton but not as far north as Cooperstown, where Kevin had had his unusual encounter with Jim Westerman. With any luck she could make an arrangement to see the Craigs and return to Crooked Lake the same day. If not, she knew that there would be a motel in the vicinity. She waited until the school day had ended and the staff would be likely to have gotten home before she called.

The woman who answered her call sounded nothing like the one who had attended the memorial service. She either had a cold or she was unusually tired at the end of a long day in the classroom. Carol hoped that her lessons had had to do with a Shakespeare play or sonnet rather than the declension of some noun.

"Hello, Betty - I'm right, aren't I, this is Betty?"

"That's right. To whom am I speaking?"

"We met at Abbey Lipscomb's - the memorial service for Franklin Pierce. I'm Carol Kelleher, Abbey's friend on Crooked Lake."

"Oh, yes, the sheriff."

"I'm afraid so, and I must confess that I'm calling because I've been asked to by the police down in Barbados, the ones who are investigating Mr. Pierce's death. This isn't a job I enjoy, but for obvious reasons they can't do it themselves. I guess you could say that I've been deputized by the Barbadian authorities to talk with Mr. Pierce's friends and try to find out what they know about what he was doing the day he was in their country. The day he died."

"*You're* investigating Franklin's death?" Mrs. Craig sounded as if she couldn't believe her ears.

"I was as surprised as I suspect you are when the inspector in charge of the investigation called me and asked for my help. He wants me to meet with those of you who were with Mr. Pierce in Barbados, see what you all remember about what he was doing the day your ship was there. I'm calling because I would like to drive over to Cortland and meet with you."

"But why you?" It was, of course, a very good question, predictably necessitating more candor than she had produced in Abbey's parlor.

"As luck would have it, I was, like you, a passenger on the *Azure Sea* when it docked in Barbados. The inspector down there learned that I was a fellow passenger who happened to live in upstate New York and also happened to be a sheriff. The inspector isn't a specialist in American geography, but he seems to think that it won't be too hard for me to drive around upstate New York and interview all of you who were traveling with Mr. Pierce. I doubt that my experience as a sheriff will prove very helpful, but he's in a bind and he's been reduced to grasping at straws."

"Forgive my language, but I'll be damned. May I assume that you're now mixed up in this matter because the Barbados authorities have't yet found Franklin's killer?"

"Their assumption, from the very beginning, was that one of their citizens, presumably somebody down on his luck, assaulted Mr. Pierce for his wallet and, in the ensuing tussle, killed him. But they haven't found the killer, so they're anxious to learn what they can about where on the island he went and with whom that day. In other words, might any of you have seen or heard something which would provide a clue to what happened."

"If I were you, I wouldn't be very optimistic."

"I'm not either, but I agreed to talk with each of you. Which I'm now doing. Is there some time soon when I can meet you in Cortland? I have no intention of urging you to come back over to where I live."

"Are you talking about me or Stuart and me? We were together that day."

"I'd prefer it be both of you - only because in my experience people often tend to remember things differently."

"I think you'll find our minds run in the same channels, but that's okay. We have what they call a teachers' day on Wednesday; no classes, time off for projects, so on - you wouldn't be interested. What about that afternoon, something after two?"

"I'll be there. Just give me your address. GPS will do the rest." Carol already had the Craig address, but once more chose to create the impression that she hadn't done her homework.

"So you spent the day over at Bathsheba," Carol said, after sharing Inspector Williams's letter.

"More or less," Stuart answered. "We found a good place to eat, watched the surf for a while. Frankly, I was ready for a siesta, but figured it'd be better to walk off my lunch. So I decided to hike up to Cattlewash. It's just a short walk up the coast."

"I don't know that part of Barbados," Carol said. She didn't like to lie if she didn't have to, and not knowing the area was slightly less dishonest than not having been there. "An enjoyable place?"

"Personally I prefer that side of the island," Betty said, "although the swimming is more dangerous. Stuart and I didn't want to risk it. But Bess did."

"Bess Stevens was with you?" Carol, of course, knew that the therapist-boxer had accompanied the Craigs to Bathsheba.

"Oh, I thought I'd mentioned that," Stuart said. "I think I speak for us all when I say it was a great place for soaking up the atmosphere."

"Did any of you see Mr. Pierce? I mean In Bathsheba or while you were up the coast at Cattlewash, Mr. Craig? Or perhaps you heard him say where he was going that day."

"I don't recall seeing him or talking to him at all when we were in Barbados." Stuart looked at his wife, and she nodded in agreement. "In fact, I don't think we saw any of our group other than Bess until we got back to the ship."

"Did anyone else mention him? Report they'd seen him or heard what he was up to?"

"Didn't hear a thing until the ship didn't get away on time and he turned out to be the problem. If you're supposed to be helping the Barbados police, it sounds like you're running into a stone wall."

Mr. Craig was right about that, but Carol preferred to leave the impression that there may have been some progress.

"I've never had to play second fiddle to a Caribbean policeman," she said, seeking to downplay her role in the investigation, "so I'm not really sure how I'm doing."

Stuart looked questioningly at the sheriff.

"What is it you usually do? I mean what's it like to be a sheriff in upstate New York?"

"Not as exciting as TV and crime novels would have you think. For all I know I deal with more paper work than you teachers do. That and policing the highways and keeping bar brawls to a minimum. But I've never done what I'm doing today before, and I'm glad it's not what I do for a living."

Carol was anxious to get back to the reason for her visit to Cortland.

"There's another question that I feel obligated to ask, in view of my assignment from the Barbados RBPF. It has to do with Mr. Pierce's plan to assemble a sort of memorial to his friends - to those of you who have accompanied him on these trips to places like Barbados. You're familiar with his intentions, and I've visited his consignment shop and seen where things stand. I've also read the file he's kept on his correspondence with all of you, and that's what I want to discuss. You do know what I'm talking about, don't you?"

"Of course," Stuart said with no enthusiasm.

"Did you and Betty donate anything?"

"The courteous thing was to go along, so we saw that he got a few things. Nothing important."

"I take it you weren't enthusiastic."

"No, and why should we have been? Franklin was something of an odd ball, and this was definitely an odd ball idea. Why should a bunch of Syracuse alums put meaningless stuff on display at a former classmate's business? Nothing would have any value. He wouldn't be able to sell it, his customers would ignore it."

"Yet Mr. Pierce made it a point to let you know that it was important, didn't he? In urging you to donate to the display, he even told you it was in *your* interest as well as his. Why don't you tell me what he meant?"

In spite of their best efforts, neither Betty nor Stuart Craig was able to keep their face from reflecting their reaction to what the sheriff was saying. Both of them recovered quickly, but there had been a moment of - what? Anxiety? Whatever it was, they had been taken by surprise by her quotation from Franklin's appeal for support of his plan. If she knew this, what else might she know?

It was Stuart who answered Carol's question.

"To be honest, I have only the vaguest memory of his invitation to help him with the display project. After all, we got his letter months ago, way back in the early fall. I don't remember how he worded his request, and I can't imagine what he meant by the words you just quoted.

I assume he was trying to make the best case for a bad idea. In any event, Betty and I dug up a couple of mementos and mailed them to him. It's a shame, I guess, that he'll never have a chance to enjoy what we all donated to his store."

Betty had been silent through all of this. At last she spoke up, echoing her husband but offering a hint of something more.

"Strange man, Pierce," she said. "I never did figure out just who he really was, or why he did what he did."

"How does it happen that the two of you knew him, that you became part of his alumni group?"

Betty and Stuart looked at each other as if they thought the other was better able to answer that question.

"We didn't know him, not like you're thinking." It was Betty. "I had one course with him. It was a class on French Lit, you know, Flaubert's *Madame Bovary* and everything from Stendahl to Proust by way of *Les Miserables.* God, I'll never forget that one, three times as long as the musical."

"No, dear," Stuart interrupted. "You're thinking of someone else. Your only class with Franklin was chemistry."

"Oh, that's right." Betty sounded as if she'd made a major blunder. "It was chem. Both of us were simply trying to satisfy a distribution requirement."

Chemistry, French novels, whatever. Carol had the feeling that both of them were making too much of an elective Betty had shared with Pierce back in the day.

More was said about how they and others had come to know Franklin Pierce well enough to become part of a group that vacationed together. The Craigs' explanation was similar to that of Roger Edgar, who had suggested that Pierce might have pulled his small list of traveling companions out of a hat. Unlike Bess Stevens, Betty had never dated him, or so she claimed, and the odds that Stuart had were so thin as to be laughable.

Carol's thoughts as she drove back to the lake could be summed up in eight words: 'Sorry, inspector, but I'm still at square one.'

CHAPTER 40

It had been bothering John Bickle ever since the memorial service. He had raised the issue with his wife on the way back to Skaneateles that afternoon, and they had had a silly argument about it. Well, not exactly an argument, but a discussion in which he had made fun of her for thinking that someone she had seen in a checkout line was the star of a recent film. What bothered him wasn't that Ann's imagination was in overdrive, but that his own memory was failing him.

Why did Carol Kelleher, the sheriff he had been introduced to at Abbey Lipscomb's, remind him of someone he had seen recently? No, that wasn't quite right. She didn't *remind* him of someone he had seen recently. She *was* someone he *had* seen recently. The more he thought about it, the more certain he was that he was right. It was, of course, unimportant, so why should he have so much trouble putting it out of his mind. Or was it unimportant?

It was nearly two weeks later that it finally came to him: the woman who had been helping Abbey organize and run the memorial for Franklin Pierce had been aboard the *Azure Sea* on its cruise in the Caribbean. Therefore, she had been on the ship when Pierce had missed the ship's departure from Bridgetown. John had no doubt about it. This woman, now identified as the sheriff of Cumberland County, was not simply Abbey's neighbor. Nor was she at the memorial service just because Abbey needed some help. For some reason, she was a player in what people were now calling the Pierce case. Why? It was suddenly a matter of some urgency that he meet with her. There were questions he would like to ask, not to mention things he wanted to say to her.

There was no reason to involve Ann. The only decision he had to make was whether he should call and invite himself over to Crooked Lake or simply arrive at the sheriff's doorstep, unannounced. Inasmuch as it was a long drive and he had no idea if and when she would be available, he opted for a phone call. Abbey would be sure to have the sheriff's number, but he didn't wish to talk with Abbey. He tried the Cumberland County sheriff's office instead, and to his surprise within five minutes the woman he had met at the memorial service was on the line.

"Sheriff Kelleher here. My assistant says that you are John Bickle and that you need to speak with me. What would you like to tell me?"

"Hello, sheriff. I'm not sure I *need* to speak with you, but I would like to if you can spare the time. We barely said hello the day we met at Abbey Lipscomb's, and you didn't tell us that you had been a fellow passenger on the *Azure Sea* this past winter. What I'd like to do is come over to Crooked Lake again, not to see Abbey this time, just you. My schedule is always flexible. Is there a date that would work for you?"

"I'm pretty flexible myself. I'm at my office in Cumberland Monday through Friday, and at my cottage evenings and usually all day Saturday and Sunday, so why don't you look at your calendar and pick a time."

"How would day after tomorrow be, let's say a little after noon? One o'clock okay?"

"Looks good. Tell you what. Why don't you come to my cottage, not the office. We won't have to deal with interruptions that way. I live on Blue Water Point. It's on the west side of the lake, not quite seven miles south of West Branch. You can't miss it - my sheriff's department car will be conspicuous."

"Looking forward to it," Bickle said and hung up.

Carol had planned to make an appointment to visit the Bickles in Skaneateles, but he had made it easier by suggesting that he, not she, do the traveling. That he needed or at least wanted to see her was encouraging. Edgar, Stevens, and the Craigs had been cooperative, but none of them had seemed particularly anxious to have her at their door. Bickle now knew that she had been on the same cruise ship as the SU alums, not surprising in view of the fact that she had already shared that information with four others. The grapevine was obviously in business. He hadn't, however, mentioned her role as a partner of the RBPF in the investigation of Pierce's death. Carol found this puzzling. Why had someone called him with the news that she had been on the *Azure Sea* but not mentioned the fact that she was now working with the Barbadian authorities? Or had his source failed to mention it? And if so, why? Her meeting with John Bickle promised to be an interesting one.

As the clock on the office wall ticked off the remaining minutes of the afternoon, Carol found herself returning again and again to Bickle's call. Much as she abhorred uninformed speculation, she kept asking herself why this man she barely knew, and who barely knew her, was so interested in driving all the way from the easternmost of the Finger Lakes to talk with her. She was sure it would have something to do with what had happened to Franklin Pierce. She hoped it would help her to better understand Pierce himself, not to mention other members of the 'Barbados Eight.' Perhaps it would even lead her to an understanding of what it was that was troubling Abbey.

———

Before Bickle arrived at the cottage two days later, Carol went back to the files to reassure herself that Franklin hadn't tucked in that additional paragraph - those words that read like a veiled threat - in his letter introducing his proposal for a group display. There were no mementos for the display at the consignment shop except for John's handcrafted corner cupboard, and it was still under lock and key in Newark.

The cottage was in fairly good shape, so Carol felt no obligation to neaten up. She prepared a pot of coffee and found an unopened six pack of root beer in the back of the fridge. Then she sat down to wonder about the reason John Bickle was so anxious to talk with her.

The CPA turned furniture maker arrived almost fifteen minutes before one o'clock. He obviously knew that he was early, because he stayed in the car rather than come to the door. Carol put an end to this needless attention to the precise time they had agreed upon.

"Mr. Bickle. Good to see you," she said as she greeted him at his car door. Bickle shook hands and followed her into the cottage. They exchanged banal comments on the improvement in the weather and she offered him coffee, which he accepted. She expected him to offer compliments on the cottage or express his appreciation for her willingness to see him on such short notice. But he did neither. This was going to be a straight forward, no nonsense conversation, and he was going to get right to the point.

"I hope you don't think I'm out of line," he said, "but I don't seem to cope well with things I don't understand. And right now I don't understand your role in Franklin Pierce's death. First there was that business at the memorial service, you being a sheriff. And then there was your presence on our cruise ship. I knew something was wrong, but it took me awhile to figure it out. What was wrong was that I knew I'd seen you somewhere but couldn't remember where. Then it finally came to me - you had been on the same cruise Franklin and the rest of us were on. After a week at sea you recognize people you see over and over again in the public places. Especially when they're attractive, and if you'll forgive my saying so, you do stand out in a crowd."

Carol chose to ignore the compliment.

"You remember seeing me on the ship, not learning I'd been on the cruise from your colleagues?"

"Did somebody else recognize you? Nobody said anything at the service."

"I take it that you haven't spoken to any of your fellow passengers since our meeting at Abbey's."

"That's right. We aren't in the habit of communicating."

"Then you aren't aware of my role in the Pierce case. Let me show you something." Carol got up and retrieved the inspector's letter. "Here. This should explain a few things."

"I see," Bickle said after reading it. "I thought there was more to your presence at the memorial service than either you or Lipscomb let on. She doesn't dissemble well, and I thought you were covering for her when she let drop that nonsense about you being the local *Law and Order* lady. So how's it happen that you're mixed up in this business?"

"I think the letter in your hands explains it very well. The Barbados authorities seem to think I may be of some help, my being a sheriff and living a lot closer to Pierce's companions than they do. It is quite likely that I'll be of much less help to them than they hope I will."

Bickle's face reflected the fact that he wasn't satisfied.

"You have a role in the matter because Barbados believes Franklin's killer is one of us. Right?"

"I'm operating on the assumption that one or more of you knows something about what Pierce was doing the day he was killed - what his plans were, where he was, something that will help narrow their search for his killer. Why would you think one of your fellow alumni was his killer?"

"Because of your presence at Abbey's, sheriff. It's pretty logical, isn't it? You were there to watch us, listen to us, form an opinion of us. And you weren't about to let us know that you're a sheriff until Abbey blew your cover. How come you're now admitting that you're helping the people in Barbados?"

Bickle had given the matter some thought, and he had pretty much gotten it right. There was no reason to pretend otherwise.

"It was almost certain that it would all come out soon anyway. I just didn't want to shift the mood at the memorial from sadness that you'd lost Pierce to a focus on me."

Bickle's laugh was hollow.

"Sorry," he said. "I'm not trying to make light of what we seem to be calling a memorial for Franklin. But you were there. I didn't hear any outpouring of sadness. Did you? I assume that Abbey has filled your ear with stories of our old school ties. Don't believe it. We may have gone through the motions. And once in awhile there may have been a moment when somebody had a passing feeling of nostalgia for what used to be. But we took the cruise out of force of habit. Maybe curiosity out of how people were aging, coping with life's problems."

"You have obviously thought a good deal about the group. Would you care to share your thoughts about its members? I mean, how does it happen that these particular alums became members?"

"I'm no psychologist, sheriff. What I do know is that the membership in our little group was all Franklin's doing. He knew all of us, in different ways of course. It wasn't just a matter of being in the same frat house or having the same major. Just look at us - we're an odd bunch, different careers, different interests, different life stories. But in every case there was a connection to Franklin that he seemed to want to keep alive. I knew a bit about those connections when I was an undergraduate at

'Cuse. In other cases I learned about the connection later. Sometimes accidentally, sometimes because I knew there had to be a reason and tried to figure it out. I can't explain what it was in every case, but I know enough to know that it wasn't random chance that brought us together."

"Mr. Bickle, you obviously know more than I do about your friends in the Syracuse alumni group. Now that you have come all the way to Crooked Lake from Skaneateles, I'd be very grateful if you'd let me have another hour of your time and share with me what you know about your colleagues in the group. And I'm confident that Inspector Williams, the man in charge of the Barbados investigation, will also welcome your input. I can even rustle up some lunch."

"That would be very nice of you. Please remember, however, that what you shall hear is one man's opinion. While I am confident that I know what I'm talking about, others may disagree. And that may include Abbey Lipscomb."

CHAPTER 41

Carol had to admit that she hadn't been as responsible as she should have in stocking the refrigerator. With Kevin down in the city and her own schedule impossibly hectic, she had let shopping slide, which made her offer to produce lunch for John Bickle a bit problematic. Nonetheless, she was able to put a few edibles on the table, and she soon found herself wondering if she might possibly be feeding Franklin Pierce's murderer.

She quickly set that macabre thought aside and urged Bickle to tell his story. The lunch was palatable. Bickle's account of the circumstances which brought Pierce's group together was fascinating. Was it true? That was something else, and Carol had determined to listen with an open mind and to be appropriately skeptical.

"Just so we understand each other," she said as they settled down at the dining room table, "my task in this investigation is not to capture Franklin Pierce's killer. I have no authority in the matter. For reasons which should be obvious, however, the people down in Barbados who do have the authority need information that they hope I can help them gather. For the most part that information pertains to the tour group Mr. Pierce was traveling with when he visited Barbados. You seem to be in a good position to provide me with some of that information. So why don't you go back to the beginning and tell me what you know that might conceivably be helpful."

"I'll do my best, starting with Franklin himself. I'm sure Abbey has told you that he's a prince of a fellow. I wouldn't put it quite that way. Franklin was an interesting guy back at Syracuse. Full of fun, a real character, bright enough but not a scholar. I knew him like many people did, not because we were friends but because if he was anywhere around you couldn't not know him. And he always seemed to be around. What's more, he had an uncanny ability to absorb information about people. I'd be willing to bet that he knew more about more people than anybody else in his class. He'd talk with you for ten minutes and he'd remember where you were from, what you liked and didn't like, who you were dating and whether you were pinned, whether you'd had a dog as a kid and what its name was. It wasn't always apparent at the time, but some of the things he knew about you - things he got pleasure from knowing - were things you'd rather he didn't know."

"I think you're suggesting that maybe he was in the habit of collecting other people's problems. Is that fair?"

"Oh, yes. What's the German for it? Schadenfreude, I think."

Carol remembered a college professor who had added the word to her vocabulary because he had used it so often. Deriving pleasure from someone else's misfortune.

"Was Franklin in the habit of gossiping about other people's problems? What shall we call it - spreading the dirt?"

"That's a hard one to answer. It was more like he had a tendency to file the dirt away for future use."

"And I take it that he sometimes *did* make use of such information?"

"Let's just say that he was capable of doing so," was Bickle's answer.

Carol realized that she had just heard a motive for Pierce's murder.

"You were going to tell me something about the alumni group that you and several others shared with Franklin, the ones that cruised with him in the Caribbean. May we go back to your undergraduate years. How did you all get together?"

"At the time," Bickle said, "there was no plan for anything like a reunion. I doubt that Pierce had given any thought to it. Most of the relationships among us were no more than 'hi, how're you doing.' I barely knew him, then one day he cornered me and asked if I'd heard about Betty Rasmussen. She's now Betty Craig. Seems that she'd been hauled before the disciplinary committee for plagiarism in a Lit class he was also taking. Plagiarism was pretty common, and this was even before Wikipedia made it easy. Anyway, Betty got off lightly - failed that course but no other punishment. Ironic, isn't it? I was just getting to know Franklin, because of an econ class we were taking, and then, thanks to him, I knew something about another member of what would be our traveling alumni group."

Carol had interviewed the Craigs only two days earlier, and her conversation with them was still fresh in her mind. She was sure that Stuart had said that Betty's only class with Pierce had been in chemistry. But Bickle had just said that she and Pierce had been in a Lit class together and that she had plagiarized a paper in that class. Carol made a quick mental note to give this contradiction some more thought. Meanwhile, Bickle was going on.

"But about how we *all* got together. As I remember it, I got a letter from Franklin one day about seven years ago. It was a hand-lettered invitation on some pretty fancy stationary - sort of rose colored, I think it was. I don't remember the exact wording, but it was something to the effect that I was invited to attend a real reunion, not the kind of mass affair SU stages every year. No names were mentioned, but it was clear that I wasn't the only one to get an invitation. The affair was to take place in Key West over Labor Day weekend, no rain date."

"Sounds like one of those unsolicited phone calls that tell you you've been selected for a free week in the Bahamas."

"That's pretty much how I saw it, except it said nothing about being free. I'd probably have stuffed it in the wastebasket if I hadn't had a phone call from Harry Pringle. Do you remember him from the memorial service? We'd known each other fairly well at university. To my surprise, he was interested in Franklin's idea, said he'd been in touch with him and gotten some more information. We still didn't know how Franklin had made up his list, but apparently it included about 15 alums, both men and women. Between us, Harry and I knew about half of them. Anyway, Franklin had told Harry that it was time his friends - that was his word - got reacquainted, and no better way to do it than to schedule an occasional trip together."

"Franklin's friends, yet you weren't really a friend," Carol commented.

"You're right, but it wasn't my list, and if Franklin wanted to see me as a friend, so be it. Harry talked me into giving it a shot, and damned if it wasn't more fun than I expected it to be. I don't remember how many took the trip to Key West; not many, maybe six or seven. But word got around and the next time there were quite a few more."

"Why do I have a feeling that interest in these little junkets is now waning?"

"Because it is. The membership has always fluctuated, but I guess that what once looked like a clever idea now seems rather stale."

"Stale? Or have the members come to realize that they aren't really that close?"

John Bickle had been ready to take another mouthful of quiche, but put his fork down and smiled.

"You're right. Were we that obvious?"

"I've talked to some of your colleagues - Roger Edgar, Bess Stevens, the Craigs - and I expect to be seeing everyone before long. Predictions may be dangerous in a case like this, but I suspect that had Mr. Pierce lived the next trip would be one of the more poorly attended. Of course now that he's dead, there probably won't be any more 'reunions.'"

"I think that's a safe bet."

"You've indicated that Franklin may have derived some pleasure from other people's problems. Like maybe Mrs. Craig's plagiarism in a Lit class. By the way, are you sure it was a Lit course?"

"Quite sure."

"Could you identify any of Franklin's other 'friends' as people whose problems gave him pleasure?"

"Oh, yes. I mentioned Harry Pringle, who urged me to take the trip to Key West. He's the best example of what I'm talking about. Harry fell in love with a coed at Syracuse, name of Terry Barkley. I never knew the girl, but according to Harry she was the real thing. Trouble is that she was what you'd call a very proper young woman, someone who wasn't about to put herself in a compromising position. The way Harry tells it, she took her virginity seriously. Very seriously. And Harry, he was so crazy about her that I guess you could say he took a vow of celibacy. Then Pierce entered the picture, and one night when Harry and his girl were at a frat party Franklin suggested that the time was right for them to slip up the stairs for a good make out session. He was drunk, of course, and he made a bad situation worse by telling the girl about Harry's bedroom escapades. That was Harry's last date with the love of his life."

"I can't imagine why Mr. Pringle wanted to accept Pierce's invitation to go to Key West. Or any place else."

"Apparently Franklin had apologized profusely. I'm sure Harry never forgave him, but he probably wanted to get close enough to him to see what made him such an s.o.b."

"Nobody was effusive at the memorial," Carol said, "but Pringle's remarks struck me as perhaps the most respectful."

"I wouldn't take what he said at face value."

"How about the others that were on the cruise?"

"You said you've talked with Bess Stevens. Now there's a weird case. She and Franklin are both gay, but wonder of wonders, he claims to have dated her once back at 'Cuse. She doesn't deny it, but he's the one who's milked it for laughs. I've never discussed it with Bess, but I'm sure she wishes he'd shut up. And now he has."

Carol had, of course, heard this from Bess herself.

As it turned out, this pretty much exhausted Bickle's theory that Pierce's 'group' was related to his desire to enjoy an advantage over his 'friends.' He talked about one or two of the others, but his stories didn't really reinforce his point.

Carol hadn't gotten around to quizzing Bickle about where he and his wife had spent the day in Barbados before he 'discovered' that he had to be getting back to Skaneateles. They had had a long discussion, not to mention a leisurely lunch, but the sudden need to hit the road struck Carol as unnecessarily urgent. No matter, she said to herself as they said good-bye. She would be talking to John Bickle again. Perhaps several times.

While she cleared the luncheon table, Carol reflected on what she had learned. It was obvious that she had much to think about, even to share with Inspector Williams. But she didn't sleep well that night, and the reason wasn't what Bickle had told her but Bickle himself.

CHAPTER 42

Abbey Lipscomb finished unloading the groceries, closed the trunk of her car, and went to the mail box to retrieve what she was sure would be bills and catalogs, neither of which were welcome. She took what she found there into the kitchen and sat down at the kitchen table to sort things into piles, one to pay, the other to dispose of. There was only one item that didn't fall into one of those two categories. It was a postcard, and it was in dreadful shape, so badly smudged and streaked as to be basically illegible. Why had it been delivered to her? Her name wasn't on it, nor was her address, only one or two words and a few letters and numbers that had not been wiped out or otherwise rendered unreadable. The same was true of the brief message on the opposite side of the card.

Curious, Abbey turned the card over. The picture was not in quite as bad shape as the address and message, and that was simply because it was easier to make out a photograph, however defaced, than it was someone's handwriting. She had no idea where the photo had been taken, but it contained what looked like a couple of palm trees and a strange form which had once been white and might have been a sailboat. Abbey guessed it was a tropical scene, perhaps an island. It was when 'island' occurred to her that she thought of Franklin and the cruise. Could what she was looking at be a postcard from him that had somehow been lost between the time it had been mailed and the time it showed up in her mail box many weeks later?

The stamp, too, was almost impossible to read, but it might be from the Caribbean. If the card had indeed been from Franklin, it would have been mailed from some island south of Fort Lauderdale. Abbey experienced a moment's excitement at the thought that she might be holding a posthumous message from Franklin in her hands. But that feeling vanished quickly. Even if he had written the card, how could the postal service possibly have figured out that she was its intended recipient?

Abbey tried to approach the postcard as if it were a coded message. She found a sheet of paper and set herself the task of writing out every letter that she was confident she could identify, spacing those letters as close to the way they appeared on the card as she could. Several minutes later, the paper looked like this.

Ab   mb
Bla   nt
E   ke   d
Y   er

"It's me!" she said aloud. "It's definitely me - Ab is for Abbey, and the 'mb' is the end of Lipscomb." She said the rest to herself. 'The next line could be Blalock Point, hence the 'nt' at the end. And once you've got that much, it's easy. It'll be East Lake Road, and then the key part of the address - Yates Center and the rest.'

As it turned out, this was the easy part of the puzzle, and she could not be sure that she had it right. But once started, Abbey was unable to stop. She tackled the message and was immediately aware that it would be much harder to decipher. Blocking out the lines and putting in the legible letters was relatively easy. Making sense of what they said and meant was something else. Her meticulous effort to copy the unreadable postcard revealed a patchwork message that looked like this.

Hi -This   t trip
if it we   erman
Why m   mned
diffic   n my
case si   uder-

dale, te	con-
signm	opics
are lovely	vely.
All the	

It meant absolutely nothing. There was only one thing to do. She would call the sheriff.

Unfortunately for Abbey, Carol was not in the office. When she returned an hour later, JoAnne passed the word that Abbey Lipscomb had called and had insisted that it was 'terribly important' that the sheriff return her call at the earliest possible moment.

"Did she say what it was about?" Carol asked.

"No, but she made it very clear that she had to talk with you immediately. She sounded excited, almost breathless."

"Okay. Give me a couple of minutes, then put her on."

It was as JoAnne had said. Abbey was indeed excited.

"Oh, thank you, thank you," she said. "I was afraid you had gone out of town. You'll think I'm crazy, but it's true. I just received a postcard from Franklin."

"You can't be serious."

"But I am. It must have been lost somewhere in the mail, and it was so illegible that the postal service would have had a hard time figuring out what to do with it."

"Losing mail's been known to happen, Abbey. Where was it sent from?"

"I have no idea. Like I said, it's almost unreadable."

"When does the postmark say it was mailed?"

"I can't read that either. At first I didn't think it even had a postmark."

Carol was beginning to feel some of Abbey's frustration.

"How about the message? Can you read that ?"

"Not a single sentence, just a few words and a letter or two, same as my name and address. That's why I'm calling. I thought you'd be able to make sense of it."

"Abbey, let's just stop and think for a minute," Carol said, trying to make sense of what she was hearing. "If the postcard is so hard to read, how do you know it was intended for you? In fact, how do you know it's from Franklin?"

"I spent a long time working on it, like maybe it was in code. You know, trying to figure out what the words I couldn't read must have been. But I'm sure it was intended for me."

"The post office doesn't typically spend a lot of time trying to figure out illegible names and addresses, especially on a postcard. But I think I'd better have a look at it. Are you going to be at home so I could come by?"

"I wish you'd come over. I won't go anywhere."

"Good. I'll be there within the hour."

Carol had a feeling that Abbey was all worked up over nothing. But she could hardly dismiss her. It was even possible that this illegible postcard from heaven know's whom and knows where could be relevant to the Pierce case, much as she doubted it.

When she finally held the postcard in her hand, the sheriff knew at once that Abbey was probably right that the card was intended for her. After all, Abbey had the advantage of guessing that her own name and address might be among the various letters on the card. How the postal service had figured it out, or why it had even tried, was another matter. But the message, or what there was of it, was another matter. It told Carol absolutely nothing. She knew that she would be spending the evening trying to decipher it, but she was doubtful that she would be able to do so.

Her greatest disappointment, however, was the condition of the stamp. That portion of the card was almost black. If only she could identify the island which had issued the stamp, she'd be in a better position to know whether the card had been written by Pierce. She had never been particularly interested in stamps, and personally knew no philatelists. But she remembered that someone had once told her that an octogenarian who lived on the far outskirts of West Branch was something of an authority on stamps. She couldn't remember the name, but thought it likely that she could find him. When she left Abbey, she took with her the postcard and a promise to give some serious thought to the garbled message. Then she set off for West Branch, where someone would be sure to know who the old stamp collector was and where he lived.

The third person she asked was a young boy who looked to be about twelve. He turned out to be a budding stamp collector who was a friend of 'Uncle' McDermott, who had apparently encouraged his hobby as a philatelist.

"Uncle Mac knows everything about stamps," the boy said. "He even has some from places that don't exist anymore."

His place of residence identified, Carol drove about two miles north of town and located the McDermott homestead down a dirt road not far south of *The Cedar Post*.

Uncle Mac was not only home. He was sitting on the porch, bundled up in a big sheepskin jacket, a large pipe clenched between his teeth. He watched the police car as it approached, and when Carol shut off the engine he leaned over the porch rail and knocked the ashes from the pipe.

"What can I do for you, officer?" he asked in a surprisingly strong voice.

"I don't believe we've ever met," she said, stepping out of the car. "I'm Carol Kelleher, and I'm the sheriff in these parts."

"I hope you aren't here to arrest me."

"Now why would I want to do that? No, I'm here because I understand you collect stamps."

"Well, that I do. You, too?"

"I'm afraid not. Mind if I come up on the porch?"

"Excuse my manners, Ms. Come right on up."

Carol knew this might take more than a few minutes, so she helped herself to a seat. Uncle Mac resumed his seat beside her.

"This is a funny question, and quite frankly I don't expect you to be able to answer it. But I have a postcard that's been pretty badly disfigured. The stamp's almost impossible to read. I thought if anyone around here would have an idea of where it's from, it would be you."

She produced the postcard and settled back to watch his reaction.

"Where'd you get this?" he asked.

"It was delivered to somebody here on the lake. She's stumped, and so am I."

"Mind if I get my magnifying glass?" he asked and went into the house without waiting for her answer.

Back in his chair, the veteran collector proceeded to study the blackened stamp that had paid for the card's journey to Abbey Lipscomb's mailbox.

For close to ten minutes he made no sound other than an occasional 'um' or 'oh.' Finally he put glass and postcard in his lap and shrugged his shoulders.

"No collector I know of would touch it," he said. "Of course if an expert was sure it was an inverted Jenny, that would be something else, but this is no Jenny. It looks to me like something a tourist in one of those Caribbean islands would stick on a 'wish you were here' message to someone back home. But I don't specialize in things like that, and even if I did I'd be guessing at who issued it. Want a guess?"

"I'd love one."

"Okay, maybe St. Lucia or Antigua. But like I said, that would be a guess."

"Any chance it could be Barbados?" Carol asked.

Uncle Mac shrugged again.

"Could be. Probably not. How did something in this condition ever get delivered? Most mail carriers would just drop it in the nearest trash can."

It was about what Carol had expected. And it still left her with a task which looked comparably impossible: deciphering the message on the card.

CHAPTER 43

Abbey herself had figured out that the postcard had in fact been addressed to her, although how a postal clerk had determined that remained a mystery. In all probability the card had not been rendered illegible until late in its journey to Crooked Lake, and some clerk had chosen to treat its condition as a challenge. No matter. Abbey had received the card, found its message indecipherable, and turned it over to the sheriff in the hope that she could discover who the sender was and what his message had been.

That one of the Syracuse alums, probably Pierce, had written and posted the card seemed almost certain. Abbey had been unable to think of anyone else, other than a few family relatives who weren't close, who could possibly have written the card, and given the fact that 'the group' had recently been on a cruise, its members were easily the most promising candidates, and Franklin by far the most likely. Something like the Enigma code would have been way out of her league, but Carol had the feeling that this postcard from some tropical location would be another matter. It was with a feeling of cautious optimism that when she got home she poured a glass of Chardonnay and sat down on the couch with the postcard and a yellow pad in front of her.

The letters that she could read were on the left and right hand edges of the message; the middle of the message was pretty much a black smudge. A few of the letters were grouped in such a way as to make recognizable words, primarily on the left hand side of the postcard. She listed them on her pad: Hi, This, trip, if, it, we, why, my, case, lovely, All, the. But there were places where a word was suggested by a grouping of letters which did not by themselves constitute a word. Three came to mind on her first attempt to make sense of things: diffi was probably difficult, consignm obviously consignment, and opics almost certainly tropics. Assuming that she was right about these words, the card had certainly been written by Franklin, who would have been thinking about his consignment shop, even while cruising in the Caribbean, and something - the shop? - was in some kind of difficulty or perhaps posing a difficult problem.

Carol was encouraged by where this was taking her, but she wasn't there yet.

Then another word popped into her mind, another hyphenated word: Lauderdale. Yes, the trip had begun in Ft. Lauderdale, but what did that tell her that she didn't already know? The two lines that were most puzzling were the second and third. What word ended in erman? And what was the question beginning with Why? Regarding the word, German made no sense. She started going through the alphabet and came immediately to Herman. Somebody's name? Carol closed her eyes and there it was: Westerman.

She went back to what she had learned so far, and quickly decided that 'we' wasn't one of the words - 'if, it, we' aren't used together like that. How about 'if it weren't'? Suddenly the beginning of the message was clear. 'This would have been a great trip if it weren't for Westerman.'

Carol put the yellow pad down and refilled her glass of Chardonnay. A few more minutes of cogitation and she had decided that the 'why' sentence became a question regarding Jim Westerman's behavior, a question which would have something to do with the consignment shop.

An hour after tackling the garbled message, Carol thought she had it. Or most of it.

> Hi - This would have been a great trip
> if it weren't for Westerman.
> Why must he be so damned (?)
> difficult? He's been on my
> case since we left Ft. Lauder-
> dale, telling me (something about) the con-
> signment shop. Otherwise (?) the tropics
> are lovely and the ship (?) lively.
> All the best, Franklin

Carol was confident that Franklin had dropped Abbey a postcard from some stop between Ft. Lauderdale and Barbados, lamenting the fact that Jim Westerman had been a problem, and that the problem had to do with *Upstate Consignments.* She was sure that it wasn't the consignment shop per se that was the problem, but rather the corner of it that was to be devoted to the contributions of the Syracuse alumni group. And just what was Westerman's problem with the display of the group's treasures? Franklin didn't say, perhaps because there wasn't room on the postcard. Or was it because Abbey would know what the problem was?

Carol knew what she had to do next. She had to revisit the boxes which she had brought back from *Upstate Consignments.* She was particularly interested in everything with Jim Westerman's name on it. Some of the alumni group had contributed nothing. No one had contributed much. Westerman's contribution, she remembered, had consisted of a framed photograph and three books, all in hard cover and a paper dust jacket, each bearing his name in large capital letters: *The Mohican Boy, The Loyalists and the Iroquois,* and *The Frigate Compass.* She removed them from their box and opened them, one at a time, looking to see when they had been published and if the author had autographed them. Westerman's signature appeared in none of the books, but what caught Carol's attention was the fact that the earliest publication date was in *The Mohican Boy.* She wasn't sure why this surprised her until she remembered Kevin's story that he had seen copies of that book conspicuously displayed in Westerman's house on Otsego Lake. There had been no copies of the other two books. Strange. Wouldn't it be more likely that the author would have his latest book on the coffee table rather than one that had been published years earlier? She checked the dates of publication again and noted that none of the books bore a recent date. Westerman had apparently stopped writing years ago and for some reason had chosen to give pride of place to his first literary effort.

There was nothing in the thin file of correspondence between Pierce and Westerman which offered any clue to the difficulty they seemed to have experienced on the cruise. Carol might have dismissed it as a minor matter of no consequence except for the important fact that Pierce had been killed only a few days at most after the card had been written and that Westerman was a person of interest in the case. She thought it unusual that Franklin had spent most of a six line message on an issue that had nothing to do with the pleasures of the cruise. Perhaps Abbey would be aware of whatever issue the two members of the group had been arguing about and Franklin would have known that she would be interested in an update. Perhaps it was only a reflection of the difficult personality of the only member of the group who had been on the cruise but had not bothered to attend the memorial service.

She would talk with Abbey again about Westerman, but chances were that the only feature of the postcard that was worth thinking or talking about was that Abbey had even received it.

CHAPTER 44

It was now obvious that Carol would have to meet Jim Westerman. Such a meeting would have been a part of her schedule in any event, but it assumed new importance in view if the fact that Abbey had just received a long delayed postcard from Franklin Pierce that devoted most of its message to Westerman. Given his apparent reluctance to come to Crooked Lake, she would be driving to Cooperstown. But the fact that he had declined to attend the memorial service at Abbey's was nothing more than an excuse for her decision to meet him at his home. He had emerged as the most mysterious of the Barbados Eight, and, rightly or wrongly, she was convinced that she would get a better picture of the man if she could see him on his own turf.

He had been in the habit of ignoring Abbey's phone calls and letters, but she suspected that he would pick up the phone if the caller weren't someone he knew and wished to avoid. She doubted that he would know who Carol Kelleher was. The lack of a response to her first two efforts to reach him almost convinced her that she was wrong, that he was simply antisocial. It was on her third call that he picked up the phone. His voice betrayed some reluctance to be interrupted at whatever he was doing.

"Yes? This is Jim."

"Mr. Westerman, so glad to have reached you." Carol hurried through her introduction. "This is Carol Kelleher. We haven't met, but I've been tasked by the police in Barbados to speak with the members of the group who were on the cruise with Franklin Pierce back in the winter. I'm the sheriff in upstate New York who met with your colleagues at a recent memorial service for Mr. Pierce."

"I've heard of you. What is it you want?"

"Like I said, the Barbadian authorities have deputized me to help them solve Mr. Pierce's murder. I've talked with most of your partners on the cruise, but we haven't met yet. I would like to arrange to see you, and with that in mind I propose to come to Cooperstown at your early convenience. When might that be?"

Her question elicited nothing but silence, and for a brief moment Carol worried that Westerman was debating whether to hang up.

"What is it that we need to talk about?" he finally asked.

"They - that is the police in Barbados - need to find out what Mr. Pierce's traveling companions know about his whereabouts, his plans for the day when you were all in Barbados. Unfortunately, they are down there and you are up here, so it seems to be my lot to do the interviewing. As I said, I would like to come up to Cooperstown and meet with you."

Another silence.

"When did you have in mind?" It was a grudging way to say that, at least in principle, it might be something he'd consider.

"As soon as possible, Mr. Westerman. They've been pestering me for a report, and I think they're afraid that their case against a suspect in Barbados will suffer if I don't hurry up."

"I see." He paused, perhaps to consult his calendar. "I think I could make it tomorrow evening, or if that doesn't work possibly the next day. It would have to be after five, you know."

Carol didn't know, but she was willing to accommodate Westerman's work schedule.

It was finally agreed that she would make the trip the next day and arrive at the address he gave her sometime around seven o'clock. The arrangement necessitated an overnight stay in a local motel. Westerman mentioned two, the phone numbers of which she took down.

Less than half an hour after her conversation with Westerman, another of the alumni group called her.

"Hello, sheriff. This is Stuart Craig. Surely you remember me." Indeed she did. Was her role in the Pierce case suddenly gaining momentum?

"Hello, Mr. Craig. What can I do for you?"

"I've thought of something I should have mentioned when you talked with Betty and me. I'd like to come over and discuss it with you."

"I appreciate your call. Why don't you tell me what this is about."

"I'd rather not do it over the phone. Could I come over tomorrow? You name the place, your office or your home."

"Of course we can meet here, but unfortunately I'll be out of town the next two days. How about Friday or this weekend?"

Craig sounded disappointed.

"Well, of course. I thought it might be important - that's why I mentioned tomorrow. Let's make it Friday."

Carol found it interesting that Craig was willing to take a day off from his classes at the high school to come to Crooked Lake. It might indeed be important, but so was her interview with Jim Westerman. In any event, she had now committed herself to meeting with two of the Barbados Eight, all in the space of three days.

———

Carol pulled up at 5:30 pm in front of the Cooperstown motel where she had made her reservation. She had remembered where Kevin had stayed and elected to stay there. She was tired from the drive. Given Westerman's directions, she was sure there would be enough time for a hot shower before heading up the shore of Otsego Lake to his home.

When she gave her name, the smile on the face of the young woman at the check-in counter broadened.

"Oh, yes, Ms. Kelleher. I have a message for you."

She produced a sealed envelope with Ms. Kelleher scrawled across it. Carol ripped it open and proceeded to read a short handwritten message.

Dear Sheriff: I am sorry to have to apologize for a slight change of plans. Fortunately, it shouldn't affect your schedule too much, inasmuch as you'll be staying overnight anyway. The problem is that I've been confronted with a minor emergency and have to leave town unexpectedly. I couldn't reach you because you were on the road and I didn't have your cell phone number. I shall be back tomorrow morning by at least 8 or 9. Thanks for your patience.

Jim Westerman

Carol's initial impulse was to be annoyed. But that wasn't fair. An emergency is an emergency. And he was quite right; her plans would hardly be much affected by the delay from 7 pm to 9 the following morning. Her shower would be more leisurely and her dinner both earlier and also more leisurely. She signed in, collected the key to her room, and set off down the corridor for the elevator to the second floor and room 22.

When she reached the old white house with the widow's walk, Westerman's car was already there, parked in the circular drive. She stopped behind it and was in the process of mounting the front steps when he opened the door and welcomed her.

"Good morning, sheriff. So sorry to have inconvenienced you like this. I appreciate your understanding of my dilemma."

"No problem at all, Mr. Westerman. I hope your emergency wasn't too serious."

"It wasn't as bad as it sounded when I got the call. All's well that ends well. All it cost me was a few hours of sleep and the opportunity to meet you last night. Come on in."

Carol followed him into the house. He escorted her to the living room, where Kevin had presumably sat with him when they had discussed opera and Westerman had lied about his knowledge of Pierce's death in Barbados.

"I haven't had time to do anything about breakfast, but I can offer you coffee and a sweet roll."

"Thanks, but I had breakfast at the motel. I would enjoy another cup of coffee, though. Black, no sugar."

"Fine. Just give me a minute."

Carol surveyed the Westerman abode, and was interested to see, as Kevin had, several copies of a book entitled *The Mohican Boy*.

"So, you are questioning Franklin Pierce's friends."

"I am, and it isn't the way I would choose to spend my time. But before I begin, I wish you'd take a look at this."

She pulled Inspector Williams' explanation of her role in the investigation from her pocket and handed it to him.

"This is the official Barbados document justifying my role in the case. I'm sure they wish I had more to report, but quite frankly most of your colleagues aren't able to recall with much precision just what they did while in Barbados."

She did not add that frequently the problem wasn't failure of memory but a preference for obfuscation.

"This paper says you were on the *Azure Sea* with the Syracuse alums. Now that's a real coincidence."

"It certainly is," Carol, who was skeptical of coincidences, agreed. "That's why I'm here. I have several questions, Mr. Westerman. Why don't I begin by asking you why you weren't at the memorial service for Franklin Pierce."

"Was my absence a major topic of conversation?"

"As a matter of fact it wasn't. I think most of the group assumed you wouldn't be there."

"Really. Well, I suppose I should have come, but frankly I'm not comfortable at these public grieving events. We should let the dearly departed rest in peace."

"Actually, there wasn't a lot of grieving going on at the memorial service. I have the impression that Mr. Pierce was not a close friend of many of your colleagues. Is that a fair assessment?"

"A close friend? No. We're an odd group. To the best of my knowledge we only see each other every couple of years when Franklin decides it's time to take another trip together. It's a matter of habit. I very much doubt that anyone is going to step up and take Franklin's place. I know that I don't intend to. I strongly suspect that we've taken our last trip."

It was a familiar refrain. Carol would have been surprised had Westerman said otherwise.

"Let's talk about Barbados. How did you spend your day there?"

"I'm sure you can appreciate that after a cruise with seven or eight island stops it's hard to remember what you did where."

"Of course, but let's try. How about highlights? What would you say was the most memorable sight?" Westerman had not said that he stayed on shipboard or simply spent his day shopping in Bridgetown.

"Well, I like rum, and like most of the islands rum is big there. I believe I spent most of my time in the places where they bottle the stuff and let you sample it."

Carol didn't like rum. She still found it hard to believe that Westerman had done no significant sightseeing.

"What about your colleagues? Any of them join you on your round of the rum shops?"

"No, and that's not unusual. Ask around and you'll get the same story. We tend to do our own thing."

"How about Pierce? What did he do that day?"

"No idea. In fact, I don't know where anybody else went when we left the ship. The last members of our group I saw were the Bickles, and they were still arguing about what they were going to do."

"How'd you get about? Hire a cab?"

"Of course. You're taking your life in your hands when you ride those crazy buses."

"I guess I was lucky. The bus driver I rode with was a jewel. By the way, what's the going rate for a taxi in Barbados?"

"I couldn't tell you. All those islands, every one has a different system. Considering that they've got the tourists at their mercy, prices aren't too bad."

"I heard a story - can't remember which island - that some guy shelled out a thousand bucks for a taxi."

Westerman's reaction was not that of a man who had heard of such a thing, much less done such a thing.

"That's got to be apocryphal," he said, laughing for the first time since the interview had begun.

"Getting back to Mr. Pierce," Carol said, changing the subject. "What's your opinion of that alumni display he was preparing for his consignment shop?"

"A truly dumb idea." He didn't sound vehement, but he was close.

"But you donated something to it, didn't you?"

"It would have been rude not to. But it's like our trips. There won't be any special display at *Upstate Consignments* now. Franklin was no businessman. Stand-up comedian maybe, but not a businessman."

Carol thought she could understand why Jim Westerman had skipped the memorial service. They talked for the better part of another hour, during which time she sought to flesh out her picture of him by inquiring about his college days, his life on Lake Otsego, and his career as a writer. Unexpectedly voluble for much of that time, Westerman was a different person when the conversation shifted to his novels. Even an attempt to discuss *The Mohican Boy,* copies of which lay proudly on the coffee table, failed. For some reason, his literary career was a sensitive subject.

Which left two questions. Why had he told Kevin that he didn't know that a passenger on the *Azure Sea* had been left behind in Barbados? What had he talked about with Pierce on the cruise that had prompted Franklin to comment on it in a postcard to Abbey Lipscomb? Carol knew that she couldn't ask the first question without giving away the fact that Kevin Whitman was more than an opera buff seeking information about Glimmerglass. The postcard was a different matter.

"I have another question about the display Mr. Pierce was planning for his consignment store. It is my understanding that you and he talked quite a bit about it on the cruise. Maybe talked is too mild a word. How about argued?"

"Where did you get an idea like that?" It was less a simple question than a challenge.

"From a postcard, a postcard that Pierce sent to Abbey Lipscomb."

"What did he say we were arguing about?"

"That's what I was going to ask you," said Carol, her voice in neutral.

"We weren't arguing about anything. I doubt that I talked with Franklin more than two or three times on the cruise, and we were in the Caribbean two weeks. It's possible that we disagreed about the food service or something, but I can assure you that we didn't argue."

"But the postcard was about the consignment shop, not the food service." Carol decided to hazard a guess. "Perhaps you were talking about your contribution to his display case."

Westerman managed an unpleasant laugh.

"As I have told you, my interest in that project was nil. I made a small contribution to humor him."

"And what was it that you contributed?"

It was apparent that Westerman wanted to bring this conversation to a conclusion.

"Please, Sheriff Kelleher. This is a silly subject. I gave him a photo or two, something from our yearbook, and even felt guilty doing it. Can you imagine anyone visiting a consignment store paying attention to things like that?"

"No, but you're an author. People might well be attracted to your books." Carol picked up a copy of *The Mohican Boy*. "Something like this."

"*Upstate Consignments* isn't a book store, sheriff."

"Whatever it is, three of your books were among the items Mr. Pierce had earmarked for his tribute to his Syracuse friends."

Any pretense that Jim Westerman was enjoying this meeting with the sheriff vanished.

"How would you know this?" he asked.

"I visited *Upstate Consignments* recently. And my reaction was much like yours: the tribute to Mr. Pierce's alumni friends struck me as a bad idea, a bad idea which I feel quite sure will never see the light of day."

"He never had my permission to use my books." Westerman's jaw was clenched when he said it.

Carol had come to that conclusion at last twenty minutes. earlier. She chose not to ask if that statement covered all three books or only the last two. After all, she already knew the answer.

CHAPTER 45

Carol's trip back to Crooked Lake was a case study in the erratic weather patterns which frequently occur in upstate New York between Lake Ontario and the Pennsylvania border. Cooperstown was enjoying bright blue skies. Oneonta, not that far to the south, was under a cloud cover and experiencing light rain. By the time she got to Binghamton, the sun had broken through. But just before Elmira the rain began again in earnest, and as she came within 30 miles of Crooked Lake it was what she thought of as a cloudburst. Windshield wipers going at maximum speed, it was still difficult to see the road for more than two or three car lengths ahead of her.

When she left Westerman's house, her mind had been sharply focussed on this strange man and his puzzling behavior, open and cooperative one minute, opaque and disingenuous the next. The last thirty miles of the trip necessitated full concentration on the road rather than on Westerman. She had planned to drive on to the office to see what had developed in her absence, but the storm had been tiring and she decided that everything would keep until the following morning. Instead she would make a pot of coffee and call Kevin.

She sat in the car for several minutes, hoping the rain would let up a bit. It didn't, but her neighbor, Mike Snyder, who had obviously seen her drive up, opened his back door and sprinted over to her car.

Carol opened the door and grabbed Mike by the elbow. He started to say something, but she beat him to it.

"Come on, we'll be soaked to the skin in a minute." She hustled him up the back steps, found the house key in her pocket, and held the door as they hurried into the kitchen.

"I've been watching for you. There's something -"

"First, off with your shoes," she said peremptorily. "Then we'll talk."

Mike was apparently used to his wife in cases like this. Two pair of shoes quickly lay side by side on a mat beside the door.

"The rest of me's wet, too," he said.

"No problem. I'm not asking you to strip to your skivvies. Just let me get some coffee started, and then you can tell me what this is all about."

Mike had a story to tell and was anxious to tell it, but he deferred to Carol. Coffee brewing, she was back from the kitchen in less than three minutes.

"Now, what is it that brings you out of a dry cottage and into this downpour?"

"Somebody tried to break into your cottage last night."

"Tried? I take it they didn't succeed."

"You're lucky. I'd been playing pinochle with some of the guys down the road and happened to drive up before he'd gotten in. The headlights picked him up when he was testing your dining room window, and I've never seen anyone high-tail it away so fast in my life."

"Nice timing. It sounds as if Kevin and I owe you one. Did you get a good look at him? Or his car?"

"Wish I could say yes, but it was raining sheets, just like it is now. He had a rain jacket on, but that's what you'd expect. He was driving a van of some kind, but it was parked behind the Brocks so I couldn't get a good look at it. Like I said, he was gone before I could confront him."

"Well, this is a first. We don't always even lock our doors. This time I did because I was going to be away two days. Maybe I should get some kind of alarm system - and lock up."

"That would be a good idea."

"I think I hear the coffee. Join me?"

"I'll take a pass if that's okay. But I thought you'd like to know."

My hero," Carol said as saw Mike out the door and back into the rain.

Had the burglar been successful, she'd immediately set about checking, room to room, to see what had been taken. But in view of Mike's timely arrival, they had survived without a loss. Kevin, no doubt, would be alarmed, more worried about her than about the household furnishings. And she would have to call Kevin. She had planned to call anyway to compare her visit with Westerman with his of a month before. Now she'd also be reporting on the failed break-in.

First, she needed to enjoy a cup of coffee and then get out of the clothes she'd been living in since the previous morning, clothes that were still slightly wet from the dash from the car to the cottage. That accomplished, she settled into Kevin's desk chair and made the call.

Fortunately, it was not a day when Kevin had an evening seminar. He would be at home. She good-naturedly revised that thought: he had better be at home.

"I was counting on a call," he answered. "What's new up there?"

"The time has come, the sheriff said, to talk of many things. And there seem to be many things to talk about this evening."

"Good, and I'm glad it's you, not the walrus."

"Let me begin with the weather. We're having a wild storm. In fact I drove through it for close to half the trip back from Cooperstown. It's been hammering this area for close to 24 hours. In fact, somebody took advantage of it last night to try to break into the cottage."

"I take that to mean that he didn't succeed."

"No. Mike Snyder surprised him, chased him off before he found a chink in our armor."

"Good thing you weren't there."

"Agreed. I always worry that one day I'll shoot somebody in a case like this only to find out he's simply lost and came to the wrong house."

"Oh, come on. You'd never do that. If they gave a prize for the least trigger happy cop in the country, you'd win in a walk."

"Anyway, that's not the important news. Westerman is. Like you, I found him to be a reasonable guy. Not someone who acts or sounds like a murderer, although I'm not exactly sure that's a very reliable test. By the way, when I got to Cooperstown there was a letter waiting for me at the motel. An emergency had called him away, and he had to postpone our interview until the next morning. No big deal - I was staying overnight anyway. But the trouble with Westerman is that he's got some issues, things he simply won't talk about. You caught him out in a lie - claiming not to know anything about Pierce's missing the boat in Barbados. So did I. He denied having a running argument with Pierce on the cruise, yet Pierce spent a whole postcard lamenting the fact that he did."

"You're referring to the lost postcard, right?"

"That's the one, and I doubt Pierce made it up. But the really interesting thing is Westerman's career as a writer. He talks freely about his book *The Mohican Boy.* But he wrote at least two others - they were at the consignment shop - and he acts as if they don't even exist."

"Maybe it's time we read one of them, see if we can figure out what the problem is. I'll volunteer for the assignment if you want me to."

"Your schedule is as full as mine is, but if you can find the time I'd be grateful."

"I'll make the time," Kevin said.

"On a more positive note, I do believe that my investigation of the Pierce case is gaining a bit of momentum. I'll be seeing Stuart Craig tomorrow. I'd just been over in Cortland talking with him and his wife, but he called and said he had something interesting to tell me. Something he'd forgotten to share with me. He wanted to come over yesterday, but I was going to Cooperstown and had to put him off. And I still haven't gotten around to meet with Pringle. The inspector must be getting impatient."

"I wouldn't be too worried. You're trying to police both Crooked Lake and Barbados. The inspector will understand."

"I hope so."

"Wait a minute," Kevin said, suddenly sounding excited. "I'm having one of my occasional brainstorms. I think you said that you were in Cooperstown last night and that both Westerman and Craig knew that's where you were. Right?"

"Not quite. Westerman did. Craig knew I was out of town, but I didn't say anything about where I'd be."

"Close enough. We both know that nobody's ever tried to burglarize us, don't we? Who'd want to steal from a small pedestrian cottage like ours? Hell, we rarely lock the doors. But what if the guy who was trying to break in when Snyder drove up wasn't really a burglar? Think about it."

"I'm thinking but I don't think I'm following you. I hope you aren't suggesting that Westerman and Craig were trying to break into the cottage."

"That's exactly what I'm saying. Well, not both of them. But it's possible. They both knew you wouldn't be home. Westerman could have manufactured his crisis so he could drive to Crooked Lake and get into the cottage. Craig could have seen an unexpected opportunity to do the same thing. Either one of them might have been interested in getting his hands on some of the things that Pierce was collecting for his crazy display case. Don't you see, one or maybe both of them knew or suspected that Pierce had something that could have been used to expose him as the killer, only now it was in your hands."

"Don't you think that that's a pretty far-fetched scenario? In the first place, how would they know that I had taken possession of whatever they were worried about? And what if I had? Why would they assume that it was in our cottage rather than the office? Besides, neither of them had ever been in the cottage, yet they found it in the middle of the night, a long way from where they lived, during a terrible rainstorm. One or both of them may have been anxious about something that tied them to Pierce, but why run such a risk given the circumstances?"

"I'm not saying that either one of them was the would-be burglar. But I think it's a real possibility. It wouldn't have been much of a problem to learn whether you had visited the consignment shop or where you lived. And both of them would know what 'evidence' Pierce might have had which would be threatening."

"Forgive my skepticism, but we don't even know whether Pierce had what you call threatening evidence. Given what I've learned in talking with both of them, there doesn't seem to be any. Or at least I haven't found it."

"Precisely. You haven't found it. What have you been looking for in Pierce's files?"

"If you're asking if I've found a smoking gun, the answer is no. I've been concerned with how they've responded to Franklin's request for contributions to his special display. And surely no one, Westerman and Craig included, is going to have given him something that puts a target on their back."

"Well, if I were you, I'd go through those files again. If I were there, I'd do it for you."

"You'd do it *with* me, Kevin," Carol said, reminding him that she was Inspector Wiliams' partner, not him. "Okay. You've talked me into it. I'll do it. I'll dig into the files again, and I'll make inquiries as to whether anyone has been asking questions about the whereabouts of those files. In the meanwhile, I'll be seeing Stuart Craig again tomorrow, and I promise to keep my antennae up. I doubt that he'll be admitting that he tried to break in to our cottage."

"What's your best guess as to why he's so anxious to see you?"

"I'm not in the mood to guess. I suspect that what he has in mind won't be as dramatic as he suggests, but I can't imagine what it will be."

"Neither can I. Do me a favor, will you? Lock the doors and don't shoot until you can see the whites of their eyes."

CHAPTER 46

Kevin's idea that Westerman or Craig - perhaps both - had paid visits to their cottage on Blue Water Point while she was in Cooperstown engaged her attention for awhile, but by the time she was ready for bed she had dismissed it as unrealistic. Not that she would banish it completely from her mind. Things could happen, things could be said, which would give it a new lease on life, but for the time being she would focus on other matters.

One of those other matters was whatever it was that Stuart Craig had forgotten to tell her when she had interviewed him and his wife. Another was Harry Pringle, the only member of the Barbados Eight other then Bickle's wife with whom she had not yet had a private conversation. A third was a discussion with Inspector Williams in which she would report on her lack of progress and he, hopefully, would let her know that his investigation was making serious headway. Finally, she would resume her search for Franklin Pierce's lawyer and the will he had either drafted or not been asked to draft.

Her first order of business would be Stuart Craig, for the simple reason that he was already on her calendar. Perhaps what he had to tell her might stimulate some thought as to where she could most profitably go next. Otherwise she would get in touch with Pringle and arrange for another road trip, this time to the place where it had all begun back in college days, Syracuse.

Carol had expected to fall asleep easily that night. After all, what with the long drive and the incessant rain, it had been a very tiring day. But it didn't happen. Sometimes, she decided, one can be too tired to sleep. Or perhaps Kevin's suggestion was harder to shake off than she had expected. The most likely explanation for sleeplessness, however, was a persistent feeling that there was something about Jim Westerman that just didn't ring true. She had been aware, even as she told Kevin that he hadn't acted or sounded like someone who could be a murderer, that she still knew less about him than she did any of the other members of the SU alumni group.

It was barely 7:15 the next morning, and Carol was both trying to wake up and poach an egg. The telephone rang so unexpectedly that she almost lost the slotted spoon on the floor.

"Good morning" was all she could manage.

"Sheriff Kelleher? This is Stuart Craig. I'm very sorry to bother you so early, but we had agreed to get together today and I wanted to make sure you were back from your trip and see if we could set a time."

"Yes, Mr. Craig. I haven't forgotten. I'm just making breakfast, and had planned to give you a call sometime around nine. Do you have a scheduling problem?"

"No, but inasmuch as I'll be driving from Cortland I need to know when you will be expecting me."

"Of course." She did some quick thinking. How long would it take him to make the trip? How much time would there be to stop at the office before meeting him? "What if we make it noon at my cottage?"

"That's fine," Craig said, although his tone of voice suggested that he'd prefer an earlier hour. Cortland wasn't next door to Crooked Lake, so she pictured him as already dressed and raring to go.

He had made inquiries, apparently of Abbey Lipscomb, so he already knew where the sheriff's cottage was located. The town whistle down in Southport had just announced that it was noon when he reached Blue Water Point. The rain had stopped hours earlier, but the ground was still soaked and the sky looked as if another storm could not be ruled out.

"Good morning, Mr. Craig," Carol said as she ushered him into the cottage. "Excuse me, I think it just turned afternoon. How was the drive? No washouts, I hope."

"A lot of standing water, but it wasn't bad. How about you?"

"As you can see, I made it. The people who track these things will probably be telling us the lake level rose a few inches. Come on in and have a seat. Coffee?"

"Sounds good. Nice place you have here."

"Nothing fancy, but it keeps us happy."

"You're married?"

Craig sounded surprised.

"It helps us officers of the law maintain perspective. Let me get you your coffee. How do you like it?"

"Black, but lots of sugar."

Preliminaries out of the way, Stuart Craig began to explain his reason for being in the sheriff's living room with a caveat.

"You've wanted us to tell you what we could about what happened on Barbados. You know, where we went, did we see Franklin Pierce that day, things like that. I did the best I could, and then it occurred to me that maybe I'd approached your questions too narrowly. You've got a tough job, trying to recreate a situation when you don't know any of us. So I put myself in your shoes and gave some thought to how I might be able to help you other than telling you that I never saw Pierce that day. Would I be right that you'd welcome more information?"

It wasn't clear what kind of information Craig had in mind, but the obvious answer was yes. It might be important. It was more likely to be inconsequential.

"In my job, more information is always better than less."

"Okay, but let me begin by saying that I am not accusing anybody of anything. But what I have in mind has to do with some of our relationships with Franklin. Or one relationship in particular. I don't know whether you have talked with Harry Pringle yet."

"No, I haven't, but I expect to within the next few days."

"I'm sure he won't share with you what I want to talk about, and I think you'll understand why. Harry's a nice guy, a real prince, but he had a terrible experience back when he was in college and I don't think he's ever gotten over it. I know this because we were friends in school. The alumni group that Franklin put together, we're superficially friendly but none of us is really close. Harry and I are an exception. Or at least we were. Harry's problem is a girl."

Craig paused and smiled, a sad smile.

"Lots of us have girl problems at that age," he continued. "Someone we've fallen in love with latches onto another guy, ditches us, you understand. It happened to Harry, but it wasn't the girl's fault. Or his. He'd fallen in love with this girl, a good kid who wasn't into what they now call hooking up. Guys liked to brag about their conquests, probably still do. But not Harry; he actually seemed proud that he was respecting her virginity. Unfortunately, Pierce, a fraternity brother of Harry's, got drunk at a party that Harry and this girl were attending and told her Harry'd had sex with other girls right there in the frat house. That was their last date. He took it real hard. I guess anyone would."

Stuart Craig had assumed that he was sharing information that would be new to the sheriff. He was wrong. John Bickle had also told her about Pringle's great love affair and the cruel way in which Franklin Pierce had terminated it. If Bickle and Stuart Craig knew about it, it seemed entirely possible that the rest did as well. If what Craig had said was true, Pringle himself had willingly shared his misfortune with others. If so, the likelihood that Pierce's role in this romantic tragedy gave Pringle a motive for murder lost some of its credibility. People don't usually go around killing people after they have so casually made clear what their motive for doing so is.

There didn't seem to be any reason not to disappoint Craig by telling him that he had driven all the way from Cortland to tell the sheriff what she already knew. However, she was interested in *his* motive. He had insisted that he was not accusing anyone - obviously not Pringle - of killing Pierce. But what was he doing?

"Mr. Craig, I appreciate that you have taken the trouble to come to Crooked Lake to share this information with me. But I must tell you that I was already aware that Mr. Pringle was deeply in love with this woman - I believe her name is Terry Barkley - and that their relationship came to an end after Franklin Pierce was so appallingly indiscreet. It seems not to be much of a secret. Why did you assume that it would be?"

Craig was clearly distressed to hear this.

"As I told you, we were friends and I suppose I assumed that it was the kind of thing he'd only share with friends."

"You were right to share something you thought might help my investigation. I'm sure there are other things I should know, things that pertain to your alumni group. Now that we're having this conversation, why don't you think about what else you may know that might help me."

"I'm afraid I can't think of anything else."

"No episodes, nothing that would help me better understand your colleagues from the cruise?"

He shook his head.

"Nothing comes to mind."

"That's too bad." Carol wasn't so sure that nothing had come to Craig's mind. John Bickle had told her about what Pierce had done to Pringle's relationship with Terry Barkley. He had also told her that Pierce had tipped him off to Betty Craig's case of plagiarism. It was inconceivable that Stuart didn't know about this as well.

Craig set off on his return trip to Cortland regretting that he had treated it as a sick day and missed his classes.

Chapter 47

It was Carol's intention to place a call to Harry Pringle as soon as Stuart Craig had driven off, but before she found his number her phone rang. Much to her surprise it was Inspector Williams from Barbados.

"Hello, Sheriff Kelleher. Your office told me to try you at your home. I'm sorry to bother you when you're off duty, but they said you'd have no objection."

"Hello to you, inspector. The truth is that I'm not only on duty, I have just finished a meeting with one of Franklin Pierce's colleagues from the cruise. What I've been doing for you on the Pierce case isn't technically part of my job for Cumberland County, so I work at home as much as I can. I hope that you're calling with good news."

"I hope so, but this is just a progress report. Do I dare ask if you've learned anything that's important?"

"I'm not ready to say yes, but I have learned some things about the relationship between Mr. Pierce and some of the people who were with him in Barbados. One or two of them could be important. I've been telling myself that it's time for my progress report, but I'd rather get it into some kind of order first, so let's focus on your report today."

"Fair enough. What I have to tell you concerns the things that were in Mr. Pierce's shipboard cabin."

Carol had a sudden pang of conscience.

"I hope you'll forgive me, but I'd completely forgotten about that."

"Don't worry, so had I. The cruise company brought it to my attention a couple of weeks ago. They knew about Mr. Pierce's disappearance during the cruise, of course, and we've been in touch with them to let them know he was dead. But frankly I hadn't been interested in what he had with him in his cabin on the *Azure Sea*, so it slipped my mind until the company informed me that they couldn't locate any family or relatives who'd want his things. I'm not exactly sure where they store suitcases that get left on their ships, but they were anxious to get rid of Pierce's. Not sure whether it was protocol or guess work, but they contacted me. We considered telling them to trash everything, but the cost of having it sent to Bridgetown wasn't prohibitive so that's what we did."

"I take it you found something that's interesting."

"Maybe. His personal belongings won't be of any use, but there's something that may be. You know those photos a ship's photographer takes of every passenger when they first board a cruise ship? They post them when they're developed and most of them become souvenirs that get taken home. Fairly expensive, but once you've paid for a week or two at sea it's doesn't seem like much."

Carol knew what he was talking about. She and Kevin had bought their 'welcome aboard' shots, having decided that they looked pretty good for a middle aged couple.

"I have no idea who among the group took photos home with them, but Pierce had a photo of every one of his traveling companions in his suitcase. So for the first time I had a chance to see what these people actually looked like. The pictures are good - very clear. They give you a good sense of height, weight, features. Most of them look happy, as if they're looking forward to the trip. There are no names on the photos so I'm in no position to say who's who. So I need your help."

"Of course. Just let me know what I can do."

"I've shown the photos to Moses King. He's the man who took a thousand dollars to let a man borrow his taxi. I've spent a couple of sessions with him, trying to get him to tell me whether any of the men in the photos resemble the man who borrowed the taxi. At first he said it was none of them, and that may be the truth. After all, at this point there's no way of knowing whether one of Pierce's colleagues did it. It could have been any one of dozens of other tourists. But I had him give it another try, and this time he wasn't so sure. There's something about the way he reacts when he's looking at some of the photos that makes me think he could pick one of them. He knows I'm really on his case, that he'll be looking at those photos until he's got a migraine. I'm going to send you a copy of every photo, together with my thoughts on his reaction. You'll recognize who they are, and you'll know something about them and their relationship with Pierce. If we're lucky, this damn case may be closer to a solution."

"I'm not going to assume we're almost there, but I'll be waiting for the photos and I'll get back to you with my comments right away. At the very least this should give me another perspective as I talk with Pierce's so-called friends. I'm afraid I've been loathe to call any of them suspects."

"It still bothers me that I've roped you into this assignment, sheriff, but we can hardly turn back now, can we? Good luck."

Carol wasn't optimistic. She was concerned that Moses King would finally decide to whom he had loaned his taxi just to please the inspector and get him off his back. She immediately regretted the thought. The inspector was too smart to be fooled like that. Nonetheless she looked forward to receiving the photos and soon found herself speculating as to whom King would have fingered as the most likely to have paid him a thousand dollars for the privilege of a few hours use of his cab.

Chapter 48

In view of what Stuart Craig and John Bickle had told her, Carol badly needed to hear Harry Pringle's version of what proved to be his final date with the love of his life, Terry Barkley. Yet setting up an appointment with him proved to be more difficult than she had imagined it would be.

When she finally reached someone at the Pringle residence in Syracuse, it turned out to be his wife.

"This is Dorothy. How may I help you?"

"Hello, Mrs. Pringle. This is Sheriff Kelleher, and I'm trying to reach your husband."

"You're calling about the Pierce case?"

"That's right."

"Well, I'm afraid he's not here at the moment. There have been some problems down at the plant, and he's part of a team that's been working overtime to straighten things out. His hours have been a bit strange lately."

"But you do expect him back this evening?" Carol doubted that a 'problem down at the plant' would necessitate Harry's spending the night in his office.

"I think so, but I couldn't tell you when. Can I take a message?"

For some reason Carol had the impression that Mr. Pringle might not be coping with a problem down at the plant. Which, of course, was silly. Why would his wife go to the trouble of making up a story like that?

But some sixth sense was telling Carol that Mrs. Pringle was - what *was* she doing? Covering for her husband? Buying him time?

"As he may have told you, I have been asked by the police down in Barbados to talk with all of the people who accompanied Franklin Pierce on the recent Caribbean cruise. My colleague in Bridgetown is very anxious for me to report on what I have learned, and I can't give him a complete report until I talk with Mr. Pringle. I am not asking him to take the time to drive down to Crooked Lake, where I live and work. I will come up to Syracuse, and I need to do it very soon. Why don't we make it this Sunday? I'm sure your husband will not be expected to spend Sunday at the plant. I'd appreciate it if you would let him know that I will be there, let's say at one o'clock. If for any reason that should be impossible, please ask him to call me back this evening." She gave Mrs. Pringle the number and assured her that she already knew their address and how to get there.

Carol placed the odds that Harry Pringle would call back at about fifty-fifty. When she retired for the night at 10:30 he had not returned her call. She would be hitting the road again, missing church once more on Sunday.

The Pringle house was an attractive one, apparently recently remodeled, in a hilly section of town not far from a golf course. Two cars were parked in the driveway. A slender auburn-haired woman was in the process of pruning back old wood on her hydrangeas. She looked up when the police car came to a stop at the curb, but didn't stop pruning until Carol had left the car and walked to the front steps.

"Hello," Carol said, using what she thought of as her cheerful voice. "I'm the sheriff, here for my meeting with your husband. Should I go on in?"

"I'd ring first, just in case he's upstairs in his study."

Mrs. Pringle wasn't exactly unpleasant, but she was making no effort to be welcoming.

Mr. Pringle was not upstairs in his study. He was in the living room, reading the Sunday paper.

"It's me, Sheriff Kelleher," she said as she caught his attention. "Thanks for taking the time to see me."

"Rumor has it that you're making the rounds of our SU group, so I knew I'd be on your calendar sooner or later."

"Actually I had planned to have had this meeting earlier, but something always seemed to get in the way."

Pringle gathered up the sections of the paper, some of which were on the floor, and motioned the sheriff to a seat.

"I presume you want me to tell you just what I did when we were in Barbados. John Bickle gave me a heads up on what I think is called your modus operandi."

"That's strikes me as too fancy a term for simply asking questions. I'll get around to what you did in Barbados, but let's first talk about something else. It is my understanding that you and Franklin Pierce had a rather unpleasant experience when you were both undergraduates at Syracuse. I'd like to hear your version of it."

"I'm not sure what you're talking about," Pringle said. Carol was certain that he knew exactly what she was talking about.

"How did you happen to know Mr. Pierce in college?"

Pringle frowned at this change of subject.

"We didn't really know each other."

"Maybe not well, but you knew him. I doubt that he would have invited you to become part of the traveling alumni group if you were complete strangers. So how did you know each other?"

"We were just fraternity brothers." Pringle made it sound as if fraternity brothers were like ships that passed in the night.

"So you lived in the same house, ate meals together, tormented the same pledges, attended house parties together. Right?"

"I wasn't into tormenting pledges, sheriff."

"I'm glad to hear it," Carol said. "I was only mentioning things that fraternity brothers usually share. How about house parties?"

Harry Pringle decided that he should cut this unpleasant Q & A short.

"All right, I gather that you've heard about the time that Pierce embarrassed me in front of my date."

"I have. I have the impression that it's no secret, but common knowledge among members of the alumni group. The way I hear it, at one particular house party Pierce was drunk and said some salacious things in the presence of your date that effectively ruined your relationship with her. Why don't you tell me about it in your own words?"

"There really isn't much to tell. Franklin was out of line, and he realized it. He apologized, said it was the booze talking. We long ago let bygones be bygones."

"What about the girl? Your friends seem to believe that you were very fond of her, even to the point of talking marriage, but that she was so upset by what she heard that night that she broke off her relationship with you."

"Some things get blown up out of all proportion. This happened a long time ago, and I moved on a long time ago. It's history."

This is pretty much what Carol had expected, so she turned to what Pringle had referred to as her modus operandi.

"Where was it that you and Pierce went when you went sightseeing in Barbados?"

"I don't know about him, but I took a bus and went wherever it was going. It's what I guess you'd call a local."

"Pierce wasn't with you?"

"No. Did somebody say he was?"

She ignored the question.

"Unlike taxis, their buses have regular routes. Where did yours go? Any place you remember? Bathsheba? Harrison's Cave?"

"It could have, but I don't remember the names of the places where we stopped, just what they looked like."

"Okay. Did your bus go to the eastern side of the island, the windward side, where the surf was rougher?"

Pringle stroked his chin as he thought about it. This time there was no attempt to hide his missing finger.

"I believe it did. There were big rock formations off shore."

"How about a big deserted place, sort of like an old hotel, up a long flight of stone steps from the beach?"

No pause, no knitted brow this time.

"No. I'd have remembered something like that."

"And you didn't see Mr. Pierce at any time during the day?"

"I wish I had. We'd have tackled the island together, and he'd still be alive." Pringle's implication was clear: it was highly unlikely that the man who killed Mr. Pierce would have done so if he had had company. Of course that would have depended on whether Pierce's 'company' had been his killer.

"So you don't know where Franklin was that day."

"We never discussed his plans, and from what I hear he never shared them with anybody else."

"Let's go back to Syracuse days for a moment before I leave," Carol said. "How do you explain the fact that a few of you alums became part of a rather unusual reunion group. When I met you all at Abbey Lipscomb's you didn't strike me as friends."

"We aren't. I've often wondered whether Franklin's idea would ever have gotten off the ground if I hadn't been intrigued with his suggestion that some of us take a trip to Key West. It was his idea, but I'm afraid I made a few calls and urged people on his list to give it a shot. That was quite a few years ago, but you can see what happened - more trips and a place of honor in his consignment shop. How ironic."

CHAPTER 49

Carol had spent a lot of time with the boxes she had brought back from *Upstate Consignments*, almost all of it perusing the files pertaining to what Pierce thought of as his alumni corner. But questions that had come up regarding Westerman and Pringle led her to wonder whether she had perhaps been too selective. Might she have missed something important by concentrating on Franklin's efforts to obtain contributions from the SU alums? Back from Syracuse that evening, she decided to give all the files a thorough going over.

It was a tedious job, and, as she had expected, not a rewarding one. But she had convinced herself that it had to be done, and eventually she did come across something which was not self explanatory and therefore worth a more careful look.

That something was a single page of paper, folded over and bearing no label. She had come across it before and ignored it as irrelevant to her mission. This time she unfolded it and was confronted with words and numbers which meant nothing more to her than had those on Franklin Pierce's illegible postcard a week earlier.

There was no name on the paper, only three capital letters, ELR, and then two lines, each consisting of three letters, three numbers, a mix of eight letters and numbers, and finally five more letters and numbers, ending in PL.

ELR
LIT 321 19CFRLIT F83PL
ANT 350 NATAMCUL S85PL

The ELR told her nothing, and initially the two longer lines were equally meaningless. She spent five minutes trying to decipher ELR without success. It was when she turned her attention to the longer lines that she realized what she was looking at. Kevin would have spotted it instantly. LIT 321 and ANT 350 would be familiar to any college student; they were course numbers and titles, one in the Literature Department, the other in Anthropology. Of course Anthropology would customarily be referred to as Anthro, but the writer had chosen to limit himself to three letters, presumably because Lit had only taken three. Having gotten that far, the rest of it was easy. LIT 321 would be 19th Century French Literature and ANT 350 would be Native American Cultures. That left the five letters and digits to the right on each of the longer lines - F83PL and S85PL. How about the semesters when the courses had been taught, the fall semester of 1983 and the spring semester of 1985, respectively. Now Carol was on solid ground. All of Pierce's SU alums had graduated in either 1985 or 1986, and would therefore have been in a position to take those two courses. She had accounted for everything except for ELR and the letters PL that followed both F83 and S85.

Two minutes later she had it. This was Franklin Pierce's reminder that Stuart Craig's wife Betty had committed plagiarism while a student at Syracuse. John Bickle had told her of Pierce's allegation that Betty had plagiarized a paper in a Lit course. He had also explained that Betty's maiden name during the Syracuse years had been Rasmussen. Betty (Elizabeth) Rasmussen with a middle name beginning with L (Louise? a family name?). ELR. The PL would turn out to be Franklin's shorthand for plagiarism.

But why the reference to an Anthropology course? A course taken in the spring of 1985 in which Mrs. Craig had been guilty - or at least allegedly guilty - of committing plagiarism a second time. Carol thought about it. According to Bickle's account, Betty had failed the Lit course because of the plagiarized paper. What if she had done it again? A second failed course? At the end of her final semester had it been necessary for her to take an additional course that summer in order to graduate? Or had the Anthro professor been more forgiving, demanding only an additional paper or simply reducing her grade on the paper she had plagiarized?

Carol found herself revisiting her interview with the Craigs. There had been no discussion of possible plagiarism, of course, because she hadn't yet heard Bickle's story. But, as she thought about it, she remembered that there had been a brief discussion of the fact that Betty and Franklin had taken a class together. And Betty had said that the class was in French literature, only to have her husband correct her, claiming that it had been in chemistry. Betty had quickly agreed that she had been mistaken. At the time, Carol had not cared whether Betty had known Franklin from a Lit or a chemistry course, but now that minor disagreement seemed more important. Had Stuart been anxious to shift attention away from the Lit course because his wife, who taught Lit at the high school in Cortland, had been guilty of plagiarizing a paper in a Lit course back in college? Indeed, she not only taught Lit, she had won a prize as teacher of the year. What would the school think of her if it were to discover that she had plagiarized a paper in the same kind of course she was now teaching? Would it rescind the reward? Its view of her as a role model for her students would certainly suffer.

Not one to jump to conclusions, Carol resisted the idea that the paper she held in her hands constituted a motive for murder. After all, if Betty had plagiarized one or even two papers in college, she would have done so almost thirty years ago. Why would she have waited so long to silence the man who was in a position to reveal her secret? And wasn't it more likely that her school would regard her years of distinguished teaching as far more important than a youthful error in judgment?

Carol wished that Kevin were at the lake. She would like to talk with him about plagiarism and how members of the academic community recognize it when they see it and how they handle it. She assumed that professors would have had a much more difficult time tracking down instances of plagiarism before the age of the internet when Betty Rasmussen Craig had been in college. Yet two of them had apparently found her out. Had the substance or style of her plagiarized papers been so dramatically superior to the rest of her work that they had known she had cheated? It was an interesting question, but it was also irrelevant. In all probability Betty's teachers would have retired. They might be dead. Either way, it was highly unlikely that they would remember Miss Rasmussen. And what if they did? The important question was how Mrs. Craig viewed her long ago act of plagiarism. Was she worried that the Cortland school system would learn of it? And if it did, how would it react?

Carol wasn't quite sure how she would approach the issue, but she knew that she had to make another appointment with Betty Craig, the sooner the better.

CHAPTER 50

The pictures of the passengers that had been taken by the *Azure Sea's* photographer were, without exception, much better than those she had collected from *Upstate Consignments.* Not only were they much more recent and hence a better likeness of each of the members of Franklin's Syracuse alumni group. They also had captured everyone in a festive mood as they boarded the ship in Fort Lauderdale. Franklin himself, having once more persuaded his colleagues to come traveling with him, looked enormously pleased with himself. There was no foreshadowing of the trouble which lay ahead. Carol wondered if the smile on one of the other faces masked an intention to leave their leader behind when they departed Barbados. Or some other Caribbean island, for that matter.

This is ridiculous, she said to herself. I have no idea whether one of these photographs is that of a murderer. The inspector may be right; Pierce's killer may still be a bajan, not a tourist from upstate New York.

She was anxious to flip the photos over and see which one Moses King, the Barbadian taxi driver, had identified as the person most likely to have paid him a thousand dollars for the use of his cab. But first she had to read what Inspector Williams had to say in his cover letter. How confident was he that King's judgment could be trusted?

What the inspector had to say made it clear that he had reservations about King, in spite of the man's effort to ingratiate himself with the RBPF.

'Hello, Sheriff Kelleher:

'I sincerely hope that you are able to put Mr. King's comments on these photos to good use. You should know that he has changed his tune about where he turned his taxi over to what he is sure was a Yankee tourist. He initially claimed it happened at Harrison's Cave, and he stuck to that story until two days ago when he admitted it was actually Hunte's Garden. It's my opinion that he originally picked Harrison's Cave precisely because he hadn't been there that day. But when it dawned on him that the man who borrowed his taxi could be the killer I was after, he figured that telling the truth might be more helpful to my investigation. And that, of course, would be to his advantage. In any event, he is sure that he earned his thousand dollars at Hunte's.'

'Regarding the photos, I haven't a clue whether the man King has fingered is the one who took his taxi. I'll be interested to hear whether King's candidate is someone who strikes you as a prime suspect. One way or another, let me know as soon as possible.'

'Good luck.'
Inspector Williams

Carol would have liked to be able to compare her suspicions to Moses King's. Unfortunately, her suspicions were at best tentative, so much so that she was still referring to members of the Barbados Eight as persons of interest rather than suspects. It was true that she had, for all practical purposes, ruled out some of the eight. As a matter of fact, she was inclined to rule out all three of the women. She was already in the habit of calling the killer 'him.' But she had to admit that it wasn't that simple. Betsy Stevens was strong enough to have done it, and Betty Craig, she now realized, may have had a motive, thanks to her plagiarized paper - or papers, if Pierce knew what he was talking about. The men were harder to classify. Harry Pringle might also have a motive. Jim Westerman had no obvious motive, but she couldn't put out of her mind the lie he had told Kevin or the puzzling matter of his books, not to mention the conflict Pierce had referred to in his postcard. John Bickle and Stuart Craig had both been willing, even eager, to share what they knew about their colleagues. Had they been motivated by a desire to help her investigation or were they seeking to shift her attention to someone other than themselves? Which left Roger Edgar, and try as she would she couldn't find a reason to give him much thought, even as a person of interest.

So much for comparing Moses King's guess as to the person who had used his taxi with her candidate for Franklin Pierce's killer. She spread the ship's photos of the Barbados Eight plus Pierce on the dining room table. There was no point in trying to guess which one he had zeroed in on and turn it over first. She flipped all of them. One of them bore a check mark. The photo with the words 'best guess' beside it was that of Roger Edgar. Carol was dumbfounded. It was not that she had expected King to pick anyone in particular. But Edgar? Yet the taxi driver had actually been face to face with the person who had given him a thousand dollars, had talked with him, had argued that he wasn't allowed to do what he was being asked to do and then had done it anyway. Wouldn't he be in a better position than she was to pick the culprit from a lineup?

Carol turned the photos over again so that the now familiar faces stared up at her once more. Nine middle aged men and women, all looking pleased to be on board the cruise ship, anxious to be on their way to the islands of the Caribbean. Lying side by side on the table, they looked as if they were standing in a row. She was aware of the fact that except for Franklin Pierce and Betsy Stevens, both considerably shorter, everyone was of approximately the same height. Nor was any one of them conspicuously overweight. All were bareheaded. Only one wore glasses, and they were sun glasses - Roger Edgar

'That's it.' She said it out loud. He had told the inspector it was hard to see the man's face because he was wearing a broad brimmed sun hat and sun glasses. She was willing to bet that King had simply selected the man in the photos who was wearing sun glasses.

Carol knew that she had news for the inspector. She could ask him to have King look at the photos again, paying no attention to the glasses this time. She was sure it would do no good, but she was also sure that King was wrong about Roger Edgar.

On the other hand, for the first time she had a strong feeling that Franklin Pierce's killer was indeed going to be one of the Barbados Eight. She couldn't explain the feeling. It had nothing to do with Abbey Lipscomb's hunch to that effect, because Abbey had said nothing about being closer to an understanding of her conviction that all was not well with the Syracuse alumni group. If neither Abbey nor Moses King was being helpful, why this feeling that she had met and talked at some length with Franklin Pierce's killer, that he or she was living somewhere in upstate New York, not more than a two or three hour drive from Crooked Lake?

Chapter 51

It was 10:50 and Carol had just turned off the light, hoping for a good night's sleep, untroubled by thoughts of Betty Craig's plagiarism, Harry Pringle's disappointment in love, Roger Edgar's alleged status as Moses King's benefactor . . .

Five minutes later the phone rang. Carol was not pleased. No one she knew was in the habit of calling at this hour, which meant that it must be a thoughtless robocall or the duty officer at the sheriff's office. If it was the former, she'd simply hang up; if the latter, she'd hope the problem could be handled by Sam or one of her other officers.

It was neither.

"Hi, it's me," Kevin said. "Don't hang up. I know it's late, but there are times when I have to talk with you, and this is one of them."

"If you'd called ten minutes later I'd have been sound asleep. What's the problem?"

"No problem, except that I'm lonely and would give anything to be snuggling up next to you as we talk. I'm thinking of making up some excuse for why I have to be out of town and up at the lake for a day or two."

"You called me at eleven o'clock to tell me that? I'd love to have you here, but you could have called earlier. Or tomorrow. Right now I'm sleepy."

"I know, and I'm sorry. But tomorrow you'll be at the office, and I couldn't have done it earlier because I was reading a book."

"What kind of message is that? Finishing a book takes precedence over calling your wife? It must have been a great book."

"On the contrary, it's a lousy book. And that's why I had to call. I just finished it."

"Okay, now I'm wide awake. What's this all about?"

"It's about Jim Westerman, the Cooperstown author."

"You've been reading one of his books?"

"I'm afraid so. And not just one, but two. I'm not calling to recommend either one for a Crooked Lake book club. Let's call this official business. At least I think it qualifies. You remember that Westerman's written three novels, all of them related to Cooperstown and Otsego Lake, all of them indebted to James Fenimore Cooper. More or less. We talked about the fact that his first effort, *The Mohican Boy*, was all over his house on Otsego, but that the others were nowhere in sight."

"And you remember that all three were at Franklin Pierce's consignment shop, waiting for the opening of his alumni corner."

"Yes, and that Westerman seems to have had a difference of opinion with Pierce about the other two books. I said that I'd try to find time to read them and see if I could make sense of the problem. Frankly, I wasn't all that interested, but you know me, especially when it comes to helping make sense of one of your cases. Anyhow, I'm in a stretch when I don't have any papers to read or tests to grade, so I started working on the Westerman problem a couple of days ago. I'll bore you with all the details when I see you, but I had to give you a heads up and that's why I called you so late."

"Okay, forget the hour. The books are worth reading?"

"Depends on your criteria. If you're looking for good literature, the answer is no. If you're trying to get a better understanding of Westerman, the answer - I think - is yes. Of course I cheated. With the help of a colleague in our own Lit department, I tracked down some reviews of Westerman's books, and to put it mildly they weren't kind. But I had to see for myself whether they're any good, so I started with *The Mohican Boy* and finished *The Loyalists and the Iroquois,* his second, tonight. About half an hour ago, so this is a hot off the wire report."

"As you might guess, " Carol said, "I'm more interested in how you think the books relate to Westerman's role in the Pierce case than in their literary merit."

"I may be way off base on this, but I don't think you can separate the two. It's the quality of the books that makes them relative to the Pierce case."

"Tell me about it," Carol said, no longer sleepy.

"I haven't read his third book yet, and considering the reviews it may not be necessary. But in my untutored judgment, Westerman isn't cut out to be a novelist. His first book is better than the second, but that's not saying much. You ever read *The Last of the Mohicans*?"

"I probably know it better from the movies, but I'm sure I read it in my teens. Why?"

"There was a time when it was considered one of the great American novels and Cooper one of our greatest novelists. But his reputation has lost some of its luster, which hasn't helped Westerman, who seems to be anxious to be another Cooper. His prose is, well, too artificial, and his dialogue is just plain stilted. *The Mohican Boy* at least has a reasonably decent plot. The other one is an embarrassment. If I hadn't been doing research for you, I'd have stopped reading before I got to chapter three."

"So what does this have to do with the Pierce case?"

"Pierce had this crazy idea of showcasing his friends at the shop, and in Westerman's case that meant putting his books on display. All three of them. But Westerman, like any author, would have read the reviews, and I'm sure he was dead set against putting books two and three in the display. He probably regretted agreeing to *The Mohican Boy* as well, but it had fared somewhat better and he'd already donated a copy. It's just a guess, but I'd be willing to wager that Pierce and Westerman had a major falling out over those books. Just think about it. Westerman refused to attend the memorial service. He told me he'd never heard of the man who missed the *Azure Sea* when it left Barbados, obviously a lie. According to that illegible postcard, he and Pierce had an unpleasant running argument during the cruise. They didn't like each other. Wouldn't you agree?"

"Are you suggesting that Westerman killed Pierce because of a couple of bad books?"

"I didn't say that," Kevin insisted.

"If he did, his motive would easily qualify as one of the most improbable I've ever heard of."

"I'll agree with that. But how many other members of your Barbados Eight come across as people who really disliked Pierce? All I'm saying is that Westerman would almost certainly have wanted his books removed from Pierce's display to protect his reputation, and Pierce would almost certainly have wanted to leave them there to give his project more status."

"But given the reviews, " Carol said, "they would hardly have enhanced the status of the display."

"Westerman and Pierce would have viewed the matter differently, don't you think?"

"I was planning on having a good night's sleep, Kevin, and I think you've pretty much ruined that plan."

"I doubt that Westerman's reputation as a novelist is the stuff of nightmares, Carol."

"I hope you're right. You say you'll be finding an excuse to come back to the lake soon?"

"I have a whole repertoire of excuses to cut classes in order to see you. And I'll promise to leave Westerman out of our conversation if you like. One way or another, let's make it next weekend. I'll call and confirm my arrangements."

"Promise to call before eleven."

"Of course."

Chapter 52

Inspector Williams, not Sheriff Kelleher, was the one who didn't sleep well that night. Carol had been wide awake because of Kevin's call. The inspector had been wide awake because he had received no call. He had expected the sheriff to be in touch with him almost as soon as she had reviewed the photos and learned whom King had identified as the man who had 'borrowed' his taxi (and presumably killed Franklin Pierce).

But by the time he had showered, dressed, and eaten his breakfast the next morning, he had given the matter more thought and put the absence of a call in perspective. Unfortunately, that perspective was not comforting. He had, he realized, been naively optimistic that her research and King's memory would lead to something approaching consensus as to the guilty party. If not to who had killed Pierce, at least to who had paid a thousand dollars for the use of the taxi. By the time he kissed his wife goodbye, he had decided that the problem was that the sheriff's judgment and King's were not in synch.

There was no point in waiting for the sheriff's call. When he reached his office he would take the initiative. Perhaps bad news was better than no news. Twenty minutes later she was on the line. Twenty three minutes later his worst fears had been realized.

"I do not wish to say that Mr. King is wrong, inspector, only to tell you that I find it highly unlikely that the person he loaned his taxi to is Roger Edgar. I say that because handing over a thousand dollars for the loan of a taxicab is both strange and extremely rare. I have never heard of such a thing. It isn't something that someone would do unless he had a powerful motive for doing so. In this case, the motive presumably is murder, although we both know that the person who borrowed the taxi may not even be an acquaintance of Mr. Pierce and may have had absolutely nothing to do his death. If that is the case, you'd still have a mystery to contend with, but we wouldn't be having this conversation. So I have been working on the assumption that whoever gave Mr. King all that money so he could use his taxi is in fact Mr. Pierce's killer. But I have interviewed at some length all of the people who were traveling with Mr. Pierce, and I would swear that Dr. Edgar is the *least* likely candidate among them to be his killer. He simply had no motive that I can discern. There are members of the group I have been investigating who may have had their reasons for not liking Pierce. I have my doubts, however, that those reasons are tantamount to motives for murder, and as far as I can tell they don't apply to Dr. Edgar at all. He insists that he spent that day in Bridgetown, and none of his colleagues disputes him."

"How do you suppose King got it so wrong?" The inspector was obviously reluctant to accept what the sheriff was telling him.

Carol didn't wish to give him the impression that King had willfully picked a man he knew hadn't been involved. She reminded the inspector of the sun hat, the sunglasses, and the fact that the differences in the physiognomy of the men in the tour group were marginal at best.

"My best guess is that he was fixated on the sunglasses," she said. "Most of the people traveling with Pierce presumably wore sun glasses while they were out in the sun on Barbados. But Edgar is the only one wearing them in the shipboard pictures. I suspect that Mr. King simply picked him because he remembered the sunglasses."

"Do you have another candidate?" William asked.

"My task has been to figure out if one of Pierce's colleagues might have been the murderer. I have no idea whom King loaned the taxi to. Let's say that I've been concentrating on eight people, five men and three women. In the circumstances I'm obligated to treat all of them as persons of interest. Murder suspects is a different story. Frankly, I don't find any of the motives all that persuasive. But both you and I know that what would be brushed aside as a minor irritant by most people could drive others crazy, crazy enough to commit murder. So if I relax my definition of motive, several of Pierce's colleagues had a motive for killing him. They include one woman and three of the five men. I suppose I must begin to rank order them from suspect number one to suspect number four.

To be completely honest about it, I probably already have a vague idea, although who's on top of the list varies from one interview to the next. This isn't much help, is it?"

The inspector was unable to hide his disappointment. Perhaps the sheriff was not as competent as he had been led to believe. Or perhaps, as he had originally assumed, Pierce's traveling companions had nothing to do with his death.

"Well, I guess we'll soldier on. Just let me know if and when you think you know which of the suspects emerges as the most likely to have done it." The inspector knew he was repeating himself.

"It's not my place to offer suggestions," Carol said, "but I'd remove Edgar's glasses from his photo and see if King reacts differently. Probably not, now that he's decided that Edgar is the one, but it's worth a try."

"We shall see."

"I'm about to pay another visit to one of my persons of interest. Maybe she'll turn out to be a real suspect."

"King's positive it's a man."

"I'm thinking of the murder, not the taxi."

———

Carol's conversation with the inspector had been depressing. She was feeling guilty that she hadn't been able to offer a tentative opinion as to the identity of Pierce's killer. She didn't believe that Betty Craig would fill the bill, but the file note about plagiarism gave her no choice but to pay her another visit.

Mrs. Craig was at work, of course, and therefore unavailable until late that afternoon. But they were able, with some difficulty, to schedule an appointment for Saturday. It might have been earlier except that Betty seemed to prefer that they meet without her husband present. As it happened, Stuart Craig would be tied up with a soccer game on Saturday, and Betty was confident that she'd be able to come up with a plan that would enable her to drive to Crooked Lake without raising his suspicions as to her whereabouts. Upstate New York was still a big area, but both Carol and the Barbados Eight were becoming familiar with its many highways and byways.

"Thank you for being the one to make the trip," Carol said as she welcomed Mrs. Craig to the cottage on Blue Water Point. "It looks as if both of us had to do some juggling this weekend. My husband arrived last night, and you made the trip over here to avoid your husband. I'm interested in why you wanted to talk with me alone."

Betty was understandably confused by the news about the sheriff's husband.

"Not to worry, Mrs. Craig. Kevin teaches down in the city but is able to get away for the weekend every so often."

"I hope I'm not messing up your plans."

"Not at all. He's used to my erratic schedule. Care for a late morning coffee?"

"That would be great, thank you."

Carol saw Betty Craig to a seat and disappeared into the kitchen, where Kevin was having a late breakfast.

"You want me to show myself?" he whispered.

"I'd prefer to handle her myself. I'll call you if I need help," she said, giving him a peck on the cheek.

"Well now, Mrs. Craig, how did you manage to escape from Cortland today?" Carol asked when she reappeared with the coffee.

"My mother loves conspiracies," Betty said. "She lives in Waverly, which is on the way, and she agreed that she just had to see me. It's convenient, all of us so close."

"That seems to have been Franklin Pierce's idea."

Betty smiled, but it was apparent that she would prefer not to be talking about Pierce, even if she knew that he was the reason for her presence in the sheriff's living room.

"You said you wanted to talk about Franklin. Inasmuch as Stuart and I already had that conversation with you, I'm assuming that what's really on your mind is something else. Would I be right?"

"I've been trying to get a picture of Pierce and the rest of you when you were on Barbados. What I'm interested in today is your relationship with Pierce outside of Barbados. Don't worry. I'm not asking about any close personal relationship. But how did you know each other? How do you account for the fact that he included you in his alumni group?"

"I expect that you know the answer to your question. He knew me - I knew him - only through two classes we took together at Syracuse. I assume that you want to know what those classes were. After all, classes were pretty big, so why me instead of Pam Kirk or Donna Hester, for example. You've been working on Franklin's case for several weeks, so by now I'm sure you know all about my so-called plagiarism in a French Lit course. It's an old story, but I think you should hear it from me."

"I'd appreciate it, Mrs. Craig."

"In the first place, the plagiarism charge was unfair. I've no doubt that I'd read things that were relevant to the assignment. I have a good memory, and some of those things may have come to my mind when I wrote the paper. It happens to all of us. But I never sat down to copy someone else's work. Never! The prof who taught the course, George Francouer, was a pedantic, uninspiring man. If some of the novels we read, like *Madame Bovary*, hadn't been so good, the course would have been a complete waste of time. Anyhow, Francouer must have been having one of those days when he was reading our papers. So he decided to call me a plagiarist. The system was stacked. I was just a student - a sophomore at that. He flunked me. Pierce was in the class, and like everyone else he knew what I was alleged to have done. He made a point of commiserating with me, telling me the prof was a jerk. I appreciated his support, but I really didn't give him much thought."

"But that wasn't the end of it, was it?" Carol asked.

"Pierce was strange. He really knew me only because of that one course and that one paper. And because Francouer flunked me. We never talked much, but when we did that's what always came up. Even years later when we were together. Like the cruise. It took awhile, but it eventually occurred to me that for some reason he thought the plagiarism case gave him some kind of hold over me. Why, I don't know, but then I never did figure Franklin out."

"How about the other plagiarism case, the one in an Anthro course?"

"Where'd you hear about that?" Betty's voice had shifted into accusatory mode.

"Pierce mentions it along with the French Lit case in a file he was keeping in his consignment store."

"That son of a bitch!"

"What's the story on that one?"

"There isn't any story. Another prof had me on the carpet, claimed I'd cribbed stuff on the Navahos' long walk to Bosque Redondo. I decided to make an issue of it that time, and the case was eventually dropped. I hope you never had to put up with creeps like Francouer and - hell, I can't even remember the Anthro guy's name."

"No, I didn't." Carol suspected that Betty Rasmussen Craig was not quite the innocent author of term papers she pretended to be. "You say that Pierce may have thought he had a hold over you because of these plagiarism charges. Did he ever actually say or do anything along that line?"

"Not in so many words. It was how he managed to bring it up, like he was trying to see how I'd react to being reminded of it. Stuart took it much more seriously than I did. That's why I wanted to see you alone. I was pretty sure you'd bring it up, and I wanted you to hear me, not Stuart."

"What is your husband's view of all this?"

"He was convinced that Franklin was dangerous. Stuart worried that he'd find an excuse to poison the well at the high school, you know, get them not to think of me as a teacher of the year but as a dishonest plagiarist. Well, I can stick up for myself. I'm good at what I do, and even if there were a grain of truth in those charges, they were dealt with decades ago. Syracuse has my records. They'll show that I graduated cum laude. And there's nobody at the high school who's had a better record. I've had more students who've gone on to college and good careers than most of my colleagues put together. Stuart's a born worrier. Pierce was a joke."

"I'm sure you'd like me to change the subject," Carol said. "How about this? You and Stuart and Betsy Stevens went over to Bathsheba when you were in Barbados. Did you or your husband borrow a local taxi that day at Hunte's Garden?"

Carol was alert to any indication that the question had caught Betty off guard, stimulated a momentary twinge of anxiety. She saw none.

"Borrow a taxi? Why would I do that?"

Her answer seemed genuine.

"So your answer is no. How about Stuart?"

"I didn't know that people borrowed taxis. Besides, he walked up to Cattlewash that day. I don't think it's anywhere near to Hunte's Garden."

Actually, Carol thought, both Cattlewash and Hunte's Garden are within walking distance of Bathsheba - one just up the coast, one just a short distance inland. How did Betty know that Stuart had not visited Hunte's Garden? For that matter, how much did Betty know about what her husband had done with his worries about Franklin Pierce?

Mrs. Craig was getting ready to leave when Kevin made an appearance. Carol had assumed he would do so much sooner, but to her surprise he had abstained from joining her interrogation of the Cortland school teacher.

"Mrs. Craig, this is my husband Kevin."

"Nice to meet you. I understand that you're also a teacher."

"That's what my c.v. says, but I'm really a lake person. Incidentally, I'm sorry the cruise ended badly for you."

It was intended as a kind remark, but Betty Craig's effort to respond with a smile was a conspicuous failure.

Chapter 53

"Such self restraint!" Carol ribbed Kevin as they rummaged through the fridge for something for lunch. "I was sure you'd feel an obligation to join us well before you did. What happened? You go back to bed?"

"You know me better than that. I simply parked myself on the other side of the kitchen door and listened while she told you what a scrupulously honest student she was."

"Do you believe her?"

"I believe she thinks she's innocent of plagiarism. In any event, it doesn't matter."

"Apparently her husband thinks it does."

"Or did when Pierce was alive."

"That's the point, isn't it? What I take away from what Mrs. Craig said is that she wouldn't have killed Pierce, her husband would."

Kevin shook his head 'no.' Meanwhile he was locating the makings for a ham sandwich.

"What's his name, Stuart? He was always a better suspect than his wife. But the chances he clubbed Pierce to death are about as good as mine of winning the Boston Marathon. Can you imagine one of the Craigs - anybody, for that matter - killing someone to cover up an act of plagiarism?"

"I know," Carol said. "I'm trapped in a real dilemma, searching for a killer among people none of whom has a believable motive for doing such a thing."

"Now that I'm here, why don't we tackle your dilemma, see if we can't make sense of what looks like a senseless murder. Just give me a minute or two to make a couple of ham sandwiches first. Okay?"

Kevin cobbled together the ham sandwiches and they had lunch at the dining room table where the day before Carol had spread out the ship's photos and pondered Moses King's selection of Roger Edgar as the man who had borrowed his taxi.

"Do you realize that we've hardly had time to say hello to each other and here we are, talking murder again?"

"Fun, isn' it?" Kevin said.

"Maybe for you because it's a change of pace. For me, it's just a matter of bringing my work home. Come on, finish your sandwich so we can get down to the fun stuff."

Lunch finished and coffee poured, they considered retreating to the porch, but found it too chilly and ended up on the couch in the living room.

"Now about my dilemma," Carol began. "If it weren't for the fact that I promised Inspector Williams down in Bridgetown that I'd help him solve Franklin Pierce's murder, I would have stopped worrying about this case weeks ago. As it is, I feel I'm wasting my time, trying to prove that Pierce was killed by somebody from upstate New York. The funny thing is that it was just the other day that I thought I'd made up my mind that the killer was indeed one of Franklin's friends from SU days."

"Really? What made you think so?"

"I wish I knew. You may remember that the reason I agreed to take the assignment that Abbey Lipscomb was urging on me was that something was bothering her about Franklin's reunion group. She couldn't put her finger on it, but she was convinced that something about the group was wrong, something that made her think the killer might well be one of Franklin's traveling companions on the cruise. Whatever that something is, she still can't seem to remember it. Well, I'm in that same boat. Like Abbey, I don't know why I feel the way I do. It'll come to me, I'm sure, but in the meanwhile it's driving me crazy because none of the tour group makes sense as the killer. And that's the dilemma. How can I know that one of eight people killed Pierce and yet find no persuasive motive for any of them doing it?"

"I'm not up to speed on this one, but are you sure that literally *no one* has a motive?"

"That's an issue I've hashed out with myself over and over again. Maybe if I were a psychiatrist and put them all on a couch for a few sessions I'd discover a motive or two. But given what I've discovered in meeting, talking with them all, anything that looks remotely like a motive is - what should I say? - really far fetched. It's like you said about the Craigs. Why kill somebody because he might tell your employer you committed plagiarism in college thirty years ago? What makes it even more improbable is that other members of the group also know about Betty's plagiarism. What do you do about them? Certainly not kill them all."

Kevin saw it very much as Carol did, but he was anxious to play devil's advocate.

"But suppose you know that Pierce is a real threat to expose you while the others are simply indifferent."

"Kill Pierce and you're home free? That's probably the way it would work, but still why kill Pierce? Murder is a far riskier business than plagiarism. All I'm saying is that only a desperate fool would kill to cover up a non-crime, and these people are not desperate fools."

"What about the others? Is there anybody else that has what you're calling a far fetched motive for murder?"

"I suppose so, and please underline far fetched.Take Harry Pringle. Remember him? When he was in college he fell deeply in love with a girl who took her chastity very seriously. Pringle took her to a party at the frat house he shared with Pierce. Pierce suggested Pringle do what he'd done at other house parties and take this girl to his room and screw her, too. The girl was right there, heard it all, realized that Pringle wasn't the perfect guy she thought he was. It was their last date. Thirty years later Pringle gets revenge, murders Pierce. See what I mean?"

"I agree, it does sound far fetched. I mean, thirty years! If he's done it in a fit of anger, say in a bar brawl, a week or two later, I might understand. But decades later, that makes no sense."

"It isn't just the time. Pierce invited Pringle to join his alumni group, which he did. How does a guy forgive the man who cost him the love of his life, go traveling with him every year or two, and then break his neck in Barbados?"

Carol was just getting warmed up.

"Then there's Westerman. You know him better than any of the others, and we just had a discussion of his problem when you called me at midnight the other day."

"Yes, I know Westerman, but when I called it wasn't yet eleven o'clock. Facts, Carol, facts."

"Okay, I exaggerated a bit," Carol admitted. "But the story is the same. Only this time Franklin was determined to dress up his alumni corner in the consignment store with the best he could get his so-called friends to contribute. In view of the fact that Westerman was an author, what better for the display than copies of his books. Unfortunately, as you know from reading them, Westerman's books, particularly the ones that followed *The Mohican Boy*, had received bad, very bad reviews. It's pretty obvious that Westerman didn't want to call attention to them, much less have them on display for every Tom, Dick and Harry to see. But Pierce had no trouble finding copies of the books, and they were already at *Upstate Consignments*, waiting for the display to open. Needless to say, Pierce's death ended the plan to have an alumni corner at the shop. In other words, Westerman had a motive for killing Pierce."

"Another far fetched motive," Kevin added, "because people who write books aren't in the habit of killing people who put their books, even bad ones, on display. Is that it, or are these just the tip of the iceberg?"

"There's one other case where one might make the case that one of Pierce's colleagues on the cruise had a motive for murder, although it's an even thinner case than Craig's, Pringle's, and Westerman's, by which I mean it's so thin I haven't been giving it any thought. One of the woman on the cruise - her name's Betsy Stevens - once dated Pierce. Turns out they are both homosexual but didn't know it at the time. It seems that at first they thought of this misadventure as a joke, but she claims that Pierce enjoyed telling the story and that she eventually got fed up with his misplaced sense of humor."

"So to get him to shut his mouth she killed him?"

"Something like that. Like I said, I've tucked this one away in my dead end file. Beyond that, the only reason any of the others might be called suspects is that they've told me things which could be efforts to shift responsibility for the crime to others. But I can't find a motive, even a far fetched one, in those cases. In view of the fact that all of these people, what I think of as the Barbados Eight, travel together and know each other fairly well, it isn't surprising that they know a lot about each other's peccadillos."

"Which means that, by normal standards of logic, none of these people killed Pierce and you *have* been wasting your time."

"Except that a small voice keeps telling me that one of them did it. How do you account for that?"

CHAPTER 54

Abbey Lipscomb had decided, on the spur of the moment, to hoe out a closet which had become the repository of all kinds of papers, memorabilia, out of date calendars, and catalogues which she had saved for reasons she couldn't remember. It was a task which should have taken no more than half an hour but, as always seemed to be the case, she was managing to turn it into a morning long enterprise because she had to revisit each catalogue and reread each letter. As a result, it was nearly lunch time and she was thinking of putting things back in the closet and finishing the job another day.

Fortunately, one of the last items she encountered before calling it quits was a bundle of Christmas cards, held together by a rubber band. It was immediately apparent that the cards came from a Christmas well past. Seven years to be exact. She started to read them, thought better of it, and was ready to toss them into the discard pile when she recognized the handwriting on a card showing a flock of chickadees feasting at a bird feeder. All the words slanted sharply to the left, their p's forming little balloons below the line, their b's doing the same thing above the line. It was from Burt Driscoll. She hadn't heard from him in years. She pulled the card from the bundle.

> 'Merry Christmas, Abbey,
>
> 'I hear you are joining Franklin's traveling circus. I'm afraid we shall miss each other. Alice and I are moving to California - more about that later. Anyway, I hope you get along with Franklin's crew. If the Key West and

> Myrtle Beach excursions are a taste of things to come, I'll wager that these biennial outings are destined to come to no good end. Watch your back!
>
> 'Best in the new year.'
> Burt Driscoll

Abbey smiled. More about the move to California had never materialized, but then she and Burt had never been all that close. And then she remembered the feeling she'd had after Franklin's death that something about the Syracuse alumni group was bothering her. It had been one of the factors that had led her to urge the sheriff to help the Barbados authorities find Franklin's killer. And now she was looking at the message from Burt Driscoll which had first alerted her to the possibility that all might not be well with the upstate New York alums. The Caribbean cruise had demonstrated that Burt had been on to something. The biennial outings had indeed come to no good end.

She had never had an opportunity to ask Burt to explain himself. She herself had occasionally been troubled by an undercurrent of tension on their trips, not to mention the fact that there had been little real camaraderie among people who were presumably good friends from college days. There had been many dropouts, not just those like herself who had physical or professional problems that caused them to miss trips. But those dropouts had usually been replaced by others Franklin recruited. She herself had been one of them.

Driscoll's Christmas card didn't, of course, presage Pierce's murder. But it told her that she must get in touch with the sheriff. Perhaps she would be able to make something of it. At a minimum it would help keep her attention focussed on the members of the group who had been on the cruise. Abbey regarded this as important, because she had begun to worry that in the absence of hard evidence to the contrary, the sheriff was losing interest in Inspector Williams' assignment.

She quickly stuffed things back into the closet and went to the telephone. JoAnne informed her that the sheriff had stepped out, but that she would have her call back. But while she was giving Abbey this disappointing information, Carol walked in.

"Abbey? Good to hear from you. I'm sure you've been hoping to hear from me. I may be making some progress, but perhaps you have something important to pass along."

"I'm not sure whether it's important, sheriff, but do you remember that there's been something about Franklin's tour group that's been bothering me? Something that I can't quite remember? Well, I discovered something today that I'm sure has something to do with what's troubling me. It's not all that specific, but you ought to hear about it. Would it be possible for you to come over?"

"Give me half an hour and I'll be there."

"Good. It may amount to nothing, but I need your opinion."

Carol's reaction fell somewhere between cautious excitement and an all too familiar skepticism. But she had no idea what to expect, so she chose not to start guessing what Abbey's news would be. Instead, she tried to take her mind off the Pierce case while she drove by thinking about the wonderful weekend she had just had with Kevin.

Abbey met her at the door with a torrent of words and the Christmas card in her hand.

"Whoa," Carol said, "not so fast Let me get comfortable."

"Of course. Sorry, sometimes I forget myself. Would you like some coffee?"

"No thanks," Carol said, helping herself to a seat on the couch. "You say you've remembered why you thought somebody in Franklin's tour group might have been responsible for his death. Needless to say, you've got my attention, so let's hear it."

"Better that I show you." She handed the sheriff the old Christmas card. "I think you can see why I've been concerned"

Carol read Burt Driscoll's brief message and found herself unsure as to just what to say. Driscoll obviously had not been thrilled to be part of what he called Pierce's 'traveling circus,' but nothing in the card conveyed what seemed to her to be a warning of imminent danger. Abbey, it seemed, interpreted it differently.

"It sounds as if your friend had lost his interest in these trips."

"Yes, I guess he did, but what got my attention was his statement that they would come to no good end. And now look what happened - they did! It's almost like he was clairvoyant."

"And you remembered what he had said after hearing that Franklin had been killed in Barbados."

"Not at first. It's like I told you. I couldn't think of what was bothering me. And then I was throwing stuff out and came across this old card."

"I take it you didn't give this man Burt's message much thought at first. I mean you accepted Franklin's invitation to join the alumni group."

"That's true. I hadn't been on any of the trips, so I didn't really know what he was talking about. Actually, I guess I was pleased to be invited, thought it might be fun. But you can see why what happened to Franklin got me to thinking."

"You ended up taking a couple of these trips, I believe. Did you see anything which told you that Burt was on to something? That you should watch your back?"

"Not really," Abbey admitted. "I realized that most of us hadn't been particularly close in college, still weren't. That probably accounted for the fact that the members changed over the years - people dropping out, new members joining, like me. But as you've discovered, I'm easy, get along with just about everyone, so I didn't pay much attention to the petty disagreements. I'd forgotten all about Burt's warning until now. To be honest, I doubt I would have remembered it was Burt if I hadn't been housecleaning and found this card."

"I know that this message is an old one, but does reading it again give you any idea of why these trips that Pierce organized would come to no good end?"

"I wish it did, but it doesn't."

Carol was disappointed. She had been hoping for weeks that Abbey would remember what was troubling her about the Pierce case. Unfortunately, what had been troubling her was a former friend's belief that Pierce's biennial trips were in some kind of trouble and wouldn't last long. Well, they had been in some kind of trouble, and they had recently been brought to a gruesome end. But why? And by whom? As she drove back to the office she felt like a dog chasing its own tail.

CHAPTER 55

Spring was now three weeks old, even if the temperature on Crooked Lake remained unseasonably cool. At least all of the ice had left the lake. A few hardy souls had taken their boats out of storage and the sound of power boats could once again be heard.

It was two days after Kevin had returned to the city, and Carol had shaken off the bad mood which had come with Abbey's false alarm. She had arrived at the office determined to shove the Pierce case aside for a few days and concentrate on neglected county business.

The Pierce case proved to be tenacious, however. Twenty minutes after the the morning squad meeting ended she was on the phone with a Rochester attorney named Seymour Simmons. Her effort to discover whether Franklin Pierce had made a will finally came to an end. He had not, and had died intestate. Simmons admitted that Pierce had contacted him, not once but twice, over the last two years and had expressed an interest in drawing up a will. But nothing had come of it. Simmons allowed that Pierce could have contacted another lawyer, but doubted it for reasons which Carol found persuasive. She wasn't surprised. She experienced a moment of sadness, but it was not her responsibility and she turned her attention to her agenda for the day. Or tried to.

What distracted her was a recollection of something she had seen when she left Abbey's cottage the day before. It was a pile of magazines on a table in the foyer. More to the point, it was the magazine on top of the pile. In fact, it wasn't exactly a magazine, but a publication the cover of which said something about Syracuse University. It had barely registered as she left the cottage. But now, while she was trying to refocus on her in-basket, it came to mind again and she had the distinct impression it had been a copy of the university's alumni news.

Carol would have dismissed it without a second thought except that it occurred to her that it might contain a brief obituary for Franklin Pierce. Curiosity told her to call Abbey and ask if she might take a look at it.

"You can have it," Abbey told her when she called. "I was going to throw it out along with a bunch of other magazines. They're all old. That one goes back to last fall. I'm trying to discipline myself, rein in my hoarder instinct before people confuse me with the Collyer brothers."

Carol laughed at the reference to the infamous hoarders who had been found dead in their New York brownstone in the midst of more than a hundred tons of accumulated stuff. Her interest in the alumni news vanished when she heard it was the previous fall's issue, but she jokingly offered to help Abbey get rid of it.

That would have been the end of it, except that Abbey surprisingly dropped by the office the following morning, the copy of the alumni news in hand.

"I considered bringing along some other things," she said with a smile, "but I suspect I've already asked too much of you."

"Thanks for making the trip. This will give me a chance to learn something about your alma mater."

"The issue with a notice about Franklin's death will be along in another month or two. I contacted the woman who handles news for our class. I have to run - you have a good day."

"You, too. And thanks."

Inasmuch as there would be nothing in the fall issue of the alumni news about Franklin Pierce, Carol set it aside and made yet another effort to focus on her primary job as sheriff of Cumberland County. Not surprisingly, it wasn't easy. Barbados was threatening to become more important than Crooked Lake, the RBPF's Inspector Williams more important than her own deputy sheriff, Sam Bridges. That thought sent her scurrying down the corridor to Sam's office with yet another apology for dereliction of duty.

"Hi, Sam. Long time, no see," she said as she pushed his door open and walked in.

"Do I know you?" he said, a twinkle in his eye.

"Oh, come on. I have't been that bad, have I?"

"Of course not. You really should be drawing overtime. I'm amazed you aren't out on your feet, coping with two jobs for close to three months."

"It hasn't been that bad. When it's over, I'll treat you to a lesson in how not to handle crimes in the Caribbean."

"Beginning with avoiding cruise ships?"

"No need to go that far. Just don't let anyone know you're an officer of the law. But seriously, how's everybody coping?"

"We're all fine. It's actually been a quiet year so far. Probably because there hasn't been a single murder on the lake."

"That's why I went to Barbados," Carol said. "Look, I've got a full in-basket, and I should let you get back to work."

She blew him a kiss and disappeared.

Carol had no book going that evening, so after a pick-up dinner she decided to read the Syracuse alumni news. She quickly discovered that one doesn't exactly read a copy of alumni news. Sampling is better, meaning that you can skip articles on campus development plans, farewells to retiring faculty you don't know, kudos to former students who have made their mark in the larger world. But she did learn a few things about the university Pierce and most of the others had attended until she reached the inevitable obituary notices. To her surprise these included two from the class of 1935, meaning that they had lived to be one hundred. Carol hoped to be so lucky. Remembering Abbey's friend Burt Driscoll, she checked the class of 1985 to see if he were still around. Apparently he was, but there on the same page were the names of two people from the class of 1987. One of them sounded familiar. Carol had always taken pride in her memory, and once again it proved helpful. The name was Terry Barkley.

Some of the obits were fairly long, long enough to remind readers that the deceased had been a football star or had later served in the House of Representatives or been the CEO of some firm. Barkley's obit was brief. It conveyed little information about her except that she had lived in Toledo, Ohio, and apparently had no spouse or children.

Carol settled back on the couch and gave some thought to what she remembered about Terry Barkley from her conversations with members of the alumni group. Her name had come up in connection with Harry Pringle, who had dated her in college. John Bickle had described her as the love of Pringle's life, only to have their relationship founder when Franklin Pierce informed her that Pringle had a history of sexual escapades with other women. Harry himself had not been so specific, but he admitted having loved Barkley and claimed that he had forgiven Pierce for his role in ending their affair. It was this relationship and the way it had ended that had prompted the sheriff to consider treating Pringle as a suspect in Pierce's killing.

But Carol now found it even harder to picture Pringle as Franklin Pierce's killer than she had when she and Kevin were discussing suspects. If, as he himself put it, Pringle had long ago let bygones be bygones, why would he kill Pierce once Barkley had died. Wouldn't her death be the ultimate form of closure for him?

Logically yes, but she couldn't put the death of Terry Barkley out of her mind. Perhaps Harry had never seen the copy of the alumni news which contained Terry's obituary. Or he had seen it but hadn't bothered to read the obits. But this was uninformed guess work. If Pringle was a member of a Syracuse alumni tour group, he was likely also to be a good enough alum to read the news mag regularly, including the obituaries. This train of thought led her to question her assumption that news of his former girl friend's death would bring his obsession to an end. Was it possible that it would do the opposite, that it would stoke the fire of an old grievance?

Once more Carol found sleep elusive. There had been too many such nights since she had agreed to help Inspector Williams in his investigation of the Pierce murder. It might not solve her insomnia, but it was obvious that she would have to make another appointment to see Harry Pringle.

CHAPTER 56

Much as she would have liked to arrive at the Pringles' door unannounced, she knew that she needed to make an appointment or run the risk of making the trip for naught. Mrs. Pringle had not been welcoming the last time she paid Harry a visit, and she hoped that she wouldn't be the one to answer the phone. No such luck. But while she didn't sound happy, she made no attempt to prevent the sheriff from talking with her husband.

Mr. Pringle was more difficult. It was obvious, even more than it had been earlier, that he didn't want to see her.

"I understand," Carol said. "You must be as anxious to put the events in Barbados behind you as I am. But I can't simply walk away from a commitment I made to the authorities in Bridgetown. The situation seems to be somewhat different than it was when we last talked, and it is imperative that I see you again."

Only when it had become apparent that she was coming to Syracuse, ready or not, that he finally agree on a date a week later.

"I'd do it sooner," he said, "but I have to be out of town for several days."

Carol could not recall a week which had dragged by so slowly. She tried to concentrate on other things, but that proved to be all but impossible. She couldn't set aside the feeling that this next visit to the Pringle residence in Syracuse could be decisive. Was it only wishful thinking, or was her mission for Inspector Williams nearing an end?

She took some of her impatience out on Kevin, calling him every night of the week but one, and that because he was tied up with a seminar. When the day came to make the trip, she awoke without the help of the alarm clock and then had to kill time so as not to arrive at Pringle's way too soon.

Dorothy Pringle once again welcomed her, but her demeanor was conspicuously different this time. She looked as if she were worried. Carol apologized for the intrusion, but Mrs. Pringle didn't appear to hear her.

Harry was not in the living room, but upstairs in what looked like a combination study and storage room. He moved an old chair with wheels into a position where Carol could sit facing him.

"So, sheriff, we meet again. I hope I wasn't too off-putting when we arranged this meeting, but I wasn't in a position to change my schedule."

"That's perfectly all right," she said. No reason why he should know how frustrated she had been by the need to wait a week.

"Rudimentary hospitality says I should offer you something to drink. It's too early for anything alcoholic, but I'm sure you don't drink when you're on duty anyway. This is a duty call, isn't it, not just a friendly chat?"

No offer of coffee or tea was made, so Carol simply shook her head and produced her folded copy of the Syracuse alumni news.

"I thought you might like to see this," she said. "Or perhaps you already have seen it."

Carol had the distinct impression that Harry was trying very hard to look disinterested.

"It has something about Franklin?" he asked.

"No, it's last fall's edition. Do you subscribe to it?"

"It's what all alumni do, unless you ask that they take you off the list."

"Then you've read this edition?"

"I always give it a quick once-over, but as I remember it there didn't seem to be anything that was worth my attention."

"Well, I'm not that familiar with Syracuse, so I read most of it. Not that I learned a lot. But I did spot one item that stuck in my mind. Here."

She handed it to him, folded open to the page with Terry Barkley's obituary.

"What do you want me to see?" He no longer looked disinterested.

"Right there under the obituaries for the class of 1987. I thought you'd be interested in the fact that Terry Barkley had passed away."

"She did? ? That's a shocker. So young, too."

"You told me that you knew her well, so I assumed that news of her death would come as a surprise. A sad one."

"It certainly does. I hadn't seen her in years, hadn't even corresponded with her. Probably should have. She was a nice girl."

"As I remember our last conversation, you dated Miss Barkley for awhile in college. There was something about Franklin Pierce's involvement in your relationship."

"Wait a minute." Pringle suddenly sounded testy. "Have you come here today to suggest that I might have killed Pierce?"

"Actually, the Barbados authorities gave me this assignment in part because they wondered if one of Franklin's colleagues on the cruise might have been his killer. That always seemed unlikely to me, but after all I knew none of you, including Franklin, so I had to keep an open mind. I'm still seeking information."

"Fine, but you'll remember that I also told you that Franklin and I had patched up our relationship years and years ago. If we hadn't, do you think I would have gone on all these trips with him?"

Yes, Carol said to herself, you might have done so precisely because you had never forgiven him.

"I believe that Miss Barkley lived in Toledo. The obituary doesn't say much about her, but it does give Toledo as her address at time of death. If my memory is accurate, you also began your post-college career in Toledo. Which reminds me," she said, having decided to test an idea which had come to her a couple of days earlier, "we're meeting today because you were out of town this past week. Where did you go? Toledo?"

It was an agitated Harry Pringle who responded.

"All right, I did read about her death, by why on earth would I have gone to Toledo? I was on business in Cleveland."

"That's okay. Cleveland's a nice city. I just thought you might have wanted to pay your last respects to Miss Barkley in Toledo. It isn't that much further west."

"I find this insulting, sheriff. I've already told you that the Barkley woman was a friend in college, and that that relationship ended many years ago."

"Of course. But it occurred to me that you might have wanted to go to the cemetery and say good-bye. Don't worry. I can check flights from Syracuse to Toledo. I'm sure they'll confirm that you never took such a flight."

Harry Pringle began to bite his lower lip.

"All right, I don't know why I'm trying to hide it. I did go to Toledo, and I did it because I had read the alumni news and knew that Terry had died. It seemed like a decent thing to do. It was no big deal, you just put me off with your insinuations. No, let me take that back. I'm not angry with you. You're just doing your job. And I'm sure you're right, nobody in Franklin's tour group will have had anything to do with his death. I'm sorry you're frustrated that the investigation is going nowhere."

No, Carol thought, it isn't going nowhere. You have now lied to me twice within the space of half an hour. You *had* read about Miss Barkley's death, and you *did* go to Toledo. What other lies have you told in answering my questions? It was at this point that the sheriff did something she didn't like to do, she shaded the truth a bit.

"When last we spoke, you claimed that your transportation on Barbados was one of those colorful buses. Most of your colleagues opted for taxis. You sure you didn't use a taxi at some point in your travels that day?"

"No, I stuck to the bus. As you say, they're colorful - in every sense of the word."

"The inspector down in Barbados has discovered that one taxi driver violated his company's policy and loaned his cab to an American tourist that day. What makes that arrangement most interesting is that he was given a thousand dollars by the American for the privilege of using his cab. Now wouldn't you agree that that's unusual? A thousand dollars! That would be a king's ransom for someone in a country where jobs don't begin to pay as much as they do here in the States."

"It does sound like a lot of money."

"It also strikes me as such a large amount of money that the American didn't hand it over to the taxi driver just so he could brag that he had driven a cab in Barbados. He must have had a very important and urgent reason for doing so. Such as needing his own wheels to help him kill Franklin Pierce."

Carol paused, waiting for Pringle to comment. Instead he shook his head, presumably in disbelief.

"Which brings me back to my question as to whether you might have spent some time that day in a taxi."

"You are apparently still determined to treat me as Franklin's killer, is that it?"

"Not at all. I'm just interested in collecting as many facts as I can in order to help the inspector who's in charge of this investigation."

"Well, good luck with that. Just remember that I had nothing to do with borrowing a cab, much less doing it for a thousand dollars."

"As it turns out, we may get lucky. Franklin bought a set of those photos that the cruise ship's photographer takes of its passengers when they first come on board. He apparently wanted pictures of all of you for his display at the consignment shop. The inspector found them in Franklin's suitcase. He'll have the taxi driver study them and identify the person to whom he loaned his taxi. Oh, and who gave him a thousand dollars."

Of course Moses King had already 'identified' his benefactor as Roger Edgar. But Carol had technically not lied to Pringle, just shaded the truth a bit.

Only time would tell whether it had worked, but whether Harry Pringle had been troubled by what the sheriff had just told him was not in doubt. In her decade plus in the law enforcement business, Carol had learned to spot the signs of fear on the faces of murder suspects. The man who sat across the desk from her in the crowded study was afraid.

Chapter 57

It was time to have the conversation with Inspector Williams that she had been avoiding. She wanted to tell him that she thought she knew, was even quite sure that she knew, who had killed Franklin Pierce. Telling him why would be considerably more difficult. It wouldn't do to chalk it up to something as elusive as intuition, and it would necessitate pressing the inspector for assurances that he had confidence in Moses King's story, including the 'gift' of a thousand dollars.

She pulled out the ubiquitous yellow pad and wrote down the questions she wanted to ask. There was no point in forgetting something and having to make a second call. That done, she took a deep breath and signaled JoAnne to get in touch with the RBPF in Bridgetown.

The inspector, as usual, sounded hopeful.

"Is this going to be my lucky day?"

"For both your sake and mine, I hope so. But I have a question or two first."

"Why am I not surprised? Go ahead."

"The big question, the one that subsumes the others, is how confident you are with what Moses King tells you. Is he one hundred percent reliable?"

"If you mean do I believe him, the answer is yes. We've been over this before, and like I've told you, I've been very hard on him. He knows that he's in serious trouble if I'm ever to discover that he has withheld information or lied to me. So, yes, he very definitely took a thousand dollars from a tourist on the day the *Azure Sea* was in port and he very definitely loaned the man who gave him the money his taxi for what turned out to be several hours. And there's no question about it, this transaction took place at Hunte's Garden. Obviously, he doesn't know who the tourist was - that, I hope, is where you come in. He originally thought it was someone named Edgar, but when I told him you were sure it had to be someone else, he backed off, saying that that was his best guess in the circumstances. I see no reason to think that his picking Edgar was anything but an honest mistake, given the pictures he had to work with."

"When you informed Mr. King that the American could not have been Edgar, did he hazard a guess on someone else?"

"Not really. I thought he was going to finger somebody. But he insisted that the men in the ship's photos looked pretty much alike, and in the end he refused to go with someone other than Edgar."

"That seems to leave what we might call the tangible evidence, for what it may be worth. The wallet and the rock you found in the taxi."

"They're still in my possession, sheriff. The only explanation for the rock would seem to be that whoever borrowed the taxi used it to kill Pierce, shoved it under the driver's seat, and forgot to get rid of it before returning the taxi to King. I've been hoping that one of Pierce's companions will give himself away when you mention that we found the rock. As for the wallet, I long ago concluded that Blackman, the man who claimed he found it on the beach, was telling the truth. I suppose it's theoretically possible that he's the killer, but that just doesn't square with the business of the swap of the taxi for a thousand dollars. By the way, I can't remember what I told you about the stuff in the wallet, the credit cards, the membership cards, things like that."

"Nothing much. Just that whoever took the money left everything else. I take it there was nothing worth keeping."

"Just the cards and a few unimportant things. Restaurant tabs, filling stations receipts, an invoice from an office supply store, a brief obituary that had been clipped from some newspaper. What I -"

"Wait a minute," the sheriff interrupted. "An obituary?"

"Right, something about a woman from Toledo. Funny thing to carry around in a wallet."

"Do you remember the name?"

"Barkley, I think. Why, was she a friend of Pierce's?"

"Not exactly, but it's interesting nonetheless. Like you say, it's a funny thing to put in your wallet - unless you knew you planned to meet Pierce and wanted to show it to him."

"I don't understand."

"I have a hunch I can enlighten you."

Carol proceeded to tell the inspector about the old college-days intersection of the lives of Harry Pringle, Terry Barkley, and Franklin Pierce. She wished Williams had been in the same room with her so that she could have watched his face as the story unfolded.

"Are you telling me that this man Pringle is my murderer?" he asked, obviously trying to avoid sounding too excited.

"I'm telling you that he has emerged as my number one suspect. That's not the same as saying I'm accusing him of murder. But I can tell you what I'm going to do next. I intend to have yet one more meeting with Mr. Pringle, and I plan to let him know that he has been identified by a Barbadian taxi driver as the man who paid him a thousand dollars to borrow his cab."

"But King never claimed that it was Pringle."

"I know, and I shall be very circumspect. There are ways of making a point without resorting to blatant falsehoods. Like the Barbadian police, we officers of the law in the United States never lie. We simply plant seeds in the minds of suspects and hope they will germinate."

CHAPTER 58

Time to plant those seeds, Carol thought, as she headed for the cottage at the end of a long and promising day. She had been spending a lot of time recently with Harry Pringle. In light of what she had learned from Inspector Williams and what it added to what she already knew, she was destined to be seeing him at least one more time, and this time it would not be at his home but in the Cumberland County Sheriff's Office.

She was anxious to place the call to him as soon as she reached the cottage, but there was a good chance that he wouldn't be home yet, and she had no desire to have another conversation with Mrs. Pringle. So she poured herself a glass of Chardonnay and took it out to the deck, where for a change it was warm enough to enjoy the late afternoon sun. Two neighboring kayakers paddled slowly past the dock, and watching them made her smile. Such a delightfully welcome contrast to what she was sure lay ahead when next she saw Harry Pringle.

It was just past 6:30 when she dialed the Pringles' number. Fortunately, Harry himself answered the phone.

"Hello, Mr. Pringle, its me again." She didn't have to identify who 'me' was.

It was only with considerable effort that Harry suppressed the urge to hang up on her. He was less successful in controlling his language, which led to a half-hearted apology.

"You needn't apologize, Mr. Pringle. I've heard much worse. I have no intention of ruining your dinner, in case you haven't eaten, or your digestion in case you have. I need to see you, so I'm calling to schedule an appointment."

"Don't you think enough is enough? I've talked with you more frequently of late than I have with my wife. And frankly, I'm tired of being harassed."

"I, too, would rather do other things with my time, Mr. Pringle, but I have a job to do and at the moment that job consists of bringing the investigation of Franklin Pierce's murder to conclusion. You can help me, and I'm afraid I must insist that you do so. Unfortunately, time is of the essence, so I shall also insist that we have our meeting within the next 48 hours."

"I, too, have a job, you know. Not to mention a family. But I am obviously at a disadvantage here, so I shall do as you say." His voice fairly dripped with sarcasm.

"Fine. You are welcome to use tomorrow to make adjustments in your schedule. I'd like to meet the next day at my office in Cumberland. Let me give you the address. Do you have a pen?"

———

Carol knew that there were still a few i's to dot and t's to cross, but barring developments that seemed unlikely, she hoped to be confronting Harry Pringle with the news that Inspector Williams would soon be seeking his extradition to Barbados to face charges that he had murdered Franklin Pierce there back in January.

Harry Pringle saw things differently. If the sheriff was not of the opinion that he had murdered Pierce, she at least harbored a strong suspicion that he might have, and he knew that he had to disabuse her of such an idea. And doing so would necessitate a very different approach than the one he had taken when last they had met. Instead of acting as if he knew nothing about what had happened in Barbados, he should have seized the initiative and told *his* story. He should have taken advantage of her questions to recast events in ways favorable to him. The problem was that to do so now he would have to admit that he had not been truthful.

The more he thought about it, however, the more confident he was that he could bring it off. He would have to explain that he had at first feared that admitting he had been with Pierce that day in Barbados would simply reinforce her conviction that he was guilty. Hence the lies.

The result was that Carol set about tying together loose ends of her case against Pringle, and Pringle turned his attention to confronting the sheriff with his version of what had happened on that fatal day in January.

"Does the fact that we're meeting in your office mean that you are planning on placing me under arrest?" Pringle asked as he settled into the chair across the desk from the sheriff.

"An arrest in the Pierce murder is the responsibility of the authorities in Barbados, Mr. Pringle. I am simply doing my job as the RBPF's American partner in the case. Would you care for coffee?"

"Of course, and I prefer it with cream and sugar."

Coffee served, Harry killed a few minutes complimenting the sheriff on the framed photos of Crooked Lake which helped to brighten up an otherwise drab room. Carol thanked him for his kind words, but made no attempt to encourage a conversation about something other than Franklin Pierce.

"Let me tell you how things stand, Mr. Pringle," she said. "Whether you once forgave Mr. Pierce for his role in ruining your relationship with Terry Barkley I do not know. But knowledge that she had recently died seems to have rekindled your hatred for him and led to his death. You acquired possession of a taxi on Barbados by giving the driver the staggering sum of a thousand dollars, and managed to use that taxi to take Mr. Pierce to an isolated corner of the island known as Harrysmith. It is our contention that that is where you killed him, after which you thoughtfully returned the taxi to its driver and rejoined your colleagues for the next stage of your cruise. Do I have it about right?"

"Surely you don't expect me to congratulate you for your detective work, sheriff." Pringle made no attempt to hide his anger. "No, you do not have it about right. Not even close."

"Why don't you, then, tell me what actually happened."

"With pleasure," Pringle said, setting his cup down so hard on the desk that some of the coffee spilled. "In retrospect, I should have told you what really happened that day in Barbados when you visited me in Syracuse. I didn't for what I am sure is an obvious reason. You saw me as a suspect in the Pierce case, and I thought it best to act as if I knew nothing. I'm here today to tell it like it is. That may be a dumb expression, but in this case it's the truth."

"Good. Telling it like it is isn't dumb. It's a good idea."

"Don't patronize me, sheriff." He took a deep breath and launched into his story. "Let me begin at the beginning. Franklin and I *were* together that day. I didn't have any plans. Just had a leisurely breakfast, stood by the rail and watched people disembark for their shore excursions. It was while I was standing there that Franklin came by - caught me by surprise. I really hadn't seen much of him on the cruise, and there he was. He said he'd been looking for me.

"What was on his mind was the news that Terry Barkley had died. I'd seen the obit in the alumni news; so had he. I know I told you I hadn't heard the news when you first mentioned it, but that was just part of my effort to look like I was out of the loop. Anyway, Franklin knew that Terry used to be a sore point between us. As you know if you've been paying attention, we'd put it behind us years ago, but there on the deck of the ship he wanted to tell me how sorry he was about Terry's death and apologize all over again for his boorish behavior back at Syracuse. Those were his exact words. Then he suggested we go look around the island together. We had never been close, but he sounded sincere and I was grateful that he was trying to be sympathetic. So I said yes.

"We caught a taxi without much trouble, but neither of us had any place in particular we wanted to go. Franklin finally suggested Harrysmith. I'd never heard of it, but he said it was supposed to have a nice view, that it'd be a good place to talk, get reacquainted, that sort of thing. And he was right. Quiet place, an old ruined hotel, kind of overgrown, nice small beach. Trouble was, Franklin was in a mood to stay awhile, and our driver wasn't interested in sticking around. After maybe twenty minutes he began to insist we move on. Like I said, Franklin wasn't ready, and the two of them began to argue about it. We were on a stone walk that went down to the beach when the driver came down to tell us he had another scheduled pick-up, that we had to get going. Next thing you know they were shouting at each other. Franklin took offense and pushed the driver. Only the steps were kind of steep and he lost his footing. He went down real hard and hit his head on the stones. I was trying to get them to calm down, but the real problem was that Franklin was hurt. He just lay there in an awkward position. I told him to get up, but he didn't move.

"The driver was obviously scared, probably figured he'd be sued or something when Franklin or I reported the altercation. He panicked. Just turned around and ran back up the stairs to the taxi and took off."

Pringle was using hand gestures to accentuate the story he was telling.

"I tried to do something about Franklin," he said, "but he didn't respond. You can't imagine how horrible it was when I realized he was dead. Anyway, then *I* panicked. What was I going to do? No place to go for help, no one else around. I knew I was in trouble, and then I did something really stupid. I decided to get out of there before somebody came along and found me with a dead man on the Harrysmith steps. I know I was thinking about myself, not Franklin, but what would you have done? So I sort of hurriedly buried him in that foliage that was growing along the path and got the hell out of there."

Pringle looked at the sheriff as if he needed her understanding of his predicament. Carol was aware that he hadn't finished his story, so she chose not to comment.

"You need to understand that I was in a bind," he said. "If someone had been there and seen what had happened, he would have known that I had nothing to do with it. But just the two of us, well, it looked bad. I set off on foot down the road back toward Bridgetown. Of course it was too far to walk, but I hoped I'd catch a bus if I stayed on the main road. And I did, after about half an hour. By the time I got back to where the cruise ship was docked, I realized that hiding the body had been a mistake, but it was much too late and too dangerous to go back. Besides, I was sure the taxi driver wouldn't dare go to the police or tell anyone else. At least that's how I felt when I reached the ship. It never occurred to me that he would cook up some cock and bull story like loaning his taxi to some tourist for a thousand dollars."

A cock and bull story like you're telling me, Carol thought. In his effort to demonstrate that he was innocent of Pierce's death, Pringle had admitted that he and Pierce had spent time together the day the *Azure Sea* was docked at Bridgetown and that they had visited Harrysmith. Otherwise the tale he had told sounded like pure invention. But almost immediately she had second thoughts. Was Pringle's story really so far fetched? Certainly no more than King's that he had loaned his taxi for a thousand dollars. Was it possible that Pringle was belatedly telling the truth and that Moses King was the one who was lying? She had been assuming that she had at last discovered Pierce's killer. But what if she were wrong, and the killer was going to be a bajan after all? And that Pierce's death had simply been a tragic accident?

Pringle was going on about how he had managed with some difficulty to say nothing about his day with Franklin when he rejoined his ship mates. Carol was thinking about how certain Inspector Williams had been that King had told the truth. It was time to tell Harry Pringle about Hunte's Garden, the rock under the taxi's seat, and Roger Edgar.

"Very interesting, Mr. Pringle," she said. "But you won't be surprised that I have a question or two. One of them has to do with where the taxi driver claims he loaned his taxi for all that money. It was a place called Hunte's Garden. Ever hear of it?"

Pringle shook his head. Carol saw no hint that the question posed a problem for him.

"The thing is," she said, "Hunte's Garden provides rum punches for people who visit there. After giving up his taxi, the driver hung around for two or three hours, using the excuse that he had to get a new battery, when obviously he was waiting to get his cab back. What he did with his time was drink rum punch, and the Hunte's people remember him. That would seem to confirm the taxi driver's story, don't you think?"

"So what? Franklin and I didn't borrow a taxi. We caught one in Bridgetown and the driver took us to Harrysmith and then left without us after Franklin had his fall. You're talking about two different taxis, two different drivers."

"Perhaps. In any event, my second question has to do with the unusual presence of a large rock under the driver's seat of the taxi." Carol was paying close attention to Pringle, hoping - expecting? - that he would betray his concern that he'd forgotten the rock. "How do you account for it being there?"

"I have no idea, because, as I just explained to you, we are obviously talking about two different taxis, two different drivers."

"I thought I should ask, inasmuch as it seems to be the weapon which was used to kill Franklin Pierce."

Pringle didn't comment, but by the look on his face he was enjoying this game of one upmanship with the sheriff.

"My other question concerns photographs. You will recall that when you and the other members of Mr. Pierce's group boarded the *Azure Sea*, a ship's photographer took pictures of all of you."

"Yes?"

"Franklin bought one of those photos of each member of the group. The Barbadian police recovered his suitcase, and it contained the photos. The taxi driver who loaned his cab for a thousand dollars was shown those photos and asked if he recognized the man he'd given his taxi to. Would you care to know which of you he picked out?"

Unlike the matter of Hunte's Garden and the rock, Pringle was clearly having trouble with this question.

"I don't see its relevance."

It was a strange response. Pringle surely knew that he and his story were in trouble if the driver had picked him.

"I very much doubt that identifying someone from a picture like that is reliable," he said. "It'd be like those line ups you see on cop shows. I read somewhere that people pick the wrong person much of the time."

Pringle seemed to be determined not to answer the sheriff's question. He must have assumed that he had been the one the driver had picked, but he had nothing to gain and very possibly much to lose by saying so. Which meant that Carol had quite fortuitously not had to tell a lie. However, she couldn't resist the last word on the subject.

"I think we know whose photo we're talking about."

CHAPTER 59

The atmosphere in Inspector Williams office in the RBPF building was gloomy. His colleagues had been trying for several days to jolly him out of his funk, but the inspector was becoming increasingly discouraged by Sheriff Kelleher's inability to assure him that her number one suspect, Pringle, was in fact Pierce's killer. It was now April, and it was beginning to look as if he was dealing with what was destined to become one of those dreaded cold cases.

Then the phone rang.

"You have a call from the States," his secretary announced. "It's that sheriff from Crooked Lake."

The inspector experienced a brief moment of optimism before his sour mood reasserted itself.

"Hello, sheriff. I don't suppose you have good news for me."

"You sound discouraged."

"I suppose I do. So, what do you have to tell me?"

"Let me put it this way. I was sure I had finally determined who Pierce's killer is, and then he paid me a visit and told me something that would make my theory impossible. Do you have time now for me to run this past you?"

"Of course I do," he said reluctantly. "So let's hear it."

Carol proceeded to brief the inspector on both versions of what had happened at Harrysmith. The inspector listened attentively, declining to interrupt.

"That's it," she said after some twenty minutes. "It's possible that both Pringle and I are wrong, but it's obvious that both of us can't be right."

"And what is your opinion, sheriff? Is this man Pringle's story convincing, or are you sticking to your version of events? Why do I suspect that you called me because you hope I'll make the decision."

It was obvious that the inspector knew he was in no position to make the decision.

"That's not fair of me, is it?" Carol said. "If he's guilty, Pringle has every reason to make up a story that will lead us astray, and that's what I've assumed he was doing. But it could have happened like he says. At least from where I'm sitting it looks that way. So I need your input."

"What I think is based entirely on what Moses King has told me and how persuasive he is, because I've never met Pringle, much less talked with him. King was anything but straight forward when I first met him. I wasn't impressed, so I've had him on the carpet so often he probably knows exactly how many threads it's got. Anyway, he's come around. His story rings true now, and he's consistent. Doesn't matter how I put my questions, I can't trip him up. But that's not all. Remember that rock, the one we found under the seat in the taxi? I'd say it supports King. What's more important is that King claims he turned the taxi over for all that money at Hunte's Garden, and then spent more than two hours there. Says he had a couple of rum punches while he waited for the taxi to come back. And that's true. I wasn't going to buy the 'rum punch at Hunte's' story without checking, so I took him over there to see if anybody recognized him. I was lucky - or maybe I should say King was. One of the attendants remembered him as a driver who was stranded there while his taxi was getting a new battery. It seems that King didn't take the tour, just drank some of their rum. They actually had to refuse him a fourth punch."

"So you believe Pringle is lying."

"I'd like to think so, but - and unfortunately it's a big but -while King's story may be true, he can't prove it was Pringle who gave him a thousand dollars for the use of his taxi. It could have been somebody else, in which case the the loan of the cab would have nothing to do with the Pierce case. That seems to be Pringle's argument, and how can we disprove it? All we seem to know for sure is that Pringle and Pierce were at Harrysmith."

Carol heard the inspector cursing under his breath.

"We've got to bring this to an end," he grumped. "I'm going to turn this place upside down until we nail your man Pringle. I'm damned if I'm going back to square one."

CHAPTER 60

Inspector Williams proceeded to mobilize all of the RBPF resources at his disposal in an effort to do what he had told Carol he would do. Parts of Barbados which he hadn't visited in a month would once again became part of his beat. People he hadn't spoken with in weeks would once again be subjected to a vigorous interrogation. His colleague, Inspector Brathwaite, would find himself badgered on an almost daily basis for his thoughts on the case.

It was three days after the inspector had learned of Harry Pringle's explanation of how Franklin Pierce had met his death that he chose to pay another visit to Hunte's Garden. He had planned to do so in any event, but suddenly it became an urgent priority. Why hadn't he thought of it sooner?

He was convinced that Moses King had 'loaned' his taxi to an American tourist, presumably Harry Pringle, at Hunte's Garden, and had remained there, quaffing rum punches, until the taxi came back. If an employee of Hunte's was prepared to vouch for the fact that it was King he had served, perhaps he could also vouch for the fact that it was Pringle who had dropped King off and returned for him.

The inspector said a hasty good-bye to Brathwaite, practically ran down the corridor, and within minutes was on his way across the island in the direction of one of Barbados' premier tourist attractions.

Well before he pulled into its parking lot, the excitement with which he had embraced the idea of revisiting Hunte's had cooled a bit. The taxi and the thousand dollars could have changed hands some distance outside the Garden, unseen by members of its staff. If a staff member had observed the transaction, he might well have been preoccupied with other matters and paid it no attention. The inspector could think of a dozen reasons why he might be on a wild goose chase. He had been lucky with the rum punch man; there was no reason why he should expect his luck to hold today. But he was in a position where he had to try anything and everything that might lead to the apprehension of Franklin Pierce's killer.

He walked slowly but purposefully around the entrance to Hunte's, preferring to get a feeling for where the Garden's personnel were stationed, what they were doing, and what they would be likely to see, rather than plunging into a conversation with one of them. It was a strategy destined to fail, because a slender young man, probably no older than his mid-twenties, was moving quickly in his direction, his sales pitch ready. He was not the dispenser of rum punch who had remembered Moses King when he and King had visited weeks earlier.

"Are you here for a tour, officer?" the young man asked.

"No," the inspector said, and his tone of voice made it clear that he had no interest in the glories of Hunte's Garden. "I need to talk with whomever is in charge here."

"Yes, sir, I'll get him." The attendant disappeared as quickly as he had appeared.

Moments later an older, bald, and considerably heavier man appeared. He look as if he expected trouble, and Williams was about to prove him right.

"What seems to be the problem?" he asked.

"You may remember that I paid you a visit several weeks ago. It concerned that cruise passenger who was killed while visiting Barbados. Your man who was doling out rum punch helped me identify a taxi driver who'd been drinking rum here."

"Oh, yes, I do remember. Have you solved that crime?"

"No, and that's why I'm here again."

"Don't tell me my bar tender made a mistake."

"That's not the problem. But I have another man I need to identify, a man who was with the taxi driver."

The manager, if that's who he was, looked confused.

"Where is he? This other man?"

"To the best of my knowledge, he's back in the United States. But I have a set of photos, and I'm sure he's in one of them. He dropped the taxi driver off, but as far as I know he didn't stay for a rum punch. Who normally watches the parking area?"

"They rotate. Weekes is on duty at the moment, Jason Weekes. I don't know if he was working the day you're interested in."

"Okay, let's hope Weekes is our man. If not, you can check your duty log."

It turned out to be Inspector Williams' lucky day. Weekes had been in the parking lot the day Pierce was killed, and like many other Barbadians, he remembered it well. Apparently the murder of a cruise passenger on the island was an exceptionally rare occurrence.

The inspector pulled the shipboard photos from his briefcase and spread them out on the hood of his car.

"On the day back in January when the cruise passenger was killed, a taxi with two men in it stopped at Hunte's," he said. "The driver got out and spent the next several hours here. He had several rum punches, and your colleague who served him was later able to make a positive identification. I'm here today to see if we can't make a positive identification of the other man, the one who drove off in the taxi. I'd like you to study these photos carefully and tell me if you recognize that man."

"But that's impossible," the manager said, obviously anxious to protect a member of his staff. "They all look alike, and it was a long time ago."

Jason Weekes smiled.

"Boss is right," he said. "I don't recognize any of these people. But maybe I know something you don't."

"What is that supposed to mean?" the inspector asked. The boy was being impertinent.

"If you're telling me that one of the men in these pictures was in the taxi, I do know something about him even if I can't recognize him from the photos."

"Well, come on, out with it."

"He's lost one of the fingers on his left hand. I think it's the middle finger."

The inspector stared at Weekes.

"How on earth do you know that?"

"Because I saw his hands. It reminded me of my granddaddy. That's how I remember him. He'd lost a finger cutting cane when I was just a kid. It sort of scared me whenever I saw that hand of his."

"The man who took the taxi, you actually saw that he was missing a finger?"

"That's what I'm saying. When he got out of the taxi to move over to the driver's side, he dropped a map. It's when he leaned over to pick it up that I saw his hand. You remember things like that."

Yes, I suppose you do, the inspector said to himself. Thank God. If you saw what you think you saw, we may have our killer.

"We think this man returned to Hunte's later in the day to pick up the taxi driver. Did you see him again that day?"

"No, just that once." Weekes didn't sound quite so cocky this time. "Maybe I'd gone to the bathroom or was helping one of the tourists. Is it important?"

"Yes and no. We're just trying to account for everything he did that day."

The inspector was disappointed, but his disappointment was tempered by the fact that he had learned much more at Hunte's Garden than he had expected to when he set off from Bridgetown that morning. Now if only the sheriff could put a name to the man with the missing finger.

"We should be establishing a hot line between our two offices," Williams said when Carol picked up her phone.

"I know. But one of these days we'll actually bring this damned Pierce case to closure."

"How about today?"

"Today?" Carol sounded excited. "You have some good news?"

"I hope so. It depends on whether you can answer a question."

" What's the question?"

"Do any of the members of Mr. Pierce's group that you've been talking to have a missing finger?"

"Missing finger?" If they had been playing twenty questions, Carol would never have guessed it. But she had a good memory, and it took but a matter of seconds for the answer to come to mind.

"Harry Pringle! He's missing a finger on his left hand. But how come *you* know about it?"

"I didn't know it was Pringle until just now when you told me. But one of the staff down here at Hunte's Garden remembered that the man who was riding in Moses King's taxi had lost a finger."

The inspector told the sheriff the story of his most recent visit to the spot where King had swapped the cab for a thousand dollars. Needless to say, both of them were equally shocked and thrilled to realize that this crucial piece of information had fallen into their laps so suddenly and so unexpectedly.

"It's the clincher, isn't it?" Williams said. "I went to Hunte's hoping that somebody there might recognize King's companion from those shipboard photos. No luck on that front, but thank goodness for the finger."

"Funny how these things work out, isn't it? Well, the next step is obvious. I'm going to be having another conversation with Pringle. Right away. It won't be easy. He'll stick to his story, tell me there must be dozens of people in Barbados who've lost a finger or two. But I think we've got him."

"And then we tackle extradition, right?"

"You can have him," Carol said.

"Like I told you, Mr. Pringle, there have been important new developments, and I know you'll want to hear about them. Otherwise I wouldn't have driven over to Syracuse for - what is it, the third time?"

"It seems like the tenth, but I'm counting my trip to Crooked Lake as well. I can't understand why you couldn't just have told me what's on your mind over the phone."

"It's like I said, some things are better shared face to face. and I think you'll agree that this is one of those things. In any event, I'm here again, and I have news for you."

Pringle chose not to comment. His face betrayed no hint of what he thought might be on the sheriff's mind.

"I had a call from Inspector Williams in Barbados yesterday. He and I have been in close touch for almost three months. He keeps me apprised of what's going on in his investigation down there, and I let him know what I've been learning about Franklin's friends, the ones who accompanied him on the cruise. That includes you, of course. In fact, our conversation yesterday was all about you."

Carol paused, smiled. Pringle maintained his silence.

"The inspector already knew that a taxi driver named King had loaned his cab to somebody we thought was you. Remember? That's when the thousand dollars were exchanged. It happened at a tourist spot called Hunte's Garden. Then just the other day the inspector decided to go back to Hunte's and see if anyone on their staff could remember the other man in the taxi."

Carol studied Pringle's face as she spoke.

"Interestingly enough, one of the staff did remember the other man. Not because the face was familiar, but because the man was missing the middle finger on his left hand. Do you know anybody like that?"

Pringle, without giving it a conscious thought, stole a glance at the hand in his lap.

"You're not only a poor cop, sheriff, you're a dishonest cop." Harry Pringle had made a snap decision as to how he was going to handle this. "Somehow you found out that I lost a finger, and now you're trying to use it to get me to confess to a crime I didn't commit. Well, you won't get away with it. Now get out of my house."

Pringle was angry. Or feigning anger. Carol knew she had the upper hand.

"I think not. The Barbadian authorities have done their homework. And they are scrupulously honest. What is more, they do not relish having tourists damage their country's reputation as a safe, peaceful place to visit."

"They can't prove I killed Pierce, and neither can you. Besides, I'm a citizen of the United States, not Barbados."

"That may be true, but the United States and Barbados have an extradition treaty. It may take awhile, but I suspect that in due course you will be standing trial for murder in Bridgetown."

CHAPTER 61

The last vestige of winter had long since disappeared. June was proving warmer than usual, the canoe now sat on the beach, and Kevin, back from the city and another year in the trenches of Madison College, was in the process of ridding himself of the pallor from another long gray season.

He and Carol were sitting on the end of the dock, feet in the water, enjoying doing nothing.

"Tell me you missed me," he said.

"I've already told you I missed you a hundred times."

"Not that, I mean as your crime solving partner."

"Come on, Kevin. It's not my fault Pierce met his end in the middle of winter. Besides, you did me some good by going up to Cooperstown to talk to Westerman."

"But Westerman didn't do it, so that doesn't count. I was an absentee sleuth where Pringle's concerned."

"You're jealous of Inspector Williams, aren't you?" Carol said with a sly smile.

"That's ridiculous. I'd just like to have been in on the kill."

"Yes, dear, I know. And if you don't mind, we don't talk that way in my business. It makes us sound like we're the bad guys, not the defenders of justice."

Kevin laughed and threatened to push Carol into the lake.

"Just so you know that I'm one of the good guys, I'm sorry I never got to meet the inspector. The way you tell it, the two of you made a pretty good team."

"I like to think so. Especially considering that we did it at arm's length. By the way, it looks like you'll be getting to meet the inspector after all. He called this morning and says he's going to have to make a trip to Washington to deal with some of the issues that have to be taken care of if Pringle's to be extradited. He'd like to include Crooked Lake in his journey, and I assured him that we'd be very disappointed if we weren't part of his itinerary."

"That's great. I assume he'll be staying at the cottage."

"For one night only and he hasn't settled on a date yet. By the way, I promise not to share with him my husband's brilliant idea that the guy who tried to break into our cottage that rainy night was either Westerman or Craig. No reason to undermine his confidence in my judgment."

"Okay, so I was wrong. But it wasn't that bad an idea. It's just that your suspects didn't think of it."

It was time for a swim before supper.

They were toweling off when Kevin raised the question that had been bothering him every since Carol had shared with him her good news about the Pierce case.

"I don't think I've ever second guessed you, and I'm not starting now. But are you really confident that Pringle will be convicted? After all, nobody saw what happened on the Harrysmith steps. It's pretty circumstantial, don't you think?"

"Of course it's circumstantial. Some of the most compelling cases are. But trust me, Pringle is his own worst enemy. He talks too much. What's more, there are a lot of people who are in a position to testify to his infatuation with Terry Barkley and how news of her death could have brought an old grievance back to a boiling point. And it's a virtual certainty that I'll be summoned to our favorite Caribbean island to testify. Having spent almost four months trying to figure out who killed the unloved owner of Newark's consignment shop, I don't intend to let him slip through our fingers when he goes to trial."

"How could I have doubted it?"

"I'll pretend you didn't. Let's eat."